P9-API-567

TALES FROM THE
CAPTAIN'S TABLE

EX LIBRIS

Lilja Stearg

STAR TREK®

TALES FROM THE
CAPTAIN'S TABLE

EDITED BY KEITH R.A. DeCANDIDO

Based upon *Star Trek*
and *Star Trek: The Next Generation*®
created by Gene Roddenberry,
Star Trek: Deep Space Nine®
created by Rick Berman & Michael Piller,
Star Trek: Voyager®
created by Rick Berman & Michael Piller & Jeri Taylor,
and *Star Trek*®: *Enterprise*™
created by Rick Berman & Brannon Braga

POCKET BOOKS
New York   London   Toronto   Sydney   Pelagia

POCKET BOOKS, a division of Simon & Schuster, Inc.
1230 Avenue of the Americas, New York, NY 10020

This book is a work of fiction. Names, characters, places and incidents are products of the authors' imaginations or are used fictitiously. Any resemblance to actual events or locales or persons, living or dead, is entirely coincidental.

Copyright © 2005 by Paramount Pictures. All Rights Reserved.

STAR TREK is a Registered Trademark of Paramount Pictures.

This book is published by Pocket Books, a division of Simon & Schuster, Inc., under exclusive license from Paramount Pictures.

All rights reserved, including the right to reproduce this book or portions thereof in any form whatsoever. For information address Pocket Books, 1230 Avenue of the Americas, New York, NY 10020

ISBN: 1-4165-0520-2

First Pocket Books trade paperback edition June 2005

10 9 8 7 6 5 4 3

POCKET and colophon are registered trademarks of Simon & Schuster, Inc.

Cover illustration by Mark Gerber
Cover design by John Vairo, Jr.

Manufactured in the United States of America

For information regarding special discounts for bulk purchases, please contact Simon & Schuster Special Sales at 1-800-456-6798 or business@simonandschuster.com.

*Let us raise our glasses to Plato, Geoffrey Chaucer, Lord Dunsany,
L. Sprague de Camp & Fletcher Pratt, Arthur C. Clarke, Larry
Niven, Spider Robinson, John Ostrander, Neil Gaiman, and all those
past, present, and future who know the value of gathering together,
hoisting a few, and telling tales. . . .*

Contents

Introduction: How We Built the Bar   ix
  Dean Wesley Smith

WILLIAM T. RIKER
**Improvisations on the Opal Sea:
  A Tale of Dubious Credibility**   3
  Michael A. Martin & Andy Mangels

JEAN-LUC PICARD
Darkness   49
  Michael Jan Friedman

ELIZABETH SHELBY
Pain Management   77
  Peter David

KLAG, SON OF M'RAQ
loDnI'pu' vavpu' je   107
  Keith R.A. DeCandido

KIRA NERYS
The Officers' Club   127
  Heather Jarman

JONATHAN ARCHER
Have Beagle, Will Travel: The Legend of Porthos   175
  Louisa M. Swann

DEMORA SULU
Iron and Sacrifice   201
  David R. George III

CHAKOTAY
Seduced   271
  Christie Golden

DAVID GOLD
An Easy Fast   301
  John J. Ordover

About the Authors   331

Introduction

How We Built the Bar

DEAN WESLEY SMITH

Back in the mists of history, around 1997, the Captain's Table was built, to float forever in time and space, allowing only captains of ships through the big wooden front door. If my memory serves, the creation of the Captain's Table was slow, like any construction process—a labor of love carried out over a number of phone calls between myself and former Pocket Books editor John Ordover.

John and I both loved the tradition of bars in literature, and often talked about the White Hart, one of our favorites. I'm not sure of the exact conversation between us that sent the Captain's Table into full construction, but I do remember that at one point John suggested I create the bar.

Since I had worked as a bartender and have a degree in architecture that I have seldom used, it was a logical assignment. I took the task very seriously, actually going to my architectural studio and drawing up floor plans. As I would in any good design, I included restrooms, determined the location of stairs, provided for liquor storage, and so on. Every detail, all to scale. Then John and I worked out the characters who would be regulars, who would be there to listen to the captains' stories.

We developed the rules of the bar, and how it works with captains of ships from any time and any space. We developed the tradition of captains telling tales, and many of the other details that threaded their way into the bar. Then John hired eight of his writers to bring the Captain's Table to life and write six novels. He assigned each the task of writing in first person, from the captain's point of view while in the bar.

Since I had designed the bar, I was given first choice and picked Benjamin Sisko, writing with my wife, Kristine Kathryn Rusch. The team of L.A. Graf took Jim Kirk and Hikaru Sulu, Diane Carey wrote about Kathryn Janeway, Michael Jan Friedman got to record Jean-Luc Picard's story, Jerry Oltion told Christopher Pike's, and Peter David told Mackenzie Calhoun's tale.

John kept everyone together in details and timeline, even managing to have the different books linked by last and first chapters, with one captain leaving the bar while another came in. John even had the artist put in the faces of the authors in the crowd scene behind the captains in the cover paintings and on the big poster. Only not always on our own books. (Hint: Kris and I are right behind Captain Janeway.)

As a hard-core *Star Trek* fan, this was all grand fun for me, not only the creation of the bar, but writing the novel. Since then, I have been editing *Strange New Worlds*, the annual-contest anthology that lets the fans into the professional writing side of *Star Trek*. Over the years, my biggest regret has been that the rules of *Strange New Worlds* don't allow Captain's Table stories. I've really wanted to read more about the bar that floated out there, giving the captains of ships a needed place to relax.

Now Keith R.A. DeCandido has solved that problem with this wonderful book, getting some of the best *Star Trek* writers to drop in to the Captain's Table and listen to more stories from many varied captains. I feel like I have come home.

So sit back and enjoy great stories in one of the most interesting and strange places in all of time and space. And when you leave, don't forget to tip the bartender.

TALES FROM THE
CAPTAIN'S TABLE

Tending Bar . . .

Cap was cleaning glasses as the pair entered the bar—both human, both Starfleet. The shorter, bald one, Jean-Luc Picard, had graced the Captain's Table on several occasions, becoming more gregarious with each visit. The taller, bearded human with him, William T. Riker, was new. Cap smiled, enjoying the ritual of the captain bringing the newly promoted beloved former first officer here for his first drink.

And, of course, for his first story.

Off in a corner, another human Starfleet captain, this a blond-haired woman who was drinking a succession of Orion whiskeys, sat dolefully, ignoring those who entered, even though they were known to her. Cap knew that Elizabeth Shelby's story was not one for the entire tavern. Another captain was moving to sit with her. She would pay her way soon enough, and the rules only said you had to tell a story, not necessarily tell it to all of the bar's patrons.

At the bar itself was another doleful captain, a Klingon named Klag, who was attempting to drain Cap's warnog *supply. The new arrivals were known to him as well, and nods were exchanged among them.*

As Picard and Riker approached the bar, Cap walked over to where they stood, already knowing what they would order. . . .

WILLIAM T. RIKER

CAPTAIN OF THE *U.S.S. TITAN*

Improvisations on the Opal Sea: A Tale of Dubious Credibility

MICHAEL A. MARTIN & ANDY MANGELS

"Ah, Paris," said Jean-Luc Picard after the shimmering transporter beam released him and faded from sight. He closed his eyes and inhaled deeply.

Not wishing to offend his former commanding officer, Captain Will Riker struggled not to wrinkle his nose noticeably as he, too, sampled the chill air and took in his new surroundings. The ancient, cobbled alley in which they had materialized seemed utterly unremarkable.

Except for its rather pungent smell.

"You look disappointed, Captain," Picard said, reminding Riker how unaccustomed he was to being addressed by his new rank. Captain Picard had been in the habit of calling him "Number One" for fifteen years now.

Gesturing toward a meandering, meter-long crack in the brick wall beside him, Riker favored Picard with a wry smile. "As sightseeing destinations go, this doesn't exactly measure up to the Arc de Triomphe or the Champs Elysées."

Picard strode confidently away from the wall and into the late-afternoon shadows. Despite the apparently anonymous obscurity of the alley, he was clearly familiar with the terrain.

"You've seen those things before, Will," Picard said. "I've something more important to show you today. It's a rare privilege, and you've earned it."

A rare privilege, Riker thought, stepping carefully around a noisome pile of animal droppings as he followed his erstwhile CO around a corner. *A scenic tour of an alley that smells like an open latrine.*

"You brought me here because I scratched up your yacht, didn't you?" Riker said aloud as they reached a crowded, filthy *rue* that Riker recognized as emblematic of the oldest portions of the area surrounding Paris's Gare du Nord. "You realized you wouldn't be able to put reprimands in my file any longer, so you had to find another way of getting even with me."

Pausing to let a cluster of harried, overcoat-bundled Parisians pass him on the ancient concrete-and-cobble sidewalk, Picard turned toward Riker, an uncharacteristically fraternal smile splitting his face. "I lent you and Deanna the *Calypso II* as my wedding gift. I've no regrets on that score, Will, dents and scratches notwithstanding. But the important thing is that you and Deanna had a safe and pleasant honeymoon trip."

"You know what they say, sir. Any honeymoon you can walk away from . . ." Riker said, trailing off as he returned Picard's grin. He quickly fell into step beside Picard as they walked down the *rue*, which teemed with pedestrians and old-style ground vehicles.

"Do tell," Picard deadpanned.

Still grinning, Riker shook his head. "Not even under the influence of Romulan mind-probes."

"We'll see," Picard said enigmatically, though his smile remained firmly in place.

Despite the comradely familiarity his newly achieved rank afforded him with Captain Picard, Riker found he really wasn't very keen on discussing his recent three-week honeymoon in any detail. Suddenly, a new mix of pungent aromas assaulted him, causing his nose to wrinkle like a Ferengi's—and giving him the perfect excuse to change the subject.

"I hope you don't take this the wrong way, Captain, but why does this place smell so . . . *strong?*"

Picard gestured as broadly about the *rue* as the relentlessly determined streams of pedestrian traffic would permit. "For the same reason that the people prefer to walk. Or take vintage twentieth-century ground transportation. Or live in apartment buildings that predate the Industrial Revolution."

Riker nodded, beginning to understand. "It's a museum city." He was familiar with the common French complaint that many of Earth's modern cities were too sterile and antiseptic for Gallic tastes.

"My people are known for their singular resistance to change," Picard said. "As well as for our frequent small acts of rebellion against modernity. We're fiercely protective of our language, our architecture, our cuisine. Parisians are particularly so. Did you know that food replicators are forbidden in this *arrondissement?*"

Riker sniffed the air again. Cooking smells melded with the sickly-sweet bouquet of ripening garbage—and the dog droppings he had so carefully avoided, which now seemed to be stalking him.

"Here we are," Picard said, coming to an abrupt stop before a crumbling gothic structure that might well have been a thousand years old. Looking up toward the shadowy, gargoyle-festooned roofline, Riker counted six stories and guessed that the structure had endured at least four centuries past its safe lifespan.

Riker looked to Picard, who was pointing toward a narrow flight of concrete steps that led downward to a dingy-looking basement door.

Riker found himself staring at a wooden sign whose peeling paint nearly obscured the words LA TABLE DU CAPITAINE.

This can't be right, Riker thought, blinking mutely at the sign.

Picard had evidently noticed Riker's confusion. "Well, I know the exterior doesn't exactly rival President Bacco's château in the Loire Valley for beauty. But I can assure you the Captain's Table is a good deal more attractive on the inside."

Riker shook his head in disbelief. The Captain's Table was the name of the secret and exclusive bar Captain Picard had told him about—very quietly—on the very day his promotion to captain had come through. Not only was it a place that catered *only* to ship captains, but Starfleet personnel of lesser rank weren't even supposed to be aware of its existence. Riker hadn't had the heart to tell him that Captain Garfield of the *Independence* had told him about the place four years earlier.

But there was one huge problem: It was on the wrong planet.

"I thought you told me you visited this place a few years back with Captain Gleason of the *Zhukov*," Riker said, frowning. "On Madigoor IV."

Picard nodded, a puckish grin tugging at the corners of his mouth. "You're right. That's precisely where Neil and I were the first time I visited the Captain's Table."

Riker scratched his beard in confusion. "I guess they must be a chain." *A chain of exclusive, hush-hush, top-secret, captains-only drinking venues,* he thought. *Right.*

"No, Will," Picard said, his grin becoming almost mischievous. "I assure you that the Captain's Table is an utterly unique establishment." And with that, he descended the stairs and pushed the dilapidated wooden door open.

Shrugging, Riker followed Picard down the stairs, across the threshold, and into what appeared to be a dimly lit, utterly unremarkable drinking establishment.

A burst of raucous sound greeted them even as Riker's eyes struggled to adjust to the scant illumination.

"Postrelativist jazz, I think," Picard said, nodding toward the narrow, battered stage where a trio of musicians labored, respectively, over exotic brass, string, and percussion instruments.

Riker shook his head, wincing at the strains of the furry humanoid who seemed to be fighting for his life against a vaguely trombone-like instrument. From the discordant hoots issuing from the instrument's coiled metal bowels, it wasn't at all clear who was going to emerge the victor.

"Sounds more like what passes for pop music on the Opal Sea," Riker said with a wince. "Mixed with a fair amount of Sinnravian *drad*."

Riker turned away from the stage and began taking a brief inventory of the Captain's Table's other habitués. Present were humanoids representing at least a dozen Federation species, along with perhaps half that many humans. A handful belonged to races Riker had never seen before. Most of the patrons sat at tables scattered throughout the room, while a few had bellied up to the bar. They all appeared to be intent upon either their quiet conversations, the various hot and cold liquors before them, or both.

A familiar face caught his eye. Seated at a corner table was Elizabeth Shelby. A multitude of small, empty glasses surrounded her, several of them upended. Not only had she taken no notice of him, but she seemed to want nothing more than to crawl inside the half-drained whiskey bottle into which she stared.

Riker wondered what was wrong, but resisted the temptation to walk over to her and ask. *Maybe she's taken on a first officer who's as big a pain in the ass as she was for me back when the Borg first tried to assimilate Earth.*

As Riker turned to follow Picard to the bar, he began to revise his opinion of the place upward. Though the Captain's Table appeared no less worn-out and seedy than it had when he'd entered, its walls boasted autographed photos of jazz legends, including Junior Mance, Charlie Parker, and Louis Armstrong, showcased alongside the bric-a-brac of a score of obscure worlds, objects ranging from a baritone sax to something that strongly resembled (but wasn't quite) a standard Terran trombone to a zither-like stringed instrument Riker recognized as a Shaltoonian *linlovar* to the chrome fittings of various ground vehicles that surely had never come within several sectors of Earth.

How did a hubcap from a Jupiter 8 end up here? Riker thought, staring at the shining disk on the wall with unconcealed amazement as he leaned on his elbows across the bar. *In a captains-only drinking establishment that somehow transported itself all the way from Madigoor IV to Paris, no less.*

A pair of large pewter mugs thumped heavily onto the bar between Riker and Picard.

Picard raised his mug and took a generous swallow, then glanced with satisfaction at Riker before casting an appreciative smile toward the bartender.

"Perfect, as usual," Picard said, setting his drink back onto the bar. "A very dry Pentarian *dresci.*"

Riker scowled in confusion. "I don't remember you placing an order yet. You must have called ahead."

"No, that's not necessary," said Picard, shaking his head. "That's one of the special things about Cap here, and his establishment. Both always seem to deliver exactly what one needs, whenever one needs it."

As long as one is a ship's captain, Riker thought, recalling what both Picard and Garfield had already told him. He studied the barkeep, a thickset human male with a shock of short, white, and slightly unkempt hair. *And as long as one pays one's tab with a story.*

"Thank you, Cap," Riker said, raising his mug toward the bartender. He wondered how much of his story would be expected to be true.

"All part of the service, Captains," the bartender said with a knowing grin as he polished a metal drinking stein on his apron.

"How's *your* drink, by the way, Will?" Picard said.

Riker took an experimental sniff of his mug's contents, and followed it with a tentative sip.

His eyebrows rose involuntarily. "Betazoid uttaberry wine, and a pretty damned good vintage, too. Funny, but that's exactly what I was going to order."

Rough laughter swelled to a full-throated, and familiar, guffaw at Riker's immediate right. He turned, and found himself within a meter of another friendly face.

"Klag!" he said with a huge grin at the captain of the *I.K.S. Gorkon.*

"Betazoid wine, Riker?" The Klingon captain chortled. "I had thought you were made of sterner stuff."

Smelling the *warnog* in the mug in front of his old friend, Riker laughed. "I'm pacing myself."

The Klingon stared at Riker's collar. "I see you have at last changed your views regarding your own vessel."

Riker nodded. "You're looking at the new captain of the *U.S.S. Titan.*"

Smiling, Klag said, "I *did* tell you that the glories of your own ship are far superior to the reflected glory of another's." Looking quickly at Picard, Klag added, "No offense, Captain Picard."

"None taken, Captain Klag," Picard said with a hoist of his own *dresci*. "I'd say we starship commanders are a fairly fortunate lot. At least those of us who have survived in the occupation for any substantial length of time. To our absent friends."

Picard drank, and Klag followed suit with an agreeable grunt. "Hear, hear," Riker said, then raised his own cup. The face of his own recently deceased father, as well as those of far too many dead comrades, flashed across his mind's eye. Tasha Yar. Marla Aster. Susan Lomax. Matthew Barnes, Mwuate Wathiongo, Razka of Sauria, and so many others who died during the recent fighting on Tezwa.

And Data, who had been among the *Enterprise*'s most recent casualties.

So is this *what I have to look forward to as* Titan's *skipper?* he thought, suddenly feeling glum. *Decades of regrets, eulogies, solemn speeches—and drinking without my wife.*

Riker set his tankard back on the bar, a bit harder than he'd intended. He came to a decision as he recalled a recent, very hard-learned life lesson. Mere days after receiving his latest promotion, he had learned that there was far more to a captain's lot in life than grim sobriety.

"You look like a man who's ready to pay his tab," Cap observed with a wry smile.

"I am, actually." He turned to Picard. "It's about my honeymoon. Three weeks on the Opal Sea."

"I believe, Captain, that you declared that subject off-limits," Picard said, his eyebrows aloft with mild surprise.

Riker smiled. "I changed my mind. Call it captain's prerogative."

"You seem uninjured, Captain Riker," said Klag in a teasing voice. "It could not have been a terribly successful honeymoon."

Well aware of the Klingon belief that a shattered clavicle on the wedding night is a portent of good luck, Riker favored Klag with a lopsided grin. "Maybe my sickbay is just better equipped than yours."

Riker noticed that he had become the focus of the intense attention of perhaps a dozen of his fellow skippers. Carefully arranging his thoughts, he considered where best to begin his tale. . . .

That day started with the mother of all hangovers. I woke up with my hands bound behind me, facedown on moist, slippery wood with a snippet of weird Pelagian music playing over and over in my head. Trouble was, I hadn't had anything to drink.

Actually, I ought to back up a few hours and explain how I ended up in the smelly bilge of that rickety old wooden sailing ship in the first place.

Deanna—my new bride—and I had arrived on Pelagia two days earlier. You may or may not have heard of the place. It's a Class-M planet dominated by oceans. The only landmasses on the entire globe are chains of volcanic islands, and the weather is damned close to paradise almost from pole to pole, nearly all year long. The planet's single biggest vacation destination is called the Opal Sea, a place of iridescent green water, golden sandy beaches, and almost uniformly friendly humanoid natives.

And pirates.

No kidding. Pirates.

With wooden ships.

Into which they sometimes toss hostages that they catch unawares while jogging on their planet's idyllic golden beaches.

I admit, I wasn't as vigilant as I should have been. On the other hand, this *was* my honeymoon. Bridegrooms usually don't expect to get clonked over the head at times like this.

I suppose I was mesmerized by the foamy boundary between the surf and the sand, watching the dawn beginning to brighten the water, when somebody coldcocked me. The pirates must have had someone lying in wait for me at the beach, down by the rocks. I'm still not sure exactly how it happened, but I got hit from behind, judging from the pain I could still feel in the back of my head as I pushed myself up to my knees in the dim, swaying, briny-smelling room that I soon learned was the hold of an honest-to-gods Barbary Coast–style pirate ship.

My first attempt to get my feet under me sent me sprawling straight to the slick wooden deck, and the noise evidently attracted the attention of a pair of low-ranking pirates. They were male Pelagians, with the same turquoise skin coloration that Deanna and I had adopted for the duration of our stay on—

"A moment, Will," Picard said. "You never told me that you and Deanna underwent surgical alterations for your honeymoon trip."

Riker tried to react nonchalantly to Picard's interruption. "It's a pretty common procedure on Pelagia these days. It helps visitors fit in, and you can have it done on several of the main southern islands, where the tech caps that are enforced on the rest of the planet don't apply."

"I've not had the opportunity to visit the place myself," Picard said. "But I'm familiar with the technological restrictions. They don't permit any electronics on most of the planet, and limit mechanical and chemical technology to the equivalent of Earth's Napoleonic Era or earlier."

Riker smiled as he recalled the prohibition against food replicators in parts of Paris. "They have a very good reason for it, as it turns out," he said. "But I'm digressing."

"Get up, Fegrr'ep Urr'hilf," said one of the two pirates in my welcoming committee. "The captain has business with you, heh."

Like the freebooters who terrorized the high seas on my home planet around seven centuries ago, these rough, bearded men wore breeches, leather boots, rough shirts—or no shirt—and bandannas. They also fairly bristled with knives, as well as muzzle-loading pistols I recognized from a holodeck pirate scenario I ran a couple of times with Lieutenant Commander Keru, the *Enterprise*'s stellar-cartographer-turned-security-officer. They almos could have passed for the pirates of the Spanish Main.

Except for their people's characteristic turquoise-colored skin.

"You heard us, Urr'hilf," said the second pirate. "Captain Torr'-ghaff wants to talk to you about collecting the ransom, heh."

I figured out quickly that they had mistaken me for somebody else. It was an easy deduction to make, since I didn't exactly look like myself at the moment. But I hadn't adopted the name Fegr-r'ep Urr'hilf, and had no idea who the hell that was.

Still, I had to admit that the name had a familiar ring to it. Just as I had to face the fact that this Torr'ghaff, who was evidently my captor, was likely to be pretty unhappy if he were to realize I was somebody other than this Urr'hilf person.

Better play along, then, I told myself as the two pirates marched me to a ladder and then up onto the ship's main deck.

Warm salt spray stung my nose. I squinted into the aquamarine-hued sky, in which the orange sun now stood considerably higher than it had when I'd gone out for my morning jog. *Deanna knows I'm gone by now,* I thought, figuring maybe three or four hours had passed since my disappearance. *She and the others must have mounted a search by now. Surely they'll—*

"So you could count on Captain Picard to bring the resources of the *Enterprise* to bear in rescuing you," interposed Klag, who then killed off yet another *warnog*.

Riker shook his head as he accepted another uttaberry wine from Cap, who had also been listening intently. "Not exactly. At the time, the *Enterprise* was already where she is right now: in Earth orbit, undergoing repairs at McKinley Station. Deanna and the rest of us came to Pelagia in Captain Picard's yacht."

Klag scowled in confusion. "How many people do you humans customarily involve in these 'honeymoons,' Riker?"

"Just two. But Pelagia is becoming a pretty popular Starfleet shore-leave destination. Deanna and I were happy to give some of our shipmates a ride to Pelagia before going off on our own."

"Sounds like that was a fortunate decision," Picard said as Cap handed him a second *dresci*.

"Having so many people present on a honeymoon excursion

reminds me of a novel I once read when I was an ensign," said Klag. "It was a tale of interspecies infidelity that involved an Andorian and a Damiani in a romantic septangle. I think you humans would call it an 'erotic thriller.' "

"Or a bodice-ripper," Riker said.

Picard chuckled. "Or perhaps a bedroom farce."

"Set in a very large house," said Cap.

"Would it be all right if I *continued* my pirate story?" Riker said with an exasperated sigh.

"Please," Klag said.

So I had to have faith that Deanna and the others were taking steps to find me. And though I had no way to know when I could expect to see them, I found the thought enormously reassuring.

Without freeing my hands—they were still bound tightly behind me at the wrists with something that felt like slimy rope—my two pirate escorts hustled me past a group of unsavory crew members who busied themselves swabbing decks and adjusting rigging.

Shortly afterward, I stood before a man who had to be at least two meters tall, a veritable mountain of hirsute muscle. One side of his face bore an impressive, dragon-shaped deep purple tattoo that made him look even more intimidating. His clothing was a good deal more expensive-looking than that of any of his men, and he was clearly in charge.

"Captain Torr'ghaff, I presume, heh," I said.

Standing tall against an all but infinite backdrop of clear aquamarine skies and gleaming green waters, the pirate chieftain looked me slowly up and down, his dark eyes shielded from the dazzling sun by the wide brim of his long-plumed, purple hat. "Fegrr'ep Urr'hilf. Judging from the music you make in your sound recordings, I had expected you would be taller, neh?"

"I suppose my height doesn't come across except in person, heh," I said, still doing my best to nail the local dialect, which I knew the universal translator in my ear could only approximate.

"Fair enough," the pirate leader said, raising a sharp cutl—

• • •

"I wasn't aware, Riker, that Earth had universal translators during the era of wooden wind boats," Klag said with a smirk.

Riker sighed. "The Pelagian authorities have made a few exceptions to their tech caps in the interest of public safety."

"Ah. Like the 'sound recordings' your pirate captor referenced."

"No, actually. Sound recordings are made and exchanged on Pelagia by natural means. Some sort of squid or octopus that reproduces sounds with its tympanic membranes."

"They use *fish* as musical instruments?"

"Do you want to hear this story or not?"

Klag raised a hand to signal his assent. "Please, proceed."

"I am delighted that you weren't too badly injured by my welcoming party, Fegrr'ep Urr'hilf," the brigand leader said, slipping the cutlass back into the scabbard that dangled from his purple, silken sash. "I have been an enthusiastic listener for many years, heh."

Fegrr'ep Urr'hilf, I thought, considering once again the stubborn snippet of Pelagian native music that I still couldn't get out of my head. I finally understood why.

Urr'hilf was a local musician of some considerable repute. He entertained large crowds on islands and sailing vessels all over the planet. Including at the visitor reception centers located on the main southern islands.

And I realized that he was supposed to be playing at the very seaside hostelry where Deanna and I had been staying. I had seen his pictures—woodcut engravings and painted portraits, actually—all over the lobby and the lounge.

This guy had kidnapped me thinking I was Fegrr'ep Urr'hilf. And now that I understood what had happened, I realized that between my beard and my minor surgical alterations, I really did bear a better-than-passing resemblance to Urr'hilf.

Great, I thought, considering the unpleasant reality of the rope that still bound my wrists behind my back. *How pissed off is this guy going to be when he realizes how badly he's goofed?*

But I had an even more immediate concern than my personal safety.

"I assume I'm the only hostage you took from the beach today, eh?" I asked Captain Torr'ghaff, taking care to avoid provoking him. Hoping it would make my impersonation of Fegrr'ep Urr'hilf more believable, I tried to appear more than a little frightened.

"You are correct, heh," Torr'ghaff said.

I heaved a sigh of relief. *So Deanna is probably safe,* I thought. *Along with the rest of my shipmates. They've got to be planning some sort of rescue, tech restrictions or no tech restrictions.*

Torr'ghaff walked slowly around me and my pirate escorts, evidently scrutinizing me carefully. Had the difference between my height and Urr'hilf's that he had mentioned before really given me away?

"You aren't dressed the way I expected either, neh," he said finally.

I shrugged. "I don't wear my stage outfits while running on the beach, heh" was all I could think of to say.

He seemed to consider this for what felt like an eternity—time always stretches when both your arms are tied behind your back and a man who carries a lot of cutlery seems to be considering carving you into chum and throwing you into the ocean—before shrugging.

"You'd better hope your people deliver a ransom far richer than you appear to rate just now, eh?" he said at length. The cutthroats flanking me laughed. One of them half-hummed and half-brayed a discordant melody that I assumed to be one of Urr'hilf's.

"Captain!" shouted a voice from almost directly overhead. "A ship! Heading right for us!"

Everyone who stood on the pirate ship's gently swaying deck or crawled in its rigging, perhaps two dozen nasty pieces of work in all, turned toward where the man in the crow's nest pointed.

Approaching far more quickly than should have been possible for a wooden sailing ship, especially on such a calm day, was a three-masted wooden frigate, her turquoise-skinned Pelagian crew visibly busy on the top deck positioning and loading cannons. Hoisted over the mainsail was a skull-headed banner, which I took to be the local equivalent of the Jolly Roger.

As the frigate heaved to, I began to make out some of her markings. I was surprised to see that they weren't written in Pelagian. They were in English.

The ship alongside us was the *Enterprise*.

"Forgive my interruption, Riker, but I believe you told us that the *Enterprise* was in drydock, light-years away from Pelagia."

Before Riker could answer, he saw a look of sudden comprehension dawning on Picard's face. "Of course. The holodeck program I'd saved from the *Enterprise*-D. It was on the *Calypso II*'s computer."

Riker nodded, grinning. "I guessed that was the work of Commander Keru, the *Enterprise*'s former stellar cartographer. He had more experience with holographic imaging than anyone else who'd come with us to Pelagia. He also had spent a fair amount of time during his two tours of duty on the *Enterprise* running pirate holodeck scenarios. I learned later that once Deanna had discovered I was missing, she rounded up the troops and ordered Keru to outfit the *Calypso II*'s hull with dozens of small holoemitters. Keru found the wooden frigate simulation program in the yacht's memory banks, and used it as a rough-and-ready disguise."

"I'm impressed," Klag said. "Not at the holographic trickery—any fool of an engineer could do that—no, I am taken with such blatant violation of Pelagian law."

Riker glanced at Picard. His silent stare felt like an accusation.

Then Riker looked into his glass. "Exigent circumstances."

"Or barroom blarney?" offered Cap, evidently trying to be helpful.

"If you prefer to think so," Riker said, content to let the others form their own opinions about that. "But regardless, violations like this one are far more serious if one gets caught."

Klag chortled. "True."

Picard's hard stare softened into a grin. "Anyhow . . . ?"

"Anyhow," Riker said, and continued.

The other ship very quickly drew to within grappling distance, as though propelled by supernatural forces.

And she was, at least from the perspective of the locals. Canvas sails were no match for the maneuvering thrusters of a *Sovereign*-class starship's captain's yacht. As I watched the large, mustachioed Pelagian freebooter who stood on the deck of the wooden *Enterprise,* twirling a grappling line over his head—I recognized him only then as our Trill security officer Ranul Keru—I hoped that Deanna and the rest of my rescuers were using whatever energy was necessary to keep their power usage shielded from the monitoring stations on the main southern islands.

They've got to be doing that, I realized. After all, they might simply have flown into orbit and beamed me directly to safety. But had they done that, the Pelagian authorities would have detected it—and the Federation would have suddenly found itself embroiled in an embarrassing diplomatic incident.

I also realized that the yacht's crew probably couldn't use the transporter even if they had wanted to; using their shields to avoid detection by the authorities would have used far too much power for that to be possible.

So we're reduced to an old-fashioned battle on the high seas, I thought just before Captain Torr'ghaff surprised me by slicing the ropes that had bound my wrists behind me.

"Why?" I asked.

"No one should die like a helpless feedbeast bound for the spit, heh. Should we challenge the woman who boards us now, that is your likely fate, heh."

"Have you not seen the flag that flies over her mast, Urr'hilf?" shouted one of the other pirates, a scruffy, dark-skinned man.

"We are being boarded by Arr'ghenn, the Pirate Queen, heh. Have you not seen her on the deck, eha?"

I looked again. Standing beside Keru, dressed in pirate finery that could only be described as regal—in an outlaw sort of way—stood my turquoise-skinned bride. A handful of other pirates stood nearby, cutlasses and pistols at the ready, resembling a potentate's honor guard more than a band of merry cutthroats.

Thank God somebody, probably Keru, I thought, *seems to be on top of the local pirate legends.*

Now Klag threw his head back and laughed. "Your Betazoid mate," Klag said. "A pirate chieftainess?"

"That's right. Would I lie to you?"

Klag shrugged. "While telling a story, Riker, I would be disappointed if you didn't. Continue."

As the *Enterprise* moved in alongside Captain Torr'ghaff's ship, I was glad to see that the *Calypso II*'s newly installed holoemitters were working flawlessly. Torr'ghaff's men edged toward the banisters, cutlasses and other weapons at the ready, but I was heartened to see that Deanna and her crew were standing fast, with none of their own weaponry brandished.

That didn't make Keru and the others any less imposing, however. Keru was stripped to the waist and looking every bit as hirsute and tall as Torr'ghaff, though he was considerably more muscular. He stood in front of Deanna, and as they neared, shouted over to the pirate ship.

"The Queen of the Nine Seas, Arr'ghenn, greets you and wishes to declare *amicry* for the evening."

For some reason, my universal translator failed to tell me what "*amicry*" was, so I asked the pirate next to me.

"It's a truce, neh," the grizzled old man hissed through rotten greenish teeth. "What, you just fall out of the sky, eh?"

"She only has a small crew," another pirate said to Torr'ghaff under his breath. "We can take her ship and her crew before night falls, heh."

Torr'ghaff seemed to consider his options for the moment, then turned to the man who had just advised him. "We don't strike now, Tarrniq, heh. Not until we know what armaments or crew she has in the hold of her strange ship."

I stepped forward. "Smart thinking, Captain. I've heard many a tale about the might of Arr'ghenn, the Pirate Queen. Her legend could not have grown so large if she were not a tremendous force to be reckoned with."

Torr'ghaff turned toward me, and I wondered if my comment was too impertinent. "She is a woman, Urr'hilf, and thus always a force, heh. But I have conquered many forces in my life, though few as succulent as she, heh heh." He leered toward her, and I had to restrain myself from grabbing him by the throat. The presence of so many weapon-wielding brigands encouraged me not to lose my cool.

After a few minutes of negotiations, yelled across the narrow stretch of water that now separated the two ships, Deanna, Keru, and a trio of other Pelagian-disguised Starfleet officers—I recognized Chief Tongetti and Lieutenants Narin and Cruzen, in spite of their temporary cosmetic alterations—came aboard Torr'ghaff's vessel. Now that we seemed to be in no immediate mortal danger, I found myself being re-tied by my captors. Green Teeth assured me it was necessary, "for my own safety."

"And who is your captive?" Deanna asked imperiously as she strode across the deck toward us.

Torr'ghaff seemed surprised by her question. "You do not recognize Fegrr'ep Urr'hilf, neh?" His eyes narrowed dangerously. "He is only the greatest *klap'pa* musician on all of Pelagia! How can you not know him, heh?""

"Oh, *him*," Deanna said, her voice dripping with disdain as she looked at me. "We don't *allow* his music on my ship. It upsets my stomach."

This seemed to mollify Torr'ghaff somewhat. "Then we shall not have him play tonight at dinner, neh. You will join us, heh?"

Deanna was about to respond to his sleazily suggestive invitation when the crewman stationed up in the crow's nest called out yet again.

"Ship ahoy, twenty *mowhp*s!"

"I assume this other ship was sent by the local authorities, alerted by your wife?" This time the interruption came from a Rigelian captain, who had scooted his barstool closer to where Riker, Picard, and Klag sat at the bar.

Riker sighed, and took another quaff from his tankard. "No, it was a merchant vessel."

The Rigelian frowned. "So, if they weren't calling for the authorities, then why this elaborate charade if they weren't going to at least try to rescue you?"

"I suspect it all leads back to the technological restrictions," Picard said dryly.

Riker pointed at his ex-CO. "Exactly. My shipmates had to figure out how to rescue me more covertly, without violating the restrictions, and without calling undue attention to the *Enterprise*. After all, even with all the holoemitters Keru had stuck on her hull, the *Calypso II*'s disguise still wasn't perfect. She looked like a wooden sailing ship from ancient Earth, which meant that she didn't look quite the same as a vessel built on Pelagia. Once they saw me in the custody of the pirates, they must have figured out that getting me free without a fight would take some finessing."

" 'Without a fight'?" Klag slammed down another *warnog*. "How disappointing."

"I'm getting to that," Riker said.

One of Torr'ghaff's men looked through a spyglass, then turned back to us with an excited grin. "It's a *neropses* carrier, Captain, heh! From how low she's riding in the water, I'd say her holds are full, heh!"

Playing her role of Arr'ghenn to the hilt, Deanna snatched a spyglass from another of Torr'ghaff's men. She studied the horizon for a moment, then passed the tube to Keru.

"*Neropses?* Are you that desperate for booty that not only would you kidnap a puerile musician, but also plunder a ship full of *grain?*" She put her hands on her hips, and I could tell she was relishing her part.

Torr'ghaff seemed to grind his teeth for a moment. He looked back toward some of his men before replying. I suspected that he truly didn't want to appear desperate in front of such an august outlaw personage as Arr'ghenn. "Of course not, Arr'ghenn, heh. We needn't worry about such ships when we have riches of our own piled high, heh." He gestured toward me. "As for this one, it happens that not only is his safe return worth a tidy sum, but his talent is also appreciated by my crew, heh, as well as by other freebooters far and wide."

Deanna flashed a smile. "As long as he doesn't perform during dinner, I don't care. While I think it might be amusing to dine with him, if he sings so much as a note, I'll cut his tongue out for dessert."

I didn't realize it at the time, but Deanna had just made a mistake in her role-playing by mentioning me singing. Torr'ghaff and his men already appeared to be suspicious about Arr'ghenn and her crew aboard the *Enterprise,* but her complete lack of knowledge about me—or Fegrr'ep Urr'hilf, to be more precise—clearly sent up a warning flag for the pirate captain.

Nevertheless, a few hours later, Arr'ghenn and her "adjutant" Keru had joined Torr'ghaff for a meal aboard his ship. Along with several of Torr'ghaff's crew, we ate in a garishly appointed stateroom, seated around a wooden table that might once have been exquisite, but which now had so many nicks, scratches, and knife carvings in its surface that it was as rough as a cobblestone street.

Thankfully, I've eaten my share of both Earth seafood and Klingon fare, as have Deanna and Keru, so the "delicacies" placed on our plates didn't churn our stomachs—at least not *too* much.

The captain's boy also served us a pungent but apparently *de rigueur* Pelagian liquor that it seemed unwise to try to refuse, however politely. For a time, the evening was almost enjoyable. Deanna managed to deflect questions about Arr'ghenn's exploits in favor of questioning Torr'ghaff about his *own* past glories. When pressed to speak about herself, she demurred to Keru. I assume that in the time since they'd first encountered Torr'ghaff, Keru had been researching the legend of the reputed pirate queen whom Deanna was impersonating.

I stayed mostly silent, aware that I knew so little about the music or life of Fegrr'ep Urr'hilf that anything I said could reveal that I was not who they thought I was. I also kept my glances at Deanna and Keru to a minimum, lest any of the pirates recognize that I already knew them both.

Unfortunately, the Pelagian liquor seemed to be having a much stronger effect on Deanna than on anyone else. The tipsier she got, the more friendly she became.

And that, apparently, was the weakness that Torr'ghaff was looking to exploit.

"So, you are uncharacteristically modest for a woman who commands so much fear, Arr'ghenn, heh," he said, leering again. "You allow me to prattle on about my triumphs, and yet, heh, you let your adjutant speak for you when you are asked to boast about your own."

Deanna grinned sloppily. "Better to allow the legends to arise on their own, I always say." She put one hand on Keru's shoulder, and rubbed the other over his upper chest. "Besides, Keru always makes my exploits sound so much better. And what's the use of having a big strapping adjutant if he can't regale you with your own tales of terror and treachery from time to time?"

"Your mate laid hands on another man in front of you and you did *nothing*?" Klag asked, his voice registering astonishment. He took another swig from his tankard.

Riker smiled. "I'm not concerned about my wife, nor about

any attention she may have paid Commander Keru during their deception. The roles they were playing there had little to do with reality."

Klag wiped foam off his upper lip. "Can you be so certain?"

Riker looked over at Picard and grinned. Klag's question had brought a smile to the *Enterprise* captain's lips as well, and Riker was glad to have received a respite from Picard's earlier disapproving gaze.

"Captain Klag, I believe that Commander Keru would be likelier to accept a romantic overture from *you* than from my wife," Riker said. "Though you might be the one whose clavicle gets broken during that particular liaison."

Klag raised an eyebrow, but didn't reply.

Riker continued.

"So, legend or not, I'd like to know what *really* happened to the Treasure of Pamplin Rock, heh," Torr'ghaff said, leaning over his plate.

I saw Deanna and Keru exchange a glance, and knew in that moment that something had gone very wrong.

"The treasure is as safe as all our other booty," Keru said. I could see the tension in his posture.

"No matter what truce we call tonight, nor what liquor you pour us, you can't expect me to reveal *all* my secrets," Deanna said, leaning forward a little shakily. She plunked her hand on the table, as if to emphasize her point. "After all, we're still pirates."

Torr'ghaff clamped his gnarled turquoise hand down on top of my wife's hand, and leaned in closer, an angry expression on his face. "Whoever you are, you're *not* Arr'ghenn, neh. The Treasure of Pamplin Rock was captured by Green Beard Grooo'lk not three *quell*s ago, heh."

Deanna seemed to sober up quickly as she yanked her hand quickly away. "My mistake. I thought you were talking about the *earlier* treasure. The one they never reported as missing."

In an instant, the others in the room had stood and drawn

their cutlasses and daggers. Torr'ghaff stood as well. "Your mistake was in thinking we would be fooled, neh. Now you *and* your strange ship will be ours, heh."

As Keru stood, he grabbed the edge of the heavy wooden table and upended it away from him. The food, drink, and dinnerware scattered, even as three of the pirates jumped back to avoid being pinned beneath the table itself. Keru and Deanna had their own weapons in hand before the table had even hit the floor.

Since my hands had been tied in front of me to allow me to eat, I quickly wrapped my arms and bonds around the throat of the pirate nearest to me, choking him from behind. He stabbed backward with his blade, but I sidestepped his clumsy slash and managed to fling him toward one of his crewmates. Unfortunately, that man was already swinging his cutlass, and the pirate I had thrown was directly in the sharp blade's path.

The blade nearly decapitated my opponent, and he went down with a spray of purplish blood. I whirled just as another pirate took a swing at me and blocked the blow with my forearms. I straight-legged him with a quick V'Shan kick I'd learned from Lieutenant Taurik, and the pirate went sprawling backward.

I barely had time to see that Deanna and Keru were holding their own against their foes as I dived for my attacker's fumbled weapon before he could recover it. Unfortunately, both of us slipped on the pool of blood from his nearly headless crewmate, and slid into each other.

Out of the corner of my eye, I saw Deanna sparring with Torr'-ghaff, their blades sparking against each other. I could hear Keru and several others fighting behind me, near the stateroom's doors, but since my attention was focused on my own immediate survival, I couldn't see how he was doing.

Though I managed to grab the cutlass, my footing was unsteady on the slippery deck. My opponent, now divested of any weapon save his wits, swept his leg out, tripping me backward. I crashed to the deck, dazed, and the cutlass went flying.

A moment or two later, I recovered, but my opponent was on

me with fists swinging. I took several blows, but managed to twist to the side, bringing him down to the deck with one good, hard punch. As he howled in pain, I extricated myself and bolted for any weapon I could find.

Just as I grabbed a metal fireplace poker and turned, brandishing it, I saw Keru throw one of the pirates through the doors of the stateroom. But that moment of triumph went sour when I saw that Torr'ghaff had disarmed Deanna and even now had a blade pressed against her throat. A line of conspicuously red blood already trickled down her neck.

"Drop your weapon or I take the head of your false queen as a trophy, heh!" Torr'ghaff growled. "And then I will dice her body for chum, heh!"

"Get back to the ship!" Deanna yelled.

Two pirates menaced me with their cutlasses, and I realized that I, too, was backed into a corner. From where I was standing, I couldn't even reach the window to dive into the sea. Not that I would have, with Deanna in so much danger.

Keru looked to Deanna and myself, and I knew he was calculating whether the chances would be better if he tried to help us here and now, or if he should back off and try to rescue us again later. But he lost whatever moment of initiative he might have had when a roaring pirate charged at him from behind. Keru flipped his sword around and crouched, impaling his attacker and using the thrust, and the man's forward momentum, to flip his body up over his head and into two of the other pirates.

"You have made a grave enemy, Torr'ghaff!" Keru shouted as he retreated. I was amazed that he still had the presence of mind to continue talking in genuine-sounding pirate-speak.

"After him!" Torr'ghaff commanded the few of his men in the room who were left standing.

The man named Tarrniq, who was apparently Torr'ghaff's second-in-command, hesitated instead of rushing after Keru. He pointed toward Deanna's neck. "Captain, Arr'ghenn's blood is . . . *red!*"

My heart sank even further. Now they knew that she was an alien of some sort. Or, at the very least, they had absolutely confirmed that she wasn't who she'd claimed to be. I didn't have long to consider this, though; they soon hustled both me and Deanna out of the stateroom, both of us bound tightly in rope, with several sword-wielding guards paying very close attention to us.

The main deck was a cacophony of war whoops as pirates brandished their weapons and scurried to the ship's starboard side. Some were grabbing ropes from the rigging and untying them.

I saw that Keru had used one of those ropes himself to swing over to the deck of the *Enterprise*, and members of Torr'ghaff's crew were now doing likewise. Thanks to several burning torches mounted on the ship's railings, I could see that the brigands were engaging in a fierce blade-to-blade melee against the small group of Starfleet officers disguised as Arr'ghenn's crew. I was pleased to note that my people were holding their own, at least so far.

I also noticed that they were undertaking a peculiar strategy. The Starfleet contingent seemed to be gathering toward the center of the ship, disappearing one by one into the hold below. Swinging a huge pole around him in a wide arc to discourage his pursuers, Keru was the last to go down, and as he leapt into the darkness belowdecks, no one could have expected what was to happen next.

The *Enterprise* shimmered for a moment, then became immaterial. Even as the holoemitters were turned off, the pirates suddenly found that they had nothing to stand on. Then they plunged downward, slipping along the sleek sides of the *Calypso II* and splashing into the warm, briny deeps of the Opal Sea.

"Keru revealed the ship to be of Starfleet design?" This time the interruption came from Picard, his look decidedly pinched.

"Only for a few seconds," Riker said, putting up his hands as a placating gesture. He wondered momentarily if he had made a mistake in deciding to tell this story, but it was too late to stop now. *In for a penny, in for a pound,* he thought, then continued.

* * *

The moment that the pirates had fallen off the sides of the *Calypso II,* Keru reactivated the holoemitters and the visual form of the wooden, three-masted *Enterprise* reappeared.

I looked over to Torr'ghaff and saw a mixture of shock and anger displayed across his craggy features. Though he was at a loss for words initially, his loud, commanding voice quickly returned to him.

"Man the cannons, heh! Open fire on that ship!"

The men nearest to him quickly scrambled to get belowdecks, where the artillery was evidently kept, while others busied themselves trying to rescue their fellows who had been dumped into the water.

Torr'ghaff's plan might have worked, had not the *Enterprise* quite suddenly begun to speed away into the darkness. Within less than a minute, it was out of range of the cannons, and all but invisible under the wan light of three of Pelagia's six small moons.

I knew that Keru had done what he'd had to do in order to keep the *Calypso II* from being overrun by Torr'ghaff's pirates, and that he had probably taken every precaution to keep our tech violations from being noticed by the authorities. But I also knew that the next rescue attempt was going to be even tougher—and that Keru now had two people to rescue.

And transporter beams were still out of the question.

Torr'ghaff whirled on his heels and glowered at Deanna. "What manner of magical ship is that, heh? And who are you, really?"

Deanna looked at him defiantly, or at least as defiantly as she could manage given that she was still obviously as drunk as a lord. On top of that, she looked to be suffering from intense nausea.

When she didn't answer him, he slapped her across the face, hard.

I struggled against my bonds, and the two men who were holding me back. "Leave her alone!" I yelled.

She responded to the slap first by glaring at him, then by projectile vomiting all over his pirate finery.

Looking disgusted, Torr'ghaff turned to face me. "This woman is not Arr'ghenn, and she does not even bleed the proper color, neh. Her ship casts illusions, and is faster than any vessel I've ever encountered, heh. Nothing appears to be as it seems tonight, eha?"

He leaned in closer to me, his expression menacing. As was his breath. "I am forced to wonder if *you* are who you appear to be, Fegrr'ep Urr'hilf, heh. This succession of trickery began when we captured you, neh? Perhaps it's time you *prove* to me you are who you say you are, heh?"

Or who you *say I am,* I thought. I was beginning to feel very, very nervous.

I swallowed hard, knowing my moment of truth had apparently arrived.

"Get me the *klap'paspech,* heh," Torr'ghaff shouted to one of his men.

"What is a . . . *klap'paspech?*" the Rigelian captain asked.

Resigning himself to at least several dozen more interruptions before his tale reached its denouement, Riker paused to finish his third tankard of uttaberry wine.

Cap placed another in front of him before Riker had even set his empty stein down.

"A *klap'paspech* was apparently the main instrument on which Fegrr'ep Urr'hilf played his *klap'pa* music," Riker said. "Unfortunately, I had never so much as seen one before, let alone taken the time to become a world-famous *klap'paspech* virtuoso."

It was the first time in my life I'd been grateful not to be able to get an annoying tune out of my head. But as I turned the *klap'-paspech,* a weird metal pretzel of an instrument, over and over in my hands, I wondered if those weird snatches of melody I'd first heard back at the island hostelry—probably in the venerable elevator that served several of the place's eating and shopping establishments—could possibly do me any good. Come to think of it, hadn't some of the pirates been humming the same tunes?

Why couldn't this Fegrr'ep Urr'hilf have been a trombone player? I thought, though I knew I should have been grateful that Urr'hilf wasn't famous for his singing or his interpretive dance. The fingers of my right hand came to rest against a series of brass keys or stops. *Not too different from the 'bone,* I realized. *If I'm holding the damned thing the right way up, that is.*

I was becoming extremely conscious of the suspicious stares of Captain Torr'ghaff and a dozen or so of his squinting cutthroats. The same pair of freebooters who had taken Deanna belowdecks now lugged a glass aquarium tank to my side, and I could see clearly what it contained: one of the local squidlike creatures whose large brains and tympanic membranes served as the biological equivalent of a modern-day audio system.

A music library with tentacles, I thought, suddenly realizing that I was in for an impromptu recording session. *No pressure.*

I therefore made a quick command decision: Taking a wild guess as to which part of this convoluted brass taffy-pull was the business end, I placed what appeared to be a mouthpiece against my lips, closed my eyes, and blew.

BLAAAAT. The sound trailed off, dying somewhere between a moan, a gurgle, and a sigh.

Torr'ghaff reached for the haft of his cutlass and bared its blade. The other pirates growled and muttered restlessly.

Crap. I adjusted something that looked like a valve and tried again.

BLAAAAT. Louder this time. BLAAAAAAAT. I kept at it, hearing progressively more sustain and less of that gurgling hiss the instrument had been making.

Even the intonation was getting better, if that concept could even be applied to Pelagian music, as I soldiered on, trying to force the bleating horror attached to my face to re-create the discordant melody I couldn't get out of my head.

I continued for maybe a minute, though at the time it seemed like the longest set I'd played in my life.

But it seemed to be working. The grumbling among the pirates was subsiding, replaced by nodding murmurs of recognition.

Whatever shortcomings were evident in my performance I had to trust everyone to chalk up to an embouchure that had been bruised and battered by the evening's fighting.

Captain Torr'ghaff released the haft of his blade, allowing it to fall back into the scabbard. But the glint of suspicion never left his eyes.

"Why do I not recognize certain parts of that . . . opus, eh?" Torr'ghaff said after I had paused for breath, and allowed the admiring applause of the pirate crew to die down.

"I've, ah, been working on some new material lately."

Torr'ghaff sniffed with disdain. "I like your old stuff better, heh. I hope, for your sake, that I like your people's response to the ransom note I left them better still, heh. Perhaps my other hostage will reveal some news of this, neh? Before I shed the rest of her red alien blood, heh."

He turned on his heel and headed belowdecks, leaving me in the hands of several armed pirates, who—luckily for me—still believed I was the person their captain had initially mistaken me for.

But Deanna's situation was far, far worse. Torr'ghaff might kill her any minute. *Come on, Ranul,* I thought as I handed my instrument off to one of my captors. *Now would be good.*

With both Deanna and myself now in Torr'ghaff's hands, I knew Keru had to be preparing another rescue attempt. But I also knew he had to be using virtually all his available power just to elude detection by the Pelagian authorities. And the longer he took, the greater the chance of his being caught, thereby touching off a diplomatic crisis that would get the Federation forever booted off Pelagia—and the whole lot of us cashiered from Starfleet. Therefore whatever he was going to do, he was going to have to do quickly.

And cleverly.

The interruption this time came from Riker himself, when he noticed Picard's pensive, serious gaze. He felt fortunate that those stern eyes were directed at the other captain's *dresci* and not at him.

"Is something wrong, Captain?" Riker asked Picard.

Picard shook his head. "Not as long as I continue to give you the benefit of the doubt, and assume you are making up at least half of this story."

"I have never doubted that," Klag said with a big grin.

Riker said, "So if you *did* believe my story, you'd have to report our . . . infractions to Starfleet Command." Realizing he might have just put a half dozen other Starfleet careers in jeopardy in addition to his own by speaking a bit too freely, he suddenly wished he'd decided to tell a different story. How he'd *really* received that broken arm on Elamin IX, perhaps. Or the *first* time he'd been forced to dress up in feathers, at that diplomatic function on Armus IX.

"No, Will. Because to do that I'd have to break a cardinal rule of the Captain's Table."

Riker raised his mug. "I'll drink to that." After slamming down a hefty swallow of the sweet Betazoid wine, he said, "Now, where was I?"

Oh, yeah.

Torr'ghaff was about to interrogate and execute my new bride. And I was pretty damned miffed about that, though I wasn't in much of a position to do anything about it.

Except maybe to appeal to the better natures of these pirates, assuming any of them had one. Since most of them seemed to be fans of music—or what passed for it here on the Opal Sea—I was willing to wager that they did. Besides, I didn't have a lot of other good options.

But although they showed me as much deference as any hostage could hope to expect—and I was still a hostage, my celebrity status notwithstanding—my attempts to convince my escorts to intercede on Deanna's behalf came to nothing. Though the trio of large, ugly pirates who marched me back down to the smelly hold where I'd first awakened looked more thoughtful than seemed possible, none of them seemed thoroughly won over.

Then I noticed something really strange.

"You were injured during Arr'ghenn's capture, neh?" I asked one of the pirates.

"During the capture of the false Arr'ghenn, heh," he said, nodding as he rubbed at a fading scar on his neck. "You pushed me into the path of a sword."

"But I saw your injury, heh. You were almost decapitated! How did you survive it, eh?"

He looked at me as though I had just fallen from one of Pelagia's six silver-hued moons.

"I have survived far worse, and healed afterward, as has everyone else here, heh. The Small Spirits see to that, neh? I suppose the false Pirate Queen will soon discover whether or not the Small Spirits will perform such favors for offworlders, heh."

Oh, no, I thought, realizing that Deanna was actually in far more danger than I had previously suspect—

"So the Pelagians heal quickly," said Klag. "So do Klingons. What of it?"

"Klingons are tough, I'll grant you that," Riker said. "But even you wouldn't survive for long with your head nearly sawed off. *That's* how badly wounded that pirate had been."

"And?" Picard said.

"And I finally began to understand something that we verified with our scanners later on—that the 'Small Spirits' the injured pirate had mentioned were actually nanites."

"Nanites?" said the Rigelian.

"Microscopic machines," Picard said, his eyes suddenly growing wide with alarm.

"Which can be used to repair injuries and cure diseases," Riker added.

"But nanites are potentially very dangerous if allowed to run amok. They can even be used as bioweapons," Picard said. Riker knew that he was speaking from bitter experience.

"That's what the Pelagian authorities think as well," Riker said.

"Which goes a long way toward explaining their current technological restrictions. It seems their ancestors accidentally released a nanoplague centuries ago. Pelagia is still swarming with nanites to this day, though the planet's biosphere has completely adapted to their presence."

Picard started to rise from the barstool on which he was perched. "Damn this place's rules about captain's discretion," he said, looking squarely at Cap. "I need to alert Starfleet Command immediately."

Riker placed a gently restraining hand on his fellow captain's shoulder, a move he would have found unthinkable only weeks ago. "It's really not necessary. I looked into it already, and Starfleet Medical has already declared Pelagia safe for all known humanoid species. The nanites self-destruct when they're taken out of the planet's magnetic field, and they've so far proven to be incompatible with all non-Pelagian life."

Looking more annoyed than entertained, Picard straightened his uniform tunic and recovered his seat. "All right, Will. Continue."

Riker nodded. "It was the nanites, of course, that—"

—had very quickly repaired all the injuries suffered by the pirates during the recent fighting. Pirates who should have died from what would have been mortal injuries had they been suffered anywhere else *by* anyone else, were practically good as new only a few hours later. It seemed that the only way a Pelagian could die by violence here was to be very deliberately chopped into many, many pieces, or to be dropped straight into an active volcano.

And this, I realized, was the very reason why Deanna was in more danger than I previously had thought. The Pelagians' "Small Spirits" not only kept them alive despite their violent encounters, but also encouraged a certain casual attitude toward violence itself.

In other words, Deanna's interrogation was liable to be lethal in and of itself. Torr'ghaff could easily kill her without even meaning to.

And I was alone and unarmed, locked in the dank bilge of Torr'ghaff's ship, with who knew how many armed guards standing between me and Deanna.

My glum thoughts were interrupted by a visit from Torr'ghaff himself, who threw the door open with a crash. I didn't need Deanna's empathy to tell me he was very frustrated.

"My men tell me you are concerned about the false pirate queen's fate, heh? Why, eha?"

I decided to take another gamble. "You claim to know my work, Captain, neh? You ought to know that I am unenthused by brutality."

The pirate chieftain looked disappointed. "You are not at all as I imagined you, neh."

"How is the woman?" I asked, assuming that if she had been badly injured or killed, I would have sensed it through the bond we shared.

"Her answers to my questions are frustrating, heh. And she tends to giggle. My wine affects her far too easily, neh?"

I shook my head in amazement, wondering when the Pelagian booze that had got her into this jam was finally going to wear off.

"Why are you so interested in this offworld woman, Urr'hilf? Is it merely the renowned love you harbor for the females in your audience? Or is it something more, eh?"

Now did not seem like a good time to show him the front of any of my cards. "She means nothing to me, heh. Other than that she reminds me of my first."

"Then I will have my men carve her to tiny pieces. She will feed the fishes, Small Spirits or no." He turned to leave.

This was going very badly. "Wait!"

He stopped in the open doorway and looked back at me with an impatient scowl. "Yes?"

I took yet another gamble then, the only one I could think of at the moment. "Your men require diversion, neh?"

He nodded. "We have been at sea for over a fourmonth."

"Then I can help. Make landfall at your nearest friendly port.

Once there, I will entertain your men with a concert. And you can still get your ransom by proving to all the world that you have me, neh?"

I could see the wheels turning in Torr'ghaff's battle-scarred head. He must have already been planning to charge admission, and trying to figure out how many Pelagian ducats the traffic would bear.

Then a satisfied grin split his bewhiskered face. "Very well. I will not harm the woman, heh. In three days, we will reach our stronghold on Terriveyt Island. You will perform there for a large crowd, heh." It was clear to me that he meant a large *paying* crowd. "I will even supply all the instruments and costumes you will need to mount your show."

Three days, I thought. That would almost surely give Commander Keru ample time to get Deanna and me out of here. Though exactly how he would do it under the watchful eye of the Pelagian authorities, and without transporters, I had no clear idea.

"All right," I said.

Still grinning, Torr'ghaff turned to leave. But I wasn't finished with him.

"But I have one additional condition, eh?"

He sighed, then faced me again. "Oh, yes. You want all the sweets served backstage to be of a particular color, neh?"

I shook my head. "I think it might be best not to be fussy about that, under the circumstances."

"Wise," he said, nodding.

"But I want the woman to be on the stage with me. Unharmed, neh."

He nodded, a light of understanding flickering in his eyes. His grin became a leer. "Ah. You wish to serenade her before the audience. And later . . ."

I wanted to grab his tongue and pull it out by the roots. Instead, I did my best to copy his leer. "Exactly."

"Agreed! Please my men with your music, Urr'hilf, and I guarantee you a night of pleasure afterward, heh. And should your people refuse to pay the ransom, I promise to spare you all possible pain when I have you diced and thrown overboard—along with the false pirate queen."

He exited, and the door slammed shut with the finality of a tomb.

Now all I had to do was fake my way through a long live set of music I had mostly never heard before, authored by a musician I knew nothing about, using an instrument I really didn't even know how to play. No problem.

Thank whatever gods watch over drunks, little children, and former first officers from ships named *Enterprise* for the Pelagian tympanic squids.

Thanks to the popularity of Fegrr'ep Urr'hilf among Torr'ghaff's crew—and the lousy soundproofing aboard his ship—I got to hear a great deal of Urr'hilf's organically recorded repertoire. By the time the ship made landfall three days later, I was beginning to think I might actually have half a chance of pulling this off.

"You okay?" I whispered to Deanna as five cutlass-and-pistol-wielding Pelagian pirates walked us side by side down a gangplank and onto the dilapidated docks that lined an island marina. Once again, the orange sun stood high in the sky. That sun had set three times and risen twice since I had last seen her.

"I've been through worse," she looked drawn and pale, the once neat, close-cropped rows of her new Pelagian hairstyle now looking disheveled. But she no longer seemed loopy. The indigenous alcohol must have finally worn off.

"Torture?" I asked quietly, fearing the worst.

"I suppose that's debatable. Torr'ghaff has been withholding chocolate. On Betazed, that's considered a basic violation of humanoid rights and the laws of warfare."

I was glad her sense of humor hadn't suffered.

We were separated a few minutes later, as we reached a large amphitheater that had been built right alongside the docks. I presumed that Deanna had been taken to some sort of green room, to await the start of the concert.

Hordes of Pelagians—all of them outlaws and pirates, judging from their mode of dress—were already lining up and entering the bowl-shaped, open-air concert hall, and I could hear the voices of what sounded like thousands more already inside. Had our captors somehow used their tympanic squids to get advance word of this concert to the island? Regardless, Torr'ghaff obviously stood to make a fortune, assuming my performance was well received. I didn't want to think about what might happen if it wasn't.

I was escorted directly to a large, richly appointed dressing room. I *was* a celebrity, after all.

The first thing I noticed was the costume. A big, awkward, fake-jewel-encrusted suit almost entirely covered in large yellow and orange feathers, obviously the plumage of some human-size Pelagian tropical bird. I put it on, hoping my musical mimicry would be more convincing if I at least looked the part—

"Actually, Will, birds that derive from island habitats usually don't grow to such large sizes," Picard said in a quietly chiding tone.

Riker's only response was a pleading look.

"Sorry," Picard said. "Continue."

The concert itself began that afternoon, and went better than I expected—at least at first. Torr'ghaff had left an instrument with me down in the ship's hold, and I'd spent the better part of three days not only listening to a good chunk of Urr'hilf's hit parade, but also determining that the fingerings of his chosen instrument weren't all that different from those of the trombone. It was too bad the thing didn't have a slide, but you can't have everything.

With Deanna lounging on a settee that Torr'ghaff's men had placed on the wooden stage beside me—she displayed what even I thought was a very convincing "adoring female fan" expression—I got through the first couple of numbers without a lot of flubs.

But those tunes were the *easy* ones. By the third number, maybe ten minutes into the set, I knew was floundering, and I could hear enough murmuring out in the bleachers to tell me that the audience was quickly becoming aware that something wasn't right. Deanna continued to do her best to dispel that by maintaining an expression of sustained uncritical admiration.

But as Thaddius "Old Iron Boots" Riker once said, "you can't make chicken salad out of chicken shit." There was only so much even Deanna could do. It was up to me and my performance to keep these bloodthirsty pirates from booing and then rioting.

And I knew I was failing, even as I lapsed into a rendition of "Stardust," an old jazz standard from Earth. I hoped the crowd would accept it as one of Urr'hilf's new, experimental compositions.

Nope. As though thinking with one mind, the pirates who composed the audience—apparently thousands of them—rose from their benches. They surged toward the stage, trampling one another in their rage, which got them het up even further.

I dropped my instrument on the settee beside Deanna, and helped her to her feet. "We have to get out of here," I said, shedding the cumbersome, feather-and-jewel-covered jacket.

Holding her hand, I moved with her toward the wings. A trio of burly pirates blocked our way, their blades extended. We turned toward the other side of the stage. Captain Torr'ghaff and another three armed pirates stood in our path, murder in their eyes.

"Now would be a really good time for an emergency beam-out," Deanna said.

The angry shriek of the crowd crescendoed as the first of the pirates reached the stage and hauled themselves up onto it.

"Looks like we're in for a real fight, Arr'ghenn," I said.

I saw that even Torr'ghaff himself—who must have been pretty angry about his big, profitable concert event falling apart—was drawing a bead on us with his pistol. Shouting a warning to Deanna, I pulled her down behind what little cover the settee provided. Chunks of wood and brass and fabric flew as a metal projectile almost parted Deanna's hair.

We needed to get the hell out of there. But we needed weapons even more.

I turned toward the stage just in time to see the first of the enraged audience members come barreling toward me. Like a lot of the Pelagian pirates, he was a nasty piece of work, and stood a good head taller than I did. Glancing at the settee, I saw the *klap'-paspech*, which Torr'ghaff had perforated with his gun. I grabbed it.

The approaching pirate didn't use a lot of science when he swung his cutlass. I stepped in close after his first slash missed, then slammed him across the temple with my broken instrument. Dropping its shattered pieces, I then grabbed the man's arm and let his own momentum carry him over my back and onto the stage, which he struck like a cannonball. A second man behind him soon went down, thanks to a decidedly sobered-up Deanna.

A moment later, she and I were armed both with blades and with muzzle-loading handguns. But considering what we were up against, they might as well have been brooms and feather dusters.

"Don't go easy on them," I told her. "They're a lot tougher than they look."

She looked at me like I was a complete idiot. "Thanks, Will. And to think I was just going to give them a stern talking-to."

We were facing a veritable army of snarling, bloodthirsty nasties that would have made Blackbeard wet himself. For the first time since we'd come to Pelagia, I began to really believe that we were about to die.

As we became completely surrounded by dozens of armed and angry men, I felt Deanna's mind reach out to mine, apparently to comfort me during our last moments.

That's when the end of the world happened.

But if a comet really *had* chosen that moment to slam into the center of the Opal Sea, I probably wouldn't have had time to wonder what could have made such a damned loud noise.

I turned then, and saw it.

The prow of the *Enterprise*—the wooden one, not the duranium one—was suddenly plowing directly through the wall of the amphitheater that faced the docks. Bodies were scattering in all directions as the ship continued to move forward amid a great creaking and groaning of timbers and beams and pier planking and shattering bleachers and convincingly splintering holographic wood. The air was scorched by angry shouts and screams.

Keru's audacity impressed and appalled me all at the same time. Crashing into an amphitheater filled with concertgoers—even *pirate* concertgoers—wasn't exactly a by-the-book Starfleet tactic.

But if the person doing it had done some research—and discovered just how hard it really is to actually hurt a Pelagian—then what would have been an act of sheer brutality anywhere else had become instead a feat of tactical genius here on the Opal Sea.

The most important thing at the moment was that everyone in the place seemed to have forgotten us, at least for a moment. "Let's go!" I shouted to Deanna, grabbing her hand.

We ran flat-out across the stage toward the wooden ship, just as it slammed into the apron with a thud that shook the building from rafters to root cellar.

I cast a quick glance at the beams overhead, which were vibrating like banjo strings. *This place is going to come right down on top of us,* I thought. *Wonderful.*

As we approached the side of the disguised *Calypso II,* several of the unsavory audience members began to form a disorganized skirmish line between us and our escape. I could see Chief Tongetti standing on the prow above them, readying a rope ladder for us, though he couldn't lower it without inviting the wrong people aboard.

Her cutlass raised defensively, Deanna looked toward me with a stunned expression. She obviously had no desire to kill anyone, and just as obviously was not aware of the "Small Spirits" that made that particular issue a nonproblem.

I raised my own blade and pistol. "Have at 'em, *Imzadi.* They heal real quick."

Blades crashed into each other. Fortunately for us, drunkenness and surprise had acted in our favor this time, allowing us to fight our way to the ship—and Tongetti's rope ladder—just before the *Enterprise* made an apparently magical retreat back toward the docks, breaking for the green, sun-dappled expanse of the Opal Sea that lay beyond.

"Welcome aboard, sir," said Commander Keru as Deanna and I pulled ourselves over the holographic railings. Terriveyt Island, and all the cutthroats thereon, was rapidly falling away from us as the *Calypso II* skimmed along the ocean surface, powered by her heavily shielded maneuvering thrusters.

"I wonder how many thousands of pairs of Pelagian eyeballs saw what you just did, Mr. Keru," I said as we made our way belowdecks, and into the yacht's real—that is to say, its twenty-fourth-century—interior.

"Almost everybody back there is a criminal of some sort or other," Keru said. "Somehow I don't think they'll be making any reports to the duly instituted legal authorities. Which, I might add, I have taken *great* pains to evade myself."

"All in all, that sounds better than being carved into chum by pirates," Deanna said.

"My thoughts exactly," said the big Trill, a self-satisfied grin on his bearded face as he placed us on a leisurely course back to one of the visitor-friendly, tech-unrestricted islands. With any luck at all, we could make landfall undetected sometime after dark.

And then get back to our interrupted honeymoon.

But for the next several hours, Deanna and I would be aboard the yacht we'd borrowed, in the company of the colleagues who had saved our lives. I wondered if we could persuade them to give us an hour or so worth of privacy in the aft compartment. Even if that meant ordering them all to cram themselves into the cockpit. Rank, after all, hath its privileges.

"That was some superbly unorthodox tactical thinking, Commander," I said to Keru, thinking he might make a worthy addition to *Titan*'s bridge crew . . .

"And that's the way it happened," Riker said, pushing his tankard toward Cap. The uttaberry wine had built up a fine buzz, and he decided that discretion was the better part of valor now that his tale was told. He stood and straightened his uniform tunic—a habit he'd acquired from Captain Picard long ago.

"So that little adventure accounted for five days," the Rigelian said. "You haven't yet told us how you spent your remaining two weeks on the Opal Sea."

Riker grinned. "And I'm not going to. I've told my story."

"But not the whole story." The Rigelian sounded angry.

Before Riker could say anything, Klag said, "One never hears the *entire* story, does one?"

"To quote an old Ferengi saying, 'Always leave the customer wanting more.'"

Cap offered to top off Riker's tankard again, but stopped when the new captain politely declined. Setting the violet bottle down, the barkeep said, "So assuming everything you've told us is true—and even if it isn't—what's it all mean?"

"Excuse me?" Riker wasn't sure he understood the question.

"I mean, what did you learn from the experience?"

Recovering his tankard, Riker took another swallow of what remained of his drink, then offered Cap a wry smile. "Since I strongly suspect that you believe only about half of it, I'm going to turn the tables on you. What do *you* think I got out of it?"

"Seems to me you may have learned a little bit about staying cool during a tense situation," Cap said. "And about thinking on your feet."

Klag grunted. "I would say you learned to hone your improvisational skills. Tactically, if not musically."

Riker shrugged.

"I think you already knew more than a little about improvising, Captain Riker," Cap said. Riker was beginning to suspect that the burly bartender was fairly well acquainted with that subject as well.

Rising from his barstool, Picard faced Riker and said, "I think this whole harrowing episode may also have taught you something about how to deal with that fourth pip Starfleet just pinned to your collar."

"It also should have taught you to be more careful the next time you pick a honeymoon destination," said Klag with a chuckle.

Riker thought carefully about everything that had been said these past few moments and gathered his thoughts. "I suppose my story was about all of that," he said finally. "But the main thing being shanghaied on the Opal Sea taught me was something else entirely. It's something no one has mentioned yet—and I had no idea it would turn out to be so important for a newly minted starship captain to learn. But I'm glad I learned it sooner rather than later."

"And what's that?" Picard asked.

"Mainly this: Maintaining captain-like deportment is important, maybe even critically important. But knowing when to toss all that aside can be even *more* important. When, for instance, pirates force you to impersonate a bizarrely dressed alien music star, it's a good time to set decorum aside and just play your heart out. And find the notes as you go along."

"I don't believe any of it," the Rigelian said. He stood up, baring his fangs. "I demand proof that what you just told us is true."

All other conversation in the bar came to an abrupt stop. Riker saw that every eye in the place was on him and the Rigelian. He knew that there was only one thing he could do.

Draining the dregs of his uttaberry wine, Riker set his empty tankard down on the bar. He walked purposefully toward the other captain—

—and then continued directly past him. Reaching up on the wall beyond him, Riker grasped one of the musical instruments that was displayed there.

He turned and faced the Rigelian captain, brandishing a reassuringly familiar trombone as though it were a phaser rifle.

"Fegrr'ep Urr'hilf calls this tune 'Six Moons over Terriveyt Island.' "

Then he raised the instrument to his lips, played his heart out, and found the notes as he went along.

Tending Bar . . .

Cap leaned against the back wall of the bar and enjoyed Riker's impromptu concert, remembering an old human saying about music having charms to soothe the savage breast—though few truly found Pelagian music all that soothing.

When the captain of the Titan *finished his concert, there was copious applause and cheering from some of the patrons, including Klag. The presence of Riker and Picard had cheered the Klingon for a time—though partway through Riker's concert, another Klingon entered and took up a position at the far end of the bar from Klag's seat, and that had a deleterious effect on the* Gorkon *shipmaster's attitude.*

After Riker returned to the bar, Cap felt obligated to remind the man who'd brought him that he hadn't actually paid his tab yet. Picard thought a moment, and apparently decided that, since Riker was at the start of his first command, it was only appropriate that Picard tell the story of what happened after the end of his. . . .

JEAN-LUC PICARD

CAPTAIN OF THE *U.S.S. STARGAZER*

Darkness

══════════

MICHAEL JAN FRIEDMAN

With all the years he had spent in the vast, lonely reaches of space, Jean-Luc Picard couldn't remember ever having experienced a complete and utter lack of light.

Even during his ship's power failures, there had always been the rays of distant stars to provide some bit of illumination. But at that moment, with the door to the rehab bay closed behind him, Picard was in as perfect a blackness as he had ever known.

Then the overhead lighting strips went on, revealing a snub-nosed, ten-meter-long, type-9 cargo shuttle capable of transporting a crew of two, a cargo specialist, and a payload of several metric tons with the help of a twin-engine warp drive, a separate impulse drive, twelve directional thrusters, and an only slightly outdated deflector grid.

Her name, represented in neat letters on her hull, was the *Nadir*—after the Rigelian diplomat who brought the Dedderac into the Federation. *How appropriate*, Picard thought.

The doors slid open again and Erik Van Dusen, head of Starfleet's new shuttle rehab facility, walked into the bay. "Sorry," said Van Dusen, a gray-haired walrus of a man. "We still haven't got all the lights hooked up in this section."

"That's quite all right," said Picard, taking in the sight of the *Nadir*. "She was worth waiting for."

But his voice lacked the enthusiasm he intended. It was a problem for him these days, working up enthusiasm—and not just when it came to shuttlecraft.

"She's all ready for you," Van Dusen informed him. "I checked her out myself."

Picard turned to him. "You know, if I had been forced to go through the proper channels—"

"It would have been weeks before they assigned you a shuttle.

And maybe longer, considering the possibility that this would have been seen as personal business."

"I'm grateful," said Picard.

"No need to be," said Van Dusen. "It's the least I can do for my sister's old classmate." His eyes twinkled mischievously. "Of course, back at the Academy you had a bit more hair. . . ."

Picard managed a semblance of a smile. He had taken his share of ribbing about his energetically receding hairline. But then, he was pushing fifty years of age. A man was *supposed* to have something to show for all the time he had put in.

At least, that was what he had always believed. As it turned out, it was not always that way.

"So," said Van Dusen, "are you ready?"

"I am," said Picard.

Van Dusen tossed him a slim, silver remote-control device. Then he crossed the deck to its only distinguishing feature—a simple, unassuming console.

Using the remote control, Picard opened the shuttle hatch and slipped through it. Then he established a communications link with Van Dusen's combadge.

"Do you remember how to pilot one of these things?" Van Dusen gibed.

Picard had spent his share of time at the helm of a shuttle recently—something the other man might have forgotten. Still, all he said was "I do."

"Glad to hear it. Just bring her back in one—" Van Dusen stopped, looking appalled at himself. *"—or, um, two months, whenever you're done on Hydra IV."*

It was difficult for Picard to make out Van Dusen's complexion from where he sat, but he was certain the fellow had turned a deep shade of red.

"Thanks again," said Picard.

Activating the thrusters, he brought the shuttle about until it was pointed at the bay doors. When they parted for him, revealing a slice of starry space, he nudged the craft forward.

Thanks to the transparent, semipermeable barrier stretched across the aperture, Van Dusen didn't have to worry about the facility losing air. All he had to do was let Picard know when the doors had finished opening.

"All clear," he said.

Applying a little more thrust, Picard sailed into the embrace of the vacuum, allowing the doors to slide closed behind him. As soon as he was clear of the rehab facility, he laid in a course. Then he engaged the *Nadir*'s refurbished impulse drive and took her to one-quarter light speed.

The Hydra system wasn't that far away. At warp two point two, a speed the shuttle could sustain for an extended period, the journey wouldn't take more than a month.

It sounded like a long time. But then, it would have taken just as long to wait for a supply ship bound for Hydra. And then he would have had to interact with her captain—a situation he might have enjoyed at a different stage of his life, but didn't think he would enjoy now.

After all, captains liked to talk about their ships. And of all subjects in the universe, that was the one Picard was most determined to avoid.

Seven days out from Van Dusen's rehab facility, Picard transmitted a subspace message to Elizabeth Wu, letting her know that he was on his way.

Wu had served as his second officer years earlier, distinguishing herself time and again as perhaps the most dependable member of his command staff. When he first met her, her literal interpretation of Starfleet regs drove his other officers crazy. But in time she learned to ease up in that regard, and she became one of the more popular figures on the ship.

Picard was surprised when she told him she was thinking about joining her sister Victoria as a researcher at the Federation's Hydra IV colony. But then, scientific inquiry had been Wu's first love, and it had loomed larger in her thoughts with each breakthrough reported by her sister.

The captain too had possessed a passion for science once. In fact, it had nearly derailed his career in Starfleet. However, in his case, it was a love of archaeology rather than arboreal genetics, and it had eventually lost out to his yearning for the stars.

Finally, Wu had given in to her attraction and asked for a leave of absence. And Picard had granted it. But he had also left the door open for her in case she wished to return. If the life of a research scientist turned out not to be all she imagined, she could always go back to work for him.

That was nearly nineteen years ago. To his knowledge, Wu had never looked back.

But Picard had made a point of keeping in touch with her, and she had done the same with him. He served as her conduit for news about her favorite crewmates and she kept him posted on the latest developments in her field, and over time they became even better friends than when they were working side by side.

Then again, he was no longer compelled to see Wu as a subordinate. She was simply someone for whom he harbored a good deal of affection and respect.

Which was why Picard was on his way to Hydra IV. Over the years, Wu had become his sounding board, an objective source of wisdom who knew intimately the workings of a starship but no longer had a stake in what went on there.

He needed that source of wisdom now. He needed it more than he had needed anything in his entire life.

Noting an unusual blip on one of his monitors, Picard put aside his thoughts and leaned forward to take a closer look. But it was nothing to worry about. Just an ion squall, too small to justify a course change.

A good thing, he mused. The sooner he reached Hydra IV and Wu, the better.

•   •   •

It wasn't until near the end of Picard's second week on the *Nadir* that he found himself sitting upright in bed, his breath coming hard, his sheets twisted and dank with perspiration.

It had happened several times before over the last couple of months. And like those other times, there was an image emblazoned on his mind's eye.

An image of a ship.

She was rust-colored, her long, intrusive bow protruding from what looked like the back of a centrally ridged turtle shell. But it wasn't only in his dreams that Picard had seen her. He had done so in reality as well.

Her captain never identified himself, never gave even a hint as to his motive. And no one on the *Stargazer* could identify his ship, never having seen her like before.

But she had plenty of firepower. Her first volley tore up the *Stargazer*'s shields. Her second, which came immediately on the heels of the first, sent the Federation ship lurching sideways and gouged her hull.

Suddenly, Picard found himself in fiery, smoking chaos. Away from the bridge, it was even worse. A half-dozen decks were hemorrhaging atmosphere into the vacuum.

And not *just* atmosphere. On Picard's viewscreen, there were bodies pinwheeling through space, some of them dead but others still horribly alive.

His eyes burning with carbon fumes and escaped coolant, Picard had risen from his seat to get a look at his colleagues. But as he did, his foot struck something.

Looking down, he saw that it was Vigo, his weapons officer. As big as the fellow was, it couldn't have been anyone else. And there was blood oozing from a blackened gash in his temple.

Kneeling, Picard had felt Vigo's thick blue neck for a pulse. There wasn't any. The weapons officer was lifeless, inert.

"Picard to sickbay!" he had cried out. "I need a team here on the double!"

He had received an answer from his chief medical officer, but it was too garbled to make out. Apparently, the attack had damaged the intercom system as well.

And the enemy was coming about in a leisurely loop, preparing for a third and doubtless final strike.

Picard was compelled to improvise, and quickly. He had learned in his Academy days that an adversary was least prepared for a taste of his own tactics. The enemy had successfully relied on the element of surprise; Picard would do the same.

Instead of trying to expand the distance between the ships, he had his conn officer wheel and go to warp—but just for the merest fraction of a second. It brought them nose-to-nose with their unsuspecting assailant, closer even than they had been before. Then the *Stargazer* fired everything she had left in her batteries.

The enemy's core must have been compromised, because she went up in a spasm of matter-antimatter fury. The battle, strangely, was over. However, the *Stargazer* could hardly be declared the winner.

Her systems were failing one by one, most every deck a sparking, flaming death trap. The death toll was at least twenty. And it was only a matter of time before their warp core breached and they shared the fate of their mysterious attacker.

So Picard ordered everyone who was still alive to abandon ship. The survivors piled into escape craft with whatever bodies they could find and sliced into the void. Then they watched the *Stargazer* diminish with distance, her once-proud lines skewed at a sad and lonely angle.

It took weeks for a rescue vessel to pick them up. By then, the survivors in Picard's shuttle looked half-dead themselves, all of them having lost friends and comrades.

But Picard had it worse than any of them. He had to live with the knowledge that those comrades had perished on his watch.

Earlier in his career, there were those who had questioned his ability to command. At the time, he had believed them misguided. Now he wondered if they hadn't been possessed of more insight than he had given them credit for.

• • •

Two and a half weeks out from the rehab facility, Picard recalled something that had eluded him since his court-martial.

Clytemnestra, he thought. *Of course.*

It was the name of the cat that had attacked him on the gray cusp of morning as he slept with her mistress. To that point, Picard had believed that she was his friend—the cat, not the woman. Though now that he thought about it, the same could have been said of the woman as well.

After all, the cat's mistress—Philipa Louvois—had attacked him with much the same enthusiasm. However, she had done it in the course of a court-martial, where he was forced to sit and listen to her describe the charges leveled at him by Starfleet.

It was standard operating procedure whenever captains came home without their vessels. Nothing to worry about, Picard had been told. Still, it had torn him up inside.

In the end, he was exonerated in the eyes of Starfleet. But in his own eyes? That was a different matter entirely.

He could have done more, Picard told himself over and over again, numbing himself in gin mills where all the customers had scars like his—the kind no one could see. He could have seen the attack coming, he insisted in the confines of his own mind. He could have taken measures to prevent it.

It was his friend and first officer Gilaad Ben Zoma who finally pulled him out of his downward spiral, or there was no telling how low he might have sunk. However, the questions persisted.

Could he have done more? *Could* he have saved his ship?

As for the deaths of his crewmen—Vigo and Yojaleya and Satran and the others—Picard hadn't gotten over them. They lingered with him like a bad toothache, a pain that seemed destined to remain with him the rest of his life.

Somewhere along the line, he decided he didn't want to go through this a second time. He didn't want to be responsible for so many lives anymore. The loss of those who had trusted him and depended on him had stripped him of his will to command.

Ever since he could remember, he had wanted to captain a ship that sailed the stars. He had defied his father to follow that dream. And now it had turned bitter in his mouth, like ashes.

But what else was he to do with his life? He didn't think he could stand remaining in Starfleet as a paper-pusher. And if he resorted to a position in commercial shipping, he would again be taking responsibility for a crew.

Still, he had to do *something*, and he couldn't solicit ideas from those who had abandoned the *Stargazer* with him. It was too difficult to face them—even Ben Zoma, with whom he had quarreled after he pulled himself together.

It was Picard's hope that Wu would have a recommendation for him. If not, he didn't know where to turn.

Picard was three-quarters of the way to Wu's colony when he thought of Ensign Jovinelly.

Even in the twenty-fourth century, some people acted on the basis of superstition. Jovinelly's compelled her to touch the bronze dedication plaque that hung near the turbolift on the *Stargazer*'s bridge.

As a shuttle specialist working under Lieutenant Chang, she didn't get up there very often. But when she did, she ran her fingertips over the plaque before she went about her business.

To bring light into the darkness. Those were the words inscribed there, the burden with which ship and crew were charged.

Once, Picard asked Jovinelly why she felt so compelled to caress the plaque. She blushed and told him it was for good luck. "But why that?" he asked, his curiosity unsatisfied. "Why that rather than some other artifact on the ship?"

Jovinelly didn't have an answer for him.

Despite her efforts to keep her luck in good supply, it ran out the day the ship was attacked. Hers was one of the bodies they removed from the *Stargazer* before they fled from the ship in escape craft.

Picard sat back in his chair and sighed. Instead of bringing light into the darkness, he had allowed the lights of twenty-four of his crew to be extinguished. *Quite an accomplishment*, he told himself.

It was then that he saw the red-on-black engine-failure graphic appear on the *Nadir*'s operations monitor. *That cannot be right*, he thought. Frowning, he punched in a code to assure himself that it was a mistake.

But the computer said it wasn't.

His warp engines, considerably smaller than those that had propelled the *Stargazer* but powerful nonetheless, were in the process of going down—and his impulse engines weren't far behind. And while there didn't appear to be any danger of an antimatter containment breach, the *Nadir* wouldn't be able to venture much farther on her own steam.

Not even to the nearest starbase, he thought, *much less all the way to Hydra IV*.

Picard swore beneath his breath. He had initiated diagnostic cycles at all the prescribed intervals, and they hadn't alerted him to any engine malfunctions.

Working at his console, he dug a little deeper—and found that some of the diagnostic circuits weren't working either. They had deteriorated, as if something had eaten away at them.

But what?

He had barely posed the question when the answer occurred to him: *The ion squall.* Maybe it hadn't been as innocuous as it seemed. Or maybe Van Dusen's people hadn't done a good enough job insulating the craft from such phenomena.

Either way, the storm's energy particles could have gotten into the shuttle and damaged some of her circuitry—and kept Picard in the dark about the state of his engines.

In fact, the engine problem might have been attributable to the squall as well. If it had penetrated the data conduits, it could just as easily have invaded the plasma manifolds.

Either way, Picard had a problem. He couldn't remain in interstellar space—not when his only sources of generated power were running out, and his battery stores were limited. More than likely, he would perish before anyone found him.

He gauged the distance he was likely to be able to cover before the engines died altogether. Then he called up a map of all the star systems in that range.

There was only one. But among its seventeen planets was a specimen that had been classified capable of supporting human life, and according to its Federation survey—which had taken place two and a half decades earlier—it was devoid of sentience. It was more than Picard could have hoped for.

Charting a course for the system in question, he made the necessary helm adjustments. Then he sent out a distress call and hoped for the best.

The *Nadir*'s warp engines eventually ground to a halt. However, they were cooperative enough to take Picard to the brink of his target system first.

It was good timing; he would have had to drop to impulse to enter the system anyway. As he did so, keeping a close watch on the failing sublight drive, his communications monitor began to blink—indicating an incoming transmission.

Apparently, one of his colleagues had received his distress call and was responding to it. Picard wondered which of them it might be. Minshaya? Capshaw? Nguyen?

Whoever it was would have smiled at first at the chance to poke fun at him. That, after all, was what happened to captains who placed themselves in need of rescue.

Then his savior would have remembered what happened to the *Stargazer*, and he or she would have curbed the impulse to mock him. No one made fun of a man who had lost what Picard had lost. Still, at some point he would have to face their sympathy, and that would be far worse than their ridicule.

At least Van Dusen had spared him that.

Tapping a stud, he said, "Picard here."

"*Good to hear you're all right,*" said a familiar voice.

Capshaw, he thought. "Thank you for responding, David."

"*What's your situation?*"

"I have reached the outskirts of the system for which I was headed. Warp engines have failed. I still have impulse, but that will go down soon as well."

"*Acknowledged. We'll be there in a—*"

The rest of Capshaw's sentence crackled off into unintelligibility. Picard manipulated his comm controls in an attempt to restore the clarity of the link, but he couldn't. And a moment later, he lost it altogether.

He sighed. *Damn.*

It wasn't the fault of his equipment, as far as he could tell. Some celestial anomaly, then, interfering with the subspace signal. It didn't happen often, but it happened.

Nonetheless, Picard knew that Capshaw was coming for him. He just didn't know when.

Sitting back in his seat, he checked his sensors and called up a visual of the world he had identified earlier. It was mostly occluded by cloud cover, making what was underneath a bit of a mystery. For all he knew, it was impenetrable jungle down there, or a maze of savage mountain ranges.

But he didn't expect to have to stay there long. A couple of days at most, not including the thirteen or fourteen hours it would take the *Nadir* to make the journey across intervening space. By then, Capshaw's ship would certainly have caught up with him.

Then he saw something else on his sensor readouts—an unmistakable nest of ion trails surrounding the planet in question. But ion trails meant ship traffic. Why would there be so much traffic around an uninhabited world?

Unless it isn't uninhabited.

Activating long-range sensors, Picard scanned the planet. Indeed, it was populated, if only sparsely, by a single species—one the shuttle's computer couldn't seem to identify.

That put an entirely new spin on the situation. Fortunately, the Federation's noninterference directive wouldn't loom as an issue—not if those on the planet had taken to space already.

No, Picard thought, correcting himself. They had come *from* space. Otherwise, they would have shown up on that Federation survey twenty-five years earlier. So like him, they were relatively new to this world. Colonists, possibly.

However, Picard couldn't be sure how they would react to his presence. Not everyone warmed to the idea of an uninvited visitor. Of course, he had the option of contacting the authorities and explaining his plight before he put down, but ultimately he decided against it.

Better to play it safe, he thought, *and keep mum*. With a little luck, he would be able to land his craft and hide until help arrived. He frowned bitterly. *After all, I have been so lucky until now.*

Applying starboard thrusters to fine-tune his course, he headed for the planet in question.

Picard was less than twenty million kilometers from the world's upper atmosphere when he noted the presence of several small, quick ships in the vicinity. At first, he assumed that they belonged to the species on the planet's surface.

Then the *Nadir*'s computer identified the ships, matching them with file data. Picard swore vividly under his breath. Skellig raiders—four of them, converging on the shuttle's position. *No*, he thought, as yet another one registered on his screen. *Five.*

He had run into their kind before. They ran in packs like this one, preying on anyone who possessed something of value and was less than expert at defending it.

Had the *Nadir* been their primary objective, they would have closed with Picard some time ago. More likely, they had entered this system in pursuit of something else. But now that a Starfleet shuttle had fallen into their laps, they would hardly be so foolish as to ignore it.

After all, there were those who would pay dearly for Starfleet technology—even the modest sort to be found in a shuttlecraft. And if there was a dignitary or high-ranking officer inside, he would fetch the Skellig a tidy ransom.

Or so they might think. The truth was that Starfleet didn't pay ransoms, and never had.

Whatever their motivation, the Skellig came at the shuttle with their weapons pulsing. Green disruptor beams sliced through the void, forcing Picard to weave a precarious path among them.

Even if he had wanted to battle the raiders, he wasn't in a position to do so—the *Nadir* simply wasn't equipped for it. His only chance was to dip below the cloud layer obscuring the planet's surface and find a place to hide.

As Picard made a break for the planet, the Skellig dogged him with bursts of disruptor fire—and scored a tail hit that slammed Picard back in his seat. The *Nadir*'s impulse engine, which was already on its last legs, fizzled out altogether—just as the shuttle entered the mantle of cloud.

Unfortunately, it couldn't conceal the *Nadir*—not when the Skellig had sensors with which to track their prey. All the clouds did was blind Picard, whose own sensors had gone down at the same time as his impulse engine.

Just a few minutes earlier, Picard had intended to seek an effective hiding place for his craft—somewhere far from the planet's population centers. Now, screaming through the upper atmosphere with nothing but thrusters left—and those with limited life in them—all he could reasonably hope for was to survive the impact of what would certainly be a crash landing.

After what seemed like a long time, the *Nadir* was still plunging through the cloud layer, unable to find the underside of it. Fearing that it would reach all the way to the ground, Picard activated the thrusters—only to have the dense, gray vapors suddenly tear away from his observation port, revealing a rapidly approaching forest of immense orange-leafed trees.

Using what was left of his thruster capability, Picard tried to pull the shuttle's nose up, achieve as oblique a descent as possible. But gravity wouldn't let him have his way. It sent the *Nadir* rumbling through a network of thick, hard-cracking branches.

Picard was jerked out of his seat and sent sprawling across the one beside it. Then the lights in the cabin flickered and he was thrown back the other way. And that was the last thing he knew before the darkness descended.

When Picard came to, he was stretched across the awkwardly tilted deck of the shuttle, a terrible ache in one of his temples. But he was alive, and felt fortunate to be so.

Rolling over onto his back, he took stock of his situation. He seemed to be uninjured except for a few bruises and abrasions. However, he couldn't say the same for the *Nadir*.

The control panel looked dead, its lights darkened. Pulling himself up level with it, Picard confirmed the observation—there was no response to his commands. The shuttle was devoid of even emergency power, meaning it was no longer transmitting his distress signal.

Peering through the forward observation port, he saw a mess of splintered branches above him, mute testimony to the path he had taken in his fall. And yet, he hadn't perished. Apparently, Van Dusen had done *something* right.

Picard didn't know how long he had been unconscious, but the Skellig wouldn't need much time to find him. For all he knew, they had followed him down through the atmosphere and were training their weapons on him at that very moment.

With his external sensors dead, there was but one way to find out.

Sliding down the incline of the deck, Picard made his way aft to the supply locker and removed one of the three charged phasers inside it—not that it would be of much use against five ships' worth of Skellig raiders. He also secured a tricorder and affixed it to his uniform. Then he found a medical kit, took out a hypospray, programmed it for a mild painkiller, and administered it—grateful for the relief it brought him. Finally, he climbed up to the hatch and pushed the stud that would slide it open.

But the door didn't slide. It just sat there. Apparently, the mechanism had been damaged in the landing.

Picard scowled. He had contemplated the possibility of all sorts of deaths over the course of his career. Suffocating in a crash-landed shuttle was not one of them.

Grabbing the hatch's interior handle, he put his shoulder behind it and pushed as hard as he could. For a moment, nothing happened. Then the door grudgingly began to move forward.

When the opening was wide enough for Picard to get through it, he stuck his head out and looked around. All he could see were black tree branches with wide orange leaves.

The ground was a good five or six meters below, but the branches offered him a plentitude of hand- and footholds. Tucking his phaser away, he wrestled himself free of the *Nadir* and started to make his way down.

It was only after Picard had dropped the last meter or so to the forest floor and ventured out into a clearing that he caught sight of the Skellig. They had indeed followed him through the clouds and were banking in formation overhead.

But they didn't seem to be coming after him. They were firing at something else—a cluster of tall, elegant towers that Picard hadn't noticed previously. Obviously, he had managed to land in the neighborhood of a city.

So much for avoiding population centers. This was clearly a big one.

As Picard watched, the raiders lashed at the towers with barrage after barrage of emerald disruptor fire. It was obvious that the Skellig were after something the planet's inhabitants possessed. But the beleaguered occupants didn't fire back.

Naturally, Picard sympathized with the defenders. But without a starship and a crew to back him up, he had nothing to offer them in the way of help—even if he were certain it was advisable which, knowing precious little about the situation, he wasn't.

Besides, his own survival was still very much in jeopardy. The Skellig might have been occupied at the moment, but they would eventually come after him with their weapons blazing. Otherwise, he might tell the Federation what they had done, and put a Starfleet task force on their trail.

Picard looked up at his shuttle, partially hidden in the grasp of the trees' stout, interwoven branches. If he remained with the *Nadir*, it would be a bit easier for a rescue mission to find him. But it would also be easier for the Skellig.

His best bet was to get away from the shuttle and move deeper into the forest, and hope Starfleet eventually tracked him down via his combadge. With that thought in mind, he proceeded in a direction directly opposite that of the towers.

However, he hadn't taken twenty steps before he heard a deep, rhythmic hum, like a swarm of gigantic bees. Looking back over his shoulder, he saw a slender, dark flying vehicle skim just above the treetops.

For a moment, he thought it might miss him. Then it came about and stopped directly above him, making it clear that he had been spotted. And though the craft didn't look the least bit familiar, it seemed likely to contain a squad of armed Skellig.

Picard bolted, hoping he could lose his pursuers. He was no longer a marathon runner but he was still fast, and the canopy was too dense for the flyer to penetrate.

Or so he thought.

Somehow, the craft found a gap in the branches and touched down directly in front of him. As a hatch slid open in its side, he whirled and ran back the other way.

Close as Picard's pursuers were, they could easily have cut him down from behind. But they didn't fire. All they did was cry out for him to wait—in a voice no Skellig could ever have imitated.

Casting a glance back over his shoulder, Picard saw two figures standing on the forest floor. But they weren't Skellig. They were too tall, too thin, and too insectoid.

The inhabitants, Picard guessed.

It might have been wiser of him to keep running. However, his instincts told him that the insectoids meant him no harm. Stopping, he turned to face them.

The insectoids held their arms out, their narrow black hands empty of weapons. Then, their blue-black exoskeletons shining in the muted light, they approached Picard on legs that bent back at the knee like those of Terran dogs.

"You are Starfleet," said one of them, the chittering quality of his voice unaffected by the universal translator in the captain's combadge.

Picard nodded. "I am."

The insectoids stopped, inclined their long heads, and clicked the mandibles that protruded from their jaws. It appeared to be a sign of respect. Clearly, this species had made contact with the Federation at some point, either directly or indirectly. And just as clearly, the experience had been a positive one.

One of the insectoids turned to the other and exchanged words Picard couldn't pick up. Then both of them looked off in the direction of the towers.

It didn't take a warp-field scientist to figure out it was the insectoids' people who occupied the buildings, or that these two were concerned about the raiders' assault.

They looked to Picard again. "Will you come with us?"

"Where do you propose to take me?" he asked.

"Somewhere safe," they said.

He shrugged. "What are we waiting for?"

"Somewhere safe" turned out to be a different concept for the insectoids than it was for Picard. Seconds after his hosts' craft took off, it headed for the towers the Skellig were battering with their disruptor fire.

Taking note of the insectoids' vehicle, at least one of the raiders began firing on it instead of the towers. Seeing the Skellig loom ahead through an observation port, Picard braced himself for a disruptor impact.

Next time, he thought, *I will be more specific with regard to my hosts' destination. If there is a next time.*

But somehow, the insectoid pilot slipped past the Skellig's

barrage. And though the towers had to be shielded somehow if they could withstand the raiders' attacks, they appeared to be selective shields, because Picard's craft reached the nearest tower without incident.

Dropping down behind it, the insectoids landed in an otherwise empty plaza, surrounded by lofty spires with gaping vents in their sides. "Come with me," the insectoid in command told Picard.

Having learned his lesson, the human asked, "Where, precisely, are we going?"

"To meet our council of governors in their chamber."

It sounded reasonable.

Before they left, however, Picard asked about the vents. He was told that they facilitated the release of radioactive gases from the ore refineries in the bowels of the city.

"You release radioactive gases into the air?"

"We have a high resistance to radiation," the insectoid explained. "The gases aren't harmful to us."

Picard was glad the vents weren't open at the moment. His hosts may have had a resistance, but he did not.

Moments later, he found himself in a tall, windowless hall, standing before three wizened insectoids. They introduced themselves as T'torric, Ch'sallis, and K'kriich, governors of the Rhitorri, the first two being males and the third a female.

"We are pleased you're alive," said T'torric. "When we saw your shuttle crash in the forest, we didn't know in what condition we would find you."

Picard cut to the chase. "How long have the Skellig been going at you?"

"This is the third day," said K'kriich.

And yet their shields had held. Clearly, they possessed an impressive power source. "What are they after? Minerals?" That was often the raiders' objective.

"No," said T'torric. "We refine minerals here, but none of them is especially valuable. What the raiders want are our people—to sell as slaves."

"It's our resistance to radiation," Ch'sallis explained. "It makes us valuable as workers in mines and refineries, where there may be significant quantities of radioactive materials."

"I imagine it would," said Picard.

"Unfortunately," said T'torric, "the energy that drives our defense systems is nearly depleted. We shut down our weapons some time ago in an effort to conserve power, but our shields won't stay up much longer." He looked at the human with desperation in his hooded black eyes. "Can you help us?"

"I have already sent out a call for assistance," Picard said, assuming that was what the councillor meant. Obviously, there was nothing one person could do against the likes of the Skellig.

"How long will it take to arrive?" asked Ch'sallis.

Picard told him the truth: he didn't know. It didn't exactly inspire relief in the Rhitorri, but what else could he say?

He didn't have a *Constellation*-class starship at his disposal anymore. He didn't have a complement of security officers. He didn't have *anything*.

K'kriich looked at her fellow councillors, then at Picard again. "The shields will not last much longer, Captain. What will we do when they fail?"

Ch'sallis and T'torric turned to him as well. Their eyes asked the same question.

Why are you asking me? Picard thought.

All he could do was fight side by side with the Rhitorri, try to defend their city as if it were his own. But when the Skellig beamed their soldiers down, Picard's phaser wouldn't make a difference. The insectoids would fall in the plazas beneath their sky-piercing towers and be—

"Wait," he said out loud, an idea taking him by surprise. Perhaps there was a way to stymie the raiders after all—at least for a while.

"What is it?" asked K'kriich.

Picard looked at her. "Those vents I saw in your towers, the ones that release radioactive gases from your refinery. How wide can they open?"

"Very wide," said Ch'sallis. "Why?"

"I have a notion . . ." Picard told them.

As the council had predicted, the Rhitorri's shields didn't hold much longer. Perhaps an hour later, power to the emitters petered out, leaving the city undefended.

The Skellig ships were too big to negotiate the narrow spaces between the towers. However, their transporter technology could reach anywhere. And no doubt it would have, except something happened almost immediately after the loss of the city's shields.

The vents in the Rhitorri's towers opened and spewed a radioactive white gas, which the breezes spread eagerly from one end of the city to the other. Before long, the air was full of it.

And with so much radiation in the atmosphere, it was impossible for the Skellig to beam their soldiers down to the planet's surface. Their vessels crisscrossed above the city impatiently like serpents hungering for their prey. But for the moment, at least, it had been denied to them.

Picard watched all this through a window in one of the towers. Unfortunately, his vantage point wasn't insulated from the radiation. But then, given the Rhitorri's natural resistance to it, they hadn't bothered to insulate *any* part of the city.

He didn't feel any effects from his exposure yet, but he knew he would eventually. Not that it mattered. He had been responsible for so many deaths on the *Stargazer*, what was one more— especially if it was his own?

And in the meantime, he had bought the Rhitorri some time— enough to carry out the second part of their plan. After all, the Skellig hadn't been turned away altogether. They could still dispatch small craft to round up and capture the insectoids.

Which was why the Rhitorri were descending into a network of tombs below the city, where six generations' worth of ancestral remains had been ceremoniously laid for safekeeping. According to the council, the Rhitorri had emigrated to this world only twenty years earlier, but they had multiplied at a rate much faster than other species'. In fact, there were only about a hundred of them when they first arrived, and in this city alone they numbered in the thousands.

"Come," said Ch'sallis, who was standing beside Picard. "The others await us in the tombs."

The human nodded and followed him out of the windowed chamber.

Picard walked among the living and the dead in the tombs below the Rhitorri city, watching childen and the elderly hunker down amid the burial monuments of their ancestors.

There were civilizations on ancient Earth that had favored internment in underground chambers. Picard had seen a few of them firsthand. They were somber places, cramped and ill-lit and unadorned.

Not so among the Rhitorri. Their tombs were spacious and bright with both torches and artificial light sources, celebrating the dead rather than casting them into shadow. And unlike the stark, half-forgotten graves of Earth's ancient cultures, the insectoids' were marked by elegant sculptures and festooned with sprays of fresh-cut flowers.

As the Rhitorri carried blocks of uncut stone to the cavern's only entrance, hoping to keep the Skellig from forcing their way in, Picard took a moment to examine some of the sculptures. They were beautiful, the pure expressions of artistic souls.

Unfortunately, he couldn't read the sprightly-looking inscriptions on them. They were rendered in an alien language, and his translator could only work on the spoken word.

Too bad, thought the archaeologist in him.

Then, as Picard was turning to join the Rhitorri at the entrance, something on one of the sculptures caught his eye—and held it. *It cannot be*, he thought, at a loss for an explanation. And yet, there was no mistaking the evidence of his eyes.

He would have asked someone about it, except he heard cries coming from the direction of the entrance. Apparently, the scouts they had left in the tunnel had arrived—with reports that the Skellig were right behind them.

Leaving the sculpture and its epitath behind him, Picard removed his phaser from its place on his jacket and hurried to the entrance. Then, taking up a place between two of the Rhitorri, he waited.

The raiders weren't long in coming. They filled the tunnel like a flash flood in their hooded protective suits, their pinched, gray features eminently visible through the convex transparencies of their faceplates.

Picard fired at one of them, dropping him in his tracks. And the Rhitorri on either side of him, huddled behind the wall of stones they had built up, cut down a few more.

But stones or no stones, the Skellig found their targets as well. And though they were eventually turned back, they took out three times as many Rhitorri as they lost.

Normally, that wouldn't have been a problem. However, most Rhitorri weren't trained in the use of handweapons. As a peaceful trading society, they had seldom had need of them. So it wasn't just a matter of how many defenders had fallen. It was also a matter of how many could take their places.

And those were few, Picard had learned. So few, in fact, that they might not withstand even one more such exchange.

As he came to that realization, his combadge chirped. Cheering inwardly, he answered it.

"*Picard,*" said Capshaw, his voice thin and static-ridden, "*are . . . all right?*"

Picard told him that things could be worse. And as briefly as he could, he described his circumstances to his colleague. "How long until you get here, David?"

"*Maybe a . . . an hour. Can . . . out till then?*"

Picard smiled a rueful smile. "Have I a choice?"

As Capshaw signed off, the clatter of boots started coming from the tunnel. Apparently, the Skellig were ready to take another stab at it.

And Picard, who had been fine until then, began to experience the first effects of his exposure to the radiation. He started feeling cold, weary, nauseated.

But he didn't have the luxury of curling up beneath a blanket. Not if he wanted to keep the Skellig at bay.

A moment later, the raiders stormed the entrance a second time. Picard aimed and fired at them as best he could, though he was hampered by bouts of shivering and muscle cramps.

Hearing a snapping sound beside him, he saw his neighbor collapse—his chest caved in by a disruptor blast. But it didn't stop the human. He turned and fired at the Skellig again.

And again.

And again, though his physical misery made it harder and harder for him to concentrate on the task at hand. When his vision began to blur, it rendered the problem almost insurmountable.

But he kept at it. He might lose this fight. He might perish. But it wouldn't be because he hadn't tried.

Time passed like the Seine in winter, slow and choked with ice. The tunnel erupted with keening cries and flashes of phaser fire, then lay still, then erupted again. Skellig loomed and vanished.

Picard was slumped against the corpse beside him, firing in what he believed was the direction of the raiders, when it occurred to him that something had changed. The sounds of battle were different, it seemed to him. Or had his hearing begun to fail as well?

Then he felt something on his arm—a Rhitorri hand, slender and black and covered with fine, feathery hair.

"It's over," said the insectoid.

"Over . . . ?" Picard muttered, fearing the worst.

A face swam into his purview—not a Rhitorri visage, but that of a human in a Starfleet environmental suit. After a moment or two, he recognized the fellow.

"David . . . ?" he said.

"Affirmative," the human replied. Then, turning to a similarly equipped colleague, he said, "Get him to sickbay—on the double!"

As Picard was lifted over someone's shoulder, he took grim

satisfaction from the fact that the Skellig had been turned away. Then, at last, he allowed himself to lose consciousness.

Picard's convalescence from radiation sickness in the *Wyoming*'s well-lit sickbay was punctuated by only a few moments of true clarity. However, he took advantage of each one to tell anyone who would listen that he wanted to return to the planet's surface.

Fortunately, his friend Capshaw had decided to linger to make sure the Skellig didn't come back. So when Picard was finally pronounced fit for the rigors of away status, the *Wyoming* was still in orbit.

Gratefully, he beamed down to the Rhitorri city, where Councillor Ch'sallis was kind enough to descend to the tombs with him in person. By then, there wasn't anything the insectoids wouldn't do for Picard. According to Ch'sallis, the human had single-handedly held off the Skellig until help arrived.

Picard was certain that it was an exaggeration. Still, he didn't argue with it.

By the time he and Ch'sallis arrived at the entrance to the underground cavern, the stones that had fortified the place had been lugged away. The tombs were once more a free and open venue, though—sadly—there were many new ones to mark the deaths of Picard's fellow defenders.

"Which one did you wish to see?" asked the councillor.

Picard frowned as he surveyed the landscape of Rhitorri memorials in the mixed light of fire and excited electrons. "It was in this area," he said, gesturing to his right.

They hadn't gone more than a hundred paces before they found the sculpture in question. Cut into its face in unmistakable Federation Standard were six words: *To bring light into the darkness*.

The words that had graced the plaque on the bridge of the *Stargazer*, expressing an ethic by which Picard had lived more than twenty years of his life. If it was a coincidence, it was a staggeringly unlikely one.

"Ah, yes," said Ch'sallis, admiring the inscription. "This is most unusual—the only marker here that is not rendered in our language."

"There must be a story behind it," Picard suggested.

The councillor's mandibles clicked. "Indeed. It harks back to the time of our ancestors' transit, after they had left the oppression of their homeworld and set out in search of a new one. They were still a year from this star system when they realized a warship was in pursuit of them, its mission to bring them back to Rhitorrus.

"As soon as they realized they were being pursued, our ancestors' leader—the individual buried here—sent out a distress call. But as the warship narrowed the gap, no one responded to the transmission. And eventually, the oppressors' vessel caught up with that of our ancestors.

"She attacked, and our ancestors fought back. But as you have seen, ours is not a violent sect. There was no possibility of our ancestors staving off the warship on their own. They were on the verge of admitting defeat when, miraculously, another vessel appeared on their sensor screens.

"It was a Federation starship. Our ancestors weren't privy to the exchange between the Starfleet captain and the commander of the war vessel, so we can only surmise the nature of it. But we know this—the starship came to interpose herself between our ancestors' vessel and the aggressor.

"For what seemed like a long time, the warship hung there in space while her commander assessed the situation. Then she moved off—*without* the prize she had come for. The starship hadn't fired a single volley, yet she had sent the war vessel scurrying. And our ancestors were saved . . . you see?"

Picard nodded.

"Afterward, the captain of the starship established a communications link with the captain of my ancestors' transport, to see if anyone required medical attention. Fortunately, no one did."

"That *was* fortunate," Picard agreed.

"Then he and his starship departed. And had he rescued some other pack of fugitives, that might have been the end of it. However, our vessel's captain was determined not to forget what the Starfleet ship did for them.

"Alas, in his effort to memorialize the event, he found that his ship's logs had been damaged in the warship's attack. They were spotty, incomplete. This," said Ch'sallis, indicating the saying on the sculpture, "was visible, but not much else. It was displayed on the bulkhead, just behind where the captain of the Starfleet ship stood. Our ancestors didn't know what it said, but they gathered it had some special significance."

"Did they ever learn its meaning?" Picard asked.

"Years later," the Rhitorri told him, "the captain of a Tellarite trading vessel was able to translate it for them when he visited this planet."

Picard ran his fingers over the incisions in the stone. He imagined that he could feel the dedication of the stonecutter, the fervor with which he had approached his work.

"*To bring light into the darkness* . . . a beautiful sentiment," said Ch'sallis, "don't you think?"

Picard didn't remember the incident. But then, it had taken place some twenty years earlier, and he and his crew had responded to hundreds of distress calls since.

But to think that one of them had enabled this city to exist, and its people to flourish in freedom and fulfillment . . . it was remarkable, to say the least. And it reminded Picard of the good he had done occasionally, which—now that he thought about it—might possibly have outweighed the bad.

"He was a great man," said the Rhitorri of his people's savior. "A great captain."

Picard smiled for the first time in months. *Perhaps not yet*, he reflected. *But given time, maybe he will be.*

ELIZABETH SHELBY
CAPTAIN OF THE *U.S.S. TRIDENT*

Pain Management

PETER DAVID

I can still see it, everywhere I look. Still see her mangled and broken body, with blood just everywhere. Everywhere. Her ripped and burned uniform, the holes in her with the bodily fluids seeping out of her by the liter.

I see it in my mind's eye when I'm awake, and I see it in my dreams when I'm asleep. Right now I'm sitting here at the Captain's Table, staring into my empty glass that had once been filled with Orion whiskey . . . the new illegal beverage of choice, since Romulan ale became legal during the Dominion War. You could pack Orion whiskey into a photon torpedo, blast it at an enemy vessel, and watch it eat through their shielding and hull. I can feel it inside me even now, scorching its way through my chest, plunging down toward the lining of my stomach. Any solid matter I have in my body from an earlier meal will be devoured by it . . . probably along with whatever internal organ it may be hiding in.

So anyway, there's the empty glass, and you'd think my own reflection would be looking back at me. But no. Instead I see her, which may be a bizarre trick of the light, or the Orion whiskey lifting her image directly out of my conscience and plastering it into the glass so it can haunt me.

You want to hear about it? I mean, you're sitting there across the table, looking at me with this weird kind of expression that says you don't know whether to pity me or feel disgust for me. Which is fine because, honest to God, I don't know which one to feel either.

My name? Name's Shelby. No, not that Shelby. I'm the other one, Elizabeth Shelby. Captain Elizabeth Shelby, which of course you probably know, what with this being the Captain's Table and all. And the thing I'm talking about . . . that is, what I was just discussing with you . . . happened just a few months ago.

We were in a war. You may have heard. No, not that war. The smaller one. The Selelvian/Tholian War. Two races working in concert with each other, and hauling in a few underhanded allies to boot, such as the Orions, to go toe-to-toe with the Federation. Basically the Selelvians tried to take over the Federation with organized mind control, and the Federation—big shock here—was peeved upon discovering that. And the Tholians took the Selelvians' side, possibly because they were in cahoots with them from the outset, or maybe they just really, really hated the Federation's collective guts and saw this as an opportunity to make a move against them.

I swear, to some degree, I haven't the faintest idea what's truly at stake or what we're fighting about. It's almost as if we're fighting just to fight. It's a colossal waste of time and resources. Almost self-indulgent, if you ask me. But no one did, because I don't get asked things. I, like any good Starfleet commander, go where I'm told and do what I'm told. And I do that at the helm of the good ship *Trident,* the best damned ship in the fleet. I'm fully aware that other captains will say the same thing about their vessels, but the advantage I have over them is that I'm actually right.

When I'm not on her . . . when I'm not standing on her bridge, watching the stars fly past us as we move . . . it's painful, you know? Phantom pain, like what you feel when you lose an arm or a leg, and you could swear that it's hurting you when it's gone. Same thing. When the *Trident*'s not there, it's like a piece of me is gone. But I learn to manage it. To deal with it. You have to; you can go crazy otherwise.

So the *Trident* wasn't gone per se, but she was out of commission. We'd just taken a pounding in an ambush arranged by a Selelvian and an Orion ship, but we'd managed to cut our way out and leave the wreckage of two enemy vessels floating in space behind us. We were barely able to limp to Starbase Bravo and put in for repairs there.

Bravo had just about the best repair facilities in the area, and the CO there is an old friend, Frank Kittinger. Frank, or "Kitt" as I sometimes called him, had been Bravo's first CO, and had come to see the station as his child. Well . . . a large, floating child. He'd told me any number of times that when he finally eased himself into retirement—which he suspected would be within the next year or two—his greatest hope was that someone like me would take over for him. I told him I can't see myself leaving the starship life behind but, hey . . . you never know where Starfleet's going to send you.

There we sat at Bravo, feeling the frustration of inactivity that always dogs you when you're waylaid and in for repair. And then, the next thing I know, Kittinger is summoning me to his office, telling me he's got someone who wants to talk to me. So I showed up at the requested time of thirteen hundred hours, and my eyes went wide as saucers when I saw who was standing there.

"Soleta! My God!" I said. I moved forward as if I was going to hug her, and Soleta just stood there and gave me the strangest look. And if you saw Soleta, you'd know why: the long, elegant, pointed ears, the upswept eyebrows, that telltale expression of quiet superiority . . . all signals of her Vulcan heritage. I stopped before I got within hugging distance and remembered that I wasn't likely to get any sort of demonstrative behavior from her, even though I'd known her since the days when we'd served together on the *Excalibur*. She as science officer, me as second-in-command to my future husband, the inestimable Mackenzie Calhoun. "I wasn't expecting to see you here," I said.

"There's no reason that you should have," she replied. "A scientific conference was held here, to discuss the research that was done on the Beings and their 'ambrosia.' As one of those who had a very close association to both, it was felt I would be an ideal speaker on the subject."

"Lieutenant Soleta was about to head back to the *Excalibur* and was wondering if you'd be interested in hitching a ride," Kittinger said. He had a slightly lascivious look in his eyes, and I knew only too well what was going through his mind. He confirmed it when he added, "After all, I'm sure you miss your husband and wouldn't mind a brief . . . conference?"

I was too annoyed with Kittinger's remarks to say anything at first, but fortunately I didn't have to. Soleta stepped in and said, "It is a happy aspect of human nature to be with one's loved ones . . . just as it is an unhappy aspect of human nature to act in a smarmy or juvenile manner about it. How fascinating that the two of you lived up and down to your respective potentials."

Kittinger mimed being shot to the heart and, after confirming that the *Trident* would not be up and running for at least a week, I decided to take Soleta up on her offer. The *Excalibur* was on active patrol along the border of Thallonian space, since Starfleet was concerned about possible Tholian incursions. Soleta was in a long-range runabout, so the trip back wasn't expected to take that long. "Thank you, by the way," I told her as she fired up the runabout's engines.

She looked at me curiously. "For what?"

"For throwing yourself on that stupid grenade of a question that Kittinger said. About me and Mac . . ."

"I did not consider it a grand gesture of self-sacrifice," Soleta replied. "He was acting in a boorish manner, and I criticized him for it. Not much need be said beyond that . . . although, should it be required that I do throw myself upon a grenade on your behalf, I hope it will be over something of more import than a foolish comment from a foolish coworker."

"Same here."

As we headed back to the *Excalibur*, Soleta filled me in on all that had been happening on the ship since my departure. Soleta wasn't exactly one for eager gossip. Rather than reveling in the details, she simply ascribed equal and unenthused importance to everything. Not for such as Soleta was the excited whisper of "Oh, and you'll never believe what else happened!" She laid out all the latest juicy bits of business in the same matter-of-fact way that one would be entering information into the captain's log.

I knew it was pointless to mention this to her, or ask her to spice things up a bit. I truly didn't think she'd have the faintest idea what I was asking her to do.

Matters, however, very quickly moved beyond a litany of the latest doings on the *Excalibur.*

We had been in space a bit under an hour, with perhaps another two hours or so to the rendezvous point where the *Excalibur* was to meet us. Suddenly the proximity alarms on the runabout went off. I jumped, startled, but Soleta was far too controlled to allow even the slightest concern to be displayed. "We have company," was all she said, studying the readings. "A single vessel, but larger than us, moving in fast to starboard. An Orion raiding ship, if I'm not mistaken."

A monitor on the visual array flickered and there was a craft of the unmistakeable thrown-together variety that characterized a raiding vessel typical of the Orions. Think of the Orions as sort of the anti-Borg. Whereas the Borg absorb, or "assimilate," diverse technology and reshape it into a seamless whole, the Orion grab what they can, where they can, slap it together, and force it to work through damnable ingenuity coupled with sheer willpower. They want people to recognize where they got various pieces of technology from. It's similar to old-Earth gunmen who would carve notches on their weapons to advertise the number of kills they'd made.

It wasted no time, diving in fast and unleashing a volley of pulse weapons that pounded us. A runabout is a swift and sleek vessel, but it's not designed for heavy-duty combat against a superior, aggressive foe. Soleta had gotten the shields up barely in time, but the runabout swung wildly under the assault. I swear, every damned systems warning light that existed on the control panels lit up at the same time.

"Losing shields," announced Soleta, and a heartbeat later, she added, "and stabilizers. And we have a coolant leak."

"I'll take helm," I said. "Can you get the stabilizers and leak under control?"

"We'll find out together," she informed me, even as she vaulted, staggering, from her seat, and made her way to the emergency access hatches.

The runabout lurched fore and aft as their pulse weapons exploded around us. Soleta was practically bent in half, the flooring pulled up as she extended her arms and upper torso into the maintenance hatch. "Good evasive maneuvers, Captain," she called out, her voice muffled.

Evasive maneuvers, my ass. With the stabilizers going out, it was all I could do to keep the ship from rolling. I struggled with the controls, caught a glimpse of the Orions darting toward us, and banked hard to starboard.

They're steering us somewhere, I suddenly realized, and then I saw it. "Soleta!" I shouted over the runabout's sirens that were warning us of the dire situation, as if we didn't already know. "There's a planet, dead ahead! Under the current circumstances, what are the odds of my landing us safely?"

Soleta hauled herself out of the hatch, her face smeared with dirt. "That depends. Is the surface of the planet made entirely of foam rubber?"

"Probably not."

"Then the odds aren't great."

Another explosion slammed us, and the computer voice—calm, naturally—informed us that we'd just lost our aft shields.

"I'm betting they're better odds than our lasting out here," I told her, and angled for the planet.

"I would be hard-pressed to disagree."

"Give me as much of the stabilizers as you can, and make damned sure the landing thrusters are functioning."

"Aye, Captain."

The next few minutes were among the most harrowing of my life. Understand that back in my Starfleet Academy days, there was no cadet who could beat me for cool-under-fire when it came to operating a simulator. I was so skilled that for a time I was even considering focusing on becoming a helmsman until my parents said, "No, you're heading on command track, end of discussion," which is admittedly another story for another day.

For that matter, I've handled helm on all manner of vessels, and on more than one occasion with the damned things practically exploding all around me.

But a high-speed landfall on a barely functioning runabout . . . well, that was something else entirely.

They teach you in Starfleet never to wonder, "Is this it? Is this how I'm going to die?" Because to have such thoughts can wind up actualizing the concern. In other words, opening the door to wondering it can end up causing it. It was difficult not thinking that, though, I have to say, as I desperately muscled the runabout down toward the planet. With the shields unreliable, bringing us in at the correct angle was vital. Too shallow and we'd skip off the atmosphere; too steep and we'd burn up. The runabout shook violently, and I heard the screeching of metal as the ship fought to keep itself together. My uniform shirt was soaked through with sweat as the ship's interior heated up, a sign that we were coming in too fast. The screen in front of me flared red. "Soleta! Do we have reverse thrusters?"

"After a fashion," she replied, convincing me that there existed no predicament about which she could not be sardonic.

"Give me what you have! Now!"

The thrusters roared, helping me to correct the ship's angle. The heat began to subside, and then I heard a sputtering as the thrusters proceeded to give out. Soleta muttered that rare thing— a Vulcan curse—and started to shove herself back under the flooring.

"Never mind! We're out of time! Secure yourself!" I called out, for the upper atmosphere had given way to the lower sections, the blackness of space being traded for what might well be breathable air. There was darkness all around us; we were coming in on the nightside. Wonderful. In the dark on a strange planet. Certainly there was no better place to be, especially with Orions on your tail.

I rerouted all power to the thrusters, trying to shore them up from the control panel, as Soleta clambered across the floor and belted herself into the copilot's seat. She glanced at what I was doing, but if she had any second-guessing about how I was handling it, she kept it to herself. Instead she simply inquired, "Do you require assistance?"

"I've got a handle on it, thanks." I risked a fast glance at her. "How are you holding up?"

"I've had far preferable days."

"Yeah. Me too. Hold on!"

"To what?" she inquired.

I braced myself as I tried to force the helm to heed my commands. "I don't know! It's what we say at times of stress!"

"Humans," muttered Soleta. "You always have to say *something*."

My annoyed response was to say nothing, which likely suited Soleta just fine.

We plunged down, down, and then all too fast we were right there, crashing through what looked (as near as I could tell from my brief glimpses in the dark) and sounded and felt a lot like the tops of trees. We'd come roaring into some sort of heavily forested area, and the trees cracked and splintered and collapsed under us as we created an extremely impromptu landing strip with the weight and speed of the runabout. I was certain I heard things breaking away from the ship—vital pieces of the warp nacelles, no doubt—and we were both slammed back and forth in our seats as I did everything I could to slow or steady us. Truthfully, my efforts added very little to the proceedings as the thrusters gave out entirely and we continued to annihilate a considerable chunk of forest real estate. Always a great way to introduce yourself to the local flora and fauna: Destroy a portion of it.

Then we hit something and I heard a horrifying crack. I think we glanced off the mother of all the trees, and the impact sent us tumbling. It slammed me backward against the seat and then forward so hard against the belt that I thought it was going to bisect me. I cried out in pain and fear. Yes, fear. Soleta said absolutely nothing. I didn't see her, but there wasn't so much as a whimper out of her. How the hell she managed to do that, I couldn't begin to guess.

The runabout hit the ground, flipped over and righted itself and flipped again, rolling over and over, and I had no choice but to white-knuckle it and pray that we came to a halt before we rolled over the edge of a canyon or something. Smoke billowed from everywhere, stinging my lungs, causing my eyes to water. I started coughing violently and dwelt on the irony of surviving the landing, only to burn to death or suffocate, and then decided that it wasn't irony at all, it was just lousy luck.

And then finally, finally, we stopped rolling, but I didn't realize it at first because my head was still spinning. Suddenly Soleta was right in front of me, shouting, "Captain! Can you hear me?" I forced a nod, and she grabbed at my restraining harness and pulled it open. She was standing at an odd angle and when I tumbled from my chair, I understood why. I could see that Soleta was clutching what appeared to be a small box under her arm, and then recognized it as the emergency homing beacon that usually resided in a panel under the control board.

I staggered, trying to keep myself upright, as Soleta triggered the emergency manual override and forced open the escape hatch.

"We haven't checked the atmosphere," I managed to say, my voice hoarse.

"This is Alpha Omega IV. Class-M, no intelligent life . . . unless you count us, and the jury is still out on that." She held me by the elbow and aided me in climbing out of the sideways runabout. Before she followed me out, she handed the beacon through to me, then foraged about the interior of the ship and emerged with two phasers—which were all the vessel was equipped with—and a lantern that had, miraculously, not been shattered upon impact. She also had a sack filled with emergency rations, and a tricorder clipped to her belt.

Rain was cascading down upon us. Naturally. Not only had we landed in darkness but in rain. I leaned against the runabout for a moment, coughing violently and letting the smoke clear out of my lungs. I suppose I should have been grateful that we survived, but ankle-deep in mud and already soaked to the skin, swatting away annoying bugs that seemed to have materialized from nowhere, I wasn't exactly awash in gratitude. Still, there was no reason I couldn't count our blessings.

"They say any landing you walk away from is a good one," I said.

Soleta stared at the overturned, crumbled vessel, and replied, "They lie."

I forced a nod. Then I picked a direction at random and started walking. Soleta followed me without a word, for really, what was there to say under the circumstances? I had taken the lantern from Soleta and held it up, casting light in front of us. The energy cell powering the lantern was enough to give us light for a good thirty days, so I wasn't concerned about using it up.

The broad leaves of the trees whipped against us, and several times I used one of the phasers to cut us a path. Soleta did the same, taking care to call out a warning each time she fired so I wouldn't think we were under attack.

"They're going to be after us, you know," Soleta said.

I nodded, my face grim. There was no way the Orions were going to let us out of our predicament that easily, although it was difficult to categorize what we'd endured thus far as "easily."

Finally I could see that the forest, or at least the part we were in, was thinning out. I paused, holding up the lantern to cast as much light as possible on our path, and saw what appeared to be shelter: a small cul-de-sac of rock in front of us and the darkened entrance to a cave. The rock stretched up in front of us and to either side. It appeared to be the base of a mountain.

"Shelter," I said. "Provided something isn't inside the cave, ready to eat us."

Soleta was as soaked through as I, her long, dark hair plastered to either side of her face. The IDIC pin she wore in her hair was sideways, barely managing to hold its place. "I cannot say that I am overly enthused about the positioning," she said. "If the Orions find us, we would effectively be trapped in there, presuming there's not an exit out the back."

I nodded, but then pointed out, "On the other hand, the entrance is defensible, so we might be able to hold out there for some time. And if we stay out here, I don't know about you, but I'm going to catch my death of cold."

"Can humans die of a cold?" she asked. She seemed to be genuinely interested in the biological realities of the question.

"I don't know, and I don't actually care to find out," I replied. "Come on."

I made my way toward the cave, and Soleta followed me, crouching low and watching the upper reaches of the rocky entrance cautiously. I paused at the entrance to the cave, and then Soleta stepped in front of me with the tricorder out and used it to study the interior of the cave before we set foot in it. Finally she nodded in approval. "Empty," she said, "with no indication of previous habitation."

I entered the cave, holding the lantern high. It was . . . well, it was a cave, really. Not much to say, except that it went about thirty feet into the side of the mountain, was wide enough to accommodate both of us and high enough that we only had to crouch a little to make our way into it. "This is nice," I said tentatively.

Soleta glanced around, not looking particularly impressed. "Yes. At last my search for my retirement home is at an end."

"Would that our clothes were as dry as your wit," I replied.

For response, Soleta aimed her phaser at several nearby oversized rocks and fired a steady beam of low intensity. Within seconds, the rock was glowing with heat, suffusing the entirety of the cave with warmth.

We removed our clothes and draped them over one of the rocks, speeding up the drying process. A steady wind whistled by the front of the cave, but fortunately we were far enough in that it wasn't gusting to where we were. I crouched as near as I could to one of the glowing rocks, warming it once more with my own phaser when the heat seemed to be dissipating. Soleta was on the other side of it, holding up her hands. I have to admit, in the reddish glow of the phaser-generated light, she looked almost Satanic.

"Naked women in a cave," I muttered. "It doesn't get more primitive than this."

"At least a prehistoric male didn't drag us in here," she replied, rubbing her hands briskly in the warmth.

"I presume you activated the homing beacon?"

"Of course," she said. "Ideally only Federation vessels will possess the necessary frequency to detect it. Our best hope is that the *Excalibur* will trace our route once we are overdue and find us here."

I paused, then said, "I'm impressed that you knew what world this was, and also knew right off the top of your head the specifics of it."

"Were you?" she asked, an eyebrow raised.

"Yes."

"Then you are easily impressed."

I laughed softly at that. "I suppose so."

We were silent for a time, and then Soleta said softly, "They did not lie."

"About what?"

"Your landing. It was a good one, considering what it was you were dealing with."

"Thank you."

"And you will see him again."

"What?" I stared at her in curiosity. "What do you mean?"

"Captain Calhoun. You will see him again. I simply will not permit you to die a pointless death in a rocky hole without ever seeing your husband again. It would be . . . illogical."

"I appreciate that, Soleta," I assured her, "and believe me, I have every intention of trying to make it out of here. But I want it to be both of us."

"As do I," she said. "However, if it is to be only one of us, obviously it must be you."

"Why obviously? Because I outrank you?"

"No. Because you deserve to."

I made no attempt to hide my surprise at her statement. It was as if, naked as she was, Soleta had been stripped bare of any pretense or artifice. Not that she had ever been reticent over speaking her mind, but still . . . her bluntness bordering on self-pity was confounding. "And you don't deserve to?"

She just gazed at me for a long moment, and then said, "It is . . . complicated."

"Soleta . . . has something happened? Something I should know about?"

"Many things have happened, Captain. Not all of them—indeed, most of them—are not worth discussing."

"Does this have anything to do with what happened with the Beings? I know you became involved with them. That you ate that stuff they called ambrosia . . ."

"Captain, I would prefer not to discuss this now."

"Something like that can turn your life on its side, I know. But if you—"

"Captain," she repeated, this time with more force, "I would prefer not to discuss this now." She was up and moving, and she grabbed our clothing off the rock on which they'd been warming and tossed me mine. "Quickly." She was already pulling hers on.

For an instant I wondered what was happening, and then I realized. Soleta's superhuman hearing had detected someone approaching, and the chances were sensational it wasn't someone we were going to be pleased to see. I dressed as fast as I could, the uniform having mostly dried. "Orions?" I said, although it wasn't all that much of a question.

"That would be my surmise," she said briskly, pulling her uniform shirt on over her head. Oddly, she smoothed it so it lay properly. I couldn't help but find it a bit amusing that she was concerned about how she looked just then.

We crouched back in the cave, keeping our phasers steady. "They couldn't have traced the beacon," I said, although I wasn't a hundred percent certain of that.

But Soleta shook her head. "They would not have needed to," she said. "Their sensors would have told them generally where the runabout was wrecked. From there, they simply would have been able to track us by scent."

"By *scent?*" I could scarcely believe it. "What are they, animals?"

She looked at me grimly. "Do not ask questions, Captain, to which you do not truly want the answers."

I heard nothing outside except the pounding of the rain, but Soleta never lowered her weapon. She kept it focused, rock steady, at the entrance. And suddenly, with no warning whatsoever, she fired. The cave flared with light from the blast of the phaser, and I didn't know what she had just shot at.

But then I did, for there was a strangled shriek, and I saw the large form of an Orion stagger two steps in, clutching at his chest which was a puddle of melting flesh. Smoke rose from it and he looked blindly in our general direction before falling flat and lying there, arms splayed out to either side.

Very softly, so that only I could hear, Soleta said, "Now, *that* was impressive."

I had to agree. Her sharp ears had detected his approach even though his footfall was so soft that I hadn't heard a thing. There was a bend in the cave so that our view of the entrance was not perfect, but Soleta hadn't needed anything save her hearing to guide her.

Dropping any pretense of not being heard, the remaining Orions conferred just beyond the entranceway in low, angry growls. None of them bothered to drag their fallen comrade away. Obviously they had other matters on their minds, or what passed for their minds.

"Come out!" one of them called angrily.

"Oh yes. That is likely to occur," murmured Soleta.

"We know there's only two of you!" came the same voice. "We know you are females!"

Soleta had been right. The Orions had impressive olfactory prowess, having been able to detect our scents despite the steady rain that should have helped to wash them away.

"Come out," continued the Orion, "and we will not harm you!"

"I suspect," Soleta noted, "that he is lacking in candor."

But then the same speaker said, much to my surprise, "Captain Shelby! You're worth more alive to us than dead! Don't do something stupid like stage a fight here that you won't win!"

Soleta and I exchanged surprised glances. Well, truthfully, I looked surprised. She just appeared curiously thoughtful. I mouthed, "How the hell . . . ?"

She shrugged and mouthed back, "Passenger manifest."

Of course. Having found the wreckage, they might well have been able to extract information from the computer, even in its battered and broken state. That information would have included the name and rank of the personnel aboard the runabout. Their little stunt about knowing that it was "just us girls" hunkered down in the cave seemed slightly less impressive now.

We made no reply. What would have been the purpose? It wasn't as if I was about to surrender to them, and I had little incentive to engage in any sort of give-and-take with Orion pirates. They'd shot us down, for God's sake. What was there to say to them?

I ran the mental image of their ship through my head. Based on the size of the ship, I estimated that they probably had a crew complement of anywhere from eight to ten. So they outnumbered us, at most, five-to-one. The problem is, once you're outnumbered, it almost doesn't matter by how much once you start getting above three-to-one.

"No one is going to find you! No one is going to rescue you!" continued our unseen opponent.

"This is a waste of time!" I heard another voice say. "Let's just kill them and be done with it!"

"She can be a valuable hostage!"

"And what are we supposed to do with her?" snapped the new speaker. "Even if we do hold her up for demands, what do you think the Federation will do? Knuckle under? They will not bargain with us. So we kill her. So what? The Federation will just promote another to take her place."

"I wonder if it will be me. I'd be so honored," Soleta said. Despite the dire circumstances, it was all I could do not to smile at that. It was hard to believe she was able to perceive anything vaguely humorous about the situation.

"So what do we do? Walk away from opportunity?" asked the first one.

"I'll show you what we do. . . ."

I did not like the sound of that. I liked it even less when a hollow, *tink tink* sound echoed through the cave, and then I saw it.

A bomb, rolling right toward us.

To be specific, it was a thermal grenade. Spherical and about six inches in diameter, the moment it exploded it would flood the cave with enough raw heat to bake the both of us. I could have tried to fire my phaser at it, but the instant any sort of beam came into contact with it, it would detonate . . . as opposed to our current situation where we have about five seconds to react.

Soleta was just staring at it, apparently frozen in indecision.

I didn't hesitate.

I launched myself forward, not having the slightest idea as to whether it would work or not, but knowing I had to try. I threw myself flat upon the sphere, smothering it with my body, desperate to shield Soleta from the full intensity of the blast.

Just as they always said it would, my life flashed before my eyes. Mackenzie Calhoun filled every moment of it, even the parts he hadn't been around for. My mind just dropped him in there, as if nothing in my life that had transpired when he wasn't around mattered, and so he might as well have been there for it all.

Soleta continued to make no move. Instead she went on staring, but now I was seeing there wasn't indecision in her face. Rather than that, she looked almost mortified, even slightly annoyed.

That was gratitude for you. Here I was throwing myself upon the grenade in a desperate bid to save her life, and all she could do was look at me scoldingly. What an ingrate. What a useless . . .

It was by that point I realized that the grenade was not detonating. It would have done so by that point, should have done so. I moaned softly, realizing.

Soleta was ahead of me, and had been the entire time. "Why," she asked reasonably, "would they simply blow up someone they want to take hostage? Obviously . . ."

"They would not. They'd roll in a dud first as a warning that they could kill us if they were so inclined." I rolled off the grenade, held it up, and turned it over. The firing mechanism had been removed. Clever. After all, they wouldn't want us to be able to turn around and lob it back out at them. "I do not think," I said softly, as Soleta came over to me and took the grenade from me, studying it, "that I have ever felt quite so stupid as I do right now."

And Soleta looked at me with something as close to incredulity as her personality would allow her to display. "Stupid? Without hesitation you threw yourself upon a destructive device with the intention of saving me. You might label it as 'misguided,' perhaps. I, and any other rational being, would call it 'heroic.' "

I shrugged, slightly mollified, but not by much.

And then the rough voice of one of the Orions bellowed through the night. "Listen to me!" he called out. "We're not going to spend forever at this! Grabbing you as a hostage is one thing, but we're not putting our own necks on the line, and we're not standing out here forever! Hostages are a dime a dozen, and if we don't take you, we'll run into another sometime! The next bomb we lob in there will not be disarmed, I guarantee it!"

Soleta had her tricorder out and was studying it, glancing every so often in the direction of the Orions.

"This is your last warning!" called the Orion. "You have one minute to come out of there, slowly and with your hands over your head, or you can take a good long look around you to see what your tomb will look like! And we'll take what bits of you are left and send you to the Federation with a note attached, boasting of yet another Starfleet officer we killed. It's your decision!"

"His bioreadings are remaining consistent and within the norm," Soleta informed me quietly. "He is not bluffing."

"So we die in here," I said slowly, "or we go out, get captured, be helpless prisoners of the Orions as they do whatever the hell they want to us, and end up either returned to the Federation bereft of pride and possibly parts of our bodies, or we die anyway."

"You make it seem a far less attractive choice, put that way."

"You know what I say?" I told her, and I held the phaser up and set it for maximum power. "I say we take out a few of them as we go."

"You are aware," she said, "that even if we break through into the open, it is only logical that they have sharpshooters positioned at strategic points above and around us."

"Yes. I'm fully aware of that." I took a deep breath. "What's the Klingon saying? 'Today is a good day to die.'"

She rested a hand on my shoulder and said, "That may well be the case, Captain." And then, before I knew what was happening, consciousness spun away from me as Soleta added, "But not for you."

Everything went black and stayed that way for a time . . . I didn't know how long. When I awoke, it was on the floor of the cave, and everything was different. The rain had stopped. Shadows had shifted enough to tell me that dawn was breaking. I could smell the moisture in the air . . . and more . . . I smelled death in the air as well.

I staggered to my feet, my head whirling. The Vulcan nerve pinch. She had dropped me with that damnable nerve technique. I'd always wondered what it would be like to come around from that, and now I knew: My head was splitting and my mouth was dry. It was like a hangover, except without the part about waking up in someone else's bed and wondering how you got there . . . which is yet *another* story for another time.

I started to call out her name, but instantly kept my mouth shut. There was no telling what to expect. I glanced around and saw that both phasers were gone. I was weaponless. But since time had passed and I wasn't inside the bowels of an Orion ship, I knew that I wasn't in enemy hands.

My legs were stiff, my muscles sore, so it wasn't the easiest thing in the world to proceed with caution. But I did my best, leaning against the wall of the cave, trying to peer around the corner to see what I could see.

There were large feet in evidence, attached to an equally large body that was prone. That was the one that Soleta had killed earlier, but then I could see others as well. At least two more, lying there unmoving. Some sort of insects were buzzing around them, and more were coming by the minute.

I drew closer, closer. One of them had a weapon still gripped in his paw, a huge-barreled, fearsome-looking blaster of some sort. Hardly possessing the sophistication of a phaser, but it would blow a hole through you just as easily as anything else. I pried his gun from his cold, dead fingers. It was incredibly heavy. I didn't even bother trying to pick up a second, because it required two hands just to hold the one I'd salvaged.

Stepping carefully around the bodies, I made my way out of the cave, squinting against the daylight.

More bodies. More Orions.

And Soleta.

She lay there in the open, staring up at the sun. Her arms lay flat, her hands open, a phaser resting in each palm. She was covered with green blood . . . her own. I couldn't even begin to count the number of wounds she'd sustained.

I jumped, thinking that out the corner of my eye, I'd seen an Orion. And I had, but he wasn't moving. He was on an upper ridge, slumped forward, and there was another near him, and yet another off in a corner. All dead. And more Orions, having ringed the immediate area, all blown to hell and gone.

I realized what had happened. Soleta had come charging out of there, phasers blasting. She had sustained various hits from the Orions, but that hadn't stopped her as she'd mowed through them, made it into the open, targeted and fired upon the sharp-shooters and snipers that she'd correctly intuited would be there. Whether she'd depended upon her own heightened senses or her tricorder, I couldn't say.

They'd wounded her, and she kept coming. They'd killed her and yet she hadn't allowed the mortal hits to stop her as she picked them off one by one. I could see it in my mind's eye, and for some reason it was all in painfully slow motion, blasts tearing the air around her, ripping through her, and she simply would not be stopped.

I knelt next to her and moaned in grief as I looked down at her lifeless eyes.

An instant later I let out a very un-Starfleet shriek as those lifeless eyes shifted every so slightly and gazed straight at me.

"Oh my God," I breathed, "oh my God. Soleta . . . are you . . . can you talk . . . ?"

She breathed two words then, and I had to strain to hear them, but I was able to make them out.

"No . . . pain . . ." she whispered.

For a moment I had no idea what to do. Moving her seemed unthinkable. But I couldn't just leave her there. Nor could I just sit and wait around to see what would happen next.

The tricorder lay near her and, miraculously, was undamaged. Quickly I used it to do a sensor scan of the area and within seconds had located the whereabouts of the Orion vessel. I dropped the heavy blaster, picked up both phasers, attached both of them to my belt, and then crouched and picked up Soleta. She tried to shake her head, and the words "Leave me" rattled in her throat, but I wouldn't hear of it. Instead I lifted her up and then slung her over one shoulder. Despite the fact that not a single muscle in her body was functional, she felt as if she weighed nothing. I couldn't help but worry that it was because she'd lost just about every bit of blood she'd had.

I staggered through the forest, almost slipping several times in the mud, monitoring the tricorder to make sure that we remained on track. Several times I was convinced that Soleta had breathed her last, but just when I thought she was gone, she would murmur those two words again—"No pain"—and I knew that, for a little while longer, she was with me.

I made it to a clearing and there, big as life, was the Orion vessel. Gently I laid Soleta down and put a finger to my lips, indicating that I didn't want her to speak. The hatch was open and slowly I made my way into the ship.

The hatch opened right up onto the bridge, and I could see immediately that the controls were so simple that I could have operated them before I'd finished my first year at the Academy. There was plunder, for lack of a better term, all over the place, scattered around heedlessly.

But the slovenliness of their living situation wasn't of consequence to me. Rather the biggest problem I had to deal with at that moment was the general smell of the place, which was almost enough to make me retch. Just as I felt the few remaining contents of my stomach begin to roil in protest, an Orion strode forward from the rear of the ship, whistling aimlessly, hitching up his pants in such a way as to indicate he'd just emerged from the facilities.

He glanced up, saw me, gasped, and before he could even reach for his weapon, I shot him. He was blasted back off his feet and slammed against the far wall. He slid to the ground, his chest still smoking, and I wasted no time in pitching him off the ship. I didn't know if he was alive or dead, but I suspected dead, and I didn't care in either event.

Quickly I checked the rest of the ship to make sure he'd been the only one left on guard. Such was the case, as it turned out, and quickly I brought Soleta in and rested her in one of the chairs. I switched on the homing beacon I'd brought out of the cave, closed the hatch, fired up the engines, and in minutes had us in space.

Setting the autoguidance system for Bravo, since we were still closer to there than to the *Excalibur* rendezvous point, I rummaged around until I found what I'd hoped I would—a Federation medical kit. I had no idea where they might have stolen it from and, at the moment, I wasn't in a position to care. I moved toward Soleta, fully expecting to find that she had died during takeoff. But no. How she was clinging to life, I could not even begin to guess. It seemed there wasn't a square inch of her uniform that wasn't soaked in blood, and I realized I was now covered with it as well, having carried her.

"No . . . pain," she whispered yet again.

"You're not feeling any pain?" I asked gently, tending to her wounds as best I could with the materials at hand.

From somewhere deep within her, she found the strength to answer the question. "Oh, no . . . pain . . . is there. I am . . . managing it. Ignoring it. That is how . . . one deals . . . with pain. You do not let . . . it get the best . . . of you. Do . . . whatever . . . it takes . . ."

Then, having exhausted herself in replying to me, she allowed her head to sag back in the chair. Her eyes closed and only the tricorder, and the barest rising and falling of her chest, told me that she still lived.

It seemed an endless time until we got back to Bravo Station and, naturally, the first thing that happened was that they were ready to blow us to bits on sight. Fortunately enough the com system was functioning, so my own messages—combined with the fact that we had an emergency beacon on board that was sending out a distress signal—convinced them of our identity.

As I guided the ship into a landing bay, I turned to Soleta and, even though I didn't know if she could hear me or not, said "Hang on . . . we're almost there."

"Don't . . . tell them . . ."

Her voice was rattling once more, and I said, "What? Don't tell . . . ?"

"Don't tell them . . . you knew," she said. "They'll . . . crucify you . . . don't tell them . . . swear you'll say . . . you didn't know . . . swear it . . . on your life . . . on Mac's life . . ."

"Soleta, what . . . ?"

"*Swear it!*" she spat out, and blood was oozing from between her lips, her body trembling with urgency.

"All right! I swear it! I swear!" I told her, not having the faintest idea what we were talking about.

She let out a sigh of what could only be relief, and her head sagged once more.

A medical team was rushed to the landing bay when we came in, and even these hardened veterans gasped in shock upon seeing their latest patient. "No pain," Soleta was murmuring, as if it had become her own personal mantra. They whisked her away while I headed up to the CO's office to tell him what had happened. Kittinger shook his head several times in the narrative, and told me how lucky I'd been, and how heroic Soleta had been. I agreed with both sentiments, and said that I wanted to go down to the sickbay to be with her.

"No," Kittinger said firmly. "Captain, I don't know if you've looked in the mirror lately, but you look like three miles of bad road. Go back to the quarters you had here, and shower, and change, and rest. I'll have fresh clothes brought to you. Get yourself together. Soleta is in the best hands right now, and there's nothing you can do for her. So go take care of yourself right now. That's an order."

I nodded reluctantly, but resolved to do what he said as fast as possible so that I could get back down to her. I returned to the quarters, showered, changed, and lay down on the bed and closed my eyes, just for a minute. The next thing I knew I was being woken up from a sound slumber by an urgent chiming at the door.

"Come," I said, sitting up and trying to smooth my hair, which had dried into uncontrolled disarray.

Kittinger entered, and he looked deadly serious.

"Is she—?" I began.

Kittinger stood there, arms draped behind his back. I braced myself for grave news, and so was surprised when he said, "Believe it or not, it appears she's going to pull through."

"Well, that's . . ." I stood, relief flooding through me. "That's . . . amazing, I . . ."

"Elizabeth," said Kittinger with that same grim tone, which I couldn't understand considering that the news had been good.

"Our physicians . . . they had to do a lot of work on Soleta, practically had to piece her innards together like a jigsaw puzzle . . . and they discovered . . ."

"What?" I said. "What did they . . .?"

"Soleta . . . she's half-Romulan."

And the first words that were about to leave my mouth were "I know."

And I did know. Soleta had told me, ages ago. Back when we were both convinced that Mackenzie Calhoun was dead. She'd told me when it was just the two of us in a bar, and she was wondering just how dedicated I was to the principles of Starfleet as compared to the principles of friendship and trust. She had not known of her mixed heritage when she'd enlisted with Starfleet, but when she had learned of it, she had kept it to herself. And routine examinations did not turn it up since Vulcans and Romulans are so similar biologically.

Still, Starfleet regulations were quite clear that she should have made full disclosure, even though it would likely have cost her her starship assignment. Romulans were a known hostile race, and someone with perceived affiliations to them would never be allowed more than desk duty. She didn't want that for herself. And I didn't want it for her. I cared about the woman, not her genetics, and so kept her secret to myself, which was also in violation of Starfleet regs. Which essentially made me a co-conspirator in what was, to my eyes, a nonconspiracy.

But an instant before I opened my mouth, Soleta's words slammed back to me. *They'll . . . crucify you . . . don't tell them . . . swear you'll say . . . you didn't know . . . swear it . . . on your life . . . on Mac's life . . .*

And I'd sworn it. I'd given her my oath, sworn it, and realized that Soleta had seen this coming, and she'd also been aware that Starfleet might very well not see it as a nonconspiracy at all.

It took me a moment to realize that Kittinger was still speaking. "What?" I said, my mind still racing. "What . . . did you say . . . ?"

"She dropped you with a nerve pinch, you said?" Kittinger inquired. When I managed a nod, he continued, "That left you helpless, you realize."

"Helpless . . . ?"

"Have you considered the possibility," Kittinger continued, "that what she did wasn't heroic at all? That she put you down so she could try to negotiate some sort of deal with the Orions that would benefit both them and the Romulans? And when the proposed deal went sour, she was suddenly just fighting for her own life?"

"That's *insane!*"

"Is it?" he said, scratching his chin. "This opens up all sorts of possibilities. It would explain a lot of things, about difficulties the *Excalibur* has landed itself in . . ."

"Kitt, you are way off base here! There's no way . . . no! Soleta was just determined to do it herself, that's all. She didn't want me out there risking myself, and was convinced she could . . . what you're saying . . . it's . . . no! I know her!"

"Do you?"

"Yes."

"Did you know she was half-Romulan?"

Swear! Swear on Mac's life! Swear it . . . they'll crucify you! Swear!

"How could I possibly know that? Do you think she would have just told me?"

Kittinger half-smiled at that. "No. No, of course not."

And that was that.

On that day . . . that day that Soleta almost died . . . I lost a part of myself. Not an arm or a leg. Not a limb.

No, a piece of my soul died that day. That day, attendant to my promise but also gut-wrenchingly afraid for my own career . . . I, who had thrown myself on a bomb to save a crewmate, backed away from another type of bomb and let it go off with me nowhere around.

Soleta recovered, only to face a hearing . . . a hearing that resulted in her leaving Starfleet for good. I testified on her behalf.

I swore up, down, and sideways that I would be a prisoner of the Orions, or worse, if not for her. But their damned suspicions overrode everything I said, and everything Mac said in her favor as well, and Soleta left.

And recently, word has filtered through to me from Starfleet intelligence that Soleta has gone over to the Romulan Empire . . . that she now works directly with the Romulan praetor. . . .

I don't want to believe it. It is unthinkable to me. But really, we left her nowhere else to go. I know Soleta, and she is someone who needs a cause to be a part of. Someone to fight for. And if that cause is the side of her heritage that will accept her, then that is where she will be.

And so I sit here and think of what is to come. And I drink deeply, feeling the liquid burning within me. I feel for Soleta, the woman whom I was so slow to call friend, whom I now call rescuer, and whom I then willingly cut loose like a rotting extremity. And I think of the lost bit of my soul that I can still feel every now and then, ghostlike, accusing me in silence of failing to stand beside Soleta, even though it might have cost me my rank, my assignment, everything.

I try to tell myself there was no other choice while knowing that there are always choices.

And I get myself stinking drunk. Because it's the only way I can think of to manage the pain.

Tending Bar . . .

Before long, Picard, Riker, and Shelby had all departed, Shelby somewhat unsteadily. Another human Starfleet captain came in, an older man with white hair and bushy eyebrows, but Cap knew that David Gold would not be drinking anything for quite some time.

Others came in as well, culminating in two more Starfleet personnel, a familiar human male and an unfamiliar Bajoran female. Cap knew that his place wasn't to every captain's taste, its ability to visually conform to the wishes of the patron notwithstanding, so it always did his heart proud to see a regular patron like Benjamin Sisko bring his friend and comrade Kira Nerys along when she made captain.

These two were different from Picard and Riker, though. Where Riker had taken to the place without hesitation, Kira seemed uncomfortable despite Sisko's best efforts. They took their seats next to Klag, who had been sullen since Riker's concert. Cap quickly brought the new arrivals their drinks. He welcomed Sisko back, and expressed his joy at Kira's patronage. Sisko was all smiles, but Kira remained apprehensive.

Cap had faith in his place's ability to knock down the walls, as it were.

He also noted that Klag's warnog mug was almost empty. . . .

KLAG, SON OF M'RAQ
CAPTAIN OF THE *I.K.S. GORKON*

loDnI'pu' vavpu' je

KEITH R.A. DeCANDIDO

"Another *warnog*."

Wiping his hand on the apron he always wore, Cap brushed a lock of unruly white hair out of his eyes. "That was your tenth *warnog*, Klag."

"Eleventh, actually." Klag snorted. "If this were truly the Klingon tavern that it appears to be, you would not be keeping track."

Cap smiled wryly. Each captain who came through the establishment's doors saw his or her own ideal watering hole, which in Klag's case meant a public house within the Klingon Empire, the wooden walls covered with various edged weapons as well as the heads of *trigak*s, *klongat*s, *targ*s, and other game animals.

Klag continued: "And I'm still quite sober, as your transparent lie was obviously designed to test, so kindly give me another. I'm not nearly drunk enough yet."

"Maybe, maybe not. But you know the rules, Klag."

A Boslic freighter captain muttered, "Like a Klingon ever follows the rules."

Slamming a fist into the bar, Klag whirled on the Boslic. "Klingons value the power of story far more than your mongrel race, woman!"

She smiled coyly. "Prove it. Tell us a story."

"Oh no," muttered a Bajoran solar sailboat master. "Every time I come in here, it's another Klingon story. They're always about fighting and killing and honor."

A human timeship captain chuckled. "They aren't all like that—just the ones they tell in bars."

Sneering, a Romulan outpost commander said, "Do Klingons ever do anything other than tell stories in bars?"

Another Klingon captain, sitting at the far end of the bar from Klag, said, "Yes—sometimes we defeat Romulans in battle."

"Doesn't matter," Cap said before the Romulan could reply to the other Klingon's insult. "Only rule in this place is that everyone who comes in tells a story, and Klag's been here for eleven *warnog*s and several stories. It's his turn."

Klag let out a long breath that was half-sigh and half-snort. "Very well. I will tell you all a tale." He gave the Bajoran a sharp look. "It is a tale of fighting—a tale of killing—and a tale of honor. During the Dominion War, I served on the *I.K.S. Pagh* as first officer to an honorless *petaQ* named Kargan. At the Marcan system—"

"Oh God, no," the human timeship captain said. "Not that story *again*."

"You told that story the *last* time you were in here," a Chalnoth kill-ship captain said with a snarl.

A Ferengi DaiMon added, "*And* the time before that!"

"We've all heard it a thousand times," a Telspong shipmaster said.

"And each time," the Romulan said snidely, "the number of Jem'Hadar that you kill with but the use of one hand and a *mek'leth* increases. I believe it was two dozen the last time."

As he poured Klag a twelfth *warnog*, Cap couldn't help but smile. Klag told the story of his victory on Marcan V the first several times he came into the bar. It was a huge hit the first time, but less so with each subsequent telling. Cap silently agreed with his customers: It was time for Klag to spin a new yarn.

Klag took a long gulp of his drink, then turned toward the other patrons, who slowly quieted down. The dozens of conversations that made a wall of sound now faded into an equally solid wall of silence.

Once Klag had a captive audience, when the only background noise was the clunk of drink containers on tables, he began to speak.

"I am the firstborn son of M'Raq, and now the head of the House that bears his name. But M'Raq and his mate, my mother Tarilla, had a second son only one turn later: Dorrek.

"That year that separated our births was as nothing to us, however. We were as inseparable as twins, though we looked nothing alike. Dorrek inherited our mother's crest, where mine matches that of our father. To look at us, you would not know we are of the same House, much less the same parentage—but to *see* us, anyone would know instantly that we were brothers.

"We learned to wield the *bat'leth* together. We mastered the *d'k tahg* together. We read together and studied all the great operas together.

"And we learned to hunt together.

"Our father's uncle was a one-eyed old razorbeast named Nakri. As a youth, Nakri served under General Koord, and later was a warrior in the service of General Kerla. After losing his eye in battle against the Kinshaya, he left the Defense Force and became a professional hunter. For seven years running, he won the competitions on Zakorg."

A Triexian transport captain asked, "What's Zakorg?"

The Romulan said, "A planet in the Klingon Empire, *obviously*—where they no doubt hold idiotic contests in outmoded activities."

Klag smiled. "I would expect a *veruul* such as yourself to characterize the hunt as 'outmoded,' Commander."

Cap wondered if the Romulan would respond to the insult, but he seemed more taken aback by Klag's use of a Romulan curse than by the insult itself.

Klag turned to the Triexian. "However, he is essentially correct. Zakorg is the home of the finest preserve in the empire, and only the greatest hunters are even allowed to *apply* to compete there.

"Once, when I was six and Dorrek five, we were sent to live with our great-uncle for a season. Father was serving in the Defense Force, and Mother was recovering from an illness. It was their wish that Nakri teach us how to hunt properly. At the time, I had thought the notion absurd. We had both participated in the hunt, and each of us had taken down *targ* cubs and a few *ghISnar* cats—not worthy of an adult, of course, but as good as our peers.

"The first thing Nakri said when we arrived at his estate in the

Talthar Highlands was 'I have seen your hunts, children. You are both fools and incompetents. I am embarrassed to call you kin.'

"We were outraged, with the petulance that only children can achieve, and tried unsuccessfully to defend our honor.

" 'None of the others in our class were able to bring down any *targ* cubs!' I wailed.

" 'And our *ghISnar* cats were the biggest ones!' Dorrek cried.

"Nakri laughed at us. 'And is this record of battle supposed to impress me? I can train a Pheben to hunt down a *ghISnar* cat.'

" 'Our instructor—' I started, but Nakri laughed again.

" 'I know your instructor. He is a lying *toDSaH* who fools his students into believing that small accomplishments are other than that.'

" 'Other than what?' Dorrek asked.

" 'Small. You are warriors! You are the sons of M'Raq! You are of noble blood, not common children whose deeds are to be measured against the unworthy.' He fixed each of us with a one-eyed glare that would make Chancellor Martok envious. 'Starting tomorrow, I will teach you. You will leave this place one of two ways. One is as the best hunters on Qo'noS.'

"He was silent for several seconds. Looking back, I know now that he was testing our patience, seeing how long it would be before we would speak out of turn. Being a youth, it was not especially long before I blurted out, 'What is the second way?'

"He smiled. His teeth were sharper than the finest *tik'leth* blade, and when he bared them, I knew a fear like nothing I'd ever felt in my six years.

" 'Dead—with dishonor—at the hands of an animal.' "

"Wait a minute," the Triexian said, "he would've *killed* you?"

Again, Klag smiled. "No—our prey would, if we failed. That was the challenge Nakri put before us."

The human timeship captain glowered at the Triexian. "Are you going to keep interrupting, or are you going to let him tell it?"

Putting up all three hands defensively, the Triexian muttered, "Sorry."

Klag took advantage of the distraction to swallow the rest of his *warnog*. Cap, anticipating his need, had his thirteenth ready for him before he put the mug down. Giving the bartender a nod of acknowledgment, Klag continued his story:

"The next morning, we were awake before the sun.

"We had been taught how to distinguish the scents of different types of beasts—Nakri taught us how to tell the specific breeds and genders apart. Once we could only tell a bird from a reptile. Now, we could tell a *ramjep* from a *taknar*, a *wam* serpent from a *ghIq*, and a male *targ* from a female *targ*.

"We had been taught to be aware of shifts in the wind—Nakri taught us how to read the signs that indicated that the wind *would* shift, or that it wouldn't.

"We had been taught to aim for the heart, regardless of the animal—Nakri told us the folly of such an approach, as the hunt was truly to procure food, and the hunter was best served by limiting the damage to the portions of the animal that were not eaten, such as the head and the neck.

"We had been taught to throw small spears—Nakri taught us how to get in close with our *d'k tahg*s.

"Once, I tried to convince him to let us hunt with a *bat'leth*. Before coming to Nakri's, we had both participated in a Young Warriors *Bat'leth* Tournament, in which we came in first and second."

"Which one of you came in first?" the Boslic woman asked.

Cap smiled, even as Klag's facial expression soured.

"That year, Dorrek did. But the previous year, it was I who triumphed. In any event, Nakri refused to let us hunt with those weapons, despite our proficiency. 'The *bat'leth* was Kahless's sword,' he told us. 'It is to be used only by those who are worthy. You are not.'

"After many weeks, however, Nakri decided that we *were* worthy. He declared that we would hunt on our own—with *bat'leth*s. We were sent out into the grounds before dawn to find *targ* and bring it home in time for the midday meal. Armed with our *d'k tahg*s and our *bat'leth*s, we went forth.

"For hours we searched, trying to scent a *targ*, but smelled only smaller, weaker prey. Nakri had sent us deeper into his estate than we had ever gone before. His lands were in a huge valley in Talthar, and this hunt brought us very close to the mountain face. *Targ* do not climb mountains, so if we did reach the base of the peak, we would find nothing.

"Then Dorrek caught wind of a *klongat*." Turning to the Triexian, Klag added, "Before you ask, a *klongat* is a huge beast, the size of an adolescent Klingon, with immense strength, razor-sharp claws, and a vicious temper.

"When I too caught the scent, the first words out of my mouth were 'We should try to bring it down.'

"Dorrek sniffed the air. 'It smells very large, brother. And Nakri has forbidden us to hunt anything so large on our own.'

"I laughed. 'We are not on our own, brother—we are together.' Remembering Nakri's words from our first day, I added, 'We are the sons of M'Raq. Is there anything we cannot do?'

" 'If there is,' Dorrek said, 'we have not yet encountered it.'

" 'Exactly. I am sure that, if one of us did try to hunt the *klongat* on our own, that one would die. But we are together—we are strong.'

" 'But, Klag—'

"I could see that my brother had not yet found his resolve. I removed the *bat'leth* from my back scabbard, and held it aloft proudly. 'I am the *older* brother, Dorrek. When Father is away, I lead our House. We *will* hunt this beast.' Slapping him on the back with my other hand, I said, 'Do not worry, brother—we shall subdue the creature with little difficulty.'

Skeptically, the Romulan said, "Little difficulty? You were *children*."

"Yes, Commander, we were. And my boast proved accurate only if one considers dozens of broken bones, several blows to our heads, the tip of one of my brother's fingers sliced off, and half of my own hair ripped out to be 'little difficulty.'

"But the *klongat* fell. It beat us, it clawed us, it blocked our blades, but it *did* fall."

"How?" In contrast to the Romulan, the Telspong was so rapt, he dry-sipped from his empty cup and didn't notice. Cap discreetly prepared another Saurian brandy for him.

"Only when we unleashed our *bat'leth*s did we wound the creature. At first, we stalked it, myself in front, Dorrek behind it. Dorrek swiped at it with his blade, causing the creature to turn toward him, seeing him as a threat. Then I threw my *d'k tahg* at its head, hoping to kill it with one blow.

"The *klongat* was too fast. The blade struck only its shoulder—and that served only to anger it. It attacked me, and might have killed me—but Dorrek grabbed its tail, giving me a moment to scramble out of its way, blood seeping from the many wounds its claws inflicted upon me.

"Then it yanked its tail out of Dorrek's grip and went for him. Unsheathing my *bat'leth*, I swung at it.

"We kept this up for some time—we would each distract it from the other, whittling away with our blades to provide minor wounds. Neither of us could get close enough to do any serious damage, but it was able to do plenty to both of us.

"Then, at last, Dorrek sliced open one of its paws with his *d'k tahg*. This disoriented it—it could no longer walk on all four paws—and its subsequent clumsiness allowed me to ram the two front *bat'leth* blades into its skull.

"Nakri was furious with us for disobeying his instructions, but he could not deny our victory. We dined heartily on *klongat* that day, and that night and the following day, as well. For together—" Cap caught a note of bitterness in Klag's tone. "—Dorrek and I could indeed do anything."

The life suddenly draining out of him, Klag grabbed his *warnog* and downed the rest of it in one massive draught.

After a pause, the Romulan sneered again. "That's *it?* You drink thirteen *warnog*s and in exchange you tell us how you killed a stupid animal? That's hardly what I'd expect from someone who claims to put such great stock in storytelling."

As he poured a third bloodwine for the Klingon at the other

end of the bar, Cap debated whether to interject. Technically, Klag *had* fulfilled his end of the deal—he had recounted a story.

But Cap had been tending this bar for as long as it had been here, and he knew when one of his customers had more than one story to tell.

Sure enough, Klag turned back around and regarded the Romulan with an unusually oblique expression.

"Very well," he finally said. He took a gulp of his drink and then started his second story:

"When one discusses the noble Houses of the empire, it is unlikely that the House of Koghima is ever mentioned. That was true even before Koghima himself, the head of the House, was killed in a brawl at the B'Alda'ar Base tavern. The killer stabbed Koghima in the back, and so the warrior died not knowing who sent him to his death.

"Koghima had been accompanied by the House *ghIntaq*, a warrior named Kazho. Kazho did see the face of the *petaQ* who killed his master, but was unable to find him. Instead, he returned to Qo'noS to tell Koghima's mate, Gosek, what had happened.

"Gosek was a proper Klingon Lady. Though the House into which she had wed was of no great moment in the empire, she still ran it honorably. Koghima had died before he and Gosek could bear any heirs. With her mate dead by dishonorable means and no children, she was also honorless. She had only one recourse: to take vengeance against her mate's killer. She instructed Kazho to accompany her, which he would have done even were he not sworn to obey all those of the House of Koghima. You see, Kazho was madly in love with Gosek, and had been since the day he first laid eyes upon her.

"Together, they searched the empire. They used all the meagre resources at the disposal of the House of Koghima. For years, they traveled to different worlds, to taverns, to space stations, to starships—all in search of a man whom Kazho knew only by face.

"Traveling alone together for so long, they, predictably, became lovers. Kazho's passion was all-encompassing, but Gosek's motives remained inscrutable. She declared no love for Kazho, no passion for him—yet she never once refused him when he asked to come to her bed. Kazho did not care, as long as those requests were fulfilled.

"They continued to live off the House's ever-dwindling reserves, but were never able to find the murderer. It seemed a lost cause, but Gosek would not surrender. Her honor needed to be served—with Koghima dead, it was all she had left.

"Kazho grew weary. Indeed, he was weary of the quest the moment it began, and that soon overcame his loyalty to the House and to Gosek. He implored Gosek to cease this insanity. They could forget their obligations to a dying—truly, a *dead*—House and perhaps be farmers on some planet in a dark corner of the empire. It did not matter to him if Gosek was forced to forfeit what was left of the House of Koghima to some other warrior, as long as they were together.

"But Kazho's importunings fell on deaf ears. Gosek called him a coward, and he relented.

"Many times Kazho could have left, but the twin obligations of his oath to the House and his love for Gosek kept him at her side as they continued their futile quest.

"Eventually, they arrived at Mempa IX. While dining in a restaurant there, Kazho saw two warriors, one of whom had a similar crest to that of Koghima's killer. Thinking this might be a relative, Kazho abandoned his heart of *targ* and, without a word to Gosek, rose from his table and confronted the two men.

"When he asked their names, one of them said, 'I am Klag, and this is my brother Dorrek—we are the sons of M'Raq.' "

"It was you?" the Triexian asked redundantly.

"Yes," Klag said with a smile. "And what's more, I recognized my questioner. I had seen him in the company of my father many turns earlier, before Kazho left the Defense Force in order to become the *ghIntaq* of a minor House.

"I looked at him and said, 'I know you—you are Kazho.'

"Before he could reply, Gosek had caught up to us. She

demanded to know who these people were. When Kazho told him we were the sons of M'Raq, Gosek went into a rage. 'Is this M'Raq the one who killed my mate?'

"Dorrek stared at both of them. 'Our father was taken in battle by Romulans. He is no doubt in *Sto-Vo-Kor* now.'

"I added, 'And the only people he has killed are enemies of the empire. Of what are you accusing him?' "

Klag hesitated. He opened his mouth, then closed it.

"Well?" the Boslic captain asked.

The human Starfleet captain next to Klag said, "You *can't* stop the story there."

Shaking his head, Klag said, "But I must."

Cries of irritation sounded throughout the tavern.

"That's crazy."

"Was M'Raq the killer?"

"Did Kazho or Gosek get their revenge?"

"If it wasn't M'Raq, who was it?"

"Why didn't Kazho say anything if he knew M'Raq?"

Klag shook his head. "You do not understand. The story cannot have a good end. If M'Raq was the one who killed Koghima without showing his face, then his sons would share in the disgrace of committing so dishonorable an act.

"But there was no proof, so it was only the word of a lowly *ghIntaq* of a minor House against two decorated officers from a noble one.

"If M'Raq was not the killer, if Kazho simply chose Dorrek and me in a desperate attempt to cease their continuous travails and at last bring an end to their quest—either in Gosek's arms or in *Sto-Vo-Kor*—then Kazho would be dishonored.

"And what if M'Raq killed Koghima as a favor to his old comrade Kazho to give Kazho a chance to became the head of the House of Koghima, mating with the woman he loved, and replacing a useless old fool who was driving their House to ruin? How was he to know that Gosek would insist on the right of vengeance against the killer of a man she never even *liked*, much less loved—or that she would carry it through to the bitterest of ends?"

The Romulan shook his head. "First a poor tale, then a tale with no ending. Were I the proprietor of this establishment, I would consider retrieiving my drinks from your gut."

"Were you the proprietor, Commander," Klag said with a vicious grin, "I would not be in it telling any tales at all, and there would be no one here to tell them to."

The Bajoran woman who sat on the other side of Klag asked, "C'mon, Klag, the story has to have *some* ending."

Klag drank some more *warnog*, then slammed the mug onto the bar with a loud clunk. "Yes," he finally said. "The truth of the matter is, Kazho and Gosek left the restaurant on Mempa without another word. I never did find out what happened to them after that. Perhaps they search the empire still. Perhaps they found their farm. Perhaps they gave each other *Mauk-to'Vor* to get out of their mutual misery. Or perhaps they insulted someone they should not have, and were killed for their effrontery.

"However, Dorrek's words to Kazho turned out to be mistaken. M'Raq was *not* in *Sto-Vo-Kor*. He yet lived, a prisoner of the Romulans who was not permitted to die. Eventually, he escaped and returned to Qo'noS."

Once again, the Romulan sneered. "I doubt that any Klingon could escape a Romulan prison on his own."

Before Klag could respond to this slander, a Rigelian hospital shipmaster asked, "If your father did return after your encounter with Kazho and Gosek—were you able to learn the truth from him?"

Klag looked at the Rigelian for several moments, then at the Romulan, then at the Klingon at the far end of the bar. He turned to finish off the drink in front of him. Cap gave him a fourteenth moments later.

"There once," he finally said, "was a great warrior. A proud man, the head of one of the finest Houses in the empire, he was nonetheless cursed with two fools for sons.

"The warrior tried to teach his sons well, but they were quite foolish indeed and there was nothing to be done with them. He tried sending them to another great warrior to learn, but they were disrespectful of their elder and flouted his instructions at every opportunity, refusing to benefit from his wisdom. Instead, they hunted a creature they were too stupid to realize they could not defeat.

"By right of birth, they were able to study to become officers in the Defense Force, and so the warrior sent them to train, in the vain hope that it would make honorable men of them.

"Somehow, they managed to get their commissions. They became adequate warriors, but nothing worthy of song. The younger fool worked his way up the ranks slowly, unable to distinguish himself. The older fool was promoted more quickly, becoming the second officer of a fine ship, under the command of a scion of a noble House. Fool that he was, he had thought that he was on the path to honor with this appointment.

"In the meantime, their father the great warrior fought many battles, including one against the empire's greatest foe. So great a warrior he was that the foe refused to allow him an honorable death, for they wished information from him. But the warrior would not yield, and he eventually made his escape." Klag said this last while staring right at the Romulan commander, who said nothing as he sipped his ale.

Klag went on. "The warrior's oldest son, meanwhile, thought himself fortunate. The first officer under whom he served was a fine warrior, who stood for the crew. When she died in battle, an exchange program with the Federation brought a most odd replacement: a human.

"It was while serving under the human that the depth of his foolishness was revealed to him, for the captain under whom he served was not worthy of his House, his station, or his brave crew. Based on the flimsiest evidence, the captain provoked a conflict with the Federation flagship, and only quick thinking on the part of the human kept us from dishonorable death.

"When the human's tour ended, the fool was made first officer, and he was soon after visited by a *bekk* of no consequence, who revealed himself to be an agent of the captain's House. 'Be warned, Commander,' he said, 'that your captain is a man of tremendous influence. You will obey his orders and serve him in all things—as your predecessor did. *Any* action you take not in accordance with the captain's wishes will result in you suffering a most ignoble fate—as your predecessor did.'

"What, you might wonder, did this fool do? Was he a worthy son to his father, who stood against his foe and would not give them what they asked? Would he defy the words spoken to him by a secret assassin working for an honorless coward? Would he live up to the reputation of his House by showing that the path of honor will win the day over those who would besmirch everything that the empire stands for?

"You can guess the answer—for time had made him a bigger fool than any could possibly imagine. And so, for ten years, he remained the lapdog of this cowardly *petaQ*, covering up the captain's dishonor just as his predecessor had. So long was he trapped under this *toDSaH*'s bootheel that his younger brother had achieved the same rank in due course.

"Meanwhile, the fools' father returned home from his captivity. He could have gone back to his life as a warrior, but, as was his right, he chose not to reclaim his honor. He had fought his battles, and he had two sons to carry on his name.

"But his sons were very great fools indeed, and they bickered and argued. The older son refused to see his father, thinking him a disgrace; the younger son would not do his filial duty and obey. So where once the two were inseparable, where once they were able to achieve great things together, now they achieved nothing.

"Eventually, the warrior died of natural causes. That only made things worse. The older fool had lost his arm in the same battle that claimed his dishonorable captain. Having at last achieved the captaincy he had waited his entire life for, the older fool, in a misbegotten attempt to salvage his family's honor, had his father's arm grafted onto his own body.

"The younger fool excoriated him for it. He tormented his

brother, even took up arms against him in a battle on behalf of the Order of the *Bat'leth*. Unable to allow his disobedience to continue, and with his position as head of the House now secure with the great warrior's death, the older fool was forced to remove his younger brother from their House.

"He had no choice, which only made him more foolish.

"Was he right to refuse to see his own father? Was he right to take arms against his own brother? Was his father truly a coward who killed another warrior without showing his face in a barroom brawl? Was his father truly able to escape the Romulans, or did they let him go? And if so, did that disgrace lead him to avoid reclaiming his honor?

"And did any of that matter?"

With the very same arm that once belonged to his father, Klag raised his final *warnog* and drank it all down. "A fine House has been sundered because of two children who did not learn the lesson that Nakri taught them: that they were warriors, and that warriors do not obey blindly, but do what is right. When they were children, the two fools knew that they could defeat the *klongat* even though Nakri told them they could not. Because, though it is honor and duty that guide us, they should not shackle us.

"Duty to her husband compelled Gosek to continue her mad quest for Koghima's killer when there was no reason why she should. Duty to his House compelled Kazho to follow her through to the bitter end. Duty to his ship compelled the older fool not to challenge his captain, even though he was an incompetent who deserved to die. And duty to his honor compelled the fool to shun his own father when he refused to reclaim his lost glory—and to cast out his brother when he did not follow the elder's lead.

"Regardless of the motives, regardless of the truth, regardless of the misunderstandings, regardless of the disobedience in the face of righteousness, regardless of the obedience in the face of dishonor—the result is the same, and the result is tragic. And little can be done about it now.

"Because the older fool realized too late that his father was dead, and that he would never be able to speak to him, to be with him—to learn from him ever again. Whether or not he was an honorable man, whether or not he stabbed a man in the back, whether or not he truly escaped from the Romulans—the fool, once again and for the final time, failed to learn the lessons his father tried so hard to impart to him. Instead a great warrior died thinking his oldest son hated him. At the very least, he was spared the sight of his son, a Klingon warrior, admitting to a room full of friends and strangers—and others—that he misses his father."

With that, Klag rose from his stool, turned, and left the Captain's Table.

Cap took Klag's *warnog* mug and dropped it into the dirty-dish bin. As he did so, the noise in the bar started, slowly, to build, as the patrons realized that the story was at last over, and regular discussion could resume until such time as someone else was asked for their payment.

"An interesting story," the Triexian said.

The Romulan once again sneered. "Your criteria for interest are considerably less exacting than my own. I found the first story dull, the second aimless, and the third maudlin."

"Well, I liked it," the Boslic woman said.

"Which one?" the Telspong asked.

"All of them."

The Bajoran solar sailboat captain shrugged. "It was just more fighting, killing, and honor."

Cap walked over to the end of the bar where the other Klingon still sat, brooding. "Another bloodwine?"

The Klingon shook his head without looking up.

"What about a story? Do you have one?"

Finishing his bloodwine and then casting the mug aside, the Klingon rose from his bar stool and said, "My brother just told it."

With that, Dorrek, son of M'Raq, left.

Tending Bar . . .

Cap had observed Kira throughout Klag's story. Something in Klag's tale struck a chord with the Bajoran woman, and Cap knew that she had found her payment, even if she herself didn't realize it. Refilling her drink, he watched her thoughtful expression, even as her companion, Sisko, told a story about a young man—Sisko's own son, Cap knew, though the captain left this fact out—who had lost his father and, in an attempt to find him, traveled a great distance and had many adventures on a vessel called the Even Odds in a place thousands of lightyears from his home. In the end, the young man did not find his father, but brought two lost souls back to the place that all three had called home. Cap had already heard a version of this story from the Even Odds' own captain a while back, and he enjoyed hearing the different perspective.

When that was done, Kira announced that she had her own story and that the tales of Klag and his brother inspired it. The Romulan commander blanched at the notion, but everyone else in the bar listened as Kira began. . . .

KIRA NERYS
CAPTAIN OF DEEP SPACE 9

The Officers' Club

HEATHER JARMAN

I felt his eyes on me. Even surrounded by four office walls and no windows, I sensed his presence. I saw cabinets and curiosities from my seat in the examining chair and the attendants bustling about with their tools, impassively taking their measurements and notes, poking at me as if I were a specimen. He'd always been exceedingly good at playing make-believe and persuading others to go along with his games; it's how he managed to stay comfortable while the rest of us went without. He'd left me—left all of us—what was it, ten years ago? But I still had issues with him. Prophets knew I saw his face on every collaborator I pummeled with my fists, heard his voice in the gurgling gasp of death I dealt each traitor. I couldn't escape him, though I'd certainly tried.

Even this examining room, abundantly stocked with the latest medical supplies and sterile instruments, expressed his nature perfectly: He loved excess. He always sought to add more to what he already had and he refused to share because it meant he would have less. But who could blame me for hoping that he might have changed? I still cared about him in my own way regardless of what he'd become (and if the gossip was true, he had his share of identities, including collaborator, pimp, black-market dealer, thief, and arms dealer). Let me be clear: I didn't forgive my brother. I just hadn't given up hope that he could still be of use to the cause.

So when Shakaar asked me to run an operation for the resistance by infiltrating one of the most powerful organized crime syndicates on Bajor, I accepted without hesitation. The mission was straightforward. I would worm my way into a nest of collaborators to facilitate the kidnapping of one Glinn Gundar. We'd heard through back channels that Gundar was being dispatched from Central Command to upgrade the Bajoran Sector

Communications Network encryption algorithms sometime in the next sixty days. Preventing Gundar from completing the systems upgrade was critical.

Running a resistance is difficult when you can't eavesdrop on the enemy's conversations.

My job was to remove Glinn Gundar from Doblana Base and place him in Shakaar's custody. No idea what would happen next; once Gundar was in the resistance's hands, I was done. But I had a vested personal interest in this specific operation that gave me an extra motivation to succeed.

First, bringing down the Cardassians by using the collaborators sweetened the deal considerably. I loved nothing better than bringing those bottom-feeders to their knees and making them beg for mercy. Second, since my brother Reon stood at the top of their festering ranks, I had the chance once and for all to settle the score. He could support our cause, honor his Kira name, and help me, or he could hold ranks with his corrupt cronies. If he chose the latter, he would suffer for it. The Fire Caves would be a pleasant way to die after I was done with him. There might be some hint of the Kira *pagh* left within him or there might not be. I would find out soon enough.

The first phase of my mission had been successful. On the grounds that I was seeking employment, I'd bribed my way onto a supply transport headed for the Doblana Arctic Base complex, a large facility tasked with managing critical pieces of the Occupation's infrastructure, including communications. The Plin Syndicate ran their primary facility side by side with the Cardassian base, a business called, innocuously enough, the Officers' Club—the facility I anticipated working for. Ostensibly, the outward purpose of the Officers' Club was providing an abundant supply of the usual vices to the Cardassians assigned to Doblana. In our briefing, Shakaar had stated that the comfort women, gambling, drugging, and drinking didn't even account for a tenth of Plin's revenues—it was just the proverbial foam on the *raktajino* and a cover for the real business: a major hub for the Alpha Quadrant black market. Talk about an abundance of opportunities for the resistance!

I just had to survive the job interview.

Only a mission that promised such a lucrative outcome could have induced me to tolerate the treatment I was being subjected to. Under normal circumstances, I'd be more inclined to knee a groin or two and get the hell out. I kept reminding myself, though, that I was enduring this humiliation for Bajor.

As Doctor Liawn pried my mouth open, he recoiled at the "stink of jumja rot" emanating from my decaying, blackened teeth. Recently, I'd had a few sores inside my lip, but I'd lanced them with my knife blade and burned out the puss to keep the infection from spreading. The doctor had shuddered when he'd observed the remains of those wounds.

He bid me to close my mouth with a wave of his hand and took a step back. "You're in terrible shape."

"No one ever said the caves of Dahkur were luxury suites in Ashalla."

Liawn exhaled loudly and shook his head. "If it were only your teeth, I wouldn't be concerned. Cosmetic treatment, and your molars will be white as *sova* shell, but the rest of you isn't much more than cadaverous skin and bones—I could see through your cheekbones to the back if your skull if I shone a light through your sinuses. I've known wire scrubbers less coarse than the skin on your hands, elbows, and knees."

As he prattled on, I clenched the edge of the examining table wishing for all of Bajor's stolen latinum that I could leap off and strangle him. What held me back was the conviction that Shakaar, perhaps most of Bajor's resistance cells, counted on me to pass Liawn's scrutiny and go to work for Plin Patra. I needed this job. I had to be hired even if I had to sleep with half the staff to do it.

Leaning forward, I widened my eyes, affixing him with my best version of an earnest, innocent look. "If repairing my teeth isn't a problem, there must be some mud bath or oil treatment that could help my skin. And Prophets know that I'd gain weight on a diet of something other than *teep* grass." I batted my eyelashes, offering him a shy but pleading grin that I kept in my arsenal for those rare occasions when smiles worked better than a punch to the jaw.

A dimple creased Doctor Liawn's doughy cheeks. He found my pathetic attempts at flirtation amusing, I could tell. "If it were only your appearance that troubled me, I'd advance you to the next interview."

I toyed with the lace ruffle around the wrist of his jacket. "I have many skills, Doctor Liawn. I'm certain I could satisfy all your doubts."

"My experience with you refugee types is that malnutrition compromises your bone density—even muscle strength," he said, taking a step back so as to be out of my reach. "Don't take this personally, but this isn't a position for a weakling. Our employees have to be able to hold their own in any one-on-one they might be thrust into."

"Test me," I said, tossing my hair, confident that I could pass any screening an Officers' Club could devise. Hell, I'd gone hours in hand-to-hand with soldiers twice my size and weight and escaped with little more than a scratch. I could manage a tray full of *kanar*-filled snifters and run a dabo game wearing high heels— no problem.

His lip curled as he considered me for a long moment. "Fine then. Step behind that partition." He nodded toward the rear of the medical bay. "You'll find the appropriate attire to change into. I'll call ahead to make sure the arena is ready."

Arena? I pondered the implications of the word while I peeled away the layers of patched and faded cloth I'd fashioned into a tunic and breeches. I deposited my yellowing, sweat-stained chemise onto the chair and paused to look in the mirror mounted on the side of the partition. I don't know how long it had been since I'd had the luxury of a mirror. Maybe a year, maybe two since my mission to the space station Terok Nor when I'd been forced to assassinate Vaatrik. Appearance didn't rank high on my list of concerns, didn't get the job of freeing Bajor done. What I needed was a stalwart heart, strong legs, good fists and the willingness to use them; that I had. But beauty . . . Doctor Liawn had assessed me fairly. The emaciated creature reflecting back at me bore little resemblance to the Nerys of my memory. The filth embedded into my nail beds, in the skin crevices of my wrists and neck where my flesh was exposed to the elements stood out in stark relief against my pale upper arms, legs, and torso. The nearly translucent skin stretched tight over my ribs, the knobs of my joints, and my desiccated muscles. I could see my pulse fluttering in my veins. I studied the reflection, wondering whether it was my hatred for the Cardassians or my passion to see Bajoran independence that kept the waif in the mirror alive and fighting. Did it matter? I was alive.

I pulled on the unisex shorts and tank top Liawn had left behind and emerged from the partition. His assistant waited for me. I followed her through several sets of doors into a long hallway where Liawn stood outside yet another door that I assumed opened into the arena. He attached sensors to my circulatory and respiratory regions, then placed a headband around my forehead and temples, informing me that the band would monitor my neurochemical levels.

"So what will it be: Klingons, Cardassians, or Romulans?" he asked.

Understanding occurred; Liawn wanted to know who I hated most. New confidence filled me and I smiled. "No question. Cardassians."

"Hardly surprising," Liawn said with a snort. Without further explanation, he activated the doors and gave me a gentle shove into a spacious room. The spongy give in the floor beneath my feet reminded me of what I'd been told a hoverball practice court was supposed to be like. I still struggled to acclimate to the recirculated air; my lungs rebelled against inhalations free from the spores, dust, smoke, and pollutants I'd lived my whole life with.

A hissing door interrupted my thoughts. I spun around to see a burly Cardassian, stripped bare to the waist, striding through the doorway. Part of my brain registered that this couldn't be a flesh-and-blood Cardassian. Hadn't Liawn asked me to choose an opponent like I might a random card in a game of *triuval?* I'd heard stories about holography and the ability to create lifelike characters out of light and energy—the bar on the space station was famous for its holosuites—but I'd never had firsthand experience with the technology. My eyes and slamming pulse validated the illusion's realism; the familiar sensation of adrenaline coursing into my limbs energized me.

He held his elbows at right angles, his hands in fists; he didn't smile.

But I did. The familiar burn of molten anger energized my limbs. I found it delicious. No love, no dream of freedom motivated me, only unadulterated hate. I snarled, charged my enemy, drew first blood. Each blow, each bruise fueled my fury. Years of scratching, biting, breaking my enemy had prepared me for this combat. What I lacked in brute force, I made up for in cunning as I ducked, dodged, and parried his blows.

How long our hand-to-hand combat lasted, I can't recall. When I finally snapped the Cardassian's neck, the door hissed open and I staggered out into the hallway. I gratefully received assistance from a waiting attendant who offered me a basin to spit a mouthful of blood and tooth shards into, and quickly spirited the distasteful mass away. I probably bled internally, perhaps I'd sustained a fracture or a concussion. I didn't care. Endorphins numbed my pain. I exulted into the hallway, confident that I'd proved my worth to these sniveling collaborators. Ten of them wouldn't be worth one of my fellow resistance fighters. Plin wouldn't dare turn me down now. She would have to hire me. If that was the worst she could throw at me, I knew I would triumph.

The look on Liawn's face said differently. "Peri will fix your teeth and attend to your wounds. I took the liberty of procuring you new things. Your old clothes are hardly fit to wear. I've had them recycled. I've also provided you with enough credits to transport wherever on Bajor you want to go. They're in the pouch next to your boots. Go with the Prophets." He turned on his heel and headed away from the arena.

I refused to accept failure.

Chasing after him, I shouted, "I mopped the floor with that Cardassian. What else do you want from me? How dare you turn me away! I want this job! I *need* this job!"

Liawn paused, exhaled, clearly annoyed. "Besides the fact that the sensors indicated both microfractures due to porous bones and weakness in your pulmonary vessels with increased stress making your fitness questionable, you lied."

My eyes widened. *How dare this betrayer call me a liar.* "I *lied?*"

"I'm almost persuaded by your indignant behavior, I'll grant you that much," Liawn said, drawing closer to me. "Why do you really seek employment with Plin Patra? Who are you working for?"

I took a step back, took a deep breath and began, "I admit: I've served in the resistance in the past and you might think that's why I'm here now. But you have to believe that I'm done with it." I dug deep into my gut, remembering every mistake I'd ever made, every failed op as I tried conjuring a defeatist mind-set. "I can't take it anymore. The suffering, the futility of it all, the endless cycle of death and destruction. I've had enough."

His eyes glinted through narrow slits, his face puckered in a frown.

I sensed his disbelief; I reached deep within my *pagh* and opened up the place of my darkest fears and most despairing failures. I had to convince him. I turned watering eyes up at him. "Any belief, any dream I had—" A tight, pained gasp escaped my throat. "—that we could end this Occupation is fading. I don't think we can break the backs of the Cardassians in my lifetime." I grabbed Liawn's arm, forced him to face me. "I'm exhausted. You've seen me—I have an old woman's body. Without this job, I have no way out of the cold and mud and starvation. I need the *litas* to go off-world and start over somewhere else." My shoulders slumped, I raised my hands to my face, breathing deeply to steady the sobs I wanted Liawn to believe were threatening to burst through.

From behind me, I heard clapping.

"Well done," a throaty female voice spoke behind me. "I don't believe a word of it, but our Cardassian members might."

Raising my face, I turned to see Plin Patra standing behind me. We'd never met face-to-face, but I recognized her from the rare opportunities I'd had to scan the newsfeeds. From time to time, she and her entourage showed up in the Cardassian News Service propaganda standing beside Prefect Dukat or socializing with visiting dignitaries. The Cardassians offered Plin's warm associations with them as proof that they could work and play well with the Bajorans.

So this was the woman who helped the Sulati acquire bioweapons and kept Dukat's bedmates in silks and baubles. Soft living kept her milky complexion satiny and unblemished; she looked like she was my age, though I knew she had children older than I was. No adornments mussed her long chestnut brown hair worn up in a tightly pinned chignon. Up close, she lacked the imposing presence she exuded in her public persona. I'd expected she'd be much taller. Even her clothing avoided pretentious displays of wealth; her plain jewel blue trousers and short jacket, both impeccably tailored, cut a fluid line over her slender form. I suppose I expected more glitzy whore and less entrepreneur. For a moment, her seeming simplicity disconcerted me.

Noting my scrutiny, she raised an eyebrow. Finally: "Change your clothes, let the nurse fix your wounds, then come back into my office and we'll talk."

Her office had more in common with a luxury suite of living rooms than a boxy, utilitarian space with a desk—what I thought of as an office. Past twining sunset colored orchids in cloisonné vases, hand-carved furniture, and wall-size frescoes of pastoral Bajor, Plin led me into her library. She motioned for me to take a seat in a high-backed chair upholstered in dark green Tholian silk before taking her place across the room in a similar-style chair. I heard burbling water somewhere in the background.

"You're not worried that my scrubbing-brush-like skin is going to snag your fabric," I said, pausing before sitting down.

Plin laughed. "Reon told me you had a sense of humor."

"I'm sure Reon's had more fun than I've had over the last ten years. Not much amusement in liberating the oppressed and brutalized."

"On that, we agree." She poured wine into a pair of goblets sitting on a tray beside her chair and walked over to offer one to me before returning to her own glass. Raising it in the air, she said, "To good business."

"To good business," I agreed, and waited for my hostess to take a sip before taking a sip of my own. Feeling neither cold nor uncomfortable, I sat poker-straight in my chair, sharpening my focus on Plin, refusing to allow ease to lull me into sloppiness.

Plin tilted her head thoughtfully, offering a half-smile. "You trust no one. Good. That will make this easier."

"This?" I raised my wineglass to my lips.

Daintily, she crossed one leg over the other, smoothing her trouser leg. "You don't want a job. You're not leaving Bajor. You're here on assignment from the resistance."

I swallowed too much wine, coughed, and quickly raised the back of my hand to my mouth in hopes that I'd covered my surprise, but obviously, Plin was too clever or too well connected for me to fool her. How could she possibly know? My operation was known only to the highest echelon of resistance leaders.

"You're wondering how I know."

"Do you read minds as well?"

"I read people. That's my business, and as you can see from looking around you, I'm an expert at doing business. You want me to tell you about yourself?"

"Reon—"

"I don't mean vital statistics. I mean the fact that in twelve years in the resistance, you have never once faltered in your loyalty. You've been watched, even approached by agents looking for vulnerabilities in that seemingly impenetrable moral armor you protect yourself with in the hopes that you might be turned–"

I gasped. I'd been approached?

Plin smiled smugly. "Your invulnerability–your single-mindedness–makes you blind in some respects, Nerys. All of those in my circles keep an eye on you, wondering not if, but when we'll wake in the night to find your knife at our throats."

"So if you assume I'm here to kill you, why am I sitting here and not in a transport on my way back to Hedrickspool?"

"Because I have a use for you."

"But what about my 'impenetrable moral armor'? Surely you don't believe you can induce me to betray those who have my loyalties with anything in this room." I smirked, waving my hand in the direction of Plin's overt displays of prosperity: Kendra jade figurines, tapestries, and the countless antique reading scrolls ensconced on her shelves.

"I share your loyalties," she said simply. "We fight for the same side."

Incredulous, my eyes widened and I snorted. "Please. You can do better than that. Pretending to be on the same team as your enemy? A pretty transparent tactic for someone who plays in your league. I thought you were good at this."

She crossed the space between us, crouched down next to my chair, leaned close and whispered hoarsely into my ear. Sitting back on her heels, she looked at me expectantly.

I blinked. Clutched the chair's armrests. Stared at Plin, my mind racing. *Was it possible?*

Plin had provided me with an emergency extraction code given to top-level resistance operatives when they needed to abort a mission. Only those who had passed tests of loyalty beyond any conceivable doubt could have an extraction code. Faking the codes was impossible, to my best knowledge.

While Bajor's resistance cells didn't run under centralized leadership, an agreed-upon emergency system had arisen over the years that allowed resistance agents to work anywhere on Bajor and be able to locate backup in an emergency situation. The codes changed weekly—the day before I left for Doblana Base, Shakaar had issued me my new extraction code.

Either Plin served the resistance or a traitor lurked in our most powerful circles. There was no other way for Plin to have the information she'd whispered to me.

I wasn't sure which option I found more surprising.

At last I overcame my shock. "How could you—"

"Can you conceive of a more ideal cover for a resistance cell than a successful business run by collaborators?" she whispered, smiling mischievously. "Once you're inside the Club, look beneath the dabo and the Cardassians parading around with their Bajoran comfort women on their arms and you'll see how perfect our setup is."

Blinking back my surprise, I sat for a minute, considered her words and realized that no, I couldn't think of a more effective cover. Then the questions started. Why hadn't Shakaar told me? How had she managed to keep such a secret for so many years without being suspected by the Cardassians? Could she be lying—playing both sides of the game and profiting from both? My expression must have borne witness to my questions because Plin patted my arm and told me that the answers would come in good time. She returned to her chair and watched me closely until I was ready to speak.

I had many questions. "But how can you avoid leaks with so many operatives?"

"Not all the employees here are operatives. You won't necessarily know who works with us, for your safety and theirs."

Immediately, I pounced on the pronoun. "Us?"

"You can work here," she said, toying with the stem of her wineglass as she spoke. "But there are no solo operations in the Officers' Club—I won't allow you to blow our cover, even inadvertently. I'll need to know the details of your op."

So it came down to me revealing all in exchange for—what? No deal. "You honestly expect me to tell you that?" I shook my head.

"Granted, you've lobbed quite an authentic-looking grenade into my lap, but I still don't trust you."

Plin laughed a deep melodious belly laugh. "Excellent. You shouldn't. In due time, however, you will be faced with a decision: we work together or you'll be on that transport to Hedrickspool, without an apology to Shakaar. Fair?"

I nodded, paused, wrestling with an impulse to ask my questions, but reluctant to reveal myself.

"You will see Reon again," Plin said quietly, willing me to meet her gaze.

I found understanding in her vivid green eyes. Perhaps she did read minds after all.

Plin slapped her thighs and rose from her chair. "One of the personnel coordinators from the Club will be up to start you on your improvement regimen."

"Excuse me?" I wasn't sure I followed her.

"I have much higher expectations for those who work for me than Shakaar does," she said, tapping information into what I assumed was a communication unit on the wall. "I have to grant that he gets results, but I feel that the journey to achieving those results should be equally satisfying."

Two Bajorans plainly dressed in *por* wool tunics materialized in the doorway. Plin introduced them as Tov and Mena and told me that they would be responsible for preparing me for work in the Club—grooming, diet, medical—

"—and especially those teeth," Plin added on her way into the anteroom.

I'd passed the first test.

I submitted to Tov's and Mena's orders without protest. After all, what's to complain about soaks in an oil tub, head-to-toe *zusah*-wood exfoliating treatments, and relaxing in *farak* steam. Having my scars mended and teeth cleaned and repaired wasn't bad either. I ran my tongue over the sleek white enamel, searching for the old caries and gaps, and found none. Even I, who lived on the opposite extreme from vanity, enjoyed a small gush of pleasure when I saw my smile. Mena had brought me a series of protein shakes formulated to help my body acclimate to eating before I assumed a regular diet of fruits, vegetables, and meat for the first time in my life. She warned me that I would need more cosmetic treatments before work started, but that at least I was presentable enough to be seen in the Club.

"Follow me to your new quarters. Your roommate hasn't started her shift yet and she'll be orienting you to the facilities and our rules," Tov said. "Madame Plin chose her specifically for you. You are fortunate she's taken a personal interest in your welfare."

She's interested because she wants something from me, I thought cynically. As I followed Tov through a series of winding service passageways, I ruminated on who Plin might have matched me with until the last hall terminated in a pair of doors.

We passed into a gloriously illuminated foyer furnished in plush, brocade settees and plump chairs offering flashes of purple, deep tree greens, and blues. On every side I saw buffet tables jammed with gleaming serving dishes and platters brimming with stuffed puffs, cheeses, steaming meats, layered desserts, and corpulent, ripe fruits. Servers flitted about, pushing carts loaded with gilded liqueur carafes and wine bottles. Overwhelmed by the fatty, spicy scents, I avoided breathing through my nose; my stomach convulsed with nausea. I forced my attention away from the food, noting instead the décor.

In essentials, the design exhibited the refined elegance of Plin's salon garnished with an overlay of crystal, shiny metallic surfaces, and colorful flourishes. From above, prismatic light shone through an ocean of vibrant blue, green, and yellow wavy glass, giving me the sensation of walking underwater. At a long-ago time many of Bajor's buildings had been as noisy and colorful as the Club, though they were no longer so—not in a day of gray Cardassian faces, the dark, glinting metal of weaponry, and the rags of an oppressed people. I was reminded of why I'd come to this place—to do my small part to help my people overcome their conquerors. But shouldn't it be harder?

A flash of guilt stabbed at me. No one here in the Officers' Club seemed to be suffering or even cognizant that so much misery existed beyond these walls. Bajorans, Cardassians, a few Trill, humans, Ferengi, and others I didn't recognize milled mindlessly around the central reception area. They flowed in and out of walkways into adjacent spaces, most likely the casino and gaming rooms or the club's notorious private suites, smiling and laughing, satiated in debauchery. Few if any that I knew from my life in Dahkur would ever have the opportunity to sleep in a safe place, never mind being offered the luxuries I'd partaken of over the last few hours. I'd even been inoculated against Vensa's Syndrome! Growing up in the camps, protection from such an illness was unheard-of. A lucky Bajoran who contracted it might lose hearing or sight; an unlucky Bajoran would be paralyzed or driven insane. Now I would never have to wonder if or when the disease would strike me. How was I fortunate when so many others weren't? What had anyone here done to deserve such privilege?

In my mind, I heard Plin's admonishment to look beneath the surface. I studied my surroundings, peeling away the shimmering layers, the grotesque excesses. The room slowly shifted, recast itself. . . .

I noted the alcohol poured in every corner; winced at the Bajoran women draped around the members' necks like medals celebrating conquests; saw the drugged haze in the faces of the Cardassians smudged in Andorian *saf*. A giggling girl sat on a gul's lap, hand-feeding him pulpy *kalava* seeds. And then it occurred to me, as I watched a comfort woman ply her Cardassian guest with more *kanar*, that from all outward appearances, the Cardassians did the indulging—the Bajorans enabled it.

Plin's people controlled the stage.

Looking beneath the façade, just for a moment, I glimpsed what power these women had over the members, how vulnerable the Cardassians allowed themselves to become in this place. Plin had done a magnificent job of crafting an irresistibly seductive environment that, over time, could beguile the most hardened glinn or gul into a false sense of security.

Talk about the perfect targets for opportunistic resistance operatives.

"Before we reach your quarters, I'll show you where you have to be disinfected at the start of shift," Tov said, interrupting my thoughts.

"Disinfected?"

"Our clients find our odors—distasteful. Our skin secretions, our musky perspiration, our hair scent." He scanned me perfunctorily from boot to scalp. "You'll have to cut yours."

I smoothed the long plait falling down my back, wondering what other indignities I would be subjected to.

"They are a fastidious people. Attentiveness to our own hygiene helps our members have a more agreeable experience."

"The customer is always right," I quipped, a line I'd heard from the Ferengi who ran the bar on the space station. A dazzling fountain combining lasers and morphing holographic plant life drew my attention away from my host. I almost didn't realize he'd stopped walking.

Tov frowned, raised his index finger to halt me. "In our club, we have members, not customers. Members receive benefits, they do not transact for services. Understood?"

I understood all right. But who was Tov fooling? Prettying up the business of selling a person like one might sell a farm animal with euphemisms and nice decorating didn't make this any less a distasteful scenario—just as calling a vole a "furry field scavenger" doesn't make it any less a pest. I knew what this job required and I was willing to take it on. That didn't mean I had to enjoy it.

A statuesque Bajoran woman clothed in a scanty, translucent drape wrapped around her torso glided by me, head held high, shoulders squared.

Will I have to dress that way? I shuddered.

As I watched her cross the lobby toward the reception desk, I realized she didn't wear her familial earring. Neither had Plin or any other Bajoran I'd met, come to think of it. Probably not allowed. Part of looking subservient to the conquerors, I reflected wryly. I wondered who she was—whether she was one of Plin's agents—and how she'd come to be in the place. I wasn't certain if I should be impressed by her beauty and confidence or pity her having to seduce Cardassians on a daily basis. Knowing my days at the Club were numbered gave me the fortitude to endure such humiliation for a season, but past that all bets were off.

All my life, I'd seen less glamorous variations on the women working the Club, hovering in the filthy corners of the space station or hanging around the barracks at military outposts, hoping for an extra ration of soup. Plin's employees, though, hardly looked like they'd suffered a day in their lives with their rounded, fleshy curves, well-powdered cleavage, and rouged cheeks.

By comparison, I felt like an emaciated river rodent.

My mission's success, though, required that I become a woman that Cardassian soldiers would admit into their private lives, thus providing a way for a clever woman—perhaps a resistance operative—to use her access to the soldiers as a way to tiptoe her way into the most vulnerable military installations on Bajor. Contemplating my new life—of opulent furnishings, plates of food filled to overflowing, comfortable mattresses, sleep uninterrupted by fire fights or explosions—I wavered between feeling that I'd made strides forward and that I'd stepped into a silken noose that would ultimately prove to be my undoing, never mind that Plin wanted me for an operation of her own. After all, as I looked at the people around me, I wondered if any of them remembered the world on the outside or if the glittering façade of the Officers' Club had seduced them with self-indulgence and luxury. I despised people so weak. And yet, I was doing my damnedest to become one—or at least give the appearance of one. *Congratulations, Nerys. You've blown up ammunition depots, lied to soldiers with the power to execute you, murdered collaborators in cold blood, stolen resources, weaponry, and anything else Shakaar asked you to take, all to further the cause of Bajor's independence. And today, you've fought for the privilege of sleeping with the enemy.*

"I suppose there's a pecking order for members. That senior officers and guls receive the companionship of someone like her." I jerked my head in the direction of the woman who had passed by. "But the lower-level personnel would have to settle for someone like—" I took a deep breath, gave a cursory glance at my negligible cleavage and skinny limbs. "—me?"

For the first time since I'd met him in Plin's office, a white, toothy grin split Tov's face. Then he laughed. Hard. "Forgive my uncouth response. It is entirely inappropriate, as the misunderstanding you are laboring under is my fault." And then he burst into another fit of laughter, collapsing forward.

While I realized that I wasn't the most polished of the girls working for Plin, I hardly considered myself *paloku* droppings, so I mirrored a more pinched version of Tov's smile back at him and waited for him to compose himself. The desk attendants across the reception area had begun eyeing him nervously. I wondered if I should shepherd him into a more private location.

His laughter hiccoughed to a stop. "My dear, don't take this the wrong way, but you are not fit to provide benefits to our members."

My smile froze. "Wait a minute—"

"Hold that thought." He raised his eyebrows meaningfully, ordering my silence. Grabbing my arm, he pulled me beyond the lobby into a quiet service access hallway and into a turbolift.

"Speak," he ordered at last.

"I'm not fit to sleep with a Cardassian."

"Sleeping is such an inexact term."

"I'm not fit to provide sexual favors to a Cardassian," I said bluntly.

He pursed his lips together, hemmed and hawed.

I held up a finger. "Just spit it out."

"You would be repugnant to them."

My eyes widened in shock. "Repugnant to them? And you

think it would be the highlight of my life to be pawed by those murderers? Why those cold-blooded, lizard-skinned—"

"I'd advise you to stop there if you ever want any hope of serving them." All signs of amusement left Tov's face.

You need this job. I took a few deep breaths, gritted my teeth, smashed my lips together, and prayed to the Prophets for patience. "So what exactly will I be doing?"

"Housemaid."

I wasn't good enough to sleep with the spoonheads; I was good enough for the spoonheads' garbage. Lucky me. I'd lived long enough to know insulting when I saw it and this situation certainly qualified. I just had to do whatever it took to elevate myself off recycler and refresher duty and into the bedroom. No matter what was required of me. I took a deep breath. "When do I start?"

Somewhere behind the illusion of the Officers' Club, Reon laughed.

My roommate hadn't been around when Tov brought me to my quarters. I took advantage of the down time to rest, though years of training myself to survive on a quasi-alert half-sleep proved hard to undo.

A clankety-clankety-clankety sounded across the room. I opened an eye.

My roommate was bent over her bed, shaking glinting metallic objects the size of my thumb out of the top of her leather corset. When the last object clanked onto her quilt, she reached into her bosom with her hand, fished around for any strays, and found at least two, which she tossed into the pile with the others.

"Hey," she called over to me when she noticed me observing her. Her voice was smoky and her eyes twinkled like the gems on her corset. "Glad to meet you—"

"Nerys. Kira Nerys," I said, scooting up against my headboard.

"Plin Teara—call me Teara, though. Everyone does." she grabbed a couple of her "treasures" off her pile and tossed them over to me.

"Let me be the first to give you a tip as your official welcome to the club. You won't see credits like this until you become a companion. But if you play nice, you'll quickly advance to the gambling rooms, where the money is better. It only took me a season to make it off the housekeeping staff and a season past that to advance out of dabo."

Plin Teara. While I was hardly naïve enough to assume that she worked in the resistance, I felt safe believing that she would be making regular reports to her mother. My initial impression was that she appeared to be a gregarious young woman with spiky purple-black hair and a penchant for a severe, dark-colored wardrobe of angular jackets and tightly fitting short tunics.

Teara jammed her fists into her waist. "Say, you want to come with me to turn these in to Mory? I can show you around the place after. I spent long enough cleaning up after the members that I know every shortcut and back way into every section of this building."

Not wanting to appear too excited about the prospect of a guided tour, I swung my legs over the edge of my bed and walked over to Teara. "Mory?"

"He's the cashier, accountant—all-around money guy. Issues you your weekly pay credits. Invests your tips if you want."

"Definitely someone you want to be your friend."

She grinned. "You learn fast, Nerys. You might not have to wait a season before you're working dabo or *tongo*."

Teara was as good as her word. Within days I knew my way around the Club better than some of the maids who'd been working for two or three seasons. My supervisor noticed too and quickly promoted me out of the casino and into the private suites where the companions took the members.

A maid servicing the suites had one adage to live by: Above all else, avoid disturbing the member dates. When a yellow notification light appeared on the grid in the service hallways running behind the suites, it indicated a suite was ready to service. I'd come in with my supplies to sterilize and straighten and quickly vacate the premises. Once the yellow light was cleared off the grid, the companions would know that the suite was available for use.

I quickly realized that my initial frustration at being rejected for a companion job was misdirected. I suspected that Plin had known what she was doing when she directed Tov to start me at the bottom. Being a housemaid suited my needs much better than companionship did minus the nasty requirement of sex with the members. My job provided me with daily opportunities to learn everything a good operative needed to know about her target. Who had what job and worked what shift. How to access the public areas without being seen. Even better, I had almost limitless access to gadgets. Oh sure, to the uneducated eye, my cleaning tools appeared to be effective ways of repairing upholstery, eliminating stains from our fine *amra*-skin rugs, and removing microparticles of skin and hair from upholstery in an effort to prevent our Bajoran stink from offending our members. To a resourceful resistance fighter, I finally had access to up-to-date submicrotransistors, photonic power cells, sensor chips, and all the quatranic tubing I'd ever need to split a line off a transmitter. I quickly learned who among the members held high enough rank to be in the know at the base and where the companions hosted those officials. I made mental notes, knowing that as soon as I acquired my target, I'd be able to move quickly to accomplish my mission. So far, none of the companions had mentioned Gundar and I hadn't seen his name on the schedule. Plin and I talked from time to time, but she didn't offer any details about what she needed from me. I remained equally closemouthed.

Though I had access to almost every Club area, I had yet to meet my brother, who'd apparently advanced as high as Plin's second-in-command. I heard his name murmured in the same reverential tones as Plin's wherever the Club's employees gathered. Half the staff was trying to get into his good graces for promotions or salary increases, the other half was trying to get into his bed. Ten years hadn't lessened his charms.

My curiosity about my brother's new life grew by the day, fueled by my knowledge of a resistance cell operating out of the Club. I spent part of every day studying my coworkers, wondering who among them was a sister in Bajor's cause, so it was natural that I wondered the same about my brother. But Plin ran a tightly controlled operation and there was nothing she controlled more than information, especially personal information. Employees talked at length about the day-to-day goings-on at the Club, but offered little or nothing about who they were beyond the roles they played. Weaknesses had to exist in Plin's carefully constructed illusion. I probed diligently to find them, but had yet to make inroads.

I wasn't without hope, though. I like to believe that if you're following the Path, the Prophets give you a nudge now and then to help out.

I felt such a nudge when I was awakened a few hours before my shift started to finish the work of a casino maid who had abruptly taken ill. Why I had been chosen didn't make much sense, considering that I hadn't worked in the casinos for weeks, but I accepted the request without question, pulled on my uniform, and stumbled down to housekeeping to be dispatched to my post.

Being unobtrusive in the gaming rooms was easy because of the lowered lights, the noise, and the single-minded focus of the gamblers. Keeping members under surveillance could be done without them ever noticing. My extra shift passed without anything notable happening until I unexpectedly saw him slip out from behind a velvet curtain over by the *tongo* pits to resolve a conflict between a member and a table attendant.

At first I believed that my eyes deceived me as they had many times in the weeks before. Not a day passed when I didn't imagine that, from time to time, Reon watched me on the security sensorcams. I also believed, though without any logical reason, that he deliberately scheduled his time to avoid any unplanned encounters with me. Housekeeping wouldn't have necessarily known this when they called me to fill in at the last minute. Narrowing my eyes, I studied him while forcibly tamping down on the agitated emotions his presence stirred up. I could hardly focus! I cursed my incompetence, believing that as an operative I obviously wasn't worth a damn if I couldn't keep my personal issues separate from the job. Maybe I was wrong. Maybe I was seeing what I wanted so desperately to see.

Then again . . .

The longer I scrutinized, the more I saw his resemblance to our mother, especially around the forehead, though he had our grandfather's height. Like Plin's, his clothes had an understated elegance that communicated his importance without being garish. Mesmerized, I watched, studying his gestures, the animated way he punctuated his words with his arms and hands. He had such an expressive face. . . . No one within an arm's length could wrench their eyes away from him. Even I could feel his magnetism from across the room.

He didn't even know I was there.

I looked away, tossing the shards of a broken goblet I'd been cleaning up into the recycler. How many weeks had I been here without so much as a word from him? Clenching my jaw, I bit back the impulse to challenge him to an out-and-out confrontation in front of everyone. I checked out my surroundings, trying to determine what my next task would be, but I found my gaze irresistibly drawn back to him. I had too many questions that wouldn't wait any longer.

I scuttled my tools, save a crumb sweeper, inside a storage compartment built into the wall and began working my way through the crowd toward the *tongo* table, keeping my eyes averted from the revelers. A crumbled appetizer, then a glance over at Reon, the remains of a pastry . . . I moved around high-stakes game tables, neatly negotiated drink servers, eluding notice from all around me, until I stood within meters of the *tongo* table. Once again I thanked the Prophets that Plin had assigned me to housekeeping.

Reon continued his earnest discussion with the member when I watched him pause and hold up a hand to halt the member's diatribe, his forehead wrinkled. Twisting his head slightly askance, he cupped a hand against his ear: I presumed he'd received a page on the communication unit he wore in his ear. He didn't look happy. He motioned a drink server over to the member, removed a stack of high-value chips from inside his jacket, and placed them in the member's hand. As the drink server slipped a large bottle of wine out of a chill sleeve and poured a glass for the member, Reon nodded toward each individual at the *tongo* table, then backed toward the service hallway.

My mouth opened with an unvoiced shout. He couldn't disappear, not now, not before I knew him.

I chose in a split second.

At a discreet distance, I followed him through the service exit and into a maze of passageways. I quickly realized that he was heading toward the suites. Only a serious problem would warrant Reon's direct intervention; in my time at the club, I had never heard or known of anyone more senior than a floor manager handling a conflict. Gut instinct told me that whatever was going down upstairs was something I needed to know about. Thankfully, the passageways hummed with activity relating to the forthcoming shift change, allowing me to tail Reon without raising suspicion. He eventually stopped at the back entrance of the club's most luxurious suite, touched his palm to deactivate the security lock, and moved inside. I checked the grid. A red light showed the room in use by an anonymous guest and employee, with no names indicated on the schedule. Odd. Usually the computer listed the daily suite assignments. In a matter of minutes, I'd observed at least two serious deviations from protocol in a place that ran by tightly enforced rules.

What next?

I could wait, hoping that Reon exited through the back way, confront him if he did; or I could short-circuit the front door, forcing him out of the back exit.

Or . . .

I called up the suite's floor plan on the grid terminal. A small antechamber preceded the door into the main room where a companion would entertain her Cardassian guest. Conceivably, I could enter through the same door Reon had, check out the situation, and then decide whether to pursue him further. I might even happen on intelligence that might prove useful to my own mission. If I got caught, I risked being sent back to Shakaar, mission aborted.

An unforgivable error.

What factors tipped my decision, I couldn't say, but before I could fully think through the ramifications of my actions, I called up the computer's command menu and changed the suite's status light from red to yellow, providing myself an alibi, however flimsy, if circumstances required it. Within seconds, I'd used my housekeeping pass to admit myself to the suite.

I took cautious, quiet steps through the darkened antechamber, training my breath into a shallow, soundless rhythm. Voices murmured up ahead—definitely one female. A meter more and I risked exposure. I still couldn't see! What was the point of coming this far only to fail when the objective was in reach? I took a cautious step forward—

A hand went around my mouth, yanking my head back; an arm hooked around my waist and forcibly dragged me into the suite before throwing me forward, sending me stumbling toward Reon.

"You were right," Teara said behind me. "You were followed. Keep out of this, Nerys." She released her grip on me and pushed me toward a settee, sending me stumbling.

My brother crouched down on the floor beside an unconscious Cardassian, holding a medical scanner in one had, a hypospray in the other. He glanced up at me briefly, his eyebrows arching in what might have been surprise, before returning his attention to his scanner's readout. I assessed the room, noting a broken carafe bleeding its fermented contents onto the rug beside the half-dressed Cardassian. A neatly made bed. A serving cart piled with empty dishes, a vague remnant of sour brandy in the air.

"Well, Reon?" Teara stalked toward him, hands on hips, her expression tense with worry. "Will the overdose kill him?"

Reon shook his head. "To the contrary. His system is processing the antidote too quickly. He could regain consciousness any minute. We'll have to move him."

"Muss the bed," Teara said to me.

I shifted my gaze to Teara. My confusion must have shown on my face, because she cursed my nosy intrusion before saying irritably, "Make the bed look like someone's been in it, then get over here and help us."

I did what I was told, though I still couldn't figure out what was happening, making me feel exceptionally dense.

"Next, Nerys," Reon said, "we need to move Gul Tulk over to the bed. He can't wake before he's had a memorable encounter with Teara."

"At least I'm already undressed, thank the Prophets for small blessings," Teara said. Wearing a loosely tied dressing gown, split open to the waist, she bent over and grabbed one of Tulk's beefy arms. Reon cast aside his instruments and took a position opposite Teara.

I grabbed Tulk's boot-clad feet and held them up while Teara and Reon dragged him toward the bed. The three of us hefted him off the floor and pushed him onto the fur coverlet.

"Undress him," Teara ordered. She had started unfastening his breeches and pushing them down over his hips.

Repulsed by the sight of Tulk's body, I recoiled, turning away from the bedside.

"Boots!" she hissed angrily.

I grabbed a boot and pulled, then the other. To avoid looking directly at Tulk's cold, scaly flesh, I watched Reon push aside a holopainting to reveal a hidden cupboard. He removed a neurotransmitter headset and several sensors. The odd behavior was starting to make sense. . . .

Tulk grunted unintelligibly and flopped over onto his side, his hand grasping at Teara's robe and yanking her down onto the bed. Startled, I stepped backward, nearly tripping over the boots I'd dropped on the floor. "He's waking up!"

Gingerly, Teara extracted Tulk's hand from her hip and watched Reon expectantly. "Hurry," she whispered.

I sensed her fear.

"My dear Gul Tulk, just give me a moment longer," Reon said as he attached the sensors to the Cardassian's chest. He then slipped the neurotransmitter headset onto Tulk's forehead and pressed the activation button. A row of lights blinked to life as the headset beeped. Tulk breathed deeply, visibly relaxed, and emitted a sigh of pleasure.

"How long did you set it for?" Teara asked, examining the headset's readout with a frown.

"Half an hour should be enough to get this place cleaned up and allow you to be in position so when he wakes up he'll be extraordinarily happy that he visited his favorite lady Teara this morning."

She rolled out of bed with a sigh. "I need a drink."

Reon turned to me.

I crossed my arms over my chest, hugging them tight against my body.

The most ridiculous grin spread over his face.

"What could you possibly find amusing about this?" I shouted.

He shrugged, chuckled softly. "You. Always off on some damn fool nosy quest to save the world. You've hardly changed in ten years."

"Wish that I could say similarly, but you're pretty much a stranger to me at this point. Never mind that I've been around for weeks . . ." My voice cracked with emotion and I cursed quietly. I let him get to me; I hated my weaknesses.

"Plin sent me away on business—supplying the Club requires trips to a dozen worlds."

"Lucky you."

Our eyes held for a long moment.

Teara cleared her throat. "Ummm . . . maybe you all could have this family reunion another time?"

Reon dropped his eyes to the floor. "Since you insisted on being nosy, you might as well get your cleaning things and help Teara get that Saurian brandy out of the rug before he comes to. I have to keep an eye on his vitals."

I obeyed without comment, though I had dozens more questions on the tip of my tongue. I located a spare housekeeping carryall out in the hallway and rushed back into the suite. Teara had retrieved the worst of the broken crystal and was tossing it into the recycler as I came in. I attended to the sopping mess on the carpets.

She sat on the edge of the bed, studying me with an indeterminate look; whether it was amusement or annoyance, I couldn't say. "Reon said you had an impulsive hothead side. Seems like he was right. You could have blown this op, Nerys."

I said nothing. She was right. I glanced over at Reon. He studiously ignored both of us, remaining engrossed in his scanner.

Teara continued. "Before my mother hands you your head on a platter, I might as well tell you what was going on here. I was supposed to get information from Tulk. That brandy you're cleaning up is laced with something that helps loosen our Cardassian boyfriends' tongues a bit. Unfortunately, someone added triple the usual quantity to that carafe, Tulk had a seizure, and that's what brought Reon up here." She paused, studying me intently. "I was trying to find out when Gundar was supposed to arrive."

I tried not to look too interested by her revelation. "Hmmm. Who's Gundar?" I said as I continued to erase the remainder of the stain from the carpet.

She threw back her head and laughed. "Oh please. You've been waiting for that information since the day you got here, and don't bother with the innocent act because it's the only thing worth risking an operative of your caliber for. There've been dozens of officials of higher rank and wielding more power than Gundar in and out of here since you showed up. He's the only one that makes any sense. Mother just wanted to get a head start on you."

Sitting back on my heels, I saw Teara, not as Plin's daughter but as a fellow operative. "Why not use Gundar yourselves?"

"I asked Mother the same thing. She says she needs you to do a favor for her, so she's letting you have Gundar in exchange. I can't imagine what you're qualified to do that one of us isn't."

I knew that "one of us" referred to Teara. Whatever Plin needed, she hid it from her child, who, from appearances, was one of her most skilled and trusted operatives.

Reon turned away from Tulk. "His vitals are changing. I think he'll be coming out of the scenario sooner than I'd hoped. Teara, you'd better undress and be ready to welcome our friend Tulk back from happy land."

"I'm sure we had a wonderful time," Teara said, dropping her robe on the floor and crawling into the bed beside Tulk. "You need to find out who doctored that brandy, Reon. It almost killed him."

Reon nodded, his sober expression conveying the seriousness of what had almost happened here.

The strangeness of the unfolding scene mesmerized me. Plin wasn't kidding about the illusion of the Officers' Club. Placing false memories in the minds of Cardassian members. Using the guise of pleasure to facilitate interrogations. The operation was pure genius.

"Later?" Teara said, her eyes soft. I heard a plea in her voice that told me a good deal about her connection to my brother.

"Page me," Reon said, "I'll come find you." He hooked his hand to my elbow, pulled me through the antechamber and out into the service passageway. After he'd changed the suite's status indicator back to red, he fixed an inscrutable gaze on me. "We're going to Plin." He gripped my forearm and tugged me a few steps away from the suite toward the exit.

"I expected as much," I said, prying his fingers off my arm and stepping away from him. "You know what she wants?"

He gestured for me to follow him into the turbolift and waited until the door closed before whispering the answer in my ear.

A shock of anxiety electrified me and I shivered. I met Reon's serious gaze with my own questioning one. For while Reon's answer had retired one of the most pressing questions of my own—where his loyalties lay—it raised more troubling questions, questions that I wasn't sure I knew how to find the answers to.

I sat in Plin's office, where an interconnected series of jamming devices would thwart the efforts of any eavesdropper.

"You're the only one outside my operation that's in a position to identify the double," Plin said. She rested her elbows on her desk, linked her hands together and waited for my reaction.

"How can you know for sure that your operation's been compromised?" I said. I knew from observing other cells that sometimes paranoia at the mere suggestion that a group had been infiltrated could do as much damage as the alleged traitor might. Accusations were made, loyalties tested. Some cells never fully recovered.

"About six months ago, Doblana Base had a visit from Central Command. Not an unusual occurrence except that a military medical official was brought along as part of the group. In more than a decade, he'd never been here. And while I pride myself on the excellence of the services we provide at the Officers' Club, Doblana isn't exactly a prime R&R destination for the Cardassian military. Because the doctor didn't have any obvious reason to visit, we kept a close eye out hoping that his presence didn't signal an epidemic or a new regime of medical experimentation on prisoners or those in the labor camps.

"When one of my girls had him alone, she loosened him up, got him talking, and he let it spill that he was visiting to follow up on a special patient, a Cardassian who had been surgically altered to resemble a Bajoran. Beyond bragging about what an accomplishment it was, he wouldn't provide any specifics." Plin spun her chair to the side and tapped an alphanumeric series into a touch panel by a shelving unit that deactivated a lock on a wall safe. She removed several tablets and passed them across to me.

Paging through reams of data, I gave the contents a cursory glance. Plin had conducted a thorough investigation. It was also the first time I had a sense of the breadth of her operation. Talk about impressive. She had her fingers in almost every aspect of the Occupation. Placing an agent in her ranks would be a huge coup for the Cardassians.

Plin sat back in her chair with a sigh. "We don't know if the patient was male or female. We combed through every surveillance recording, every computer log, and talked with every witness we could find to see if we could compile a timeline as to where the doctor was when and with whom, but came up with nothing. The only individuals we could specifically identify him having contact with were my senior operatives."

"So there are two possibilities: Either the meeting happened and you didn't know about it or one of your senior operatives is a plant," I said, drawing my conclusions from the data she'd given me.

Plin nodded.

"And since I've never been here and I have a well-documented track record with Shakaar, I might be able to see something that you can't because you're too close to it."

"Precisely."

"Teara's on the list, isn't she?"

"As are Reon and about ten other of my most trusted agents. Right beneath them are the names of a dozen employees who aren't involved in our resistance work but who have access to the most sensitive areas of the Club. Any one of them could destroy what we've built."

"I'm one person and you run a massive operation. I don't know how much help I can be."

"Be my eyes. Have an open mind."

I inhaled deeply, considering Plin's request. How could I possibly know what was unusual behavior at a place like the Club? Layers within layers of deception made it nearly impossible to know what was real and what was gauzy illusion. Push away one curtain only to reveal another. "I'll do what I can," I said at last, "but my own operation comes first."

"As it should. If you succeed in using Gundar to stop the communications upgrade—or even better, install a backdoor to the network—the resistance could shift the balance of power within months." Plin shrugged, flipped her palms up as if to say "Who knows?"

Laughing, I looked over at my boss. "You're sure you're not part telepath? Because you have an uncanny way of knowing my secrets."

"Under different circumstances, I'd be running your op with my own people. Unfortunately, I don't know who I can trust. I'm waiting for you to tell me."

"I'll do my best."

Reon waited for me in the foyer outside Plin's office. I watched him pace the length of the room, carrying on a conversation with an unseen person speaking into his earpiece.

"Two dozen won't do, Derna. You'll need to up our order for the next transport." A pause. "I don't care what it costs, take care of it." A longer pause. "Fine then. We're done. Don't get back to me until you have it fixed." He sighed deeply, then switched his attention to me. "So we meet again, Nerys."

I couldn't let him get off easily. "We wouldn't be meeting if I hadn't followed you out of the casino."

"I wasn't planning on waiting much longer. I've been back less than a few days." He placed his hands behind his back. "I wanted to figure you out first. See if you were still the headstrong, bossy big sister I remembered."

"Hardly fair considering I'm the one in strange territory."

"Ah yes, but now that you know what we're up against, can you blame me?"

Not wanting to reveal what Plin had told me, I shrugged. Reon *was* on her list.

"I like your haircut."

"Really?" I ruffled the shaved hair at the base of my neck, smoothed the layers above my ears; I hadn't quite become accustomed to the short length.

"Most definitely. Though I was very young when we lost Mother, I remember she had kind of a coppery tint to her hair." A distant look in his eyes took me back to our childhood in the camps. He continued, "It glinted in the firelight when she would hold me in her arms and rock me to sleep. She sang that song—the sea maid and her farmer prince?" After humming a few atonal bars, he stopped, probably noting my pinched expression. "Never was a singer."

"True. You weren't. You aren't." I offered a polite smile: one that invited him to continue our discussion, but one that withheld my full trust. I wanted—*needed*—to believe what my eyes saw, that Reon had truly become the person I wanted him to be. Yet so many years had passed that I couldn't let go of my doubts so easily.

"I can't undo the past, Nerys," he said softly. "And I won't make excuses for my choices, so I feel safe in disabusing you of any notion that you might be receiving an apology from me. But we can start from now."

He needed to know the stakes. "Our brother died."

"I know."

"This place you have here—this life you've led. You had the resources to save him and you didn't come for him."

"I know that too. I did what I had to."

I studied his handsome face, probed his blue-green eyes, whose color evoked a memory of summer sky in Dahkur. My heart still grieved for the child he had been.

After a long pause, he said, "We'll talk more over brunch in my apartment. It's better than what they serve in the lounge, and since I'm the boss, I can excuse you from your next shift." He winked, then offered me an arm.

I inhaled deeply, paused. The impulse to forgive and move on warred with the impulse to demand more answers.

"Come on, Nerys. Grant your brother clemency—at least for the duration of brunch—and if you still hate me when we're through, at least you'll know my side of the story." He shrugged. "Since we're working for the same cause, at least we have that in common."

I slid my arm through his. "So it appears."

After the morning when the mishap with Tulk occurred, I didn't talk with Plin—or Reon for that matter—for several days. I knew what Plin expected from me, and frankly, I needed space to process what Reon had told me. His conversion to the resistance cause had happened gradually. By the time he'd grown to his majority, he understood why Plin took the risks she did running a resistance cell and why a mercenary existence would ultimately be unsatisfying to him. He hadn't been a *legna* since he left me, living the luxurious life of a collaborator to its fullest. I was loath to call his reborn devotion to Bajor an "atonement" for his choices, but I did sense that he was trying to make amends for the past. I accepted him for what he'd become and determined we would start again. Unfortunately, what I'd fixed with Reon had broken with Teara.

Since my intrusion on her interlude with Tulk, she kept her shields up, deflecting my friendly overtures with what I could describe only as cynical distrust. Her attitude didn't make sense to me—after all, weren't we now linked by devotion to a common cause? Instead, she became territorial, as if my presence at the Officers' Club threatened her personally.

I didn't realize how threatened she felt until one morning when I checked in with my supervisor and discovered that my cleaning assignment had been changed from the senior suites, where I'd been since before the Tulk incident, to the junior suites. The change didn't make sense. My tips had steadily increased over time; the girls seemed happy with my work. More important, my missions for both Plin and Shakaar were easier to do when I had access to the high-ranking officers hosted in the senior suites. I monitored who visited and the companions they arrived with. Since I anticipated Gundar's arrival any day now, I couldn't afford to be moved from the senior suites. I asked my supervisor why the change had been made and she mumbled some noncommittal explanation.

At mealtime later in the day, one of the girls, who had just spent a few hours with the base commander, stopped by my table to tell me how sorry she was to see me transferred and that she hoped I'd be back soon.

"I don't know what Teara's problem is," she said, "but I wouldn't take it personally. She gets in these moods sometimes."

I sat for a long time wondering what possible reason Teara would have to ask me to be reassigned unless she felt threatened by me. When I finished my shift, I sent a brief note to Plin simply informing her that I'd been reassigned to the junior suites. I trusted that she'd follow up. She did.

Teara stormed into our rooms later that night.

"Keep my mother out of this!"

"You stay out of my work, I'll stay out of yours," I said.

"I don't know why she has such faith and in you—her and Reon both. But to me, it was just a little too providential that you showed up when you did. She's so desperate to protect our work here that she's grasping at whatever slender hopes she can, never mind that your presence here puts us all at risk."

"Believe what you want." I wouldn't defend myself against baseless accusations.

"My mother will do what she needs to do," Teara said, her eyes boring into me. "But I'll be watching your every step."

I looked up at her placidly. "No you won't. 'Cause I'll be behind you—watching yours."

I returned to my old position the next day, adding close monitoring of Teara's clients and schedule to my daily routine. I expected her to keep a low profile, and she did. Several days passed before anything unusual happened, and when it did, it was explosive, though at first it appeared fairly innocuous. . . .

In my review of the daily suite logs, I discovered an irregularity. Supervisors usually glossed over the reports; as long as everything appeared to be in order, no one raised an eyebrow. I knew, however, from my shift that one of the companions listed as entertaining a guest had abruptly taken ill midshift, but the logs didn't indicate her departure. I asked around and found that another girl had been called in to take her place: Teara. Suspicion overtook me. I had to know what she'd been hiding. Early in my club days, I'd used some of the components in my cleaning tools to split a feed off the security sensors. I checked the pictures from time to time, but until now it hadn't been critical to my operation, since Gundar hadn't shown up yet.

I wandered through the residential wing until I found an empty apartment. The employees who lived there worked nights and wouldn't be back until dawn. I patched in to my feed through the club's intranet, sorting through the day's data, frame by frame, watching companions come and go without incident. After hours of examination, I had despaired of ever finding the answer when at last a frame appeared that illuminated Teara's motive to doctor the logs.

I considered my options. Plin had a vested interest in protecting her child. She might or might not take my concerns seriously. If Teara was tipped off about my suspicions, any hope I had of my op succeeding would effectively end. An accusation of this magnitude had to be backed up with incontrovertible proof before I could move.

Reon could help me. The conflict with Teara had preoccupied me for the past few days; I hadn't spent a lot of time thinking about my brother. Maybe I'd been avoiding it. But now I needed him. He might ridicule my request—especially since I suspected that he and Teara were lovers. One fact was indisputable, though: If he wanted me to trust him, he would need to trust me. He owed me that.

I found him in his office attending to the bureaucratic details that running an operation the size of the Officers' Club entails.

Surprised, he looked up from the tablet he was reading. "Nerys?"

"Can I talk?" The implication being, "Can anyone overhear what I'm about to say?"

Reon pressed a series of buttons mounted on his desktop and studied me expectantly.

"She called him 'Father.' "

He blinked, his mouth puckered in confusion. "Who?"

"Teara. I saw it on the visual sensor readings from this afternoon. She called Gundar 'Father.' "

"Gundar's here?"

I nodded, taken aback that such a high-profile client had made it into the Club without Reon knowing. "Teara had him in the suites this afternoon."

"Are you sure you heard her correctly?" He looked dubious.

"No question."

Reon rolled his eyes. "Our members have all kinds of odd sexual predilections, Nerys, who's to say that he didn't ask her to call him that as part of some warped fantasy—"

"She called him Father in *Cardassian*."

When Gundar showed up the next day, I was prepared. Reon, without consulting with Plin, had provided me with access to any surveillance feeds and data I wanted. I spent the greater part of the night combing through every Cardassian database the Club had, searching for information on Gundar. What I discovered didn't bode well for Teara. Not only did Gundar have a daughter—Kayana—but his daughter had reputedly joined the Obsidian Order after graduating from an elite military academy. All recorded traces of her vanished about two years ago. An intercepted Central Command communiqué had a vague reference to Kayana being on a deep-cover intelligence assignment.

If indeed the woman I knew as Plin Teara was Kayana Gundar, she'd have a vested interest in keeping close tabs on my every move, protecting her father from the resistance. She'd make sure she was assigned to be his companion, providing him with alibis and cover should any questions be raised. In short, she'd behave exactly as Teara had been behaving since the Tulk incident. I just had to make sure that next time Gundar showed up, I was watching.

Gundar's physical appearance surprised me, though I didn't quite know what I should have expected from a Cardassian academic. From all reports, Gundar's mathematical genius had protected the empire's communications from prying Federation eyes for years. I'd envisioned him as a razor-lean, pensive, scholarly type. So when a husky, squarish glinn with drooping jowls and a protruding belly showed up at the reception desk, I checked the feed twice after I heard him identify himself as Gundar. On a monitor provided by Reon, I watched Teara approach him, her arms outstretched; Gundar folded the willowy Bajoran woman into his embrace, practically lifting her off the floor. She took him by the hand and guided him toward the turbolift. Within minutes, they'd be in the suites and within five meters of my position.

If Teara was an Order operative, she wouldn't be foolish enough to break cover anywhere in public, so I watched the sensor feeds from the turbolift with marginal interest. Once she was in the suites, though, I'd have to be prepared to move quickly if I perceived that Teara's behavior might put my mission at risk. Yes, I'd agreed to help Plin find the double in her operation; my first allegiance, though, was to Shakaar, and nothing—*nothing*—would prevent me from fulfilling my promises to him.

The suite door opened. Leaning forward in my chair, I hovered within centimeters of the viewscreen, hearing Gundar cross the floor behind Teara's buoyant footsteps.

She spun around, her hands clasped together beneath her chin. "I'm so pleased to see you again," she said, rocking back and forth; she gazed on Gundar with a shy smile.

"And I, you. I feel as though I've waited a lifetime." His voice was round and melodic, like tones pulled from the strings of a Trill *cyn lara*. "Come, my child. Sit on my lap and we will talk as we have before." He dropped down onto a couch and patted his thighs with his hands.

She moved fluidly across the room, draping her legs over his lap and curling into his shoulder.

Imagining that Teara might be the double made the scene bearable to watch. Otherwise, the mere suggestion that Gundar found Teara's childlike behavior titillating disturbed me; I shivered, disgusted at the depths of Cardassian perversity. Whatever Shakaar had planned for the glinn he deserved. Their giggles and whispers continued. I watched, bored by their small talk, wondering when—and if—Teara would reveal herself.

She broke from Gundar's embrace so she faced him straight-on. I couldn't see what she was doing wi th her hands, but it looked like she reached into her jacket pocket to remove something. "I kept this for you since last time."

"What a lovely girl you are, to be so thoughtful," Gundar said. "Hopefully I can repay your conscientiousness. . . ."

I ordered the computer to zoom in on Teara's hand. She passed a medallion to Gundar—maybe a military honor of some sort. Teara's behavior set off a warning beacon for me. I knew I'd seen what had just passed between Teara and Gundar before. *Think, Nerys.* . . . I sorted through hundreds of memories until I found a match.

Years ago, in Hedrickspool, I'd been sent to retrieve a weapons shipment. The dealer was a mercenary Bajoran who preyed on the weaknesses of Cardassian supply clerks. When the arms merchant visited the weapons depot, he had removed an amulet from around his neck, flipped the back side up, and passed it to the clerk. Within minutes, the whole deal had fallen apart; I'd barely escaped with my life. I hadn't thought about the event in ages, but now, as I replayed Teara's behavior, I recognized the gesture for what it was: a signal. What precisely she told him, I couldn't say, but I had my suspicions.

I ordered the computer to focus on Gundar's face: barely concealed panic.

With haste, but quietly, I exited my hiding place, a supply closet on the suite floor. The computer kept the audio feed from the suite looped into my communication headset, so I focused intently on the conversation unfolding within. On the surface, the discussion seemed innocuous enough, but I could hear the tension in Gundar's voice. *What the hell is Teara up to?* I paused outside the door, touched the weapon strapped to my thigh. Closing my eyes, I mentally ran through the possibilities of what I might find when I opened the door.

I liked none of them.

Here goes nothing. . . . I waved the all-access pass Reon had given me up to the security reader, drew my weapon from the hidden holster, and pivoted into the suite.

Teara stood before me, phaser drawn. "Took you long enough. I thought I'd have to start the party without you."

"I prefer making a dramatic entrance."

She smirked. "Put down your weapon or I'll kill Gundar. What use will he be to your cause then?"

"You people never cease to amaze me. You're right up there with the Romulans in terms of loyalty."

"I don't know what you're babbling about, but I'll be damned if I let you destroy my life's work." Her flinty eyes narrowed to slits.

I knew she wasn't bluffing.

An instant before she squeezed the trigger, I dove for her legs, sending her toppling to the floor. I pushed up from the ground. Her weapon had landed on the floor beside Gundar, who reached for it. I aimed my boot for his stomach, throwing him back against the wall, winded. Teara scrambled up onto her hands and knees. Both Teara and I reached for the phaser, but her tightly fitted tunic inhibited her progress. I reached the weapon first, slamming it with my fist, sending it skidding across the floor into the corner. Gundar coughed and sputtered, clutching at his stomach, collapsing onto the couch. Teara charged toward me; I opened my arms to catch her by the shoulders and force her head down.

I wrapped my hands around Teara's neck, squeezing her throat.

She clawed at my wrists; I overpowered her, angling her neck and slamming her skull hard against a stone table. A stomach-twisting crack broke the silence. I watched Teara's head swivel limply onto her shoulders as she toppled to the floor. I stood up and looked over at Gundar, who still wheezed like an invalid.

"I didn't kick you that hard, you big baby," I snapped. "Get up. We've got to get out of here, and I'm not carrying you."

Though how I'd move Gundar out of the club compound without being noticed I'd yet to figure out. I searched the room for something I could use to secure Gundar's hands and feet with, and finally settled on using his own weapons belt. While I knotted the leather strap, his limbs trembled incessantly. I used Teara's scarf to gag him.

This operation had gone down so quickly, I hadn't even had time to signal Shakaar to let him know Gundar was on the way. Glancing over at Teara's corpse, I wondered how Plin would take the news of her daughter's death—never mind her betrayal. When Teara had been kidnapped and doubled was unknown and might never be now. Asking Plin for help at this point could be risky. One last time, I had to trust Reon to help me escape the club.

Minutes felt like hours until he arrived. I knew, though, as soon as he came through the door, that he'd conceived an ingenious solution for moving Gundar. He'd brought with him a food transport hovercart—about a meter and a half long and a meter tall. The servers used them to move food from the kitchens and replicator stations into the banquet areas. I quickly helped Reon empty out the cart's interior. Out of the corner of my eye, I watched, amused, at Gundar's fear playing out over his face. Reon removed a hypospray from his pocket and pressed it to Gundar's neck. The Cardassian slumped over, passed out cold. Together, Reon and I managed to heft him off the couch and into the transport cart's hollowed-out interior. Once Reon secured the lid on the top, I sighed, relieved. "Can he breathe?"

"The cart's designed to vent steam. He shouldn't have a problem," Reon said distractedly.

I followed his gaze; he stared at Teara or Kayana or whoever she might have been. "I'm sorry, Reon."

"So am I," he said. "Though I suppose I'm not entirely surprised. She's been behaving strangely for a while now. I can only guess that she was doubled on one of our offworld supply trips."

"The real Teara might still be alive."

"You don't believe that."

"No, I don't."

He took a deep breath. "We'd better get going."

I nodded.

"We probably shouldn't travel to the shuttlebay together; I typically don't accompany housemaids or servers on their duties. Though I don't know how I'll find you—" He paused, dropped his eyes to the ground, his brow furrowed in concentration, then abruptly looked back up. "I'll activate the tracking device on your communication unit. I'll monitor your progress from my office and catch up with you once you're out of the way of regular club traffic."

"What about—" I jerked my head in the direction of the body.

"I'll take care of it," he said softly.

Using the service lifts, I made it out of the suite wing without incident. I then needed to clear the maintenance areas, pass through the lobby, and then move toward the transportation center. My gray Club staff uniform drew no notice from those around me. I did what hundreds of workers did every day, though part of me expected to be stopped and accused of murder at any moment.

I'd killed for the resistance before, and more than a few of my kills had been premeditated; I wasn't squeamish about dealing death. Why this time felt different I couldn't say. I replayed my confrontation with Teara over and over as I walked until I realized what bothered me.

Teara had never confessed to being the double.

I had suspicions and fairly damning circumstantial evidence, but no absolute proof. Reon might be able to check her physiology with one of his medical gadgets, but until then, there loomed a pos-sibility in my mind—however slight—that I might have been wrong. Or not. As long as I met my mission objectives, did it matter?

Wishing away the confusion, I closed my eyes. Turmoil seethed within me.

Teara might have been framed.

I might be heading for an ambush for myself or Shakaar.

My chest tightened. Too many questions nagged at me; so much was at risk. I ducked into an alcove, out of hearing, and entered Plin's page code into my comm unit.

"*Yes.*"

"Teara's dead," I whispered.

Silence.

"I killed her because I had reason to believe she was the double."

"*You should have come to me, it didn't have to end this—*"

"Listen—I might have been wrong. There's a chance Teara was set up. You have to check the internal communication network and see who Gundar's been talking to since he arrived."

"*We shouldn't be talking this way. Why don't I meet you and we can do this together?*"

"I'm gone, Plin. The only reason we're having this conversa-tion is because I want justice."

I clicked off the com link and headed toward the lobby, pick-ing up my pace. I had about a hundred and fifty meters before I reached the shuttlebay and had no time to waste.

Before I moved Gundar through the public areas, I had the sense to stop at a replicator station and collect a few platters of Denobulan scallops and *yamok* sauce. Years of running ops for the resistance overcame my nerves. An almost nonstop internal monologue—reminding me to stay calm, keep the needs of the mission first—played in my head. Passing through the edge of the reception area, an inebriated officer pawed at one of the plates before lifting the whole tray of seafood off my cart. I smiled in acknowledgment and continued to move forward. Only a turbo-lift and a few passageways before Gundar would be boarded on a shuttlecraft headed for the resistance. Fifteen steps, fourteen steps . . . eight . . . three . . .

Heart thudding in my throat, I guided the hovercart into the turbolift and ordered the door closed. I cleared my throat and said, "Shuttlebay." A nearly imperceptible jerk and the turbolift started upward. The door parted soundlessly and I exited.

Not surprisingly, the transport-center waiting area was desolate. The comings and goings of Club members ebbed and flowed with the shift changes on Doblana Base. Another few hours and I'd be hard-pressed to find a place to walk. I directed the cart past dozens of rows of empty chairs, my shoes clicking against the glossy stone-paved floors. A shadow darkened the wall. I paused. No one appeared. I continued moving forward until I reached the VIP boarding area. Using my security pass, I activated the doors and I stepped through.

Reon waited for me. An amused half-smile crossed his lips as he glanced at the cart. "The scallops are a nice touch. I like your style." He stood up. "If you'll follow me through to the airlock to your shuttle, I'll help you secure Gundar. You've contacted Shakaar to arrange the rendezvous?"

I shook my head. "I'll do that once the shuttle's in flight."

"Can you risk waiting that long?" he said as we walked together.

"I don't have a choice."

"You do. If you want to go ahead and talk with the pilot, I'll put Gundar in the holding area. We need to get out of here. Fast."

I sensed anxiety beneath the poise. "What's wrong?"

"I'll tell you once we've cleared Doblana's defense grid."

I didn't hear footsteps until we stood beside the airlock. I knew without looking that Plin was behind me. *What the hell—*

"You decided to throw a going-away party without me. How unlike you, Kira!"

"What are you doing?"

"I wanted a witness to your betrayal, Reon. You set Teara up. Made it look like she was the double when she was really following your instructions. You're not going to get away with it."

I turned to face him, forcibly ignoring the pain carving up my insides. Plin must have checked the internal communication records. I should have known. He never changed. I wanted so desperately to believe that he wasn't a collaborator that I'd allowed him to deceive me.

"I've got him covered." Plin's voice echoed through the waiting area. I heard her unsheathe her weapon.

"So, Nerys, you're back to believing that I've lived down to all your expectations." Laughing bitterly, he took a step toward me, holding open his hands to show that he wasn't armed. "Feeling morally superior to your collaborator brother about now, eh?"

"You've always bailed out when circumstances became too hard." Reon's inscrutable expression made it impossible to guess what his next move would be. I spat on the ground. "Collaborator."

He flinched as if I'd struck him.

Anxiously, Plin said, "We only have a brief time before the shift changes. Nerys—you take my weapon and I'll secure Gundar in the shuttle hold."

I reached behind me to take the weapon from Plin. I heard the low hum of the hovercart moving forward shortly after she passed by me, followed shortly by the dull thud of a closing door.

"This time your inability to let go of the past may be your undoing," he said, his voice low; he took another two steps toward me.

I unfastened the phaser's safety. "Don't move any closer—" Before I could react, he plunged forward; I gasped. He threaded his hands behind my head, smashing his mouth into my ear.

"Listen to me. *There is no double*," he whispered. "I scanned Teara's corpse—she's as Bajoran as you and I. She was set up and there's only person who could have done it."

My eyes widened. *Prophets let him be wrong.*

"Gundar is bait," Reon continued. "There is no systems upgrade. I checked. Plin arranged to have him sent here. She must be in trouble with the Cardassians because she's selling out Shakaar as some kind of loyalty test to save the Club."

My mouth fell open; I choked back a scream. I didn't know what to believe. My brother pulled me tight into his arms, allowing me to lean against him for support. I felt the weight of something slipped into my jacket pocket. "Once you're far away and safe, find out the truth for yourself. I've given you the map, so to speak."

Had he crafted another illusion for my benefit? All these years in the Officers' Club had made him a master of the masquerade. I pulled back from his embrace to search his face.

I heard Plin walking across the shuttle deck. She'd be back at the airlock within seconds.

"Whatever you do, don't go straight to Shakaar. Go anywhere else." He shoved me away, his eyes bright with unshed tears. "Aim your weapon," he mouthed.

Tossing my hair defiantly, I snarled loud enough for Plin to hear, "You won't get away with this, Reon or whatever your name is. You can tell your Cardassian masters that they'll have to do better if they want to break the spirit of Bajor!"

Plin emerged from the airlock, glanced between me and my brother. "The shuttle's ready to go. Shakaar will need time to make the rendezvous, and I can help you through Cardassian security much faster than you can go through by yourself."

"You have to stay here, Plin," I said with as much earnestness as I could muster. "You have to figure out what damage Reon's done to your operation—for Bajor's sake." I thought I caught a glint of triumph in her eye before she again donned a mask of earnest indignation. *Reon might be telling the truth.*

She reached for the weapon. "Go with the Prophets, Nerys."

Then I knew. Leaving Reon at the Club would mean his death. If Plin had betrayed the resistance to the Cardassians, she couldn't afford to let Reon expose her before she could cover her tracks, or she'd kill him as revenge for framing Teara. My brother would die either way.

Until I was away from the Club and could prove or disprove Reon's story, I wouldn't know the truth. And in that moment, the truth couldn't matter, because the mission came first.

I met his eyes: A hint of a smile on his lips told me that he'd made peace with his fate. Numbly, I handed Plin the weapon and moved through the airlock. I imagined I heard the metallic zing of phaser fire before the airlock doors sealed.

When the shuttle hatch closed, I checked to make sure that Gundar was still alive (he was) and then headed up to the front to check with the pilot. I gave him a fake destination, one many hours away from the Officers' Club, and settled into the copilot's chair. The authorities wouldn't touch me before I'd led them to Shakaar. I wasn't too worried about being hassled until the spoonheads figured out that they'd been duped. At that point, I'd shake whatever goons might be waiting for me and request emergency extraction. Recalling my operative codes and how Plin had shared hers with me during our first meeting, I thought of her—and Teara and Reon. Reaching into my pocket, I removed what he'd put in my pocket—an oval-shaped locket I instantly recognized as my mother's. I found a memory chip inside: Reon's map. I wondered where it would take me.

As the mission meandered to a conclusion, I wished for sleep, for drink, for any sensation that would make the memories go away. Escape eluded me for a long time. I worked for Bajor and would sacrifice whatever was required of me to assure my people's freedom, including giving my life and in this case, my brother's life. I tried being matter-of-fact about his loss and managed quite well for a time.

Tears finally spilled on the day when Shakaar, thanks to Reon's chip, slipped through an untraceable backdoor into the Cardassians' communication network. Those in my cell assumed that I wept for joy, as they all did, because at last we had in our power the ability to break the Cardassians' stranglehold on Bajor. Not so much as a supply clerk would be reassigned without the resistance knowing about it. The occupation would end.

I raised my face to the blue-green summer sky of Dahkur and remembered my brother.

JONATHAN ARCHER
CAPTAIN OF *ENTERPRISE* (NX-01)

Have Beagle, Will Travel:
The Legend of Porthos

LOUISA M. SWANN

"I'm pleased you decided to take me up on my offer."

Captain Jonathan Archer gazed at the Andorian city spread below and nodded. "I appreciate the invitation, Shran, as well as the tour of your city. Porthos appreciates it too."

"Without your help, Captain, there would be no peace agreement between Vulcans and Andorians."

"I'm glad I was able to help." Archer glanced over the beagle's head at Shran with a feeling of satisfaction. *Nice to be in a position to help two cultures work out their differences.* "So where is this place you're taking me?"

Hopefully, a nice restaurant. Archer had an aversion to most bars, especially the dark, smoky kind a lot of folks seemed to enjoy. He preferred a light ambience—not to mention a place that appreciated beagles.

"It should be around here somewhere." Shran's antennae twitched as he moved forward one step at a time.

What? Archer wondered. *Is he just expecting a doorway to suddenly appear?*

"Ah, here we are." Triumph flooded Shran's voice.

Street lights illuminated a door deep within a hooded archway a few feet away. The age-darkened wood sported an intricate metal plaque embedded in the worn grain. Archer studied the door in surprise; he could've sworn there was a wall there a moment ago.

Shran grasped a heavy metal handle and pulled the door open.

"Welcome to the Captain's Table," the Andorian said. He waved Archer forward with a tilt of his head.

Archer smiled and scratched Porthos's ears as he stepped inside.

Anticipation can often be misleading, Archer thought. He moved farther into the room, pleased to find the interior neither dark nor smoky. In fact, there wasn't even a hint of sour beer in the air, only a pleasant, sawdusty scent. "Somebody takes good care of this place."

"As it should be, Captain Archer. As it should be," a deep voice said.

The man polishing glasses behind the bar stood tall, with a breadth that matched the voice. He wore his silver hair short in a style that reminded Archer of his days back in boot camp.

"Have we met?" Archer slid onto a leather-covered barstool.

"Cap knows everyone," Shran said. His antennae dipped toward each other as he took Archer's arm. "Set us up with a round of drinks, would you, Cap?"

The bartender's eyes twinkled, but Archer suspected the man's gaze could turn water into ice if the occasion warranted. "It'll be just a moment."

"I'll take a—" Archer started.

"Scotch, neat," Cap finished.

Archer nodded and flashed a puzzled smile. "How did you know?"

"It's my business to know." Cap pulled a thin blue bottle from the shelves lined up beneath a spotless wall-length mirror. "Would you like to try the Andorian brand? Highly recommended by many customers, especially Shran."

Shran gave a quick nod.

"I'll give it a try then," Archer said. An antique propeller mounted above the mirror caught his eye. It reminded him of a remote-control model his father had given him a long time ago. "Is that a de Havilland?"

Cap nodded. "A genuine de Havilland Moth, circa 1925. The particular plane this little gem comes from flew solo from Britain to Australia."

The bartender turned away before Archer could ask any more questions. Shran led the way through assorted aliens, tables, and chairs until they came to a table with a couple of empty spaces.

"Here, have a seat," Shran said. "Ladies and gentlemen, may I present Captain Jonathan Archer, diplomat extraordinaire."

Archer tore his attention away from the antique model aircraft displayed throughout the room and nodded to the group. *Easy to get used to this place*, he thought as he relaxed into the brown leather chair, settling Porthos comfortably on his lap.

"What is *that* doing in here?" hissed a feline alien. Her scarlet mane fluffed wide around her pink-furred cheeks, and for a moment Archer thought she might just decide to take Porthos on.

"Calm your fur and relax, Prrgghh." Cap's deep voice carried a no-nonsense tone. "Porthos is as welcome as anyone else in this establishment."

A youth in long, flowing robes drifted up to the table with a tray so full Archer wondered how he managed not to spill anything. The youth gracefully served everyone without dampening the long sleeves of his robe, then slipped back to the bar.

"I assume we pay when we leave?" Archer asked.

"Not exactly." Shran's antennae wriggled. "The only payment for libation in this establishment is to tell a story."

A noxious breeze swept through the room as the outer door opened and an enormous alien oozed inside. Without a glance in either direction, the newcomer proceeded to the bar and coated three seats.

"Caxtonian," Shran said. Archer nodded and sniffed his Andorian Scotch to clear the oily smell from his sinuses. The Scotch did the job. He sipped the light amber liquid. It slipped smoothly down his throat, leaving behind a pleasant burn.

Shran watched him expectantly.

"Good choice." Archer nodded his approval. The Andorian smiled and began introductions. The Klingon female covered her surprise well when Archer gave her a traditional Klingon greeting. He smiled politely at the slender green-skinned alien and gave the feline Prrghh a cool nod.

A palm-sized gold and green spotted lizard poked its head through the white beard of the rotund man sitting opposite Archer. The lizard leapt down onto the table and raced across to touch noses with Porthos.

The man pulled a curved pipe from between his teeth and grinned. "Better watch out or Lizzy here will eat that little friend of yours."

"I'd be glad to lend Lizzy a hand," the feline muttered.

A big-eared alien wandered over and stood behind the white-bearded man. Archer groaned and refrained from hiding Porthos under his chair. The last time he'd crossed paths with a gang of Big Ears, they'd tried to kidnap the poor beagle. But the group at the table didn't know that, and neither, apparently, did the alien.

"What is that creature?" Big Ears asked.

Archer grinned. "I'd be careful if I were you. You don't want to get Porthos angry."

"Why not?" Big Ears asked. He looked the beagle over. "The creature doesn't look very dangerous to me."

"He's a first-generation clone of the original Porthos," Archer said. *If I'm supposed to tell a story, may as well do it now.* "The canine hero who provided the inspiration for the BIA—the Beagle Intelligence Agency—and a decorated member of the *Canis Beagalis* clan. Human and beagle have fought side by side against many enemies. In fact, the Beagle Brigade played a major roll in winning the Pac Man Offensive during Earth's Third World War."

Shran sipped his drink, covering a small smile. Archer ruffled Porthos's ears and continued. "Don't let his small stature and mild looks fool you. His nose is registered with the Intergalactic Sniffers' Association. His paws are licensed lethal weapons."

Big Ears smiled wide, exposing sharp, crooked teeth. "Just how did this *operative* come to be part of your . . . crew?"

The table exploded with laughter. Archer looked at the sneering faces and decided that by hook or by crook, he was going to prove to this crowd that his pal Porthos was the best of the best. If they wanted a story, he'd give them a tale to beat all tales. . . .

"As a boy I watched all the *Beagle Brigade* vids I could get my hands on, but I'd never had a chance to meet a beagle personally until four years ago. It was five a.m. Sepulveda time when I got the call."

Big Ears interrupted again. "Where is this Sepulveda?"

"It's a minor planet in the Orion system. I'm sure you've heard of it." Archer continued before the alien could question him further. "One of Earth's most prized researchers, Mary Ellen Findalot, had been abducted and taken deep into the Sepulvedan rain forest by a band of renegade aliens. Admiral Tucker needed two good operatives to find and rescue the researcher. When the admiral's personal shuttlecraft arrived to pick me up I found out he didn't necessarily mean two *humans*. I'd be working with one of the best sniffers in the system: Porthos the Great, aka Double-O One.

"I was so excited about meeting my boyhood hero, I made the admiral wait while I polished my dress shoes until they reflected my freshly whitened teeth. . . ."

The shuttle dropped us off in front of a run-down hotel in the middle of Sepulveda's wettest rain forest. The peeling paint and moldy boards of the building were only a façade: Poke & Prod Intergalactic was the birthplace of the most cutting-edge technology in the entire galaxy. It also happened to be the facility where Doctor Findalot conducted her research.

Long-tailed birds flashed blue overhead, swooping between broad-leafed trees like kids on a playground. Tropical flora draped the dark green foliage with splashes of orange, red, and yellow. A rich perfume saturated the air—tropical jasmine, maybe, with a hint of guano.

A second shuttle touched down a few feet away. The doors sprang open and a beagle jumped out.

I knew my new partner the moment I saw him. Who wouldn't know Porthos the First? Shiny black and brown coat. Neatly trimmed nails. Nice curl to his tail. He *was* smaller than I expected, but his eyes and ears were constantly alert, his little beagle body poised to leap into action at any moment.

I was looking Porthos directly in his big brown hero eyes, intending to say something earth-shattering like "Wow," when Admiral Tucker cleared his throat.

"Porthos—this here's Captain Jonathan Archer."

The beagle looked me over from head to toe—and sneezed.

I glanced down at my shoes and smiled, but my shoes didn't smile back. Time for another spit polish.

The humid jungle temperature rose two notches, ignoring the fact that my shirt was already dripping wet. I waved away a curious fly and frowned at the sun peeking between the trees.

"Doctor Findalot's assistant is supposed to be meeting us here," Admiral Tucker said. "Something about important equipment."

A funeral dirge echoed inside the hotel.

"Ah, here she comes."

A shimmery haze warped the air in front of us as a soft female voice oozed from the speakers. *"Welcome to the R&D Lab Network, where we love to take your samples."*

"Did anyone say anything to you about samples?" I asked Porthos. He shook his ears.

The hazy air coalesced into a ravishing, dark-haired angel.

"Hey, Doc." Admiral Tucker shook the angel's hand and turned to me. "This here's Captain Jonathan Archer, Porthos's new partner."

A whiff of musky perfume sent my head spinning. I forgot about Porthos. Forgot about the admiral. Forgot about everything but the woman in front of me. She looked me over from head to toe—and sneezed.

This time I didn't bother looking at my shoes.

"I'm Cari Fetchalot," the angel said. She stepped forward until we were nose-to-nose. Her deep brown eyes—like twin cesspools—drew me into a deep forbidden tunnel.

Too bad my shoes had lost their polish.

"I thought you might be needing this." The air whistled as a very broad, very sharp-looking machete flashed by my ear.

I backed around Porthos. He backed around me. Admiral Tucker backed around both of us.

"If you have no idea why you are here, please remain standing. A doctor will be with you shortly to see if you have anything we want."

Doctor Fetchalot flicked her wrist, flipping the machete into the air. Somehow she managed to catch the thing without slicing through her hand, and presented me with the butt end.

"I have something for you too." She handed Porthos an orange package. A beefy fragrance filled the air, sending my stomach into hunger spasms.

"You didn't." Admiral Tucker glanced at the doctor in disbelief, then wrestled what was left of the package from Porthos's sharp beagle teeth.

"You boys have a nice trip." The smile on Doctor Fetchalot's face lit the entire jungle. Then the air shimmered and she was gone.

Admiral Tucker groaned. I peered over his shoulder at the writing on the wrapper.

BEAGLE BURGERS—YOU NEED 'EM, WE FEED 'EM. A double beagle burger with cheese.

"Nothing we can do about it now." The admiral crumpled the wrapper into a tiny ball. "Guess you guys'd better get going. Don't want you wasting any time."

He shook out what looked like a handkerchief and handed it to Porthos.

"I know you'd rather be working alone," the admiral said. "But the captain here's a good man. You watch each other's backs and come back in one piece with our missing doctor, you hear?"

Porthos sniffed the red and white cloth as the admiral continued. "We're expecting you for dinner tonight. Promptly at seven. The wife said she'd skin me alive if you were late, and I kinda like my skin, if you know what I mean?"

The admiral looked me straight in the eye. "You can come along too, Captain. Don't want anyone feeling left out."

He started to head inside, then paused for a final word. "Porthos is good at what he does, even though he may not be entirely cooperative. You'll get along—" He grinned at the beagle. "—eventually."

The door hissed shut, the admiral was gone, and I was left holding the machete.

"I suppose we should get going." I secured my phase pistol, hefted the machete, and headed toward a path on my right.

Porthos went left—through a heavy wall of elephant-ear leaves. Who was I to question a beagle's choice of direction?

Trying not to think about spiders, ticks, ants, and assorted alien creepy crawlies I'd come to know and not be fond of, I wielded the machete with masterful ease and followed Porthos into a world of watery green light filled with squawks, screeches, and howls along with hordes of man-eating mosquitoes.

I slashed right and left, struggling to see through the dark cloud buzzing around my head. Good thing we had a licensed beagle nose leading the way.

All I had to do was find the beagle.

Porthos bayed, his voice low and rich with discovery. He was on the trail of something big—hopefully, Doctor Findalot.

The jungle thrust barrier after barrier into my way—tangled bushes, matted leaves, gnarly vines—taking delight in thwarting my every movement. When the machete came dangerously close to thwacking my leg instead of the local vegetation, I paused for a moment beside a massive tree root.

The baying shifted to an impatient bark.

So much for short breaks. "I'm coming, I'm coming."

But I wasn't going anywhere. My right foot moved; my left foot stayed put, trapped in a sticky vine. A tendril snatched the machete from my hand while the main vine wrapped me up for dinner.

Double-O One had made it clear he preferred working alone, but I didn't think he'd leave me to be eaten by an alien forest.

"I could use a little help here."

Porthos—brown lace-up boot in his mouth—burst through a wall of matted leaves.

"Don't just stand there breathing," I said over the leaf supporting my chin. "Do something."

Porthos made one lazy circle around the tree, then stopped somewhere in the vicinity of my feet.

The vine relaxed its grip just as something hot and wet trickled down my leg.

Shran started coughing. *Well, they wanted a story*, Archer thought. He held back a smile as he watched the feline Prrgghh pound the Andorian's back.

Shran cleared his throat—a loud harsh sound—and finally caught his breath.

"What is it?" Big Ears didn't seem to get it. "What happened?

Archer glanced at Shran. The Andorian didn't say a word, but his antennae moved back and forth in an Andorian shrug.

"It's a highly confidential beagle secret," Archer said.

White Beard leaned over and whispered in Big Ears's big ear. The alien sucked on his pointy teeth for a moment, then looked at Porthos. "No."

"Yes," Archer said with a nod. . . .

The vine dropped off my leg like it'd been hit with a hot poker. It wound back up the tree, until all that was left was a puddle on the ground and a uniquely sour odor in the air.

"Thanks." I knelt down, reveling in my newfound freedom, and took the boot in hand. Porthos sniffed the leather a couple of times, then whined expectantly. I took a sniff, too, but all I could smell was wet feet. "Doctor Findalot's?"

Porthos gave a soft woof, reflecting his opinion of my scent-impairedness, and soldiered ahead.

I could tell we were getting into real rain forest by the way my dress shoes sloshed. An old alien once told me that the reason these forests get so much rain is to keep the ground water at a reasonable level—somewhere between the ankles and the knees. This provides ample feeding grounds for all the bugs and slimy critters, especially the fist-size leeches that seemed particularly fond of my flesh.

Blood donation hadn't been on my to-do list for the day; between the mosquitoes and the leeches, however, I managed to give more than my pint. I waded rapidly in the direction I thought Porthos had taken, pond scuzz swirling around me in dizzy circles. Suddenly, Double-O One reappeared—to the left and slightly behind. He wrestled a massive leech from the back of my knee and woofed at me to hurry up.

Ever since we'd left Poke & Prod, noxious odors of varying styles and intensities had pounded my nose: mildewed vegetation, green slime, and rotting brush. Now a new stench joined the group, an oily, oozing, putrefying-fat stench that clung to the inside of my nostrils and didn't want to let go.

The stench of death.

Porthos smelled it too. He growled, his hackles raised like a flag in a brisk wind.

Were we too late? Had Doctor Findalot gone to that great research facility in the sky?

The beagle darted forward into the tangled brush. One branch snapped. Then two. Then nothing.

"Porthos?" I whispered. "Porthos!"

No sniff. No whine. Not even a nip on the knees.

Clenching my teeth in one hand and phase pistol in the other, I forced my way through the brush, and stumbled into a clearing.

Porthos stood like a melting ice sculpture, staring straight ahead. A cat-size kitten stood beside him—fur and tail both on end. I looked to see what could convince cat and beagle to stand side by side in silence.

And froze.

Less than a hundred yards away a small herd of cattle surrounded a pile of rotting bones, bones the cows were busily consuming.

Porthos grabbed my pant leg and pulled me back into the bushes, but he was too late.

The cows turned as one entity, looked me over from head to toe, and sneezed.

Adrenaline screamed through my veins, along with a good dose of healthy panic. The kitten scrambled up my legs and onto my back. I grabbed a handful of fur and stuffed the little beast inside my shirt, then immediately regretted the action.

We tore through the jungle. Porthos took the lead while the kitten mewled encouragement. Fear made up for the lack of machete as we stumbled through bushes, fell over crumbling rock walls, and dodged hungry vines.

Nothing fazed the stampede thundering behind us.

Suddenly, Porthos scrambled over a huge log.

Always one to chose discretion over valor, I bent to catch my breath and study the takeoff.

Not a wise move.

Leaves behind me exploded, and a giant carnivorous cow stampeded right into my extended posterior, catapulting my body, kitten and all, clear over the top of the log.

That might have been the end of the story right there, but Porthos had chosen our path well. Instead of slamming into a tree, or worse yet, another herd of meat-eating cattle, the kitten and I clawed and slid our way down a mud-encrusted incline, splashing to a stop at the bottom of an overgrown ravine. Due to its location in the middle of a rain forest, the ravine had no choice but to be filled with scuzzy water, complete with the required complement of UBCs: unidentified bump-and-I'll-eat-you critters.

The kitten decided my head had a more likely chance of staying above water than the rest of my body. Tiny claws in your skull can be a real motivator. So can strange things sliding by your leg. Without waiting to try to identify the unidentifiable, Porthos and I swam toward the far end of the ravine, where there appeared to be a clearing above water level.

The brush and trees had been hacked away to make room for a shuttlecraft. I didn't recognized the hull, but I did recognize the towering aliens headed my way.

"What were they?" Big Ears asked. "The aliens I mean."

Archer shrugged and thought fast. "Nausicaans. Very *big* Nausicaans." He stretched his hand toward the ceiling. "At least twice your height and ugly enough to curl the hair on your grand-father's head."

Big Ears touched his bald head. Shran gave a knowing nod and said, "Nausicaans can be very temperamental."

Everyone around the table mumbled their agreement.

Pond scum gave way to mud. We crawled on our bellies until we reached a small stand of brush, where our surveillance team reconnoitered. I plucked and squished only five or six leeches. My leech count was down, but the mountain-size mosquito bites more than made up the balance.

A pair of Nausicaans squished through the muck, loading boxes and containers marked with the P&P insignia onto the shuttle. Bound to the shuttle's loading-ramp strut was a gray-haired carbon copy of Cari Fetchalot.

I looked at Porthos. He looked at me. We shared a partner-type thought: There was no way to know how many more of the big thugs might be waiting inside. "You have a plan?"

I needn't have asked. Porthos was a pro, and pros always have plans. He disappeared into the bushes and reappeared a moment later, dragging an enormous black cloak. The kitten promptly started inspecting the material for more leeches.

"You expect me to play Nausicaan?" I took one whiff of the fragrant fabric and declined. "I'm not wearing anything that smells like rotten petunias."

Porthos gave a low bark of disgust. He sniffed the air. Eye-balled the kitten. Vanished into the jungle.

This time he didn't reappear.

I'd just about decided to charge in with phase pistol blazing when birds exploded out of the jungle. A black and brown beagle blur hurtled into camp, followed by a very large, very irritated jungle-type cat. A cat that looked remarkably like the kitten curled up in my lap.

Nausicaans flew one way, crates flew the other as the cat twisted its sinuous length through the tangled mess. The cat yowled, a low, angry sound, and the cuddly kitten in my lap turned into a bundle of teeth and claws. The kitten headed toward Momma while I took advantage of the situation and slithered closer to the captive woman.

No reinforcements came off the shuttle to help the opposition. I studied the pair closely: one Nausicaan was a real giant, with a bushful of hair and heavy leather vest. He towered over the smaller Nausicaan, but the little guy wasn't intimidated. The smaller one's headful of tightly woven braids stuck out like frozen snakes as he zapped the burly one with something in his hand. The big one leapt forward, drawing a double-edged sword from his belt.

That's when I noticed the beagle-size box creeping along the ground.

Fortunately, the Nausicaans' attention was still focused on the cat. She dropped to her haunches and slid to a snarling stop. Her tail lashed from side to side, scattering leeches and leaves.

I slithered to the next crate and crouched in position, nerves singing with adrenaline.

The box moved in rapid bursts without slipping or sliding. It stopped the moment a Nausicaan glanced its way, moved forward when the aliens returned their attention to the angry cat.

I'd have to get him to teach me that little trick.

Mud flew every which way as the kitten dashed between its mother's legs. The jungle cat snarled once more at the Nausicaans, snatched the kitten in her mouth, and disappeared back into the jungle. Two crates stood between the captive and my hiding place. Mouth dry as the Sahara desert in spite of the humid air, I banana-slipped to the next crate, peered around the corner, and prepared to make my final run.

That's when I realized even heroes make mistakes.

My stomach clenched like I'd been gut-punched as the big Nausicaan sidled over to the box and settled into a prime lid-snatching position.

"Porthos!" I did a sliding forward shoulder roll—a move only possible in extreme muddy conditions—and raised my pistol.

But I was too late.

The Nausicaan snatched the box with one hand, leaving Porthos standing naked in the humid jungle air.

So much for the beagle stealth-box method.

Porthos attacked the huge alien's ankles. I drew a careful bead, but before I could fire, the phase pistol flew from my grasp. Pain racked my shoulders as someone wrenched my hands behind my back. I'd forgotten one of the prime rules of engagement: Never lose sight of your opponents, especially the smaller ones. The stench of rotten petunias assaulted my sinuses, and my knees buckled.

Porthos renewed his attack. He ducked in, nipped at the Nausicaan's ankle, dodged out again, but the beagle's precision timing was off by a fraction of a second. The Nausicaan landed a blow upside Porthos's head, sending the little beagle sailing into the side of the shuttle with a hollow thud.

Light glanced off the double-edged sword as Porthos's attacker prepared for his final charge.

"That's the second time you've mentioned a sword." This time it was White Beard who interrupted. He took the pipe from his mouth and frowned. "What kind of sword?"

Big Ears piped up. "Nausicaans have all kinds, lots of them really old. The double-edged serrated blades are very valuable." He sucked on his teeth and grinned.

"Swords are an honorable way of doing battle." The Klingon slammed her fist on the table and glared around the table.

"No question about that," Archer said. *Time to wrap this story up.* "They have other nasty weapons as well."

Porthos cocked his head as if to say, "Interesting story, boss. What's next?"

Archer chuckled. "There are other ways than brandishing weapons to catch someone's attention, however. . . ."

A whistle shrieked through the clearing—one perfect note so loud and shrill it knocked a purple spy bird out of the closest tree and drew the Nausicaan up short.

"Be careful with that beagle," the woman said. "He's worth more than all the junk you've got in these crates."

The Nausicaan holding me close enough to dance clamped a band around my wrists and tossed me over by the woman. Metal flashed in the small one's hand as he headed toward his partner in crime.

"Porthos is one of a kind," the woman continued. "My own creation. He's the reason you're getting paid a fortune to kidnap me."

Sun glinted off the sword as the big Nausicaan started to swing. The smaller one lunged forward with the rod in his hand. Metal connected with Nausicaan rump. Sparks flew, and the acrid stench of burning hair stung my nose. The big guy must have been zapped with a ten-megawatt jolt. I have to give him credit: He didn't fall over. He just sort of crumbled in place.

Now seemed like a good time to introduce myself. "Doctor Findalot, I presume?" I closed my eyes and turned my head as the woman looked me over from head to toe—and giggled.

I opened one eye, then the other.

"Yes, I'm Doctor Findalot, and that," she pointed at the Nausi-caans, "is Buff and Fluff. The big one's Buff. The other one's Fluff. Your not-so-typical Nausicaan couple."

I nodded and squinted at the pair. Besides the different sizes and hairstyles, it was difficult to tell them apart.

Buff was back on his feet, but his eyes weren't really in focus. He shuffled over to the loading ramp, grabbed the doctor with one hand, the back of my shirt with the other, and carried us both inside the shuttle, where he dumped us into an empty space between a stack of ragged crates and the open cockpit door.

Fluff bounced in and tossed the beagle's limp body in a small cage nearby. I swallowed hard, willing Porthos to move, but Double-O One didn't even whimper.

The shuttle was a utility model, a stripped-down hollow tube, with cockpit up front, engine compartment in the rear, and lots of floor space in between.

In spite of their constant bickering, the Nausicaans managed to haul the rest of the booty inside in a remarkably short time. The loading ramp retracted and the exterior door snapped shut as the pair filled the shuttle with their not-so-fragrant presence.

I had a pretty good view of the cockpit from my aisle seat. Fluff slipped my phase pistol into a bulkhead compartment along with an implement I didn't recognize, then came back to make sure we were comfortable.

"Welcome aboard," she said in barely understandable English. There was no misunderstanding the prod in her hand, though. She grabbed my chin and smiled. "We'll be departing shortly. Please make sure your bindings are securely fastened." She grabbed our wrists and clicked the bands closed another notch. "And bring your knees into a full, upright position." A swift kick from that lovely, size-twenty boot got us into the proper position.

"I have some breath mints," I said, trying not to gag at the stench of who-knows-what sliming my face. She definitely needed a visit to Dentists-R-Us. Failing that, maybe I could talk her into a deal of some kind. "Whatever they're paying, we'll double it."

Fluff sneered, not a pretty sight. "Enjoy the flight—it'll probably be your last." She spun around, flipping snake braids in all directions, and returned to the cockpit as the shuttle left the ground with an ear-numbing rumble.

"Feels like the thrusters need adjusting," I said to no one in particular. The acceleration pressed me tight to the floor for a moment; then we settled into a nice cruise.

Maybe now was the time to indulge in a little light conversation. I skipped the "what's a nice girl" line and got straight to the point. "So, Doctor Findalot. Do you have any idea why we're about to be sold into slavery?"

The doctor shrugged. "A few years ago I discovered a new cloning procedure. I've had one major success: my daughter Cari."

"Doctor Fetchalot is a clone?"

"The Nausicaans claim there's a transport ship out there, waiting to torture me into submission."

"Sounds terrific." I couldn't tell what direction we were headed, but I knew one thing: Once the shuttle hooked up with the transport ship, escape would very likely be impossible. I glanced at Porthos and frowned. The beagle hadn't moved a muscle since he'd been knocked silly.

"Porthos," I whispered, glancing toward the cockpit. "You're going to miss dinner."

Porthos immediately rolled into a prone position and shook his head so hard his ears flapped against his cheeks. He struggled to his feet, flipped the latch on his cage open, and slipped out the door.

"Wait a minute. How did it manage to get out of the cage? It has no hands!"

Gotcha! Archer stifled a grin. "*He* is a consummate escape artist. I'm not doing him justice, though; it isn't so much the fact he escaped. Double-O One had a flair for the dramatic. I'd swear he straightened his coat and winked as he stepped free of that cage."

"Winked . . . ?" Big Ears was flummoxed—a situation Archer thoroughly enjoyed.

"As I was saying . . ."

Porthos eased between a stack of crates and the bulkhead wall. My stomach did nervous butterfly things while we anxiously waited to see what he would do. He reappeared in the shadows near the engine-room door, clambered up a set of access rungs, shoved a vent open with his nose, and scrambled inside. All without making a sound.

At least not a sound loud enough to be heard over the burping engine.

"What is he up to?" I whispered.

"Double-O One has a few genetic enhancements that allow him to go places ordinary beagles dare not go." Doctor Findalot grinned like a proud mother.

My pulse echoed in my ears at the sight of the cage door standing open. We'd lose a major advantage—maybe our only advantage—

if they found Porthos missing. But I was helpless to do anything with my hands going numb behind my back, so I ignored the pond stench wafting off my soggy shirt and concentrated on the scraping noise overhead.

Porthos had worked his way into the ventilation system, and he wasn't being quiet about it. Before I could deduce what my partner had in mind, a noxious odor swept through the shuttle. I pressed my nose tight to my shirt and tried not to breathe.

"Did you give Porthos cheese?" I detected a slight note of accusation in the doctor's muffled words.

"I didn't give him anything." I thought about the empty cheeseburger wrapper. "Your daughter did."

"Ugh."

Up in the cockpit, the Nausicaans were being tortured. A lung-hacking cough had Buff curled in a ball. Fluff wasn't in much better shape. She'd pulled her collar up over her nose, but her color was pale—for a Nausicaan. She lashed out at Buff, her screeches echoing off the shuttle's hull. I couldn't understand a word she said, but Doctor Fetchalot thought it was something about dying.

I suggested to the good doctor that we take advantage of the distraction. We inched ourselves around back-to-back and worked on each other's bonds.

The scratching overhead started, stopped, started again. Porthos was on the move.

Slowly the coughing and gagging subsided. Buff mumbled something about running a maintenance check on the ventilation system once they'd delivered their cargo. Fluff scratched her right arm—the arm that had carried Porthos into the shuttle—and growled something unintelligible.

"Looks like one of our fearless captors has a skin problem," I said to Findalot.

"She probably activated Porthos's nanoflea defense system. If he's rendered unconscious, the fleas automatically head for the nearest warm-blooded body."

Why did every inch of my skin not covered by mosquito bites

or leech lesions suddenly start to itch? I pulled my feet close and studied the floor for tiny troops.

The vessel bucked and rolled, flinging Doctor Findalot and me against the wall.

"Maybe we ran into an asteroid belt," I whispered in the doctor's ear.

"Get off me before I give you a belt," the doctor whispered back.

My hypothesis proved wrong a moment later when Buff appeared in the cockpit doorway, smoke trailing from the seat of his pants. The doctor and I held our collective breaths as the big Nausicaan stormed past, yanked open the engine-room door, and stepped inside.

We sagged back into a tangled lump: Buff hadn't noticed the empty cage.

The shuttle lurched again, slamming the rear door shut. Porthos scrambled out of the air vent, tumbled to the floor, and disappeared behind the crates. A broomstick—an ancient Nausicaan weapon—fell across the engine-room door, lodging in the handle. After a moment of silence the door thumped.

It thumped again a few seconds later, louder this time. Then again and again until Fluffy slammed the control panel with both fists. I found myself introduced to all sorts of interesting Nausicaan curses as she staggered back to the engine room.

My breath stuck in my throat as Porthos dashed into the cockpit, shoved open a section beneath the control console, and proceeded to make a few adjustments. He ducked a few flying sparks and sizzling wires, snatched an object in his mouth, and raced out of the cockpit.

The stench of fried circuits reached my nose about the same time Porthos pressed something hard into my hand. He ducked into his cage as I curled my fingers around the cold metal. Fluff yanked the broom out of the handle and tore the rear door open, releasing Buff from his prison. Both aliens glared in our direction.

You'd have sworn Porthos was a newborn puppy, the way he

stretched out in that cage, eyes closed in feigned innocence. Even I believed him.

A brilliant display of electric blues and reds erupted from the control panel. The Nausicaans thundered into the cockpit, kicking everything out of their path.

Every cell in my body leapt into action. I managed to free the doctor and myself with the stolen key after only three attempts. Taking a deep breath, I crept up to the cockpit door and studied the situation. Porthos crawled up beside me.

My phase pistol peeked out of the compartment next to a furious Fluff. Too close for me to grab it and make a quick getaway.

I needn't have worried—Porthos was in complete control of the situation. He sauntered up beside Buff and lifted his leg, a move I definitely approved of. A wet trickle appeared on the Nausicaan's pants. Buff lunged from his chair with a roar as Porthos leapt onto the control panel and danced across the buttons. Without any warning the gravity system went haywire and everyone floated into the air, moving like a slow-motion vid.

The doctor and I drifted up to the ceiling.

Porthos drifted right into Buff's grimy hand.

Fluff hooked a foot around her chair and continued to punch buttons until the gravity system kicked back in, dropping everyone to the floor with a crash.

Porthos scrambled to his paws and swiped Buff's big, ugly face—with his tongue. He followed up with a sneeze right between the Nausicaan's eyes.

Buff let out an ear-shattering bellow and rolled to his side in agony. The beagle snatched my pistol as he dodged around the pilot's chair, then sprang for the cockpit door. Buff staggered to his feet and lunged after Porthos, but the beagle was too quick. He dropped the pistol and leapt at the Nausicaan's throat, a bristling ball of pure beagle fury. Buff yanked a serrated dagger from his belt and struck out blindly.

The two of them went down in a snarling heap just outside the cockpit door.

I dove over the wrestling pair, snatched the phase pistol from the floor, and aimed it at Fluff. It took two crackling shots to knock the Nausicaan prod from Snake Lady's hand. Once I had the electric zapper in hand, I glanced into the cargo compartment. Buff was sprawled across the floor in an unconscious heap.

Clearly Porthos had everything under control.

"Looks like you should have made that deal, after all." Quickly, I found the discarded bands and bound Fluff's wrists tight enough to get a satisfying wince.

Certain that everything was wrapped up in a neat little package, I put in a call to the admiral, gave him our coordinates, and suggested he also send someone to intercept the transport ship.

"You'd better make sure he sends an emergency team," Doctor Findalot said.

My stomach plunged as I stepped to the cockpit door and dropped to my knees. Doctor Findalot sat in a bloody puddle, Porthos's head cradled in her lap. Air wheezed in and out of an enormous hole in the beagle's side. I spread my hands and swallowed back the shock. "What can I do to help?"

Doctor Findalot sighed. "Find me the medical kit, if there is such a thing on this ship."

I put the prod to good use on its original owner and soon had the medkit in hand. I passed the kit on to the doctor and tore into the crates.

The doctor did what she could with the Nausicaan supplies and what little else we could find, but it wasn't enough.

Approximately fifteen minutes before our own troops arrived, Double-O One passed into beagle heaven.

Everyone around the table was quiet. Porthos laid his head across Archer's arm.

Finally, Big Ears spoke up. "Porthos was indeed a great warrior."

Everyone nodded.

"Double-O One gave the ultimate self-sacrifice," Archer said, satisfied he'd given his audience a story they'd never forget. He scratched the beagle's soft ears. "He traded his life for mine and the doctor's. A sacrifice I'll never forget."

"What about the doctor's daughter?" Shran asked. His antennae curled forward in the curious expression Archer had grown to appreciate.

Archer cleared his throat. Leave it to the Andorian to want the steamy details. "Cari was extremely grateful that I'd managed to bring her mother home safely, though they were both distraught at losing Porthos, as was I. It surprised me how quickly I'd grown fond of Double-O One. Doctor Findalot recognized what good partners we'd made. She promised me first pick from Double-O One's clone litter."

Archer held the beagle high in his lap. *Time for the clincher.* "The *Enterprise* is honored to have Porthos the Second on board as protector. And I am honored to call him friend."

Big Ears slammed his fist on the table. "This honored friend has yet to drink with us. A drink! A drink for Porthos the Great!"

Everyone turned toward the bar. Cap's eyes twinkled. "Maybe he'd rather have some cheese?"

Archer glanced down at Porthos. The beagle licked his lips and gave a soft woof.

"No cheese," Archer said. "He'll have Peruvian water, please. Shaken, not stirred."

Tending Bar . . .

Cap smiled as he prepared Porthos's Peruvian water. The theme today seemed to be bringing fresh faces to the bar: Picard bringing Riker, Sisko bringing Kira, and now Shran bringing Archer.

Sisko and Kira departed right after Archer's story. Gold was still sitting at his table, neither eating nor drinking, and another Starfleet human had just entered. This one had been here before, of course—but Chakotay's last trip to the Captain's Table saw him a Maquis cell leader, fighting against Starfleet. Cap wondered if the story of how he went from one to the other would be the one he'd tell this day.

Then a furtive figure ran through the front door into the pub, and Cap smiled again. This was about to get interesting. . . .

DEMORA SULU

CAPTAIN OF THE *U.S.S. ENTERPRISE*-B

Iron and Sacrifice

DAVID R. GEORGE III

She pursued him into the empty marketplace, confident of his capture as she finally closed the gap. Beneath the silvern glare of a waxing moon, she easily kept him in view. He fled past vending stalls—not staffed at this time of night—that marched between the old mortar-and-brick buildings on either side of the agora.

Not for the first time since she'd arrived at Temecklia II, Captain Demora Sulu counted herself fortunate that Strolt had made his way to this once-thriving spaceport at this time. Transporter inhibitors had always blanketed the complex, but five or ten years ago, he might have been able to find assistance here among the throngs of vendors and travelers, or at least blend in with their great number. Even at this time of night, the marketplace would have been filled with those hawking wares and services, and those looking to acquire one or the other. But the viral pandemic that had swept the population and numerous wayfarers a few years ago had triggered a dramatic decline in civilian traffic, and lying beyond Federation space, the port had never seen more than a few Starfleet vessels. So close to the Tzenkethi border, and with the Coalition's recent aggressive attempts at expansion, the spaceport had subsequently never recovered.

Now, bathed in the hoary moonlight, the open-air bazaar appeared immaculate and new, but Sulu knew better. Even in the days it had flourished, this place had been unclean and timeworn, and in recent years, the Orlenti had allowed the entire facility to fall into disrepair. The nighttime illumination revealed the surroundings in soft tones, but veiled a multitude of unflattering details.

As Strolt ran, his long coat flaring out behind him, he glanced back over his shoulder at her. Perhaps twenty or twenty-five meters separated them now, and Sulu's strong legs and aerobic stamina carried her closer with every stride. He was, like her, a human, and she felt confident that he could not outrun her.

Suddenly, though, Strolt darted left and dived between two stalls. With three sides meeting at right angles and rising up waist-high, the vending booths provided cover for Strolt to duck out of sight, but no place he could remain hidden for very long. But concealment might not be his aim right now, Sulu knew. If he could find time enough to arm the explosives he had stolen just moments ago, he could escape her—or threaten to escape her—in the most permanent way.

Sulu dashed to the left and hied along the open backs of the stalls. She wished that she had a phaser with her, or even a tricorder. As she approached the area where Strolt had gone, she slowed, calculating that he had to be in one of the next three booths. But she did not see him in either the first or the second, and so as she neared the third, she grew even more cautious.

But she found the third stall empty too.

Sulu checked out the next as well, without success, then stopped. Strolt should have been here somewhere. She'd seen the point where he'd lunged from the central path, and she'd followed quickly in that direction. He might have been able to move from one stall to another beside it, but she would have seen him had he moved more often or farther than that.

Turning back the way she'd come, Sulu bent low and studied the ground, visible in the reflected glow of the moon. A rough, cracked tarmac spread throughout the marketplace, covered in patches by sand that had blown in from the eastern desert plain abutting the town. Squinting, she could make out her own footprints here and there, but then back by the second stall, she spied the front half of a different, larger boot. She hunted around for other such tracks, and located a second, and then a third, leading off to the side, toward the building there.

Sulu looked up, expecting to see a door or window ahead, but instead saw an alleyway, extremely narrow and easily missed. Still, she had run right past it, and she chided herself now for having been less observant than she'd needed to be. Wasting no time, and concerned that she'd already lost the Federation fugitive, she charged forward.

Aware that she might be rushing headlong into an ambush, Sulu simply put such thoughts out of her mind. Temecklia hung in space too close to the Tzenkethi border for her to worry about her own safety. She would have to pick up Strolt's trail quickly if she had any hope at all of learning his mate's current location and preventing her from reaching Coalition territory.

As Sulu sped on, it surprised her to see neither doors nor windows fronting on the alley. Peering upward, past the tops of the buildings on either side, she saw a thin sweep of stars. There appeared to be no possibility that Strolt had rapidly scaled the sheer, three-story brick walls. Barely wide enough to accommodate two average-sized humans side by side, the passage seemed not quite right to her, but before she could give much thought to why that might be, she reached the alley's end.

A single door stood there, unmarked and strangely out of place. Distinctive, composed of vertical wooden slats bound together by coarse metal bands, it reminded Sulu of one at a winery on Argelius II that she'd often visited. As she slowed to a walk, she saw a slip of light along one side of the door, which obviously stood ajar. From beyond the jamb emanated voices and laughter, punctuated by what sounded like the ring of glassware.

Unwilling to abandon her pursuit of Strolt, Sulu reached out, placed her hand flat against the surface of the door, and pushed. She wished again that she carried a phaser or tricorder, or even that she wore a Starfleet uniform. While her simple gray jumpsuit would draw little attention, neither would it command any respect.

The door swung open, one of its hinges creaking. The voices and other sounds grew louder. With the same urgency as when she'd hunted for Strolt in the vending stalls, Sulu moved quickly through a small circular vestibule and into the main room of a tavern. Dark woods dominated the walls and ceiling in an old-Earth style, with several pieces of artwork hanging at tasteful intervals. Tables of various shapes and sizes sat scattered about, each surrounded by matching chairs. Along the inner wall, opposite Sulu, an ornate mahogany bar stretched almost the entire width of the room.

She peered around carefully, searching for Strolt among the tavern's many patrons. There did not seem to be an empty seat anywhere. She saw several humans, and even what appeared to be a Terran dog on one man's lap, but as she gazed about, she spied individuals from a wide assortment of other species. A pair of Gorn communicated in rasps and hisses at the near end of the bar. An Otevrel—doubtless an exile, considering her distance from home—sat alone in a corner, a half-filled crystalline goblet held before her in two of her tendrils. And at a small table near the center of the room, an unlikely quartet drank and laughed together: an Axanar, a Tholian, a Corvallen, and a Cardassian. Oddly, though, nowhere did Sulu see any Orlenti.

As many species as she could identify, at least as many she could not. But irrespective of their anatomy, quite a few of those present appeared clad in one form or another of official attire. The Tholian, the Cardassian, and one of the Gorn wore the uniforms of their particular space fleets, although the Gorn's tunic seemed well out of date. Sulu saw no obvious members of Starfleet, but she did notice on the left breast of one man's garb a familiar metallic chevron. Dressed in a one-piece, dark-gray uniform, with lighter shoulders and a crimson undershirt, the man looked essentially human, although a pattern of blue lines showed on one side of his forehead, above his left eye. Sulu thought the markings decorative, but supposed that they might be naturally occurring. Another man—similarly clad, but without the facial characteristics—sat at a table by himself.

She finished scanning the room, and saw no sign of Strolt. But she also noted no windows or doors anywhere, other than the one directly behind her, through which she'd just entered. On either side of the bar, though, two parallel halls led toward the back. Sulu randomly selected the one on the right and headed in that direction.

The short corridor led to a smaller room, also with no evident exits. Most of the patrons there crowded around a couple of gaming tables. Sulu swiftly surveyed the lively scene, then hurried back to the main room via the other hallway. She passed two doors on the way, just as she'd passed two doors in the first hall. One pair led to restrooms, and Sulu assumed that the others opened to storage areas, or perhaps to an office. Regardless, they were bounded by the front and back rooms and the twin corridors, and so likely wouldn't provide a means of escape for Strolt. To confirm her reconnaissance of the tavern, though, she approached the bar, where a lone man worked.

"Pardon me," she said. She kept the front door in view, and an eye out for Strolt.

The bartender glanced over at her from where he stood. "Help you, ma'am?" He twisted a towel in and around a drinking glass, presumably drying it. A white-haired man, he stood about the same height as Sulu did, though given his stout frame, he probably outweighed her by fifteen to twenty kilos. She attempted to estimate his age, but perceived a paradoxical blend of youthfulness and experience in his aspect, an improbable combination of innocence and wisdom. At first glimpse, she'd thought him human, but as she regarded him now, some quality she could not quite place made her believe otherwise.

"Are there any ways out of here besides through the front door?" she asked him.

"Every entrance and exit we have," the bartender said, "is right there." He raised the hand in which he held the towel and gestured toward the vestibule.

"All right," Sulu said. "Thank you." She started to move away, back toward the door, but then the bartender stopped her with a question.

"Something for you to drink, ma'am?" he asked.

Sulu looked back over at him. "No, nothing for me," she said. "Thank you." She considered whether or not she should try to enlist the bartender's assistance. She would check the restrooms herself, but suspected that the other doors in the halls might be locked. In that case, she would have to—

Rapid movement caught Sulu's eye, and she looked over at the right-hand corridor just in time to see Strolt withdrawing into it, out of her view. She hastened in that direction, careful not to run, wary of drawing attention to herself, and wanting to avoid panicking the tavern's patrons.

As she drew nearer the hall, she saw Strolt standing within it, a few paces back from the main room, staring at her. Disheveled, unshaven, and with deep circles beneath his eyes, he looked as though he hadn't slept soundly in days. His long, light-brown hair hung down around his face in matted clumps, and his russet, calf-length coat draped loosely around his lanky, perhaps undernourished form.

Sulu met his gaze, and she stopped moving at once, recognizing the desperation showing in his countenance. Verifying her fears, the renegade freighter captain reached into his coat, his hand sliding beneath the wrinkled fabric as though retrieving a concealed weapon. Sulu didn't know whether the past few minutes had provided him the time needed to arm his purloined explosives, but she could not risk assuming that he hadn't done so—not with so many people close at hand, and not in view of the stakes involved. With Strolt dead, Sulu would not be able to ascertain the whereabouts of Zeeren Tek Lom-A, his Tzenkethi mate, who would then be able to abscond back to her native space and deliver to her people the sensitive matériel, deployment, and mission information Strolt had appropriated from Starbase 143. With the Coalition forcibly trying to extend their borders and expand their territories, and with their increasingly imperialistic tendencies, their acquisition of Starfleet operational data would undoubtedly put Federation lives in jeopardy.

Sulu took a step forward, and Strolt's arm tensed. Fear appeared on his face, but so did a grim determination. The implication could not have been clearer: He would kill himself in order to avoid capture, even if doing so resulted in the loss of innocent lives.

Raising her hands waist-high, Sulu made patting movements, her palms toward the floor. She intended it as a placatory gesture, a calm, unspoken plea to Strolt that he should reconsider resorting to violence. He peered back at her evenly, but did not remove his hand from within his coat. Sulu saw the weariness in his eyes, in his posture, the aura of imminent defeat he seemed to carry with him, and she realized that, right now at least, she would have to let him go. If she didn't, he would detonate the explosives and take to his grave the secret of Zeeren's route back to her homeland—and he would kill scores of people in the tavern.

Before Sulu could begin to retreat, though, she felt a presence at her side. She turned her head to see the bartender standing beside her, holding in his raised hand a stemmed glass filled with a dark red liquid. "For you, ma'am," he said. "I think you'll enjoy this."

"Oh . . . no, thank you," she said, unhappy to be disturbed during this critical juncture with Strolt. Thinking of the most efficacious means of dismissing the bartender so that he would not return, she said, "I'm afraid I have no money."

"Money?" he said, and his mouth widened into a lopsided smile. "Here at the Captain's Table, our customers pay for their drinks with something other than money. They pay with stories."

"I'm afraid I don't—" Sulu started, keenly aware of Strolt's presence in the hallway, but the bartender interrupted her.

"Don't what?" he asked. "Don't have stories? *Everybody* has stories." Again, he proffered to her the glass of what appeared to be wine.

Around them, Sulu realized, the tavern had quieted, the conversations and laughter silenced, the shifting of chairs and the clink of glassware stilled. She peered about and saw that the collective attention of the tavern's patrons had swung toward her. At the table nearest where she stood, a pre-Shift Frunalian male rose to his feet, stepped back, and then with a wave of one chitinous hand offered up his vacated chair to Sulu.

Quickly glancing back toward the hall, she saw that Strolt hadn't moved, but continued to watch her. Suddenly, she perceived an opportunity. Had she managed to apprehend Strolt, she would have attempted to persuade him to reveal the information necessary to prevent Zeeren Tek Lom-A from crossing back into Tzenkethi space. Perhaps this moment provided her a chance to do just that.

Sulu reached out and accepted the wineglass from the bartender, the liquid inside a rich, translucent maroon. "All right," she said loudly, addressing the tavern's patrons. "I'll tell you a story." She padded over to the Frunalian's table, at which one other individual sat, an Alonis woman in a formfitting landsuit. As Sulu set down her stemmed glass and took the empty seat, she searched her memories for a tale that would convey to Strolt the appropriate message. Finding one from just two years ago, she said in a raised voice, "I'll tell you a story about one of the most difficult times in my life. I'll tell you about when I had to step down from command of the *U.S.S. Enterprise*."

By 2315, I'd already been commanding the Federation flagship for almost four years. During that time, my crew had navigated an impressive record of exploration, including a number of significant first contacts. We'd also endured our share of military engagements, although after the Tomed Incident and the Romulans' adoption of an isolationist doctrine, tensions throughout the quadrant had eased considerably. We'd all welcomed the prospect of seeing less combat, returning instead to the types of missions for which most of us had joined Starfleet in the first place: those of scientific discovery.

The *Enterprise* had just completed such an assignment, a rigorous survey of several super star clusters. We put in at Starbase Magellan for six weeks of dual R and R: rest and recreation for the crew, and repair and refit for the ship. At the end of that time, we would head out into unexplored territory, on a long-term mission in search of new life and new civilizations.

As ship's captain, I had numerous duties to tend to during the layover at Magellan. Among my responsibilities, I had to oversee the removal of the special equipment the crew had utilized to study the super star clusters, and once that had been done, I had to supervise the installation of new scientific instruments considered better suited to investigating several anomalies known to lie along our prospective flight path. I also needed to complete personnel evaluations, and at the same time, welcome thirteen new crew members to the *Enterprise*.

Except that I completed none of those tasks. On the third day in dock, I received a subspace communication routed to me through Starfleet headquarters. The message had originated on Sentik IV, a world outside Federation space. By the time the transmission reached me at Magellan—the starbase itself out on the frontier—it was already seven days old, despite having been tagged as urgent. I listened to the message at once—it came with no visual component—but even before it began to play, I knew who it must be from: Shimizu Hana, my paternal grandmother. I also knew that she must be in trouble.

Only twice in my life had I spent time with Hana, although that had been enough for me to formulate a lasting impression of her. I initially visited her when I was a young girl, maybe twelve or thirteen. I remember meeting her that first time, walking into her apartment and seeing her standing out on a balcony that overlooked the dense, modern city of Kaiseki. Small in stature—I was already taller then she was—Hana appeared positively diminutive against the backdrop of the numerous tall buildings that formed the skyline of New Tokyo's capital. And yet when she walked back inside the apartment, the room seemed to fill with her presence. Not given to emotional displays, she spoke little and in quiet tones, which somehow lent her words even more weight when they did come. I'm not sure if I ever saw her smile.

Hana's husband, my grandfather, had died a few years before my childhood visit to New Tokyo. I got to meet him just once, when he visited Earth to attend a physics conference. A kind man, a gentle man, he stayed with my father and me for two weeks, and when he left to return home, I hated to see him go. Later, I found in my room a gift he'd left for me: a poem, tenderly celebrating my presence in his life, even though he'd only just met me.

When I met Hana that first time, I guess I expected her to act in a similar manner, to be of a similar temperament, caring and expressive. I couldn't have been more wrong. Stern and stoic, she seemed more interested in maintaining her daily routine than in getting to know her granddaughter.

The ten days I spent in Kaiseki with her—a time to which I'd been looking forward with great anticipation—dragged on like a prison sentence. After my grandfather had died, Hana had relocated to New Tokyo in order to care for her older sister, Nori. And although my great-aunt was very sweet to me, her health was poor, and so I didn't get to spend much time with her. What little time we did have together was hard, since her physical condition brought her almost constant suffering. When I finally left to go back to Earth, I felt as though I'd escaped an unwarranted punishment.

I next saw Hana about a decade later, on the occasion of Nori's funeral. As far as I could tell, Hana hadn't changed much, except possibly that she'd grown even more austere, even more cold. Other than to offer my condolences, I didn't speak much with her.

After that, with most of her family gone, and the few that remained scattered throughout the quadrant, Hana relocated again. This time, she moved to Sentik IV, a far-flung world that played host to a small community opposed to the use of almost all technology. So when I received the transmission from there, I knew immediately that she had sent it.

Except that when I listened to the message, it turned out to be not *from* Hana, but *about* her. Somebody on Sentik IV, a man named Rosenzweig, had taken it upon himself to contact Starfleet with news of Hana's failing health. With everybody else in her family either dead or unreachable, the message had been directed to me.

I barely knew Hana, and since I was facing a month and a half of preparations for the *Enterprise*'s upcoming assignment, my choice seemed clear. I would find medical care for her, and send somebody to look after her, possibly to bring her to an assisted-care facility. I knew that many doctors and nurses and other health-care personnel in the Federation had dedicated their lives to tending to the elderly, the infirm, and the sick.

Except that I couldn't do that. Maybe I didn't know Hana very well, maybe I didn't even like her very much, but she was still my grandmother. And right then, at that moment, I knew that there was nobody else in the universe to whom she could turn, other than me.

As Sulu had begun to speak, searching for the right tale to tell, and the right way in which to tell it, she kept Strolt in her peripheral vision. At first, he remained stationary, doubtless not wanting to attract any attention to himself. After a couple of minutes, though, with the tavern's patrons concentrating on Sulu, she saw him begin to move.

He edged toward the front door slowly, staying close to the walls and clearly attempting to maintain a low profile. Wanting to stop him without risking detonation of the explosives he carried, Sulu paced herself, timing the introduction of Hana's predicament to the moment when Strolt passed closest to her. Carefully, as she delivered the words about being the only person to whom her grandmother could turn for help, she looked over and made eye contact with her quarry.

Strolt stopped.

Sulu held his gaze an instant longer, willing him to stay, willing him to listen to what she had to say. She knew that his mate had no one to whom she could turn but him. Once Zeeren had wed a human, the Tzenkethi people—including her family and friends—had shunned her, and the coalition had closed its borders to her. Strolt's reason for betraying the Federation was simple and understandable: he loved his mate, and Zeeren's reward for bringing Starfleet intelligence to the Tzenkethi would be acceptance—or at least tolerance—of their marriage. Strolt wanted to allow her that opportunity to reconnect with those she loved.

But Sulu could not permit that.

She took a breath, and then continued.

I requested a two-week leave of absence, which Starfleet Command granted. In order to expedite my return to duty, though, and because the *Enterprise* would be moored at Starbase Magellan for weeks, Admiral Ratnaswamy authorized me to utilize the *Armstrong*—one of the ship's warp shuttles—for my travel. Even then, it still took me three and a half days to reach Sentik IV.

When I arrived there, I found a world even more unwelcoming than I'd imagined. With a narrow habitable zone, indications of harsh summers and winters, and subsequently difficult agricultural conditions, life must have been a constant struggle for survival. According to Federation records, the lone settlement there had been established three decades earlier by neo-Luddites as a refuge from technological society. The archaic haven had been intended for hardy people seeking isolation and the chance to truly take care of themselves.

From orbit, I scanned the surface. Sensors identified a population of only a few thousand, spread out across twenty-five thousand hectares. I detected almost no electronics or duotronics, and virtually no modern equipment of any kind, save for a small subspace communications assembly and several solar-powered generators feeding it. There also seemed to be no town of any sort, although the comm station sat in a building centrally located amid the farms surrounding it.

Not wanting to create a stir in the community, I landed the shuttle in a glade well outside of the inhabited area, flying in low over a neighboring forest. From there, I used the *Armstrong*'s sensors to locate Hana's farm, the longitude and latitude of which had been included in the message I'd received at Magellan. I outfitted myself with a transporter recall and a medical tricorder, then beamed myself on my way.

I didn't wish to surprise anybody, and so I materialized on an empty dirt path leading to Hana's house. Above, a thick, gray cloud cover blanketed the sky, and a slight breeze rustled the tall grass atop the hillocks on either side of the dusty trail. In the distance just a hundred or so meters ahead stood the farmhouse and, not far from it, a small barn.

I started toward the house. The hillocks flattened as I approached, revealing fields beyond them. To the left of the path, short, red-leafed plants grew, and to the right, taller, leafier green plants. It appeared that some of the former had been harvested, but what remained of both crops looked sere and unhealthy.

When I reached the farmhouse, I saw that it could more aptly be described as a cabin. Small and simple, it had been constructed out of logs. To me, it looked like something out of a historical holo.

I walked up to the house and rapped my knuckles against the wooden planks of the door. My knocking sounded hollow, and somehow fit the cool, gray day around me. After a few seconds, I heard footfalls clocking along the floor inside, growing louder with each step, until the door opened to reveal a short, portly man, perhaps my age or a little younger. He wore large, round glasses, and a beard traced from ear to ear along the line of his jaw. He had a thin mustache, and dark brown hair receding above his temples.

"Hello, my name is Demora Sulu. I've come to see my grandmother, Shimizu Hana. I received a message that she wasn't well."

"*I* sent that message," the man said, sounding annoyed. "Almost two weeks ago."

"You're Mister Rosenzweig," I said, even as I recognized his voice from the transmission. He nodded, but said nothing more, instead regarding me for a long moment, as though deciding whether or not he could trust me. I was pleased that I'd worn my Starfleet uniform, although given the reclusive nature of the people on Sentik IV, I wondered whether my position and rank would carry any weight at all with Rosenzweig. "Thank you for sending the message. I received it only a few days ago, and I came as quickly as I could. I took a warp shuttle to get here."

Rosenzweig looked out over my shoulder at the mention of the shuttle, as though searching for a glimpse of the spacecraft. "I landed out in the forest to avoid causing any disruption," I explained.

Rosenzweig nodded again, then moved back and waved me inside. I stepped up onto the raised floor and past him, entering Hana's house. As Rosenzweig closed the door behind me, I paused, allowing my eyes to adjust to the dim interior, the only light in the room coming through a small window in the right-side wall.

I peered around and saw a place as primitive inside as it had appeared outside. There looked to be neither power nor running water. Rough-hewn wooden furniture sat scattered about, most of it arranged around a stone hearth in the center of the left wall. A round iron stove squatted in one far corner, and a washbasin in the other, with two stretches of simple cupboards between them, separated by a door. Just past the fireplace, another door stood ajar. I assumed that the back door led outside, and the side one to a bedroom. Hana's bedroom.

"I came by a few weeks ago to borrow an ax," Rosenzweig said as he moved over to my side. "Ms. Shimizu wasn't here, so I looked out in the fields. I found her there, collapsed in a heap, exhausted. She claimed it was the sun, but I don't think it was. I helped her back here, and I've been visiting as often as possible since then, but I have my own farm to tend to, and my own family to feed."

"I understand," I said, taking note that although Rosenzweig had helped Hana, he also seemed to resent having to lend such assistance. Of course, the founding of the settlement possessed something of an antisocial aspect, as did the layout of the place, which contained no real communal areas. I could not imagine living in such an environment, though I had no difficulty at all believing that Hana did so.

"May I see her?" I asked. I wanted to take care of Hana, get her moved to an appropriate facility if necessary, and get back to Starbase Magellan and the *Enterprise* as quickly as possible.

Rosenzweig—I realized that he hadn't offered his given name—pointed toward the door past the fireplace. I padded over to it and pushed it fully open. Even before I saw Hana, I heard her labored breathing. I walked into the room, which was small and almost completely filled by a large four-poster bed, its uprights reaching nearly all the way to the low ceiling. Amid heaps of pillows and linens, Hana's form was almost lost. She lay on her back, propped up against the headboard, her eyes closed. The bedclothes pulled up to her chin seemed barely to rise with her respiration. She looked even slighter than I remembered her.

I turned and gestured to Rosenzweig, who stood in the doorway. I pointed him back to the main room, then followed him, quietly closing the door behind me. "Has a doctor seen her?"

"There are no doctors on Sentik, Captain Sulu," he said, employing my rank for the first time, obviously recognizing my insignia. "I'm sure you noticed from your shuttle that there aren't many modern conveniences here. That includes physicians."

"But people must get sick or injured," I said. "Surely you must have a means of dealing with such inevitabilities."

"People do get sick or hurt, and mostly their families take care of them as best they can," Rosenzweig said. "Only a handful of people here are completely alone. As for medical personnel, there are two individuals who each have some training as a medic. Both visited Ms. Shimizu several times during the last ten days and did what they could for her."

"Do they know what's wrong with her?" I asked, hoping to get an idea of what I could do for Hana.

"What's wrong with her?" Rosenzweig echoed, clearly surprised by my question. "Nothing, really. She's just had a hard life,
and she's old."

Hana was one hundred fifteen, I knew—past middle age, to be
sure, but not necessarily so old that she should be reaching the
end of her years. In my own life, I'd known people who'd lived
robustly into their one hundred forties and fifties. Still, not everybody experienced the same things in life, nor did every person
age in the same way. I asked, "Did the medics provide a progno-
sis? Did they say whether she would recover from her fall?"

"She might recover from the fall, but she won't recover from
her age," Rosenzweig said. "She's dying."

I thanked Rosenzweig for everything he'd done, and he quickly
left, evidently anxious to return to his own house and family.
Once he'd gone, I pulled a chair from around the table in the
main room and brought it in beside Hana's bed. In the quiet broken only by her ragged respiration, I studied her face as she slept.
She looked like an apparition of the woman I'd last seen more
than twenty years before. Her pale flesh had grown looser with
time, particularly around her neck, and the complex of wrinkles
suffusing her features had expanded and deepened. No vestige of
color remained in her hair; even her eyebrows had faded to white.
Her slight form seemed smaller and more frail. Even in repose,
she appeared old and worn down, as though no longer capable of
drinking in the everyday elixir of sleep.

As I waited for Hana to wake, I peered around her room. It
contained no adornments: no artwork, no photographs, no pos-
sessions pushed into a corner or set upon a shelf, no mementos
of any kind. A window in the back wall looked out on a stand of
trees, and two large chests—one at the foot of the bed and one
below the window—probably contained Hana's clothes, but other
than that, the room was bare. I found the lack of personal items
discomfiting, though perhaps not entirely surprising.

I wondered how receptive Hana would be to my help. That she

had managed on her own for more than two decades in that demanding environment demonstrated her independence and vitality during that period. But if what Rosenzweig had told me was true, then that time had come to an end. On the journey to Sentik from Starbase Magellan, I'd researched assisted-care facilities, but I'd needed to know Hana's condition and her feelings about the situation before I could decide which would be best for her.

"Demora." At first, I couldn't even tell whether Hana had spoken, or whether perhaps I'd just heard a gust of wind or a tree branch brushing against the outside of the cabin. I looked at her and saw her eyes still closed, but then I realized that her breathing no longer came in rasps. At the same time, her lips moved, and she spoke again, louder this time. "Why are you here?" The words did not sound as though they had been offered as a challenge, but neither did they seem particularly welcoming.

"Hana," I said, and elected to sidestep her question for the moment. "How did you know it was me?" Maybe she'd heard my voice when I'd been talking with Rosenzweig, but I really thought she'd been asleep at the time.

"Your perfume," she said simply, her eyes still closed.

I felt my brow knit. I liked wearing fragrances, and while I never did so on duty, I'd brought some with me on the shuttle. When I'd woken earlier, still en route to Sentik, I'd checked the autopilot and verified my location, then washed up and dabbed on some perfume. But that didn't explain how Hana had recognized me . . . unless—

"Was I wearing this same fragrance when I saw you at—" I stopped, about to make reference to Great-Aunt Nori's funeral. "When I last saw you?" I finished. I'd been using a couple of particular scents for a long time, even since my teens, but that Hana would recall one from almost a quarter of a century ago seemed remarkable. I certainly couldn't remember what perfume I'd worn all those years before.

"Yes, you were wearing that fragrance," Hana said. She opened her eyes and looked toward me. Her slow, deliberate movements contributed to her air of fragility, as if the mere act of turning her head required both great effort and great care. Still, her gaze did not waver as it fell upon me. "Why are you here?" she asked again. "It must not be a coincidence that you've come at this time."

"No, it's not," I agreed. "Mister Rosenzweig sent a message that you weren't well to Starfleet Command, and they contacted me." I hesitated, and then added, "I came as quickly as possible."

A quizzical expression crossed Hana's face, and it was obvious why. Despite being grandmother and granddaughter, we'd had virtually no relationship at any time in our lives, and were really more strangers than family. And although I knew that some vague sense of kinship had motivated me to travel to Sentik IV, I was also aware that what drove me was more intellectual than emotional; I understood the concept of family rather than feeling the joys of such a connection.

Still, the fact remained that I'd gone to Hana, and even though I hadn't adequately explained the reasons why—either to her or to myself—she did not ask again. Instead, she shifted her attention to the reality of my visit, and to its implications for her. "Have you spoken to the medics here?" she asked.

"No, not yet," I said. "Mister Rosenzweig told me briefly about their conclusions, but I thought I'd seek them out once you and I had spoken."

"You may consult them if you like," Hana said, "but there's really no need. I'm simply old, and my health is poor. I'm going to die before long, and there's nothing to be done about that." She didn't sound angry, or fearful, or as though she suffered any of the emotions I would have expected a person to feel when they believed themselves near the end of their days.

Hana closed her eyes and straightened her head on the pillow. "I'm afraid that your trip has been in vain," she said.

Even though Rosenzweig had already said much the same thing, Hana's words should have moved me, should have elicited my sympathies, but they didn't. Hana's remoteness, her stoicism, rendered impotent any feelings prompted by her situation. Speaking as impassively as she had, I said, "I think I can help. Someone can see to your needs, and that you're kept as comfortable as possible."

Hana said nothing for a few minutes, and I thought that perhaps she had dozed off. But then she said, almost in a whisper, "Do *you* intend to stay here with me?" Her inflection told me that she thought the notion of me looking after her completely absurd.

"I thought I could take you to an assisted-care facility," I said.

A small, sharp sound emerged from Hana, and it took a second for me to realize that it had been a laugh. "Talk to the medics," she said. "They'll tell you that any trip off-planet would likely kill me. Even a journey in stasis would probably be too much for this ancient body of mine to survive."

"I will talk to them," I said. I felt totally disconnected from Hana, her closed eyes an apt metaphor for the walls separating us.

"It doesn't matter," Hana said. "Even if I could travel, I wouldn't. This place—" She opened her eyes as the bedclothes at her side moved, and she struggled to pull her arm free of the blanket. When she had, she waved her hand weakly about, clearly intending to take in the whole of her house and land. "This place is my home. It's been my home for twenty-four years. I won't leave."

I wanted to ask Hana what kind of a home that would be for her in her infirmity. Although the small population of Sentik could have provided a tightly woven community, I doubted that it actually did, or would—an estimation bolstered by my interaction with Rosenzweig. Also, according to my research, the founding of the settlement had been conceived as a flight not only from technology, but from society as well. Rosenzweig had made it clear that whatever he had done for Hana during the past couple of weeks had been an aberration, and that he would not continue such efforts. I suspected that no one who lived there would be willing to provide Hana the care she would need.

"You can't will away the fact that you need help, and it doesn't seem like you'll get much from the people who live here." I said to her. "According to Mister Rosenzweig, you don't even have much food. I saw your crops . . . they need to be harvested, and many have died. If you choose to remain here on your own, how do you expect to survive?"

"That's very simple," Hana said, and she turned her head to look at me again, the gaze of her dark eyes locking with mine. "I'm not going to survive."

Sulu shifted in her chair, using the movement to cover her glance around the tavern. Strolt continued to observe her, she saw. She'd brought him to this point in her tale, where Hana had needed help and Sulu herself had been in a position to give it, just as Zeeren Tek Lom-A needed help right now that Strolt was in a position to give.

Here, she knew, the story needed to turn.

The decisions she would soon reveal she'd made with respect to Hana could send the wrong message to Strolt, in effect validating the choice he'd made to forsake the delicate balance of power between the Federation and the Tzenkethi Coalition in order to help his mate. But those decisions Sulu had made would provide only the context of what she wanted to convey to Strolt, and not the substance of her moral claim.

For that, she would need to describe the events that had motivated her during her time on Sentik. The mission to Devron II remained classified, and so she would not be able to reveal its details: the location; the identities of the seven-member Starfleet team, which had included Captain Harriman and "Iron Mike" Paris; and the reason for the mission—namely, the Romulans' attempt to infiltrate the Neutral Zone and establish a covert base there. But even without divulging such specifics, she felt confident that she could still give an account of what had occurred, and especially of what had been sacrificed.

As Sulu charted the story in her mind, she absently reached

forward and plucked her wineglass from atop the table. She slid her middle and ring fingers around the stem and raised the glass to her lips, pausing briefly to note the wine's intense violet-red color, and to sample its strong bouquet of aniseed. She sipped it, and recognized at once the Argelian vintage, so similar to an Earth Tempranillo. It was one of her favorites, and one she'd never encountered anywhere but on Argelius.

Sulu peered over toward the bar, to where the bartender had retreated. When their eyes met, he lifted his glass, part toast, part encouragement that she continue with her story, she thought. Curious, but with no time to dwell on the odd circumstances surrounding this tavern or its host, she set the glass down and returned to Sentik IV.

Feeling as though I needed some air, I opened the front door of Hana's cabin and walked out into the dreary day. She and I hadn't said much more to each other after she'd made it clear that she would be staying there—that she would be *dying* there—no matter what I said or thought. I hadn't asked about her time on Sentik, and she hadn't asked about mine in Starfleet. Nor had she mentioned her son, my father. Walking alone between Hana's cabin and her dying crops, and figuratively between the needs of her failing life and a quick return to my own existence, I wished that I could speak with my father, seek his opinion on what I should do, draw on his strength, wisdom, and experience. But that was impossible.

Still, my choice seemed clear. The *Enterprise* was scheduled to depart on its year-long mission in five weeks, and I needed not only to be on it at that time, but to prepare my ship and crew before then. To that end, I had one week to spend on Sentik before starting on the three-and-a-half-day journey back to Starbase Magellan. I'd thought I would utilize that time to help Hana get situated in an assisted-care facility, but that obviously wasn't going to happen. She was an adult, and though she was in poor physical condition, her mind seemed sharp as ever. I had no right to impress upon Hana my opinions about what would be best for her. She was entitled to make her own decisions about her life, no matter the impact on others.

And really, how much effect would her choices have on me? That was only the third time I'd seen Hana in my forty-four years, and the truth was that I'd spent most of my existence blissfully unaware of the events transpiring in her life. And yet for all of that, leaving her there by herself in her diminished state seemed wrong.

As my stride brought me nearer the failing crops, it occurred to me that the deteriorating forms of the plants provided fitting imagery for Hana's own condition. I thought of my grandfather, recalling his poetic nature, and how he'd once touched my soul with his words. What would he have wanted me to do in that circumstance, I wondered.

Something cool suddenly struck my cheek, then slid down my face. I held my hand out, palm up, and waited, eventually feeling several other drops fall from the sky. I peered upward, and saw that the clouds had thickened and darkened, threatening a rainstorm. Not wanting to get caught in a downpour, but not wanting to return to Hana's farmhouse either, I headed instead for the barn, a simple structure not much larger than the cabin.

I passed a stone well along the way, then trotted through a large, open doorway. Inside the unlighted interior of the barn, the smell of hay and animals was strong. Birds clucked at the far end, and I heard a couple of larger beasts moving about in nearby stalls.

I turned and looked back out at the overcast day. The temperature had dropped since I'd first arrived, and my breath formed evanescent puffs of white when I exhaled. The rain grew heavier as I watched. I peered skyward again, and the image of the unbroken cloud cover quickly sent my thoughts back to a similar scene I'd witnessed at a different time, in a different place.

My mind traveled then, from the gray haze of Sentik IV to the miasma enshrouding another world.

•   •   •

I'd first seen the forbidding sight from space. The pall enveloping the planet churned and roiled, a cauldron of bleak shadows. I was piloting one of two warp shuttles, which together were taking a team of seven officers, including myself, to gather critical information from the veiled world. Starfleet Intelligence had uncovered evidence that renegades had established a covert base there, on the cusp of Federation space, and from which they intended to strike at both military and civilian targets. Our mission was to find and infiltrate the compound, obtain data detailing the plans of the renegades and the locations of any other bases, then return that information directly to Starfleet Command.

We neared the planet as stealthily as possible, shutting down the warp drive of each shuttle, employing only passive sensors, and masking our approach by riding the tail of a comet as it fell toward the system's star. When the burning ball of dust and ice passed as close to our destination as it would get, we flew the shuttles from the cover of the plasma cone. Seeking to reestablish concealment as quickly as possible, we sped toward the clouds, my shuttle closely following behind the first.

The cabin in the shuttle I piloted was quiet during the short journey, the only sounds the hum of the impulse drive and the beeps and chirps of the navigational and helm controls as they responded to my touch. I felt my weight shift as I began our descent, the planet's natural pull asserting itself over our craft's inertial dampers. As we soared through the atmosphere and into the thick layer of clouds, the view of the lead shuttle through the forward ports vanished.

Turbulence began to buffet the hull. I adjusted the trim, attempting to compensate, and succeeded briefly. But then the shuttle jolted, as though struck by something solid. The cabin began to tremble, and none of the corrections I tried calmed the movement.

"What's going on?" I asked the officer—a man named Mike—seated to my left at the primary console. I glanced over to see him operating the sensor panel.

"We're passing through a column of ash and rock," he announced after a few seconds. I looked up through the forward viewing ports again, but saw only the dark vapors I'd thought were simply clouds. At the same time, I recalled the mission briefing, which had mentioned the planet's sporadic but significant geological activity. From habit born of long experience, I reached down and grabbed hold of the strap concealed in the side of my chair, then fixed it across my lap.

"Secure yourself," I said over my shoulder to Mike and the other two members of the team aboard the shuttle. "I think we've come down in the middle of a volcanic eruption." I sent my hands feverishly across the helm controls, intending to halt our descent and take us into a wide turn, even though that would mean breaking from our planned flight path and parting from the other shuttle. But if it was a volcano below us, I wanted to get clear of the plume.

The bow of the shuttle suddenly lurched upward. I felt the safety strap tighten over my legs as my body threatened to fly from my seat, but I remained in place. I thought I heard somebody cry out in pain behind me, but I had no time to find out who it was. Around me, the cabin grew loud, the sound of the wind extreme as the shuttle hurtled through the air. Something—probably rock ejecta spewed from the volcano—had clearly struck from below, compromising the noise-suppression plating and altering our attitude.

I worked the helm to right the shuttle, easing its nose down onto a level trajectory. Ash and rock pelted the hull, the impacts audible in the cabin, like hailstones beating down on a tin roof. "Give me a direction," I yelled, raising my voice to be heard. When I received no response, I peered to my left, and saw Mike pulling himself up from the floor and back into his chair, from which he'd doubtless been thrown. "I need the shortest distance to get us clear," I shouted.

"Working on it," he called, bending over the console. "Engaging active sensors," he added, and didn't wait for authorization from the captain who led our mission. I looked up and stared through the viewports, searching for clear sky somewhere ahead. "I've got it," Mike finally yelled above the din. "Relative bearing: thirty-five degrees."

My fingers moved rapidly across the helm controls, sending the shuttle onto that course. I was grateful that our nearest exit from the plume lay before us, and not behind. I gazed through the viewports again and waited, hoping that nothing else would strike us before we made it into open sky.

Seconds passed . . . one, two, five, ten . . . and then at last the murk fell away. At once, the flight of the shuttle settled down, though with the noise-suppression plating no longer intact, it remained loud in the cabin. Smoke and clouds still covered the sky above us, and soot and smoldering pieces of volcanic rock continued to rain down, but we'd escaped the furor of the eruption itself. Below, the great green expanse of the planet spread out before us.

"We're out of it," I called back to the others. I quickly resumed our descent, visually searching for the first shuttle.

"Oh no," I heard Mike say, and before I could ask him anything, I spied the cause of his exclamation: a corkscrew of black smoke rose in front of us, different from the clouds and ash through which we'd been passing. I followed it down to its source, and saw far below us the other shuttle spinning out of control, flames streaking out of its aft section. "The other shuttle's been hit," Mike yelled. "It's going down." He called out its altitude, and then: "Twenty seconds until it hits the planet surface."

I felt a presence step up beside me, to one of the starboard panels. "Targeting transporter," I heard the captain say. Through the viewports, I saw a flare of light emerge from the first shuttle, brighter than the fires already consuming it. Two seconds later, a fractured warp nacelle pinwheeled toward us. I banked our shuttle hard to port, and we plunged past the broken engine structure, missing it by the narrowest of margins.

"Ten seconds," Mike called.

To my right, the captain said something, but I couldn't make out his words above the noise of the wind. Another sound suddenly grew in the cabin, though, even as Mike continued his countdown. Hearing the familiar whine of the transporter, I couldn't help but turn and peer back toward the small platform in the aft section of the shuttle. I felt enormous relief as three forms materialized there, all of them moving.

Spinning back to my console, I was just in time to see a fireball blaze into existence amid the greenery of the massive rain forest below us. "The shuttle's down," Mike reported.

Again, I felt a presence beside me. "Land us as quickly as possible," the captain said in my ear. "I don't care where. We can't take the chance that the active sensors, the explosion, or the transporter have given us away."

"Yes, sir," I said. I worked the helm controls, pointing the shuttle's bow down at a steep angle, at the same time taking us into a tight turn. We would spiral down to the planet while maintaining as narrow a flight profile as possible.

As we turned, the volcano came into view. The massive mountain rose high into the air, a dark, dense column of smoke, ash, and rock exploding from it and obscuring its peak. Farther below, rivers of glowing lava streamed from rents in the slopes and flowed downward.

For a moment, an eerie calm settled over the noisy cabin. I heard a moan behind me, and guessed that one of the crew members of the first shuttle had suffered injuries when their craft had been struck by the volcanic debris. I could only hope that they hadn't been hurt too badly.

"How much time until we land?" the captain asked.

I checked the altimeter, but before I could reply, Mike suddenly yelled once more. "I'm reading weapons fire."

I acted even before the captain called for evasive maneuvers, but too late. A bolt of energy hammered into the shuttle, and I felt grateful that we'd powered down the warp drive after reaching the system. Still, the shuttle sheared from its course, and I worked to bring the helm back under my control. As I did so, a second energy blast sliced past the bow, missing us by only meters.

"I've got a read on the source of the weapons fire," Mike reported.

"Aim phasers," the captain ordered.

"I'm reading just one battery on the ground," Mike continued. "Coordinates are—"

Another energy burst slammed into the shuttle, and then another. The cabin shuddered, and an overload surged through the engineering circuits. I saw the result on the readouts as the generator spiked and shut down.

The shuttle dropped a thousand meters in just seconds.

The backup engaged automatically, throttling up and braking our rate of descent.

Again, the captain spoke from a position beside me. "Crash us," he said.

"Sir?"

"Keep the shuttle as intact as possible, but make it look as though we've been blasted out of the sky, before we really are blasted out of the sky."

"Yes, sir," I said, even as I searched through my years of experience at the helm for the best possible method of complying with the captain's orders. At that moment, a burst of coherent blue light streaked past the viewports, and an instant later, another shot pounded into the hull. My readouts showed a power surge course through the circuitry again, and the transporter went down.

"Brace yourselves," I yelled to the others. I tensed my own body, and positioned one of my hands at the antigrav controls. I desperately hoped that the plan I'd extemporized would work.

Then I cut the main power, and the shuttle fell from the sky.

As I stood in the doorway of Hana's barn, peering out at the rain and thinking back to that mission, I realized that I couldn't simply leave Sentik IV. For the assignment to thwart the renegades, I'd been asked to step away for a brief time from my regular

Starfleet duties in order to take part in the dangerous, potentially deadly reconnaissance, all in the name of the greater good. Although the parallels were hardly exact, I saw a similar set of circumstances with respect to Hana's situation.

While she hadn't asked me to look after her, somebody else—Rosenzweig—had, and I had to wonder if, given the chance, my father would have done so too. In order to stay on Sentik, I would have to take a few more weeks away from the *Enterprise* and the preparations for its upcoming voyage, but Xintal—Commander Xintal Linojj, my executive officer—was more than capable enough to step in for me. Spending time with Hana might be uncomfortable and unsatisfying, maybe even difficult, but I'd obviously experienced far worse things during my lifetime. As I saw it, a greater good was involved there too: Hana's need for care might not have been as dramatic as the need for Starfleet to protect the Federation from terrorists, but it was a real cause nonetheless, and one that I had the power to serve.

I made the decision. I activated the transporter recall and beamed back to the *Armstrong*. There, I recorded a message to Admiral Ratnaswamy, explaining the situation and requesting that my leave be extended another three weeks. Since it would be days before I received a response, I made it plain that I would not depart from Sentik IV until the week prior to the *Enterprise*'s scheduled launch. I'd arrive back at Starbase Magellan with a few days to spare, time enough, I felt, for Xintal to brief me on whatever I needed to know before our mission.

Before I touched the transmit control, I thought about speaking to Hana first, but determined that I didn't need to do so. This was my choice, and though I would certainly do my best to honor her wishes during my stay, there could be no debate about her condition. She needed help, and I aimed to provide it for her.

I sent the message to Starfleet Command, then transported back to Hana's house.

· · · ·

When I walked through the front door of the cabin, I was startled to see somebody moving on the far side of the room. I initially thought that a child from the community had entered the house for some reason, and I'd taken two steps forward before I realized that the undersized form belonged to Hana. Stunned because I'd believed her confined to her bed, I stopped for a moment and stared.

Hana leaned heavily against one of the cupboards that marched along the base of the back wall. She must have heard me come in, because she looked over in my direction. As I'd noticed earlier, her sluggish, purposeful movements made her appear brittle, as though she might break apart at any moment.

"Hana, what are you doing?" I asked sharply, striding over to her. "Shouldn't you be in bed?" I took hold of her elbow, concerned that, left on her own, she might fall, as she had out in the fields.

"I thought you'd gone," Hana said, peering up at me with undisguised irritation.

"No," I said, returning her pique with my own. "I've decided to extend my leave and stay here a few more weeks."

"What?" Hana said, her voice rising and her eyes going wide. "Why would you do that?"

"Because—" *Because you're my grandmother*, I thought, but I wasn't sure that such a declaration would have convinced even me of my intentions. All I knew was that Hana needed assistance, she had nobody else, and staying a little longer was the right thing to do. "Because you need help," I finished.

Hana carefully pulled her elbow from my grasp, and then turned back to the cupboard. "I'm old," she muttered, almost too low for me to hear. "I'm not an invalid." She opened the cabinet door, and a heavy, plantlike scent wafted out. Inside the storage area sat piled several small caches of what appeared to be different vegetables, fruits, tubers, and nuts. I wondered if she had grown all of it on her own land, or had traded some of her own crops for those of others on Sentik. I suspected the latter.

As Hana cautiously bent to reach for something, her ancient joints emitted snaps and pops. The sounds seemed to me like the forewarning of an imminent collapse. "Do you want something to eat?" I asked her. "I can go back to my shuttle and prepare a meal for us with the food synthesizer."

"We don't use *food synthesizers* here," Hana said, pronouncing the words as though they were an epithet. She continued reaching into the cupboard.

"Well then," I said, "I guess I can make dinner for us here."

Hana stopped then, but she didn't offer a response. She didn't immediately straighten, either, and for a second, I thought she might topple over. Again, I reached out to steady her. As my hand settled around her upper arm, Hana stood up, reached for it with her other hand, and brushed it away. Then, holding on to the line of cupboards along the back wall, she made her way toward the table.

Once she cleared the open cabinet door, I knelt down and peered inside. I saw items that looked familiar—tomatoes and strawberries, potatoes and walnuts—and some that didn't. I recognized the squat, red-leafed plants from Hana's own fields, though I'd never seen them before my arrival there. Opening the other cupboards, I found various other foods, mostly in short supply. There were also spices, utensils, kitchenware, and several large jugs of water.

I looked over at Hana as she reached the table and dropped into a chair there. Just the short trip from her bedroom appeared to have exhausted her. I couldn't recall ever seeing somebody who seemed as old as she did at that moment.

In silence, I gathered a group of the foods I recognized, and out of which I could make a meal. I started a fire in the stove, then washed, prepared, and cooked everything. Hana said nothing as I moved about, and I didn't feel up to starting a conversation with her.

Finally, I set two plates down on the table, one in front of Hana, and the other where I would sit. Beside each dish, I put a fork, knife, and napkin, along with a mug of water, which seemed to be the only thing in the cabin to drink. Then I retrieved the chair I'd taken into the bedroom, and sat down across from Hana.

"Thank you," she said.

"You're welcome," I said, and smiled. I looked over at her, but her head was down, her gaze apparently on her meal. I shrugged, settled my napkin in my lap, picked up my fork and knife, and started eating. At least I'd finally heard a kind word from Hana.

But those were the last things either one of said for the rest of the night.

That first day with Hana set the tone for those that came after. In asking me nothing about my life, in telling me nothing about herself, in saying almost nothing to me at all, she'd made it clear that she had no interest in getting to know me. I supposed I should have expected that, considering our almost nonexistent shared history. To be honest, even though I'd gone to Hana's aid on Sentik IV, I had little desire to get to know her. She'd always been a stranger to me—as best I could tell, had *chosen* to be a stranger to me—and I knew that wasn't going to change in just a few weeks.

And so we spent most of our days in silence. I retrieved a bedroll from the shuttle and slept on the floor in the main room of the cabin, hanging a blanket over the window in order to block out the moon at night, and the sun at dawn. In the morning, before Hana rose, I'd collect water from the well, check for eggs in the bird coop at the far end of the barn, feed the animals, and get ready to prepare breakfast for us. Hana typically woke midmorning, changed out of her nightclothes, and made her way out into the main room. While she made a trip to the outhouse behind the cabin, I'd start cooking our meal.

On a couple of occasions, most often in the mornings, Hana appeared to have trouble walking, and I went to her to lend a hand. In every case, my efforts were rebuffed. In time, I learned not to bother even trying.

After breakfast, Hana would retreat to her bedroom. At first, I thought that she was sleeping through much of the day, but whenever I would check on her, I'd find her awake. Sometimes she sat on her bed, propped up against the pillows, but most often I would find her perched beneath the window in the back wall, atop the chest there. Most of the time, she didn't seem to be doing anything, although several times I spied a book tucked against the side of her leg.

In the evenings, we went through the same routine as in the mornings. Hana would come out of her bedroom, make a trip out back, and return to wash up and sit down to dinner. Afterward, she would go back to her room once more, usually without a word other than the thanks she would tender for the meal I'd made for her.

On my second day with Hana, I searched out the two medics who resided on Sentik. They verified for me the results of their examination of Hana, confirming what she and Rosenzweig had already told me, and what I'd corroborated myself with the medical tricorder I'd brought with me. She suffered from no particular health problems beyond her advanced years. Still, that was enough for the medics to conclude that a journey of any significant length—and certainly any voyage off-planet—would likely kill her.

A few days after that, I received a response to my request to extend my leave. During those days on Sentik, between making breakfast and dinner for Hana—she ate only twice a day—I would return to the *Armstrong*. Among other activities, I'd have an afternoon meal; I'd inspect the shuttle's systems as a matter of course; I'd sometimes download to a padd nonclassified data about the *Enterprise*'s upcoming mission, so that I could take it back to the cabin to study; and I'd check the comm system. When the message arrived from Starfleet Command, I was pleased to find that they'd agreed to extend my leave, though I really hadn't given them much choice in the matter. At the same time, Admiral Ratnaswamy made it perfectly clear that he expected me back at Star-

base Magellan in time to resume command of the *Enterprise* prior
to the start of its long-range mission.

On my thirteenth day on Sentik, two and a half weeks before I
would have to depart, Hana was late rising. As midday approached,
the thought rose in my mind that perhaps she'd passed away during the night. Filled with trepidation, I knocked lightly at her door.
When I received no answer, I pushed it partway open and poked
my head inside.

The bed was empty.

Surprised, I threw the door wide and stepped into the bedroom. I first looked to my right, toward the chest that sat against
the back wall, but Hana wasn't there. Before I could look elsewhere, I heard a sound. I turned and peered down, to the floor to
the left of the bed, and saw Hana on her knees, apparently struggling to pull herself up.

I raced to her, kneeling down beside her and putting my arms
around her shoulders in an attempt to steady her. She was still in
her nightclothes, I saw. "Are you all right?" I asked, and I could
hear the concern in my own voice.

"No," she replied, and I thought she meant that she'd suffered
some sort of injury when she'd fallen, or perhaps that some condition had overtaken her and caused her to lose her balance. But
then, just as she'd done on each of the occasions when I'd tried to
aid her physically, she pushed me away. *No* didn't mean that she
wasn't all right; it meant that she didn't want my help.

"Hana, please," I said, and I reached out to her again.

"No," she barked, the word louder and sharper than before. I
pulled back, struck by her vehemence, both because of the contrast with her overall infirmity, and because of the anger I heard
in her voice. But then something made me think that perhaps it
was not anger I heard, but fear. Except that didn't make any sense
to me. Hana and I might have had, at best, a strained relationship, but I could think of no reason that she would fear me.

"Hana, I just want—" I tried again.

"Get out," Hana cut me off. "I can do it myself. I'm not an invalid."

I felt my mouth drop open. Was this Hana's pride speaking? It astonished me to think that at her age she could demonstrate such foolishness.

"Hana—"

"Get out!"

I stayed there on my knees, astounded—and angry. I'd taken leave from my Starfleet captaincy and traveled light-years to see this woman I hardly knew, because I'd been told that she needed my help—and she *did* need my help—and that was how she treated me. I didn't need or even expect her gratitude, but neither did I need or expect her enmity.

"All right," I said calmly, frostily. "If that's what you want." I felt immature for saying the words, for the attitude behind them, but I couldn't stop myself. I'd tried more than once, and I couldn't force Hana to accept my assistance—not in that manner, anyway. I rose and walked from the room, then continued past the fireplace and through the front door.

Outside, the weather had grown colder as winter approached. It had rained on most of the days since I'd arrived, but it was dry at that moment, though the gloomy sky threatened to change that. I stopped and put my hands on my hips, considering what to do. I alternately felt sympathy and resentment for Hana, but going back inside didn't seem like a viable option right then.

Before me stretched Hana's crops. They were clearly dying, their leaves flagging, the surfaces of the plants duller in color than they had been, and in some cases, beginning to rot. Hana did not have much left in the way of supplies, and there before me was the reason why: She'd obviously been unable to reap most of her crops before her physical condition had deteriorated as much as it had. That she had managed to harvest any of the plants at all amazed me.

I wasn't concerned about a lack of food for Hana, at least not while I remained on Sentik, because I knew that I could supplement her supplies via the *Armstrong*'s food synthesizer. Anticipating that Hana might protest, I'd already brought some of her fruits and vegetables, roots and nuts back to the shuttle for analysis. Later, the food synthesizer would be able to reproduce approximations of them. If need be, I supposed that I could also gather some of Hana's crops myself.

Right then, though, the failing crops presented a different opportunity for me. Still feeling the adrenaline rush of my emotion, I paced over to the barn and searched through it until I found the tool I was looking for: a scythe. I grabbed it and carried it out into the fields, where I hefted it and sent its arced, pointed blade slicing through the stalks of the short, red-leafed plants nearest the cabin. The forceful, almost wild movement felt good. I moved down the first row of plants, felling one after another, then moved back the other way down the next row, all the while pondering why I'd gone to Sentik in the first place.

I'd been presented with choices, of course, first whether or not to go to Hana's aid when Rosenzweig's message had arrived, and second, whether or not to return to Magellan and the *Enterprise* after just a week there, or to stay and care for Hana a bit longer. In both cases, I'd somehow concluded that the right thing to do would be to help Hana, my reasoning no doubt based on my fundamentally unfulfilled desire for a strong, happy family.

The truth was that I hadn't ever had much of a family life. Until I was seven years old, I lived exclusively with my mother, not even meeting my father until after she died. I'd met none of my mother's relatives; if she'd even had any, she never spoke of them, deftly avoiding any questions I'd ever raised. Once I went to live with my father, I found a similar circumstance, although I did eventually meet my father's parents and aunt.

My resentment fueled by my recollections, I swung the scythe furiously, downing the plants and sending some of them flying several meters away. Chilled when I'd first come out of the cabin, my body became overheated, my skin wet with perspiration. I wanted to cry out in frustration. *Didn't I deserve a real family?* I asked myself.

But I had no family, not really, and yet there I was, leaving behind, at least for a time, the life I loved in order to meet familial responsibilities. But why should I feel obligated, I wondered, to somebody I hardly knew, I didn't like, and who obviously didn't like me? I was paying the price for being Hana's granddaughter, and yet I'd never experienced any benefits from that relationship.

After half an hour, spent from my exertions in the fields, I stopped. I lay the scythe down and put my hands on my knees, pausing to catch my breath, which came in great, gasping gulps. Once my respiration had calmed, I headed toward the barn, where I intended to retrieve some baskets in which I could then collect the crops I'd chopped down. But as I neared the barn, I thought of Hana on the floor beside her bed, and my concern rose for her once more. I switched direction and went back to the cabin.

When I walked inside, I saw immediately that both Hana's bedroom door and the back door stood open. I crossed to the far wall, verifying as I passed Hana's bedroom that she was not there. I peered outside, but didn't see her, and so I waited for a few minutes, until the door to the outhouse began to open. I quickly ducked back inside, not wanting Hana to know that I'd been watching for her.

A few seconds later, I stepped through the door. Hana was there on the path to the outhouse, her head down, shuffling toward the cabin. I noticed that she still hadn't changed out of her nightclothes.

"Hana," I said, choosing simply to ignore what had happened earlier. "I'm going to make breakfast for us now." The day had already slipped into the afternoon, but neither one of us had yet eaten.

Hana stopped and looked up.

I waved, and then not waiting for a response, I went back inside and started to prepare our meal.

That night, I dreamed of family. But not mine.

On the mission to infiltrate the renegade base, I'd brought the shuttle down hard into the middle of the rain forest. I'd let us fall from the sky, as the captain had ordered, our engine power shut down. Fortunately, although the transporter had been knocked out by the second weapons strike, the two systems I needed for my plan had remained intact.

As the shuttle plummeted toward the jungle canopy, I utilized the emergency thrusters to decelerate at the last moment, engaging them in the few seconds before we hit. The green expanse of the rain-forest cover braked us even more, and once we'd penetrated the top level of vegetation, I overcharged the antigravs. We didn't exactly soft-land—part of the frame twisted upon impact, and fractured in a couple of places—but the shuttle did come down relatively intact.

Everybody survived the landing with cuts and sprains, scrapes and contusions. The three officers from the first shuttle had been more seriously hurt when their craft was hit. All three of them had suffered burns and broken bones, and the engineer had also had the forward portion of her foot severed.

While two of us broke out the medical equipment from the emergency survival cache and treated the injuries of the crew, two others used the equipment we'd stowed before the mission and erected a sensor veil about the shuttle. Above us, the jungle canopy showed almost no signs of our violent passage through it, most of the leaves and other vegetation more or less snapping back into place behind us. It would take some time for the renegades to locate us, and with any luck, they would in the interim believe that everybody aboard the shuttle had died in the crash.

We spent the rest of the day and night in the shuttle, nursing ourselves back to health. Four of us alternated taking watch and tending to the three burn victims. It took twenty-four hours to complete the treatments for their blistering flesh.

Our planned reconnaissance and incursion into the renegade base, predicated on having a pair of shuttlecraft, had been completely undermined. We hypothesized that the collision and subsequent crash of the first shuttle, along with our use of the second shuttle's sensors and transporter, had betrayed our presence to the renegades. The only advantage we'd gained from the fiasco was learning the location of their base—assuming that the weapons battery that had fired on us was positioned on or near their compound.

That was enough for the captain.

Rather than escape once we'd repaired the shuttle—among other damage, the hull had cracked in two places, the phaser coils had melted, and the antigrav system had burned out—the captain decided to endeavor to fulfill our mission. While the engineer would remain behind to render the shuttle operational, which would likely take several days, the rest of us would divide up into teams of two and try to make our way on foot to the renegade base; the shuttle's transporter was beyond repair. Once one of the teams had retrieved the target intelligence, they would signal the others, and the engineer would bring the shuttle to recover the teams and depart. A plan fraught with risks, to be sure, but considering the importance of the mission's goal, one the captain decided that we should attempt.

In the middle of our second day on the planet, the three teams outfitted ourselves with phasers, communicators, tricorders, medkits, portable beacons, individual sensor veils, heavy broadbladed knives, bedrolls, and water. Less than fifty klicks away, the base would have been within a long day's journey had our routes to it been unimpeded. Given the dense jungle growth, though, we estimated that it would take us three to four days to reach our destination. We could have utilized our phasers to cut through the vegetation, but while the sensor veils would prevent the renegades from scanning our bodies, they would not adequately mask the output of energy weapons.

I was teamed with Mike. He and I would travel on a route that would arc west through the rain forest, while another team would arc east. The captain's team would take the central route, and therefore would likely arrive first.

Mike and I alternated taking point. Hacking through the vines, trees, bushes, and other plants was backbreaking work, particularly in the thick, humid atmosphere of the jungle. Before long, my arms ached with the efforts of forcing my long, broad blade through the underbrush, and my clothing—a formfitting jumpsuit that allowed great freedom of movement—was soaked through.

Before beginning our trek, I worried about Mike. He was a youthful man, with soft features and light hair, younger in appearance than in actuality. Although he and I were the same age, he looked probably ten years my junior. Part of that might have been the result of his small stature. But even though his size made him appear fragile, he had little trouble navigating through the dense growth of the forest, and I sometimes had to push myself to keep up with him.

Throughout our journey, we stopped regularly for water and rest, pacing ourselves so that we would make it to the renegade base with enough energy, if necessary, to carry out our mission. We didn't speak as we hiked along, our focus on achieving our goal too intense.

On our first night in the rain forest, we both tried to sleep at the same time. We sealed our bedrolls around us, and set up a tricorder to passively scan our surroundings within a ten-meter radius. At first, though, we were awakened every few minutes to deal with various creatures as they came near: reptiles, huge insects and arachnids, several small primates, and on one occasion, a lithe, six-legged beast with twelve-centimeter fangs. Fortunately, all ended up either scared of us, or uninterested in large, moving prey. After the first hour, though, we decided that one of us would keep watch for two hours while the other one slept, so that we could each get at least some periods of uninterrupted rest.

I woke on the morning of the second day of our journey in terrible pain, feeling as though my head was going to explode. As I came fully awake, I cried out, the sensation incredibly intense that the right side of my face was on fire. I reached to unseal my bedroll, but couldn't concentrate enough to do so.

"Demora?" I heard a voice say, and somewhere in the fog of my consciousness I identified it as belonging to Mike. I didn't care. I wanted one thing only: to reach up and peel the flesh from my skull. As I moved within the bedroll, though, its material brushed against my face, sending new bolts of pain slicing through my head. Again I cried out.

"Demora," I heard Mike say again, and then suddenly I was free, the bedroll gone from around me. I sent my hands up to my face, intending to dig my fingernails into my skin and claw it off. "Demora," I heard again, closer and louder, and then I found myself unable to move my hands. I struggled, without success, and a high keening sound reached my ears. Somewhere, something hissed, and then everything went dark.

When I came to some time later, Mike stood over me. The unimaginable pain on the right half of my face had mercifully faded to a dull ache—still pervasive, still torturous, but at least bearable. I raised my hand to feel the area.

"I wouldn't," Mike said crouching down beside me. "It's swollen, and probably still painful to the touch." I saw that he held a tricorder in one hand.

"What happened?" I asked, recalling the monstrous agony I'd experienced, so great that I'd been unable to form coherent thoughts.

"A creature from this planet," Mike explained. "It somehow got into your bedroll and stung you in the face. You started screaming, and I pulled you free."

"But how? You were standing watch, scanning the area." It didn't occur to me for an instant that Mike might have failed to adequately perform his duties.

"The creature doesn't show up on sensors, and I never saw it," he said. "I can't explain why."

Slowly, I pushed myself up to a sitting position. I looked around, but had trouble focusing with my right eye, and I realized that the bloated flesh of my face had pushed it almost completely closed. "Am I going to be all right?" I asked.

"Yes," Mike said confidently. "The creature pumped its venom into you, but I've managed to clean your wound of most of it.

I've administered an anti-inflammatory from the medkit, and a serum that will counteract the toxin. The swelling has already gone down considerably, and any pain you still feel should vanish shortly. You should be back to normal before long."

"Thank you," I said, grateful for Mike's assistance.

He nodded, and then said, "However badly the creature's chemistry hurt you, yours was apparently no match for it."

"What do you mean?" I asked.

"Once it stung you, it only lived a few more minutes," Mike told me. "I believe some element in your bloodstream poisoned it."

"It's dead?" I asked, and Mike pointed. I followed the line of his finger. On the ground not far from where I sat atop my bedroll, a black, many-legged creature lay unmoving, its hairy digits sprawled outward around a barrel-shaped body the size of my fist. To me, it looked like something out of a nightmare. I felt my mouth drop open at the thought of that thing slicing into my flesh and shooting its bane into me.

"It's all right, Demora," Mike said, obviously recognizing the emotion I felt.

"I know," I said, looking over at him simply because I didn't want to look at the creature any longer. "We should get moving."

"We will," Mike said, standing and backing up to sit on the exposed, misshapen root of a tree. He slipped the carry strap of his tricorder over one shoulder. "Let's give it a few more minutes, though. I don't want any leaves or branches brushing against your face right now."

"How long will we have to wait?" I asked, the importance of our mission reasserting itself in my mind.

Mike held up the tricorder and scanned me. "Probably not more than thirty minutes," he said.

"Okay," I said, and we lapsed into silence. Around us, the sounds of the forest closed in: water dripping, leaves rustling, branches creaking as trees shifted, birds chirping, other animals scuttling through the canopy far above us. I lowered myself back onto the ground and waited. By degrees, the discomfort I felt in my face diminished.

After a few minutes, Mike asked me an unexpected question. "Are you married, Demora?" he wanted to know.

I blinked. "No, I'm not," I said with a grin, "except maybe to Starfleet." I gestured with both hands at the rain forest around us, and to the right side of my face, trying to indicate that I'd obviously do anything Command asked of me. I wondered why Mike would have posed such a question to me, and then I realized the reason. "Are *you* married?" I asked.

Mike looked at me from where he sat on the root that had grown free of the jungle floor. A smile rose on his face like a morning sun peeking over a horizon. "Yeah, I am," he said brightly. "Eight years now."

"You're a lucky man," I said, and meant it. I also hoped that my statement would hold true for the rest of our mission. So far, it had not exactly gone as planned.

"Yeah," he said again, and nodded. He was quiet for a moment. Somewhere in the distance, one of the beasts of this world called out, its voice like a bass horn. Then Mike spoke up again. "I've also got two sons," he said. "One of them was born just before we began this mission. I haven't even met him yet."

"You will," I said, perhaps a little too quickly to be convincing. Mike surely knew as well as I did the dangers that lay ahead of us at the renegade base. The volcanic eruption, the weapons strikes on the shuttle, the hard landing, and my encounter with the spider-like creature this morning might only be the beginning of our travails.

"Yeah, I know I will," Mike agreed. He quieted again, peering into the middle distance for a short time. Then he seemed to gather himself, and said, "Wanna see a picture?"

"Yes," I answered eagerly, and climbed back up to a sitting position. Mike pulled his tricorder from where it hung about his shoulder, then keyed in what appeared to be a complex control sequence. The device responded with various tones, and then he entered a second code. Finally, he stood up and walked over to where I sat on his bedroll, my legs now folded beneath me. He squatted down and held out the tricorder before me.

On the display, in what looked like a hospital room, a beautiful woman with long, fiery red hair lay in bed. Sitting beside her, his legs hanging down, was an adorable little boy with full, rosy cheeks, and whose bright hair matched her own. A man and a woman, both older, stood to one side of the bed, and two men, also older, stood on the other. In the crook of the red-headed woman's arm, his face just visible within the blanket wrapped around it, was a newborn baby.

"My wife and my firstborn," Mike said, pointing. "Those are my parents on the left, and my wife's on the right."

"And *that*," I said, raising my own finger to point at the baby, "is your new son."

"Yeah," Mike said, and the wide smile returned to his face.

"You have a beautiful family," I said.

"Thank you," he said. "I can't wait to see them again."

On that mission, in real life, I'd said nothing after that. I'd just nodded and smiled, and placed what I hoped was a reassuring hand on Mike's shoulder. But in my dream, I opened my mouth to speak. Asleep in Hana's cabin on Sentik IV, I fought to keep myself from saying anything, fought to take control of my dream self, but I couldn't. "You'll see them again," I told Mike. "Soon."

I woke up with a start, propped up on my hands, and with the sensation that I'd just called out in my sleep. It took me a few seconds to orient myself, to recall that I was in my bedroll on the floor of Hana's cabin, a long distance and a long time from those days in that rain forest with Mike. I listened in the darkness for any sound from Hana's room, concerned that I might have woken her. Finally, hearing nothing, I lay back down in the bedroll, exhausted.

I tried to push away the images from my dream, but they stayed with me. Not the shuttle crash or the crew's injuries, not the hideous creature that had attacked me, but Mike sitting in the middle of that jungle, talking about his loved ones, showing me a picture of them. And I remembered envying him for his good fortune at having such a family, and pitying him for having to be away from them.

In my grandmother's house, I closed my eyes in the darkness, desperate to let go of my emotions and get some rest. But when morning came, I hadn't slept again at all.

Four weeks after I first arrived on Sentik IV, I prepared to depart. I collected the few items I'd brought from the *Armstrong* to Hana's cabin, and transported back with them to the shuttle. I charted my course back to Starbase Magellan and the *Enterprise*— back to my *life*—and entered it in the navigational computer. Then I went to bid farewell to Hana.

When I returned to the cabin, it was nearly midday, and I was surprised to see Hana's door still closed. In the last week, she'd taken to rising later in the morning than she had previously, and also to retiring earlier at night. And in just the past few days, she twice hadn't bothered changing out of her nightclothes even after she'd risen.

I tapped lightly at her door.

"Demora," came a whisper from the bedroom, barely audible. I think it was the first time Hana had said my name since we'd first spoken, just after my arrival.

I opened the door and peered inside. Hana lay in bed, and I walked over to stand beside her. When I gazed down at her, I was shocked to see tears pooled in her eyes. It seemed inconceivable to me that Hana would be sad to see me leave.

Before I could say anything, Hana spoke again. "Demora," she repeated, and a tear spilled from one eye and down her cheek, leaving behind a quicksilver trail. "I need help." The words still came in a whisper, so low that I wasn't sure that I'd heard them correctly.

"Hana, you'll be all right," I said, not knowing what else to tell her, but also believing the basic truth of my assertion. Hana was old and failing, but she could still get around, no matter how slowly. There was enough food stored in her cabin now—I'd restocked her cupboard both from what I'd cut down in the fields and from the food synthesizer aboard the *Armstrong*—and she seemed strong enough to prepare simple dishes for herself.

"No," Hana said, looking up at me with a wounded expression. "I won't be all right. I . . . I need help."

Suddenly, I understood that Hana's tears were not for me, but for herself. "What's wrong?" I asked. "What do you need?"

"I can't get up," she said, and now tears slid down both sides of her face. She wept, I realized, because she thought that she could no longer take care of herself.

"Hana," I said, "I can bring your breakfast to you here. We can prop you up against the pillows, and you can eat in bed. You don't need to get up."

"I need to go out back," she said, the very act of having to ask for such help obviously a terrible embarrassment for her.

"It's all right," I said. "I can use my shuttle's transporter to—"

"No," she pleaded.

"Well then," I said, considering how else I might be able to assist Hana. "I guess I can rig something up, bring it in here for—"

"No," she interrupted again, beseeching me. "Please . . . not yet, Demora."

"All right," I said. I leaned in over the bed and took hold of Hana, sliding one hand around her back and placing the other on her arm. I felt her recoil automatically from my touch, her flimsy body tensing, but then she relaxed her muscles. With great care, I helped her to the edge of the bed, and then up onto her feet. Her body seemed no heavier than if it had been made of paper.

It took us a long time to move out of her bedroom, through the back door, and over to the outhouse, but we eventually made it. Afterward, I walked her back into the cabin and headed for the table, where I intended to sit her down. But Hana told me that she wasn't strong enough, and that she'd rather go back to bed, if I wouldn't mind bringing her breakfast there. I did as she asked.

After we'd both eaten—she in her bed, and me at the table in the main room—I told Hana that I needed to visit the shuttle, and that I'd be back in a few minutes. I didn't know if she realized that I'd been scheduled to leave Sentik that day, but it was clear that if I did, she would not be able to survive on her own.

As I activated the transporter recall, I had no idea what I was going to do.

I sat at the *Armstrong*'s primary console, staring at it as though an answer might suddenly materialize there. On the navigational display, I saw the course I'd plotted that would take me back to Starbase Magellan, the *Enterprise*, and my crew. On the communications console, I saw the indicators that told me the system was ready to record and transmit a message.

Sitting motionless for a long time, I reviewed the impossible choice I had to make. Leave Hana—my grandmother—alone here on Sentik, unable to take care of herself; relocate her against her will, and in so doing, risk the journey killing her; or—

"Or what?" I asked myself aloud. Was I supposed to forgo living my own life in favor of somebody at the end of theirs? Somebody who'd never shown me even the slightest amount of love?

I continued staring at the shuttle's primary console, until in my mind it morphed into something else, into a control panel I'd once seen half a quadrant away from Sentik IV. It sat in the middle of the renegade base, in the middle of the immense rain forest, on a forbidden world.

For the third time since I'd arrived at Hana's, my memories took me back to that mission.

I verified the download of data from the renegades' computer system to my tricorder, the transfer rate blinking in green numerals across the panel display. Our basic mission had been to obtain details of the renegades' impending operations, and to identify the locations of any additional bases that might exist, but what I'd found in their comp system was much more than that. Once we delivered the information to Starfleet Command, they would be able to shut down the entire operation.

As I waited for the volumes of data to download, I worked the console into which I'd patched my tricorder, and from which I'd burrowed into the base's computer network. Sitting in the small room that housed a power substation, I reconfigured the display and brought up the information most vital to Starfleet Command. Reviewing it, I understood that the admirals' suspicions had wildly underestimated the scope of the renegades' strategy. Without the intelligence I had uncovered, the Federation would soon find itself at grave and possibly irreversible risk.

Abruptly, an alarm sounded, and a moment later, a male voice emerged form the comm system. "*Intruder alert, intruder alert,*" it said. "*Perimeter breach in section thirty-one alpha.*" I studied the data transfer, expecting it to be interrupted at any second, but the bits continued to flow.

Behind me, I heard the room's lone door glide open. "Demora," Mike called. "They've found us. We've got to get out of here." For the moment, I ignored him, and instead concentrated on bringing up a schematic of the base. "Demora!"

"It's not us," I declared. "We're not in section thirty-one alpha."

"That could be a code," Mike said. "They might–"

"No," I told him, tapping into the comm system in the base's command center. I grabbed a small silver speaker sitting on the panel and lifted it to my ear. I listened as one of the renegades ordered the prisoners brought to him. "No, it's not us," I said again to Mike. "They've got one of the other teams. Maybe both of them."

"Then they'll be looking for us soon," he asserted. "How much longer before you've got what we need?"

I threw down the speaker, sending it skittering across the panel, and checked the status monitor. "Sixty seconds," I said.

"I hope we've got that long," Mike said earnestly, and exited the power substation, obviously to resume standing guard for me.

Mike and I had arrived at the base on our fourth day hiking

through the jungle. Theoretically, the captain and his partner should have arrived there before we did, since they'd taken a more direct route, but we'd received no signal that they'd succeeded in the mission. The third team also could have arrived before us, but again, we'd received no such signal. And so it had fallen upon us to find a way inside in order to retrieve the data Starfleet Command needed.

As Mike and I had reconnoitered the base perimeter, happenstance had provided us a chance. Very close to where we hid in the jungle, a renegade guard had exited the compound, for no reason we could determine. Gambling that we weren't walking into a trap, we pounced, incapacitating the guard and hauling him back to the access hatch. Quickly, we utilized his hand and retina prints to breach the base's biometric safety measures. From there, it had been a short trip to the room with the computer interface.

I toggled the speaker selector, sending the command-center audio feed from the individual speaker I'd just used to a panel speaker. I listened as I heard a commotion, and then the sound of flesh against flesh. I recognized the voice of a man on our third team as he cried out in pain.

Behind me, the door slid open again. "Demora."

Over the comm system, I heard one of the renegades order both prisoners interrogated without regard to their health or survival. "Mike," I said, turning to look at him, "they're going to torture—"

"That can't matter right now," he said. "We've got to get out of here. Nothing's more important than that intelligence." He pointed to where my tricorder sat atop the console.

Knowing he was right, I turned back and checked the status monitor. "Ten seconds," I read, and then, "Five . . . three, two, one." I ripped the shielded patch cord from my tricorder. "Let's go," I said.

As Mike and I headed out the door of the power substation, I heard behind us the transmitted moans of the two people who'd made up our third team. Again, I felt the urge to do whatever it took to find them and free them, but I also knew that Mike was right about the critical importance of returning to Starfleet Command the renegade intelligence we'd collected.

And so we ran.

We didn't stop for an hour as we retraced the path we'd hacked through the rain forest. Once we'd cleared the renegade base, we'd sent a signal both back to the shuttle and to the captain's team, but so far, we'd heard nothing from either. For the moment, we could only hope that the engineer had been able to repair the shuttle and could get us off the planet and back to the Federation.

Breathing heavily and drenched in sweat, Mike and I finally slowed, and then stopped. For several minutes, we listened to the jungle around us, trying to detect any sound that might indicate that we'd been followed. We heard nothing of the kind.

"I think we're clear," I said.

"I hope so," Mike replied. "Now we just—"

A high-pitched whine suddenly filled the air, increasing rapidly in volume. I recognized it as the sound of an overload, and quickly drew my phaser and checked it. The power indicator reflected the imminent detonation of the weapon.

"Overload," I said, and I reached back and hurled my phaser into the jungle, as far from us as I could. It was quickly lost from sight, though I heard it strike several leaves in its flight. I ducked behind a tree, and Mike followed suit, taking cover a short distance from me. Several seconds passed, and then an explosion rocked the rain forest.

Mike and I looked over at each other, but before we could say anything, another whine pierced the day. Mike drew his own phaser, but even as he did so, a second and then a third whine commenced. The renegades had triggered self-destruct commands not only in our phasers, but in our tricorders as well, obviously blanketing the jungle with the deadly signals.

Mike quickly tossed away his phaser, and then his tricorder. I pulled my tricorder's strap from around my neck, then opened its storage compartment, from which I pulled a blank data tape.

"Demora," Mike called to me as the whine from my tricorder grew louder. I didn't answer, instead focusing on pushing the tape into the recording slot. Out where Mike had thrown his phaser, a second detonation occurred.

As I activated the data transfer, I knew it was too late. I hauled the tricorder back and flung it away. It exploded before it hit the ground, and then Mike's also blew up.

Mike ran over to me. "Did you get the data off-loaded?" he asked.

"Not onto tape," I said. "But I've got it up here." I tapped a finger against my forehead. "I viewed the most critical intelligence as I downloaded it at the base."

"Well done," Mike said. "But now they know where we are, so we have to keep moving."

We continued on through the rain forest.

Two hours later, as I'd begun to grow concerned that the shuttle had not yet been repaired, it broke through the jungle canopy. A great sense of relief rose within me as Mike and I stopped and watched it descend. Knowing that we would escape this place, and that we would succeed in our mission to help secure the Federation, I lamented only the apparent loss of at least two of our crew.

The shuttle lowered slowly toward the ground, its antigravs evidently returned to working order. It came down amid the enormous trunks of the rain-forest trees, and settled atop a mass of undergrowth about twenty meters from our position. Bushes and twigs cracked and snapped beneath its weight as it alit.

Once the shuttle had landed, I started toward it, reaching up with my knife to slice through the vegetation along the way, but then I felt Mike's hand close around my upper arm. I looked over at him, and he mouthed the word "Wait." I gazed back over toward the shuttle and saw the silvery white of its starboard hull visible in patches through the leaves. As I watched, the hatch slipped open with a mechanical hum audible even at that remove.

I waited, as Mike had prompted me to, and he stood motionless beside me. Nothing happened.

"Where is she?" Mike asked quietly, obviously referring to the Starfleet engineer we'd left behind to repair the shuttle. He clearly didn't trust the situation. Seconds passed, and with each one, I became more suspicious as well.

But then the engineer appeared in the hatchway. She peered out into the jungle, doubtless aware of our presence from the signal we'd sent to her, as well as from her ability to scan for the frequency of our sensor veils, which she knew. As her gaze passed over our position, she and I made eye contact briefly, although she gave no indication that she had seen me. "Captain Green," she finally called out.

I looked again at Mike, and saw on his face the same mixture of confusion and wariness that I felt. The captain who led our mission was not named Green.

"Commander Brown, Commander White, Specialist Gray," the engineer continued. "I've repaired the shuttle, and we can now depart."

Green, Brown, White, Gray, I thought. Not one of the names belonged to any member of the mission crew. *She's being coerced,* I concluded. Forced to call out to us, she was trying to warn us of the dangers, while at the same time attempting to save her own life. Had she simply refused to call to us, she likely would have been killed by the renegades.

"What should we do?" Mike whispered beside me. As I turned to respond, the shriek of an energy weapon cut through the moist jungle air. A single short burst was followed by a longer one, and a beam of intense light sliced through the vegetation directly to my left. As I instinctively ducked down, I saw the engineer collapse in the hatchway, revealing a renegade behind her in the shuttle. The man, tall and muscular, had obviously aimed in our direction based upon a scan of our sensor veils, but hadn't yet spotted us visually. Remaining in place seemed an untenable option, though, since he would doubtless sweep the area with his weapon.

As though my thoughts had driven him, the renegade leveled his weapon again and fired into the jungle. Once more, a lethal ray cleaved the air, closer to us this time, less than an arm's length away. I turned and darted for cover, and felt Mike's presence beside me as he followed.

I headed for a gargantuan tree just a few steps away, its enormous trunk at least three or four meters in diameter. Throwing myself down behind it, I thought I'd made it in time, but then intense pain erupted in my foot. An involuntary cry escaped through my gritted teeth as Mike landed on the ground beside me.

The weapons fire stopped momentarily, but then the wail of the renegade's weapon once more pierced the rain forest. Behind me, I heard the blast strike the tree, which trembled beneath the onslaught. I imagined the scorched crater that must have been opened in its trunk.

"Are you hit?" Mike asked me.

I nodded, and said, "My foot." I drew my knee up toward my chest so that I could examine the damage. As I did so, the scent of seared flesh—*my* flesh—reached my nose. I immediately felt sick to my stomach, but pushed the sensation away. I looked at my boot, where the renegade's weapon had scored a glancing strike. The upper portion of the boot's surface had been charred, and a tear penetrated through to my foot. I saw an open wound within, my skin burned black, but the energy bolt had also cauterized the injury.

"Can you move?" Mike asked me.

"I'm going to have to, aren't I?" I said, already trying to stand by bracing myself against the tree. Then the weapons fire began again, the streaks of lethal light screaming past the tree, first on one side, then on the other. When they stopped, the singed vegetation surrounding us hissed as though communicating to us whispers of death. "We need to find deeper cover," I said, well aware that the only weapons we now possessed were the broad-bladed knives we'd been using to slash our way through the jungle.

"Right," Mike agreed. He stood up and moved to my side, where he tucked a shoulder beneath my arm, helping to support me as I stood on my uninjured foot.

Suddenly, a familiar whine rose from the direction of the shuttle: a phaser or tricorder set to overload. The sound increased in pitch, and then abruptly grew louder. Beside us, I saw a glint of alloy as a phaser went arcing down and into the brush a few meters away.

I pushed away from Mike at once, intending to hobble forward, find the weapon, and toss it farther away from us. But Mike held me back and forced me down onto the ground, then raced toward the screeching phaser. "Stay there," he ordered me. "You've got the intel." He raised his long knife over his head and swung it rapidly in short arcs and thrusts, driving through the undergrowth and searching for the weapon that threatened us.

The frequency of the whine increased higher still, clearly only seconds away from detonating.

"Mike," I called, wanting him to try to find cover, as unlikely a prospect as that seemed.

At the last instant, Mike glanced over his shoulder at me, and then he spread his body wide, obviously attempting to shield me and protect the vital information I carried in my head.

And then the phaser exploded.

I saw a burst of flame bloom on either side of Mike, the yellow-red fire enveloping him for just a moment before it receded. Around me, shrapnel from the blast shot through the jungle, tearing through the plant life. I heard numerous metal fragments strike the tree behind me, and I felt one shoot into my forearm, but I seemed otherwise unscathed by the explosion.

Ahead of me, Mike fell to the ground in a heap.

I resisted the urge to call out to him, instead scrambling up onto my hands and knees and rushing toward him. Pain shot through my foot as I moved, and I felt the new ache in my arm, but I ignored the hard sensations. I concentrated solely on reaching Mike.

When I got to him, I found him on his back, his calves bent awkwardly beneath him. I quickly examined his body, and through rips in his uniform, saw his flesh in bloody tatters. A deep gash had been opened in one arm near his wrist, his hand now just barely attached. A narrow slit climbed from the tip of his chin up his cheek to his hairline, a crimson trail marking the path that a sliver of the destroyed phaser had taken across his face.

He looked badly broken.

I reached up to Mike's chest to try to gently pull off his uniform, wanting to pinpoint his severest wounds and treat them as best I could. The fabric, already burned and torn from the blast, came away easily. Beneath it, Mike's torso was shredded, his body pierced in a dozen places, his skin ragged, his blood flowing freely from his body.

As I used scraps of uniform to wipe away the red pools from his wounds, somebody yelled behind me, from somewhere near the shuttle. The meaning was unclear to me, but I absently noted that I heard neither weapons fire nor the sound of another overload. Looking back now, my training should have had me utilize the lull as an opportunity to attempt escape, but I couldn't leave Mike like that.

As I worked over him, my hands becoming soaked in his blood, the ground around him covered by it, I realized that I wasn't going to be able to save him. Distraught, I peered at his face. To my surprise, he was looking back at me.

I opened my mouth to say something, to somehow try to soothe him. Before I could, though, he took a quick intake of breath, as if gasping for air. Then he was still, and the light faded from his eyes.

Behind me, near the tree, the brush rustled as somebody approached. I spun around from Mike's body, my foot and forearm flaring in pain, and I realized that I no longer held my knife. I quickly scanned the path I'd crawled along to get to Mike, and

looked around the base of the tree, but I didn't see the blade any-
here. With no recourse, I tensed my muscles, preparing to attack
the renegade with the only weapon left to me: my own hands. A
moment later, somebody rounded the tree.

It was the captain.

He saw me first, and then Mike. "Dead, sir," I said, my voice flat.
The captain nodded, his features tensing almost imperceptibly.

"And you?" he asked. "Are you all right?"

"Wounded, but yes," I said. "I have the intel."

He nodded again, and told me that we had to go. He helped
me to the shuttle, explaining that the engineer had completed her
repairs, but then had been attacked and captured by two renegades. The enemy had apparently tracked the frequency signature
of our sensor veils from the shuttle, intending to capture or kill
us, but the engineer must not have divulged the different fre-
quencies of the captain's veil. He and the other member of his
jungle team had reached the shuttle just as the attack on us had
been launched. Using their knives, the two had overcome the
renegades, though too late to save either the engineer or Mike.
The captain also confirmed that the other two members of our
mission crew had been captured and taken to the renegade base.

In the shuttle, I prepared the helm to speed us off the planet. I
waited while the captain and the other crew member recovered
Mike's body, loading it into the aft section of the shuttle and raising a stasis field about it. Then I worked the controls, and the
shuttle rose, crashed through the jungle canopy, flew up through
the atmosphere, and headed us for home.

All the way back to Federation space, sitting at the primary
console, all I could think about was Mike's family, and how much
they had lost that day.

Back on Sentik IV, I sat at the primary console of the *Armstrong*,
the memory of what had happened on that mission as fresh as an
open wound. I could not deny the value and importance of what
our small crew had accomplished there. I believed then, and still

believe now, that our actions, our retrieval of that critical intelligence, subsequently resulted in the saving of uncounted Federation lives—and ultimately, in the saving of renegade lives as well.

But Mike hadn't survived. I'd gone to him, had tried to minister to his mangled body, but had instead looked on as he'd drawn his last breath. He'd saved my life at the cost of his own, and I've carried that burden ever since. It went beyond survivor's guilt, beyond the unanswerable question of why I had lived through our shared experience and he had not. What haunted me was the family to which Mike had never returned: parents who would have to wade through the misery of a memorial service for their child; a young boy who would grow up with ever-fading recollections of a father he'd barely known; an infant son who would spend all of his days with no father at all; and a wife whose lips would never again touch those of the man she loved.

As I sat in the shuttle on Sentik, I told myself what I'd repeated in my head so many times before: Mike had understood the risks of the mission, and despite how much he had to lose, he'd chosen to participate in it anyway. I believed that, paradoxically, he'd done it *for* his family . . . for *all* the families. He'd given up his life so that the knowledge I'd learned at the renegade base could be used to prevent the deaths of others. I'd never entirely learned how to live with that, but as I considered what to do about Hana's situation, one truth kept playing over and over in my mind: Mike had paid the ultimate price in order to help secure the continued safety of his family. Sitting in the shuttle on Sentik IV, I had to ask myself if I was strong enough to pay a much smaller price for the good of my own family.

"What are you waiting for, Demora?" I said. My voice sounded strange in the empty shuttle.

I reached forward to the communications panel, pressed a control surface there, and then turned to the starboard monitor so that my image would be recorded along with my words. "To Admiral Mahesh Bapu Ratnaswamy, Starfleet Headquarters, Earth. Admiral, this is Captain Demora Sulu of the *U.S.S. Enter-*

prise. As of today—" I peered at the chronometer on the console, then recited the time and stardate. "—I am requesting an indefinite absence from my duties, and I'm stepping down from my captaincy. Due to the needs of—" I paused, unaccustomed to the words I was about to utter. "—of my family, I cannot negotiate for this leave. If Starfleet Command is unwilling to accommodate my request—an action I can fully understand—then I withdraw my request, and instead immediately resign my commission."

I toggled the control on the panel, halting the recording. I then reached for the transmission key, but hesitated before activating it. I found that I needed to say one more thing, and I restarted the recording. "Admiral Ratnaswamy, this is not a decision I've made lightly," I said. "My grandmother is dying. She might have a day left, or a month, or even a year. However long it turns out to be, she needs help, and I'm the only member of our family who can provide it for her." I paused the recording, and thought about saying more. Instead, I reached again for the transmit control.

This time, I didn't hesitate.

By the time I heard back from Starfleet Command, the *Enterprise* had already departed Starbase Magellan and begun its yearlong exploratory mission. A veteran captain had been assigned to the ship, a man I knew and respected, and who I thought a good choice for my crew. I'd hoped that my first officer would be given the position, but Command had apparently believed her not quite ready for the promotion.

In his response to me, Admiral Ratnaswamy graciously expressed his concern and best wishes for Hana. Starfleet Command understood my situation, he said, and had elected to approve my request for an indefinite furlough from my duties. Aware of the conditions on Sentik IV, and taking into consideration that the *Enterprise* had left on its mission without the *Armstrong* aboard, the admirals had also chosen to allow me to retain custody of the shuttle until the *Enterprise* completed its current assignment.

Finally, at the conclusion of the message, Admiral Ratnaswamy emphasized that, when I was ready, Command wanted me back on the bridge of a starship. He also pointed out that he could offer no guarantee that circumstances would permit me to return to command of the *Enterprise*. He signed off by wishing me well.

I felt more than a twinge of regret. I'd been aboard the *Enterprise* during its test runs and maiden voyage, assigned there directly out of the Academy. I'd served on the ship for more than two decades, and during that time, had worked my way up from ensign to captain, from the helm to the center seat.

Still, I knew that I'd made the right decision to stay with Hana. I didn't *want* to do it, but I had no choice in the matter. Quite simply, it was the right thing to do.

The weeks I'd already spent with Hana turned into months, and with each month that passed, her physical condition deteriorated. On the day I'd chosen to stay on Sentik, she began staying in bed most of the time, taking almost all of her meals there, rising only to have me help her visit the outhouse. She also stopped changing out of her nightclothes, which I washed for her every couple of days.

After a time, she could no longer walk, even with my assistance. I fashioned an antigrav chair from components I pirated from the shuttle, and while I'd steeled myself for Hana's protest at my use of technology, she was either too weak or just didn't care enough to say anything. I began to wonder how aware of her surroundings she actually was.

Eventually, Hana couldn't even make it out of her bed and onto the antigrav unit, and I had to employ the *Armstrong*'s transporter to get her to the outhouse. When even that proved too much for her, I was forced to improvise a means for her to relieve herself in her room. In effect, I'd become her nurse, seeing to all of her needs. I felt humiliated for her. No matter the quality of my relationship with her, no matter her lack of interest in my life, no matter her hard, unemotional manner, she had always seemed a strong, proud, independent person. It saddened me terribly to see her in such a desperate situation, so completely reliant on me for her very existence. I recalled my Great-Aunt Nori's illness and incapacity, and how on my one visit to New Tokyo, Hana had appeared to pity her at the same time that she had cared for her.

As the months marched on, Hana's mind seemed to follow her body downward. As little as she had ever spoken to me, she began to do so even less. Once she'd become fully bedridden, her ability to enunciate diminished. Where once she might have offered a word to me here or there, she stopped speaking at all, apparently capable of producing only indistinct, guttural noises.

For my part, though, I spoke to Hana more than ever. As I spent more and more time with her, I found the silences intolerable. And so as I served Hana her meals, helped her with her purgation, cleaned her, repositioned and massaged her failing body to avoid bedsores, as I did all of those things, I began to tell her about my life. She never gave me any indication that she heard my words, let alone understood them, but I talked to her anyway.

I told her about my mother, a vital, enigmatic woman I'd loved and idolized, and who I'd watched die in an infirmary bed of Sakuro's disease when I was seven years old. I told Hana about those first turbulent years with my father, and finally coming to accept and love him. I told her about following my father's path, joining Starfleet Academy, graduating to a helm position, and then working my way up to starship command. I told her about various adventures and experiences I'd had while on board the *Enterprise*: my capture and apparent death at Alaskon V; my parts in the famed Coronado Mystery, both in the beginning and at the end; the ridiculous turn of events that had left me, for seven hours, as Absolute Ruler of the Universe; my fascinating and difficult first mission as captain of the *Enterprise*, when the ship had traveled to the Röntgen Wall. I even told her about Mike, and those horrible days on our mission to the renegade base.

In the end, it didn't matter whether Hana could hear me or not. I hoped that she did, but simply talking to her, telling her some of the story of my life, turned out to be something I needed to do for myself. At the same time, I wished I could have learned about her. I'd never really known her, and I realized at some point that I never would. But despite that, I decided to treasure as best I could those last few months with her.

In the springtime, I woke early one morning to bright sunshine. I rubbed my eyes and yawned, then rolled onto my side and squinted toward the right-hand wall of the cabin. The blanket that I affixed over the window every night had slipped down on one side, allowing in the rays of the dawn sun.

Knowing I wouldn't be able to get back to sleep even if I rehung the blanket, I got up, put on my boots, and headed in my night-clothes to the outhouse. Outside, the temperature was surprisingly comfortable so early in the day. On the way back to the house, I filled the water containers at the well, then hauled them inside. I then dressed, did my daily chores, and went out to the fields.

I spent the rest of the morning digging furrows. During the fall and winter, I'd reaped some of the crops, but then had ended up plowing most of them under. The work, even with the animals Hana kept, had been exhausting, but the break from tending to Hana's continual needs helped me get through that time.

By late morning, I estimated that I'd covered half a hectare, perhaps more. I looked back over the neat rows I'd dug into the ground, and felt satisfied with the accomplishment. I removed the plow from Hana's beast and boarded the animal back in its stall in the barn, then headed for the house. From the position of the sun almost directly overhead, I could tell that it was time for a meal, both for Hana and for me.

After I'd washed up, I opened Hana's bedroom door and looked in to check on her. She was still asleep, I saw. I started to leave, but then something caught my attention. I peered back over at Hana, and then stared as I saw something I couldn't ex-plain. Hana lay on her back, with her hands atop the bedclothes, resting at her sides. Beneath one hand, she held what appeared to be a small book.

I'd seen the cloth-covered volume from time to time since I'd been there, but not for a long while. I hadn't thought about it in months, probably not since the last occasion I'd seen Hana sitting on the chest below the back window, the book at her side. I wondered now where it had been, and assumed that she'd kept it in one of the chests, neither of which I'd had much call to open.

What I really wanted to know, though, was how Hana had retrieved it. She hadn't been ambulatory for many months. I gazed at her tiny, weakened form, and found it impossible to believe that she'd somehow gotten out of bed that day.

As I regarded Hana's tranquil visage, I realized something else: the bedclothes were not rising and falling with her respiration. Stunned in spite of the inevitability of the moment, I walked to the side of the bed and gingerly reached two fingers to the side of Hana's neck.

She had passed away.

Carefully, I lifted Hana's hands and folded them together across her midsection. I regarded her still features, and thought she looked more at peace than I'd ever seen her. I felt relief on her behalf that her plight of infirmity had ended. I also felt an unexpected melancholy.

My gaze drifted back to the book still lying by her side. I picked it up and examined it. It was perhaps ten centimeters wide and half again as tall, and covered in a soft, floral fabric. It had no title or writing of any kind on the exterior.

Curious, I opened it to the first page. There, several symbols marched across the white page in a handwritten scrawl put down in black ink. I recognized them as Japanese kanji, though I could not read them. Below these was a single word—*Magomusume*—presumably a transliteration of the symbols into romaji, which I could read.

The word meant *granddaughter*.

I gasped, realizing that Hana had left this for me.

I turned to the next page, which was filled with paragraphs penned in the same jagged handwriting. The words were written in Federation Standard. I quickly flipped through more of the book, and saw page after page crammed with writing. I then went back to the first page of text, and read the first line.

I was born in 2200 on Earth, on the cusp of the centuries, on the island of Shikoku.

I looked back over at Hana. I'd known her even less than I thought I had, but saw that would not continue to be the case. Unaccountably, she had left me the story of her life.

I peered down at the book again, and reread the words there: *I was born in 2200 on Earth . . .*

Below them, the first of my tears fell onto the page.

Sulu finished her tale. Around her, the tavern's patrons regarded her in silence. She couldn't tell whether she had impressed everybody—or *any*body—with her story, but she was interested in its impact on only one person: Strolt. She looked over at him, and for the first time since he'd stopped to listen to her tale, she met his gaze with her own. For a long moment, the tableau remained frozen in place.

And then the bartender said quietly, "Well done."

Unsure what Strolt was thinking, and not wanting to risk antagonizing him, Sulu broke their eye contact. "Thank you," she said, turning in her seat toward the bar.

"Another for you, Captain Sulu?" the bartender asked, holding up an empty wineglass. "You've earned it."

Sulu looked down at her own glass, which she'd emptied during the course of her story. "No, thank you," she said.

Around Sulu, the tavern seemed to come slowly back to life. People shifted in their chairs, stood up, moved about. Voices rose in conversation, softly at first, and then to more normal levels. Sulu glanced over again at Strolt.

He was on the move, she saw, walking rapidly toward the front door. As he entered the vestibule, Sulu quickly pushed back from the table and stood up. Behind the bar, her stout host asked if she was leaving, and she told him that she was.

"I hope you'll come back and regale us again," he told her.

"Maybe," Sulu answered without conviction, watching as Strolt passed out of her sight. She heard the creak of one of the hinges on the front door. Fighting the urge to give chase immediately, Sulu waited, wanting to give Strolt enough time to put some distance between himself and the tavern. When she caught up to him, she did not want to be in a position again where he could put innocent lives at risk.

"Well, Captain Sulu," the bartender said, "I owe you a drink. You really told *two* stories, not just one."

"Fine," Sulu said as she measured the time until she thought she could safely pursue Strolt. "I'll look for you next time I'm on Temecklia."

"My name's Cap," the bartender said. "But you won't have to look for me; I'm always here."

"Okay," Sulu said, and she offered him an inattentive smile. "I've got to go now though."

"Safe travels," Cap said.

Sulu nodded, then headed across the room. She moved quickly through the vestibule, then pushed open the creaky front door. As soon as her feet hit the ground, she started to run, but then stopped almost at once.

The sky had begun to lighten in the early morning hours. Up ahead, at the agora end of the alley, Strolt leaned tiredly against a wall—far enough away from the tavern for its patrons to be safe, close enough for Sulu to resume her pursuit. But she discovered that she wouldn't have to chase him. He waited for her at the end of the alley as she walked its length. As she neared him, it relieved her to see both of his hands visible, neither of them reaching into his coat, ready to trigger the explosives.

"You're right," he said when she had closed to within three meters of him.

Sulu stopped. "About Hana?" she asked him. "About Mike?" She wanted to ask about Zeeren, his Tzenkethi mate, but didn't.

"About everything," Strolt said, and Sulu thought she heard a note of resignation in his deep voice. "Sometimes it's necessary to act for the greater good," he went on. "Even if it's at the expense of what you most want."

"I know," Sulu said gently. "Believe me, I know."

Strolt nodded. "When I first stopped to listen to your story," he said, "I thought you were going to make my argument for me. Because you were all that your grandmother had, and because I'm all that Zeeren has. You did what you had to do, and I thought that demonstrated that I should do what I had to." He paused, then added, "But there was more to your story."

"Yes," Sulu agreed.

"I really am all that Zeeren has," he said. "We love each other, and all we want is to be together. But I'm not a Tzenkethi, and her family . . ." His words trailed away.

Sulu nodded, but said nothing. In truth, her heart went out to Strolt and his mate. For people to reject somebody because they'd fallen in love with an individual of another species . . . the very notion of the prejudice disgusted her.

Strolt shrugged. "They gave her a chance to return. If she could acquire certain Starfleet data . . ." Again, his voice drifted down into silence.

"Your record as a freighter captain is spotless," Sulu said. "If you take me to Zeeren now, if we can recover the data you stole before she makes it back to Tzenkethi territory, I'm sure you can be together again soon."

"But she'll still be cut off from her people," Strolt said sadly. "From her own family."

"The greater good," Sulu said sympathetically. "And frankly, with such attitudes, they don't deserve Zeeren's presence in their lives. Or yours."

Strolt pushed away from the wall and faced Sulu, then quickly reached into his coat. For an instant, she braced herself, preparing for the blast that would tear through Strolt's body and then her own. But that didn't happen. Rather, Strolt pulled out a train of four thin bundles, silver on one side, green on the other, with two small touchpads and a status indicator at one end. Sulu recognized the common packaging of the infernite-cabrodine chemical bombs. Had he detonated all four earlier, the explosion would have flattened the tavern and killed everyone inside.

Strolt tapped a sequence on the pads, then handed it over to Sulu. "It's disarmed now," he said.

Sulu took the explosives and checked the status indicator, confirming what Strolt had just told her.

"Zeeren's in the Entelior system," he said. Sulu had visited the system before, and knew that it hung in space not far from Temecklia. "She's on the fourth planet, waiting for my signal to move. I'll take you there."

It was over, Sulu knew.

"My shuttle's at the northeastern landing facility," she said. "Let's go."

Strolt exited the alley ahead of her, and then fell in beside her as they headed for the port. They walked quietly for the thirty minutes it took them to reach the landing facility. As they neared the shuttle, though, Strolt stopped and gave her a questioning look. "*Enterprise*?" he asked.

Sulu stopped beside him and glanced over at the shuttle *Mitrios*, the hull of which was adorned with the registry identification NCC-1701-B/5, and the name of the vessel to which it was assigned: *Enterprise*. "After I dealt with the aftermath of Hana's death," Sulu said, "I went to Earth, to Starfleet Headquarters. I flew a desk there for three months, and then my ship came back from its mission."

"*Your* ship?" Strolt said, and for the first time since she'd begun pursuing him, Sulu saw him smile.

"*My* ship," she said. "The crew's exploratory mission was wildly successful, and its new captain offered an admiralty as a consequence. When he accepted the position, Command proposed that I return to the *Enterprise*."

"And you couldn't refuse?" Strolt asked. Sulu shrugged, smiling now herself. She took a step toward the shuttle, but Strolt stopped her again. "And what about the book?" he asked. "What did Hana tell you?"

Sulu felt the smile melt from her face, not because what Hana had written to her hadn't been important to her, but because important as it had been, it had still been a difficult tale to take. "She told me everything," Sulu said seriously. "The story of her life: her terrible childhood, the mistake she made that resulted in her estrangement from her son, the deaths of so many people in her life, including her husband and sister—she told me all of it. It helped explain who she was, why she'd treated me the way she had, and that . . ." This time it was Sulu who let her words taper off.

"And that what?" Strolt wanted to know.

Sulu looked him in the eyes. "And that she loved me."

Strolt didn't smile again, but Sulu nevertheless interpreted the expression on his face as one of joy. "I'm happy for you," he said.

"Thank you," she said, and to pull herself from the myriad thoughts and remembrances now churning through her mind, she headed again for the shuttle. She keyed in her access code, and when the hatch opened, she and Strolt climbed aboard. Sulu immediately placed the explosives in a stasis field, then computed a liftoff trajectory and a course to the Entelior system. Once she'd contacted the port's control tower and received clearance, she took *Mitrios* into orbit. As she worked the helm, she felt the weight of Strolt's attention, and so it didn't surprise her when he asked her another question.

"Are you all right?"

"Yes," Sulu replied automatically, then thought better of her response. With her hands still moving across the helm panel, setting the shuttle on its course to locate Zeeren, she said, "I'm all right. It's just that . . ." She successfully choked back the emotions threatening to overwhelm her, then peered forward, out at the stars. "It's just that I miss my grandmother," she said.

Tending Bar . . .

The look on Chakotay's face when Demora Sulu entered the bar was telling. As Cap suspected, there was a story coming from the former Maquis, but it wasn't going to be about his days as a terrorist or how he came to return to Starfleet. The link between Sulu and Chakotay was obvious from the moment he noticed her entrance, though she herself did not recognize him, as they wouldn't meet outside the bar for some time yet.

Handing Chakotay a fresh drink, Cap asked if he wanted to go next, and Chakotay allowed as how he would. . . .

CHAKOTAY

CAPTAIN OF THE *U.S.S. VOYAGER*

Seduced

CHRISTIE GOLDEN

"They're coming today."

Blue Water Boy, an Oglala Sioux my own age, tossed this tantalizing tidbit out with as much nonchalance as he displayed when feeding the fish. Which he was also doing at the moment.

"Who?" I asked, thinking I knew and hoping desperately I was right. Sekaya, my little sister, looked up from where she lay sunning on a flat rock and glared at me.

"The Starfleet people," Blue Water Boy said. There was a slight splash as one of the red and purple fish took the piece of bread he tossed on the water.

"Who says?" Sekaya sat up and then abruptly tugged on her swimming sarong, looking embarrassed. Both Blue Water Boy and I averted our eyes. Over the last year, Sekaya's tree-trunk-straight figure had developed curves, and she wasn't used to dealing with them yet. Neither were we.

"No one," Blue Water Boy said mildly. Another bit of bread on the water; another red and purple fish gulping it down. He shrugged his shoulders. "I just know."

Such a statement was as good as any hard, cold fact as far as I was concerned. Somehow Blue Water Boy did "just know" things. And I couldn't remember any time when he'd been wrong.

Sekky and I had known the "weird kid" since infancy. We'd never had any friendships among the children of our own tribe that were as close. For one reason or another, we three were the odd ones out. Blue Water Boy was ethereal, almost mystical, and he had that strange sixth sense that often unnerved adults, who were much more inclined to challenge such things rather than just shrug and accept them. Sekaya was too headstrong and outspoken for a female in our tribe, and I . . .

Well, I was the "contrary." I came into the world backward, a breech birth that, I learned, had almost killed my mother. My father took this position to be a sign that I was destined to always challenge, always question. And he was right—I did. I asked about the other tribes. I asked about aliens. I asked about their histories, their technology—sweet fruit to a child raised by a tribe that seemed to dwell more in the past than in the present. It seemed the only thing I never questioned was Blue Water Boy's pre-science. Which was, in itself, a contrary thing to do. So we three had found each other, and we didn't seem to need much else in the way of company.

"When?" I asked. I didn't want to miss them. They came far too infrequently for that.

"Chakotay, you better not," Sekaya said, her voice a warning. "Father was not happy at all to learn that you were hanging around the Starfleet people. You remember how he acted."

"Well," I said, "he won't get angry if he doesn't know about it, will he? And who's going to tell him?"

I was bigger than either of them and had become the de facto leader of the group. I liked to think it was my commanding presence, but it was probably only because Sekaya was a girl and Blue Water Boy found anything in the world more interesting than being a leader.

"I won't volunteer that you're seeing them," Blue Water Boy said. "But I won't lie for you, Chakotay."

"Me neither." Sekaya stuck her chin out defiantly. It was meant to be a "take me seriously" gesture, but she looked too cute for it to work the way she wanted.

"Fair enough," I said. "Let's go. I don't want to miss them."

We were an hour early, but Blue Water Boy had of course been right. And when they beamed down to the official transport site, we were there to greet them.

My eyes widened. "They're all women," I hissed to my friends.

Sekaya smirked. "How very interesting. You know, Chakotay, somehow I think I could learn to like Starfleet too."

Blue Water Boy cleared his throat and the three women smiled at him. One was an elderly Asian woman. Her long hair was almost completely white and tied in up a bun, but her eyes were bright and alert. Another was a Vulcan, slender and cool. The third was a stocky Anglo woman with red hair and lots of freckles.

"Well, hello," said the Asian woman. "Are you the welcoming committee?"

"Not really," I had to confess. "Not officially, at any rate." Inwardly, I cringed. So much for a good first impression. I straightened and said, "But nonetheless, it's my pleasure to meet you. My name is Chakotay. This is Blue Water Boy and my sister, Sekaya."

"Hi." Blue Water Boy smiled sweetly. Sekaya looked like she wanted to burst, but per tribal custom, she could not speak until spoken to.

The Asian woman looked at her critically. "Don't young woman say hello on this planet?"

"We do when we're said hello to first," Sekaya blurted.

The Vulcan woman and the Asian exchanged glances. In what I was later to learn was an almost genetically inherited gesture among Vulcans, the pointed-eared woman lifted her slanted eyebrow.

"Indeed," she said.

"Well, Sekaya," the Asian woman said, choosing, I thought, to deliberately address my sister rather than me or Blue Water Boy, "My name is Captain Demora Sulu. This is my first officer, Commander T'Piran, and my chief engineer, Lieutenant Commander Anne O'Hara. We're supposed to be addressing your council shortly. Can you take us to them?"

The Vulcan, Commander T'Piran, shot me a glance under slightly lowered lids. I'm sure I gaped like an idiot, but I had never been more shocked in my life.

It was only the third or fourth time I'd ever talked to anyone from Starfleet, and in all that time, I'd never even heard of a female captain. How did she keep order? And a female first officer and engineer?

"Is your ship entirely female?" I wanted to clap my hand over my mouth and wish the words back. Blue Water Boy made a strangled sound; I think he was trying not to laugh.

"Is your tribe entirely ignorant?" shot back O'Hara, but she, too, was trying not to laugh.

I gave it up. I had blown any opportunity to get in well with this crew, learn about their technology, maybe even get a tour of their ship. Slumping a little in defeat, I said honestly, "Yes. Sometimes I think we *are* entirely ignorant."

Captain Sulu took pity on me. "The *Mandela* is not composed entirely of women, no. Would it bother you if it were?"

"No," I said. "I think it would be wonderful."

O'Hara snorted. "Spoken like a true adolescent male."

T'Piran continued to regard me, her brown eyes like deep pools. "I do not think that was what he meant," she said.

"While I'd love to host a roundtable about gender equality," said Captain Sulu, "we do have a schedule to keep. Perhaps the three of you could be our escorts."

We looked at each other. Blue Water Boy shrugged. Sekaya's eyes gleamed. I wished she hadn't come today; she would be insufferable after this exchange.

"Sure," I said. "Follow me."

Sekaya chattered like a bird the entire way home. She could not stop talking about the female captain. Blue Water Boy seemed troubled, but there was no way he could get a word in edgewise. Finally, exasperated, I snapped, "Sekky, shut *up* for a minute, okay? Blue Water Boy, what's wrong?"

He shrugged his thin shoulders. "Nothing. I just . . . I feel a change coming. That's all."

"Because of what?" Sekaya was instantly alert. She, too, trusted Blue Water Boy's hunches and feelings.

"Captain Sulu and her crew."

"Why?" I wanted to know. "We've talked to Starfleet people before."

"I know. But this time is different."

I felt a shiver run down my spine. "Good or bad different?"

"Both. Like everything." He gave me a shy grin.

"Well, I'll tell you one thing," Sekaya said, striding forward determinedly. "If Starfleet can have women captains, then our tribe can have women council members and women shamans. I'm so tired of—"

"Don't," I said sharply.

"Don't what? Don't 'don't' me, big brother."

"Don't tell Father. Please."

She stopped dead in her tracks and stared at me. "You're going as crazy as Blue Water Boy," she said. "Why shouldn't I tell Father?"

"Because he won't let us see them anymore," I replied. "You know that. He thinks they're bad enough already. If he learns that they promote women to captains, he'll—"

"There are female admirals, too," put in Blue Water Boy. "I heard them talking about it."

"Captains and admirals," I continued. "We'll be forbidden to see them."

"I won't be," Blue Water Boy said reasonably. "I'm Lakota. We get along fine with Starfleet and women captains."

I rounded on him almost angrily. My heart was racing, my palms were wet, and I didn't know why. "Your tribe isn't living a life that should have evolved," I said, almost shouting. Blue Water Boy blinked, startled. "You aren't forbidden technology, and padds, and games, and—and—and all that stuff. You don't have to sit and listen to boring old legends about the stars and—"

"I like listening to legends," he replied, maddeningly calm. "And looking at the stars."

I threw up my hands. "Fine. Go ahead. Ruin any chance for Sekaya and me to talk to them."

"I won't say anything," Blue Water Boy said, but he looked very sad all of a sudden.

Sekaya sighed loudly. "Neither will I. But you owe me one, big brother. No, wait, you owe me three."

She strode forward with renewed energy. Blue Water Boy and I hurried after her. "Three? How do you get three?"

She turned over her shoulder, and in her still-girlish face I saw the hint of the strong-willed woman she would become. Then she grinned.

"Three." She held up a slender-fingered hand and counted them off. "Captain Sulu, Commander T'Piran, and Lieutenant O'Hara."

News travels fast in a little colony, and over dinner that night—a vegetable stew of squash, beans and corn—my father, Kolopak, brought the subject up.

"The Starfleet people have come back," he said.

I studiously buttered my bread and took a big bite. If I had to chew and swallow, maybe I could think of something to say. I nodded, looking at Sekaya out of the corner of my eye.

"I know you like to see them, Chakotay. Did you?"

I hated lying to my father, but sometimes . . . But people had seen us. So, I swallowed, took a sip of water and answered with a hundred percent truthfulness, "Yes, I did."

"Hmph." Father ate another spoonful of stew. I had hoped this would be it, but he was apparently not satisfied.

"Did you talk to them?"

"Yes." *Please shut up, Father,* I begged silently.

"What did you think of them?"

What answer did he want to hear from me? "They are the same as others who have come before."

"Did you meet their captain?"

Sekaya's eyes were as wide as the bowl in front of her, but she said nothing. Only I knew how hard it was for her to stay quiet. "Um, yeah, I did." *Here it comes. The lecture on female captains. How women were special and to be cherished, and had many good and wonderful talents, but how the Creator had made them to serve their men and not to take leadership roles and—*

"What did you think of him?"

I choked on the stew. "Wh-What?"

"Their captain. What did you think of him?"

This was a gift from the Sky Spirits! Not that I entirely believed in them, but this was surely a gift. Somehow, word had not gotten out to my father that Captain Sulu was a woman. My spirits lifted and I felt suddenly giddy.

"He seems . . . like a decent man," I said.

Sekaya snorted. Stew went all over the table. "Sekaya!" snapped my mother. "Manners, child, manners! What in the world is so funny?"

I would kill her. I would just have to—

"A bug crawled up my leg and it tickled," Sekaya said smoothly. I stared at her with renewed admiration. I had no idea she was such an accomplished liar. "I'm sorry." She wiped up the stew and looked contrite. From where I was sitting, I could see one of her hands under the table. She folded up her thumb and splayed the other fingers:

Four.

The Starfleet people couldn't have timed their arrival better as far as I was concerned. Seven young men of our tribe, including myself, had come of age this year, and Father and the others were busy planning some sort of initiation ritual. I was supposed to be preparing for it myself, of course, but there was no way I was going to be holed up somewhere meditating on stones or something when I could be around Starfleet people. I was grateful that my father was occupied and that was the extent of my interest in the rite.

In previous years, the Starfleet people came solely to gather samples from our planet and run a variety of tests to ensure that the world continued to be healthy for people who were technically Federation colonists. It was routine and apparently not a very interesting thing to do; I at least couldn't imagine that it was interesting. Now, while they still fulfilled that original function, they also had begun patrolling the Cardassian border. We began to see them more frequently, which suited me perfectly. Despite the now more military reason for visiting our world, there apparently were still opportunities for "R&R" planetside. My homeworld was a great deal like Earth centuries ago—wide-open spaces, beautiful mountains and deserts and rain forests and tundra and so on. I took the world for granted, and often thought I would trade all the so-called natural wonders for a tricorder and a phaser I could call my own.

The Starfleet people also talked with the all-tribal council. Father had been invited to be a member, and in later years he would accept the honor. But now he wanted nothing to do with them. "I am an elder in my own tribe, and that is enough," he always said. That bothered me—others were elders in their own tribes and still served on the all-tribal council. I knew it was because my father disapproved of the other tribes' liberal use of technology and involvement with the "offworlders."

Most of the sessions were held, if not in secret, at least not in public. But there were a few that were open to all the colonists, and at these, Sekky, Blue Water Boy, and I eagerly gathered.

We weren't sure half the time what the Starfleet people were talking about, and frankly, I didn't really care. I just wanted to look at them—their uniforms of red and gold and blue, their combadges, their tricorders and phasers. Some of our people had similar technology, but it was old and I had explored it thoroughly.

Watching me one day, Blue Water Boy whispered, "You are hungry, Chakotay."

I looked at him, bewildered. We'd all just had breakfast. "What do you mean?"

"You are starving to get this into your life," he said. "I look at you and I see the look of a famished wolf staring at a deer."

I didn't know what a wolf or a deer was—some kind of animal native to Earth, I supposed. From his words, I gathered that the wolf ate the deer, and I had to nod. As always, Blue Water Boy was right. I was hungry for what these people had.

At one point, Captain Sulu caught me staring at her. She cocked her head and stared back, a slight smile tugging at her lips. I immediately lowered my eyes—staring at a female so intently was discourteous. My heart raced and my palms were wet. A woman, captain of a starship. It was still hard for me to get my mind around it.

When I next dared to look up, Sulu's eyes were elsewhere but T'Piran was looking directly at me. The blood rose in my cheeks and again I dropped my gaze. I didn't dare lift it again, and spent the rest of that morning's council session staring at my feet.

Sekaya nudged me and giggled. She tilted her head in T'Piran's direction and waggled her eyebrows meaningfully. I wanted to throttle her, but I couldn't even say anything—after all, I owed her four. When the council session broke for lunch, everyone headed for a large table spread with native delicacies. We waited for our honored guests to choose first, then the council members, then the adults. By the time we got to the table it was pretty well picked over.

I loaded up my plate with cut-up vegetables and bread and a few fruits. Embarrassed by being caught staring at a Starfleet captain and her first officer, annoyed at Sekaya's bold teasing, and generally in a defiant mood, I also heaped some cold fish onto my plate.

Sekaya was scandalized. "Chakotay! What are you doing?"

"Fish is supposed to be good for you," I shot back. Then I took a slice of some other animal flesh I didn't recognize.

"You're just being contrary," she said, sniffing slightly.

And that, too, annoyed me. I made a sound and turned away. She looked to Blue Water Boy for support, but my friend just shrugged. "I like fish," he said. "Everyone should eat it. It's good."

"Oh!" Sekaya stamped her sandaled foot, stared at the spread, then put some fish on her plate too.

Blue Water Boy sighed. "You're a bad influence, Chakotay."

"Hey, you're the one who said everyone should eat fish."

"Excuse me."

The voice was as cool as a river in spring and we all three started. I turned around to see Commander T'Piran. She held a carved wooden plate that bore a selection of grains, fruits, and vegetables. There was no hint of animal flesh.

"Vulcans are vegetarians," she said mildly. "There is no shame in it."

I could do nothing right. For the most fleeting of moments, I wanted to hurl my plate to the ground and storm off. Instead, I clutched it until my knuckles turned white and said, "I am not ashamed." I was pretty sure that was a lie. "I merely want to experience things other than what my tribe teaches."

"Most logical," T'Piran said. I knew that was high praise from a Vulcan, and I felt my spirits lift just the smallest amount. "You are Chakotay, is that correct?"

"Y-Yes."

"Captain Sulu would like you to join us for lunch."

I'm sure I gaped. "Um . . . of course. I would be honored." I turned to give my friends a look that I hoped was mature and confident, but what I now think was probably one of barely suppressed glee. Both of them looked surprised, but Blue Water Boy, again, had that faint look of consternation on his face that troubled me.

But I wasn't going to let it trouble me. Not today, not under a blue, cloudless sky when I was about to dine with a captain of a starship.

T'Piran took me back to a private area where the captain lounged beneath a canopy. She was reading a padd and sipping from a glass containing a red beverage when we approached. She looked up and smiled, the expression genuine, curving the wrinkles around her eyes and mouth into semicircles of pleasure.

"I'm so pleased you could join us, Chakotay," she said in a warm, friendly voice.

Like I'd say no to a luncheon with a Starfleet captain, I thought.

"The honor is entirely mine, Captain Sulu," I replied with as much graciousness as a fifteen-year-old boy could muster.

She gestured that I should sit. I perched on a carved wooden stool, awaiting . . . whatever was going to happen.

"I'd offer both of you a glass of this excellent vintage, but you're underage, Chakotay, and T'Piran doesn't drink." She sipped the beverage, clearly savoring it. At my expression, Sulu grinned. "Captain's privilege. I don't usually drink when I'm on duty, but a glass of wine now and then with a meal is good for one . . . and, well, I outrank everyone here."

I was shocked. I had imagined that Starfleet officials were a bit like my father—no bending the rules, no exceptions to anything. "By-the-book" was the term I'd heard. And yet here I was, dining with two women in positions of great power, talking about sipping wine when on duty. I felt almost as giddy as if I had drunk some of the wine.

"So a little bird told me that you are very interested in Starfleet," Sulu continued.

A little bird named Sekaya? "Yes, I am," I answered honestly.

"What is it, exactly, that intrigues you so much?"

I set my plate on my lap and looked her full in the eye. If ever there was a time to speak from the heart, I sensed it was now.

"When I was younger, it was the technology," I said truthfully. "I was fascinated by it. Phasers, tricorders—everything."

T'Piran frowned a little. "But your people have access to Federation technology," she said. "It is nothing unique to Starfleet."

I turned toward her and for perhaps the first time I fully realized what an attractive woman she was. I'd seen her before on many occasions, but always saw the officer, not the woman. She was tall, her shiny black hair pulled back in a ponytail, her ears tapered to graceful points. Her body was fit but not overly muscled; curvaceous, but not lush. Her expression was controlled, of course—she was Vulcan, after all—but there was real curiosity on her lovely, aquiline features.

My brain turned to mush for a moment, then I remembered the question. "Um . . . that's true. Sort of." *Well, that was eloquent.* I tried again. "The technology is here on the planet, but my tribe tries to involve itself as little as possible with it."

Demora Sulu, under no cultural restraints to control her emotions, drew her still-dark eyebrows together. "Don't tell me your tribe denies itself proper medical treatment?"

"No," I said hastily. Contrary that I was, I suddenly didn't want to paint my tribe as being primitive or, worse, stupid. "No one comes to harm through lack of technology. We just don't use it as much as the other tribes do."

"Interesting," said T'Piran. "What is the term among humans—forbidden fruit?"

I hadn't heard the term and looked inquiringly at Captain Sulu. "It means that often, we want what we don't have." She smiled again, and again the years dropped off her face. "We have *lots* of quaint phrases to describe that phenomenon."

I suddenly realized what they were getting at. They thought that my interest in Starfleet was that of a child—a "deprived" little boy wanting to play with toys. No, they couldn't think that—they just couldn't!

"But it's become more than that," I said quickly. "I've talked to lots of the people who have come here. I've heard their stories. I know about what's going on off this world, about the Cardassians and everything, and it fascinates me."

The two women exchanged glances. T'Piran arched that eyebrow again, and Sulu continued to hold her smile. "So you've outgrown a desire to play with toys and have graduated to wanting adventures," Sulu said.

I sagged on my stool. I couldn't make them understand. Just like my father, they saw me as a child: a little boy wanting to enact a fantasy.

"Chakotay? What's wrong?" Sulu's voice held almost a motherly tone.

I swallowed hard. I had been famished before, but now the food on my plate—especially the meat and fish—looked unappetizing. I had lost already. They had mentally classified me, and nothing I could do could make the situation better. It didn't matter now if I made it worse.

"Captain Sulu, did you invite me here to make fun of me?"

"Chakotay," said T'Piran in a warning voice.

"No, T'Piran, it's all right." Sulu fixed me with an intent gaze. My mouth went dry under that scrutiny. Suddenly I saw just why Starfleet had seen fit to promote this woman to a captaincy.

"You have a right to ask," she continued. "And I certainly did not invite you here to make fun of you. I'm a little disappointed that you even thought that."

Inwardly, I cringed. How often had I heard that? *I'm disappointed in you, Chakotay.* My father always knew that that word would crush me more than *angry* or *upset*. How often had I seen that look on his face, that sorrowful resignation? To know that I had, again, failed him as a son. No doubt he secretly wished that young Kamaran had been his son instead of me—Kamaran was so perfect, he knew all the old legends and—

"I asked you here because you intrigued us." She gestured to T'Piran. "You're not the only one on this planet interested in Starfleet, you know. But there was something different about you. Something that we both noticed. An intensity, if you will. A passion. Starfleet is not all fun and games, Chakotay. It's life and death, sometimes. It's being willing to die, and what might be even harder, being willing to kill for something you know is right. And there's boredom aplenty. Did you see the look on the faces of my crew when they came down for shore leave? We don't want to crowd Starfleet Academy with starry-eyed youngsters who quit once they get a taste of what it's all about. We don't want cadets who enrolled as an act of rebellion."

She leaned forward in her seat, her brown eyes blazing with intensity. "What we want are young people who would make fine officers one day."

My heart leaped at the unspoken words. I desperately tried to think of something appropriate to say, but my tongue cleaved to my mouth and all I could do was stare at her.

"You mentioned that your tribe rejects modern technology," came T'Piran's cool voice. I dragged my gaze from Sulu's face to hers. "What would your family think of your attending the Academy?"

It was time to choose: truth, or a lie. For a moment, I was torn, but only a moment. With a wisdom that I now marvel at, some few decades later, I knew with unshakable certainty that I would never learn to be happy staying home. I knew, too, that I would not be able to serve as I wanted there, either. My destiny lay before me: Starfleet, or tribal tradition.

I made my decision. "My father is quite forward-thinking for our tribe," I said, marveling at how firm and believable the words sounded. "He encourages me to meet and talk with you. I'm certain he'd be pleased if I were to attend."

"That is good," said T'Piran approvingly. "Perhaps we can arrange to meet your father and discuss what is necessary for your admittance."

Panic fluttered in my gut. "My father is very busy right now," I said, and that much, at least, was true. "He is involved in creating a rite of passage ritual for the young men of our tribe. I can study for the exam on my own. Once this is over I'm sure he'd be delighted to meet you."

All right, then, a little lie on the end of a great big truth. The world of black and white absolutes in which I had been raised had suddenly gone very, very gray.

The two women exchanged glances. "We will need to get his permission for you to attend if you are accepted," said Sulu. "But in the meantime, if you want to handle the studying all by yourself, then more power to you, my young friend."

To my shock, she lifted the glass of red wine and toasted me.

I drifted home that day. Secreted on my person were the contraband padds that contained the necessary information to prepare for the exam. I sneaked away as often as I could to peruse them. It was almost like reading a foreign language, everything was so different. If only I'd been born on Earth, or at least to the Navajo or Lakota or Hopi tribes here.

Any tribe but my own.

I was engrossed in a history of the formation of the Federation when a voice at my ear made me nearly jump out of my skin.

"That's five. Maybe six or seven."

Sekaya squatted beside me, her arms around her knees. She was grinning. "So what is it, a new game? Let me see."

I tugged the padd out of her grasp. "It's history," I said. Her lovely eyes narrowed.

"You hate history."

"Not this history. It's Federation history." Starfleet history.

She regarded me for a moment, chewing on her lower lip, trying to crack my secret. I usually kept very little from her, but this . . . this was mine. I gave her stare for stare, then finally she rose.

"Something's going on with you," she said. "I don't know what, but eventually I'll find out."

She strode off angrily. I watched her go. Eventually, everyone would find out, but I hoped that would not be until I was packing to leave for San Francisco aboard the *Mandela*.

A week later, I struggled into the animal skins that were to be the formal outfit for the evening, pausing to think about the unspoken hypocrisy of my tribe who would not eat the flesh of animals but did not hesitate to clothe themselves in them. Around the single candle that provided illumination in the Waiting Hut, I saw the shadows and heard the noises of the other six boys who would become men by the time the evening's ritual was over. We did not speak; that much I knew, but I was starting to hyperventilate as I realized that I had spent nearly the entire time allotted to prepare for the ritual reading padds and talking to T'Piran and Captain Sulu.

How hard can it be? At any point, just do or say the most pretentious, old-fashioned thing that pops into your head and you'll be fine.

Sekaya was a year younger than I, and madly jealous that I was going through the adulthood initiation ritual first. She ate this stuff up—the clothing, the face paintings, the ritual words. I'd seen her just the other day, following one of the shamans, chattering about something or other. The poor man looked both flattered and exasperated by her interest.

The loincloth chafed, and I felt naked with nothing on my legs or torso. Furtively, I looked around; none of the other boys seemed to feel as out of place as I did. But then, none of them *was* as out of place as I was.

Next, we pulled the ritual headbands around our foreheads, tying them securely. I was aware that my hands were shaking. For right now, I could follow the lead of the other boys, but once we got out there, I would be on my own.

Kamaran, the perfect boy as always, looked calm and in control. More than one boy was watching him, taking his cue from this youth who seemed destined to become either a tribal leader or a shaman.

I hated him with a passion.

He sat down and reached for the pots of paint. He turned to the boy on his left, and began to decorate his face. The boy sat quietly, accepting the blue and yellow and black dots and swirls in silence. When Kamaran was done, the boy whose face had been decorated turned to the boy on his own left and repeated the process.

One by one, we adorned one another. Part of me felt myself sinking into the ritual; the other part of me fought like hell. The paint dried on my face, pulling it taut. I resisted the urge to scratch.

We then sat in silence, waiting to be summoned. One by one, the Walker Between the Worlds—really the shaman's assistant Lakkam—came for us and took us out. I didn't want to be first, but I certainly didn't want to be last, either.

Finally, Lakkam came for me. "Chakotay, son of Kolopak, stand and step into manhood."

I rose, feeling this whole thing to be stupid and a waste of time, at the same time realizing I was shaking. I walked on unsteady legs to where Lakkam stood in the doorway. He took my hand and guided me to step forward, closing the door after me. When I would have continued on, he stopped me with a hand on my chest and a slightly surprised look on his face. In front of me, he drew a line in the dirt. In the flickering torchlight, I could barely see it.

Of course, the threshold. The first step in the ritual and I'd already forgotten about it. Beads of sweat dappled my forehead. I wondered if they would ruin the paint pattern. Then I wondered if ruining the paint pattern by sweating would get me kicked out of the tribe.

Calm down, Chakotay, I thought, annoyed with myself. *I bet there's no one who gets the ritual perfect. You just need to do it . . . right enough.*

I stepped over the line, then stooped and rubbed it out with my hand. "I am between the worlds," I said, remembering the words more or less correctly, "for I have left behind the world of the child forever, but I am not yet a full man of the tribe."

"You are between the worlds," Lakkam said, "and you will walk with me." He turned me around so that my back was to him, and a blindfold went around my eyes.

For a moment, I panicked. This part, I hadn't heard about, and my heart began to slam against my chest. What was going on? Lakkam gripped my upper right arm and urged me forward. I followed, nervous, my bare feet stumbling frequently.

Objects were thrust into my hands and I was asked to identify them. At first it was easy; a pinecone, a rabbit pelt. But they got harder. What type of traditional pipe was this? Identify this herb by feel and smell and name its uses.

Even the things I thought I knew suddenly deserted me. I don't know what answers I gave, but I knew they weren't right.

Suddenly I was brought to a halt and the blindfold was removed. I stood in the center of a circle of men, all clad in traditional garb, all gazing at me expectantly.

I tried not to look at my father, for I knew if I met his gaze, every semblance of calm I sought to project would vanish utterly.

I knew in my very cells that I was about to disgrace him, and I couldn't bear that.

"Chakotay, son of Kolopak," said the shaman, almost unrecognizable in his paint and animal pelts, "tell me of the Star Walker and his daughter."

Relief shuddered through me. I knew that one, at least. Sekaya used to throw it up in Father's face as a reason why women should be permitted on the tribal council. I dutifully recounted the story of Star Walker and his intelligent, quick-witted daughter. Out of the corner of my eye, I saw Kolopak relax ever so slightly.

"That is well," the shaman said. "Now, what is the story of the Bear and his Beloved?"

Confidence ebbed from me like water at low tide. I stammered out the part of the story I could remember, but I got the ending wrong.

Things rapidly deteriorated from that point. It was one of the worst moments of my life. To this day, just recounting it makes me uncomfortable. I was asked to draw a specific constellation from Old Earth, and I drew Orion instead of the requested Big Dipper. I was asked to chant a war cry, and I couldn't remember any of the words. And finally, I was asked to tell at least one story of the Hero Twins.

I made one up on the spot, and when I looked up, I saw my father had left the circle.

The shaman walked up to me and without warning upended a gourd of water over my face. The liquid was cold and I couldn't suppress a gasp of shock. He rubbed at the paint violently, washing it away. When he was done, he stepped back, contempt on his face.

"The Hero Twins," he said in a voice that reeked of scorn, "are from Navajo mythology, not ours. You should have said so, or at least said that you did not know the names. Instead, you made up a story to hide your shame, to cover your pathetic ignorance. Go from this circle, Chakotay, and remain still between the worlds. You are not a boy, but by the Great Spirit, you are most certainly not a man."

• • •

I don't remember stumbling out of the circle, but I must have, for the next thing I clearly recall was sitting by the little pool I had discovered. The last thing I wanted was to go home and face my father.

The moon was full and the water caught and held its reflection. *No doubt the shaman will catch the moon's reflection in a bowl of water and use it for some ritual,* I thought. *Some ritual for Kamaran and his kind who don't flunk out of becoming a man—*

My fingers had closed around the stone and hurled it at the moon's reflection before I even thought. I took a savage satisfaction in the splash and resulting shivering of the image.

"You shouldn't throw stones in the dark," came a soft voice. "You don't know what you might hit."

I growled. "I don't want to talk to you right now."

Blue Water Boy ignored me and sat beside me, his long legs folded up beneath him. "Sekaya told me what happened," he said quietly. I ducked my head, feeling my face grow hot for the dozenth time that night. "I'm sorry, Chakotay."

"Yeah, well, I'm not," I said fiercely, grasping another rock and tossing it into the lake's depths. "I don't need a stupid ceremony to become a man."

"Well, not to be argumentative," said Blue Water Boy, as if he could possibly ever be argumentative, "but you kind of do. I mean, after all, you're going to live your life here and—"

"No I'm not," I said. That shut him up and for the first time ever I saw Blue Water Boy whirl to stare, shocked, at me.

"What?"

"I'm preparing to take the entrance exam for Starfleet Academy," I said. I hadn't wanted to break it to him this way, but the words poured out of me. "Commander T'Piran is helping me study. And Captain Sulu has agreed to sponsor me if I'm accepted."

After his shocked outburst, Blue Water Boy stayed silent. I couldn't see his dark eyes; the moon's light threw his face into sharp relief and shadows.

I kept talking. "I'm tired of adhering to a tradition that has no place in the twenty-fourth century. That won't take a look at itself and change where it needs to. I've got to get out of here before I suffocate."

"It's not like it's over the mountains," Blue Water Boy said. "You'll be going far away from us, Chakotay. From Sekaya and from me as well as from the tradition that has no place in the twenty-fourth century."

"I'd come back for visits," I argued.

He shook his head slowly. "Not for a long time, and by then, things will be so different . . . things will have changed so much. . . ." He fell silent and stared into the now-still water. Uneasily, I wondered what he was seeing. I wasn't sure I wanted to know.

But my mind was made up. "Change is a good thing," I said. "It's good to shake things up now and then. Isn't that what Coyote and Raven are all about?"

He smiled then. "You have absorbed more about this world than you think, Chakotay. I wonder if you'll be able to let it go as easily as you think you will."

I thought about all that I'd learned in just the past few days: scientific theories and fact, technological marvels, species with characteristics I could barely wrap my mind around. Things that people in Starfleet treated as everyday matters seemed to me wonders almost beyond comprehension. That was the world I longed to be a part of; that was the world that made my heart race and filled me with dizzying longing. I was hopelessly in love with the world of Starfleet, and I had to pass the entrance exam. *Had* to.

"We'll leave it up to fate," I said. "If I pass the exam, I'll be going to Starfleet Academy. If I don't, I'll stay here."

Blue Water Boy said only, "I will miss you, Chakotay."

"Earth?" I cried. *"Earth?"*

"Central America, to be precise," my father said implacably.

"We're going to hunt for the Rubber Tree People and explore your heritage, Chakotay. After what I saw last night, I think you need a solid reminder of where you are from. If you go, perhaps I can persuade the council that next year you can try the initiation rite again."

Despair and terror flooded me. My father was going to take me away from the Starfleet people and plop me down in the middle of a wet, bug-infested Central American rain forest on a hopeless quest for people who probably never existed.

In two weeks.

I had barely begun my studies. The odds of my being able to prepare sufficiently, take the exam, and get the results back before then were not good. I wanted to rage, scream, yell at my father. I wanted to tell him right there what I planned to do, and what he could do with his Rubber Tree People and his Central American rain forest.

By some miracle of restraint, I held my tongue. "You know I don't want to do this, Father," I said quietly. Where she was sitting in the corner working on a headdress, Sekaya's eyes grew enormous at my words and at the calm manner in which they were spoken. "However, you are my father, and I will do as you say."

The words almost stuck in my throat, but I got them out. There was no way I was going to talk my father out of this, not after the spectacle I had made of myself last night, and by not arguing with him I would likely buy more time to myself to study.

I closed the door behind me and took off running, but not before I heard my father say, "Well! That was easier than I thought."

Fear at the thought of losing the sweet fruit of Starfleet that was almost in my grasp gave my feet speed. I'm sure I must have set a record running the two miles between my father's hut and the place where the Starfleet people were housed. In a typically contrary manner, I said a prayer to the Sky Spirits I didn't believe in that I would find T'Piran or Captain Sulu alone.

I was gasping for breath by the time I arrived and I caught a glimpse of T'Piran walking down the trail that led away from the Starfleet quarters to the river. Gulping air, I ran after her. She eyed me curiously.

"You are in a hurry, Chakotay," she said. "What is it?"

"Commander," I gasped, "I need . . . to take the test . . . in less than two weeks. And . . . know the results too. . . ."

That eyebrow reached for the sky again. And again, I marveled at her cool beauty.

"That does not give us much time."

Us. She said us. It was then that I realized that for whatever reason, T'Piran was as anxious as I that I get into Starfleet. Briefly, I wondered why, then let it go. It didn't matter why. The point was, she was.

"No," I managed, still breathing heavily.

"I am going to the river to meditate," she said. "You will accompany me."

I'm sure my face fell. Meditate? If I wanted to meditate I could do it by myself, or under the guidance of the shaman. At my look, T'Piran said, "I know you do not consider yourself to be as spiritual as the other members of your tribe."

She had me there, and I nodded.

"You should respect that aspect of your heritage," she said. "It is not incompatible with a Starfleet career. We Vulcans are highly spiritual and have many intricate rituals."

"Really?" I never would have guessed it.

"Logic and ritual are not opposed. Such meditation and ceremony open pathways in the brain that are otherwise not easily accessible."

"I never thought of it that way."

She stopped and faced me squarely. She was almost as tall as I was and, like Captain Sulu, had a gaze that seemed to bore into my very soul.

"The captain and I are interested in your success, Chakotay.

We both feel you would make an excellent officer. You do not have the luxury of a great deal of study time, so I will teach you how to make the most of what you do have. The meditation techniques you will learn will enable you to focus and absorb information more quickly."

"That would be great," I said, never meaning any words more. Who would have thought an old tradition from my own homeworld would help me to escape it?

If Captain Sulu was my sponsor, then T'Piran was my drill sergeant. On leave, she ignored her own interests to teach me how to meditate. She timed my runs and helped me devise an obstacle course to make sure I would pass the physical exams. Living the highly active life I did, I had an edge over more coddled cadets, though, and she quickly realized that I would do fine in that area. She graded my essay with a ruthless eye and then one day, she and Sulu had a surprise for me.

They let me come aboard the *Mandela.*

Like a child in a dream, I wandered with them from the bridge to engineering to the mess hall to stellar cartography. It was almost more than I could take in. At one point, as I stood gazing down at the blue and green orb that was my homeworld, Sulu stepped beside me and put her hand on my shoulder.

"Are you all right, Chakotay?" she asked quietly. We were alone in stellar cartography.

"Yes, Captain," I replied, but my voice, thick with tears, gave me away, I'm certain. I cleared my throat. "You have no idea how amazing this is to me." *Or how I long to be a part of it,* I thought, but did not say.

She looked at me penetratingly. I thought a tricorder couldn't have done a more thorough analysis.

"I've sent messages to your hut," she said. My blood ran cold. "I want to talk to your father about the exam and what it will mean for you, but he hasn't answered. Sekaya promised she'd give him the messages."

Bless you, Sekaya, I thought.

"You and your father do not always get along well," she said. It was a statement, not a question. My face grew hot.

"How did you know that?"

She smiled a little. "I can recognize the signs. It might interest you to know that I didn't even know my father for the first six years of my life, until my mother died. When he came to get me, to raise me, I resented the hell out of him. The word 'hate' comes to mind."

I couldn't believe she was speaking so frankly. I'd done my research on her, once I had access to information—Demora Sulu was the daughter of the famous Hikaru Sulu. To hear that even a famous father and daughter had problems was both unsettling and reassuring.

"I don't hate my father," I said, and as the words left my lips, I knew they were true.

"Good," she said. "Then you don't have as far to go as I did. I eventually did come around, learning to grudgingly respect, then like, then love him. This tension between child and parent is nothing unique to you, Chakotay, though I know it must feel as though it is. I once told a good friend of mine a bit of wisdom that I think I'll share with you. You have two families, the one you were born into, and the one you choose every day of your life." She looked at me with those eyes that seemed to see everything. "And it looks to me like you will need to leave your homeworld to find that second family."

"Will I find them?" I winced at the need behind the words.

She smiled that wonderful smile and said, "I'm certain you will." Again she squeezed my shoulder. "Come on. You haven't seen the holodeck yet. I think that's going make your eyes fall right out of your head."

I took the test in time.

I passed with flying colors.

• • •

The trip to Earth was a disaster, except for one thing: I told my father everything, and though he was disappointed and saddened, he accepted it.

Well, I told him almost everything.

When we returned, my father insisted on meeting Captain Sulu. "I want to meet the man who is going to be sponsoring my son," he said.

My gut clenched. I was still technically a minor. He could still forbid me to go, and Starfleet would never accept a student against a parent's wishes. "He—he's awfully busy," I stammered. "I don't think that's such a good idea."

"If he wasn't too busy to take such an active interest in you," Kolopak countered, "then he's not going to be too busy to talk to me for five minutes."

There was nothing I could do, once my father was set on a path. I followed miserably, wondering what would be the best course of action—confess now and prepare him, or wait and see how it all played out. I decided on the former.

"Father, there's something you need to know about Captain Sulu," I said.

But it was too late. Captain Demora Sulu herself was in conversation with Anthwara, and looked up as we approached. She smiled, and as always, the years dropped off her face as she did so.

"Chakotay," she said. "Good to see you. How was your trip?"

"Educational," I said. I took a deep breath. "This is my father, Kolopak. Father—this is Captain Demora Sulu."

My father's jaw dropped and he gasped, just as I had when I first realized who this elderly Oriental woman was. "Captain Sulu?" he stammered.

Sulu walked forward and extended a hand. "A pleasure to meet you, sir. Your son is a very gifted young man. I haven't seen entrance exam scores that high in some time, and he had so little opportunity to prepare. He'll make a fine cadet and an excellent officer, I'm certain of it."

I waited for the fallout. I waited for my father to explode, to tell everyone how I had lied to him, that women couldn't possibly be captains, that he had never known about this, that I was a poor excuse for a son and—

"Thank you, Captain. Chakotay certainly is a bright boy. And inventive." He shot me a meaningful look. "I am not as familiar as perhaps I ought to be with what he will be involved with once . . . once he leaves home. Perhaps we could meet and discuss it?"

"I'd be delighted to. Now, if you'll excuse me, Anthwara has something he wants to show me." She smiled at both of us, gave me a wink, and strode off with a bounce in her step that belied her years.

"Thank you, Father," I said, deeply moved.

"You passed, you know, Chakotay."

Confused, I said, "Yes, I know. My scores were—"

"Not just an exam. You passed the initiation into manhood." I was still baffled, and he smiled sadly. "Except . . . you chose another tribe and their rite of passage. I called you a boy on Earth; I was incorrect. Your passion in following this path is not that of an awestruck rebel, but of a man who sees his future."

"Father. . . ." I had no words.

"I still have hope that once you have thoroughly investigated this life, you will hear the call of your homeworld," he said. He didn't live to see it, but in a way, I did. "In the meantime, I think I will have to tell Sekaya she can go study with the shaman after all. A woman captain." He shook his head as we walked home.

Sekaya was thrilled when Father spoke to her, and she said it erased all fourteen of the favors I owed her. I asked her how she calculated fourteen—I knew I owed her at least three more for "forgetting" to deliver Sulu's messages to Father, but I had no clue about the rest—but that's another story.

Blue Water Boy's worry that things would change, and some things not for the better, came true. Once I left, I never saw him again. By the time I had made sufficient peace with myself to return home, he was dead, as was my father, slain resisting the Cardassians, and T'Piran, killed when her ship's warp core breached. My little sister had matured into a grown woman. But I had no hint then of the dark tone the future of my world would take. I had the innocence and ignorance of youth, and I left everything I had ever known without a backward glance in order to involve myself in the most passionate love affair of my life . . . Starfleet.

DAVID GOLD

CAPTAIN OF THE *U.S.S. DA VINCI*

An Easy Fast

JOHN J. ORDOVER

Captain David Gold of the *U.S.S. da Vinci* knew that the best way to attract unwanted attention at a bar was to sit at a table neither eating nor drinking. Gold had half-expected Cap, the bartender at the Captain's Table, to ask him to stop taking up space. Then he realized that Cap was probably aware that on this day Gold could neither eat nor drink before sundown and in any case, he figured Cap could take one fasting customer in stride. The Captain's Table was always as big or as small as it needed to be at any particular moment—which was one of its charms.

Until he had opened the door to his temporary shore quarters on Magatha IV and found himself walking into the Captain's Table, it had looked like Gold, the only Jewish member of his crew, would be spending Yom Kippur alone. The Starfleet Corps of Engineers contingent of the *da Vinci* had stayed in orbit to repair the ship's life-support system, and the rest of his crew was occupied by what meager entertainments the sparsely populated planet had to offer.

His original plan had been to spend the High Holy Days on Earth in his wife Rachel's synagogue with as many of his children and grandchildren as could make it there, followed when it was all over by a sumptous meal prepared by Rachel in their house in the Bronx. But the problem with the ship had forced them into orbit around the nearest available planet, with no chance of getting home in time. Given that, the Captain's Table was an acceptable, if unexpected, second option.

While Cap seemed to have no problem with his neither eating nor drinking, a couple of the other patrons of the bar did, specifically those who had, over the course of the many hours he'd been there, offered to buy Gold a drink and had been politely rebuffed by the captain. They had grown increasingly curious as to his reasons for refusing, especially a Boundarian captain whose round, beach-ball-like body quivered with insult when Gold turned down his offer.

"Too good to drink with the likes of us?" the Boundarian asked. Gold knew this species. Despite their comical appearance and their voices, which hit high squeaky notes as they issued forth from a valve on the top of their heads, they took matters of honor and insult as seriously as any Klingon—perhaps more so. A quick explanation was in order.

"Not at all," Gold replied, "and as soon as it's sundown, I'll not only drink with you, I'll buy the drinks myself." The Boundarian seemed mollified, but curious, so Gold continued. "Among my people, this day is called Yom Kippur, the Day of Atonement. On this day we think back over the previous year and consider all our actions, so we can atone for those that were, uh, less than honorable, according to our code of laws. To aid ourselves in focusing, we take neither food nor drink during that day."

"Interesting," the Boundarian said, "and honorable. I had no idea that humans lived by such codes."

"Not all humans follow the same codes," Gold said, "which is one of the things that some find confusing about us. Nevertheless, once a year, from sundown to sundown, those who follow my path must take neither food nor drink."

Gold's explanation had drawn the attention of an Olexan and a Telspong, the first from yet another warrior culture, one often at odds with the Boundarians, the second from a culture known for its gentle consideration of all sides of each issue.

"How old is this tradition?" the Telspong asked.

Gold shifted a bit in his seat to face the Telspong. "Ceremonies of atonement go back six thousand to ten thousand years, dating back to before my people had acquired a written language."

"Ah," the Telspong said, "then you are still waiting to see how it works out. I wish you luck, and would suggest that—"

What the Telspong was going to suggest was drowned out by the sound of the bar door swinging open violently enough to slam into the adjoining wall. As a radiant figure stepped through,

Gold found himself automatically reaching for his phaser. The Boundarian, meanwhile, looked like he was about to take out what Gold knew was a compressed-air stun weapon, and out of the corner of his eye Gold noted Cap reaching under the bar for heaven only knew what weapon he kept there.

"Hey, there," Cap said pleasantly, "what can we do for you?"

The figure stepped forward. Closer up, Gold saw that he—the figure looked male—was humanoid in shape, with a crown of horns sticking out of his head, empty holes where Earth humans had nostrils, and weblike ears that were pointed forward in what Gold could only guess was anger. His species was hard to place; he looked like a number of different races kluged together.

The figure was clothed—or perhaps, Gold thought, a better description would be "cloaked"—in a flowing uniform that seemed to be made from a generated light pattern. At first Gold could place neither the creature's time frame nor the uniform, but there was something about the latter—something familiar—that led him to venture a guess.

"Starfleet?" Gold asked the figure. "But from the future?"

"Starfleet, yes," the figure said, "but from the present. You, however, are from the far past. Perhaps two or three hundred . . ." The figured stopped. "I know where I am," he said.

"Excellent," the Telspong said, "but may I ask in what sense? Personal location is subject to mental variables, spatial ones, even points of view. Could you elaborate on . . ."

"I'm in the Captain's Table," the figure said.

"Right the first time," Cap said from behind the bar. "What brings you here?"

The figure glanced around. As he did so, Gold followed his gaze around the bar.

"I am looking for Captain Mak Dav Al," the figure said. "He found his way to my *skreee*, and has *terwelled* me once again. This time for the last time."

"I'm sorry," Gold said, "he found his way to your what now, and did what?"

The figure regarded Gold intently. "I do not believe," he said, "that the concept of either has been developed as of your time, and it would take far too long to explain, and perhaps violate Starfleet regulations covering time-space contamination. Trust me when I say it is a vile crime in my time, and that Mak Dav Al must be made to pay for it."

To one side of him, Gold saw the Telspong writing down "skree" and "terwell" on a tiny personal padd.

"So you are on a mission of vengeance, and your trail led you here," the Boundarian squeaked. "Excellent. How may we assist you?"

The figure moved to an empty chair at Gold's table and sat down heavily, clearly exhausted. "I am not sure. My quarry ran down an alley with many doors, and I was pulling them open one by one when I found myself looking into this place. Why I am here now I do not know."

"Sometimes," Cap said from behind the bar, "you wind up here 'cause here's where you need to be."

"Interesting," the Telspong said, and added more notes to his padd.

"That," the figure said, "is highly unlikely."

"And you say that because?" the Telspong asked, his fingers ready over his padd.

"Because I can see," the figure said, "that my quarry is not within this establishment, so once I catch my breath, I will have to pursue him elsewhere."

"Is that really what you want to do?" Gold asked evenly, his eyes looking right into those of the figure in front of him. "Vengeance is a dish best served cold, they say, and like any other cold dish, it can fail to warm your heart."

"A somewhat tortured turn of phrase," the Telspong said as he joined the two others at the table, "but worth writing down anyway." Both Gold and the figure across from him ignored the Telspong.

"Look," Gold began, then stopped. "Do you have a name? Hard to talk to a man without knowing his name."

"Mak Dav Al."

Gold was taken aback for a moment. "I thought that was the name of the man you're after?"

"It is," Al said. "My problem with him relates to a method of resolving personal identity conflicts that you do not as yet practice."

"Fascinating," the Telspong said, tapping once again at his padd.

"Okay, Al," Gold said, "I have a story to tell you. I owe Cap one anyway. It's not about someone who had his *skreee terwelled*, or at least I don't think it is, because I don't know what that means, but it is about a man who had been offended in a way that gave him at least as much right to seek vengeance as you seem to have. It's about a friend of mine. Call him . . . Abraham Silver. Abe. Great guy. This story starts quite a while back, when he was on his first shore leave from a Starfleet vessel, and . . ."

From behind Gold, the Boundarian suddenly squeaked, "Is this a tale of betrayal and death and revenge?"

Gold smiled. "In its way."

"Excellent," the Boundarian squeaked, as he half-climbed, half-bounced into the one remaining seat at Gold's table. "My apologies for the interruption. Please go on."

Captain Gold continued.

The problem began when Abe was an ensign on the *Gettysburg*. He'd been out of Starfleet Academy for only about six months when the ship pulled into Cathius IX for shore leave. For one reason or another, Abe's assignments tended to run more toward cleaning out Jefferies tubes than exploring strange new worlds, and the poor guy hadn't been off the ship the entire time. Shore leave on Cathius IX, a world known for its exotic charm, sounded very good to him. He'd come to the ship straight from Earth, you see, and had never even been on a planet outside his own star system before.

So there Abe was, young and handsome, ready to take on a

whole new world. Problem was, Cathius IX saw Abe coming a light-year off. A fool and his money are soon parted.

Soon he found himself in a little out-of-the-way establishment ordering drinks for a scantily dressed, raven-haired young woman who seemed to imply that their evening would culminate in a trip back to her place.

First, though, she wanted to have some fun. There was gambling in the back of the place, some Carthian game that Abe had never played and didn't really understand, but the young woman was more than helpful at suggesting where and how to place his chips, and soon his red chips were replaced with blue ones, then gray, then black. When his stack of black chips had reached—oh, a goodly number, and Abe was beginning to sober up a bit, he decided it was time to cash in his chips and take the woman to somewhere more private.

His first clue that something was wrong was when he tried to tip the Gallamite gamemaster with a chip and got a nasty look in return. The manager, a Katcherian, then stepped over, counted up his chips, and demanded a number of credits larger than all the credits Abe had saved up over the last six months.

Red chips, they explained to him, represented positive numbers, as did blue chips and gray chips. But black chips were negative numbers, representing money owed to the house. When Abe looked around for the young woman to verify this, she had vanished. It was just Abe, the gamemaster, the store manager, and a hired Mausetite goon.

Abe realized he had just been conned, and conned good, and he was young enough to resent it greatly and take a stand for truth, justice, and so on. Rather than negotiate a sum that he could afford—the standard operating procedure in these circumstances—he refused flat out to pay a single credit, and turned to head for the door. He hadn't gotten four steps before he was struck from behind by the leg of a chair or some equivalently solid, clublike object.

Now, remember, Abe was young and strong and trained in

combat at Starfleet Academy. And what's more, he couldn't take a hint, so of course he responded with anger and violence. He turned back to his attackers and, using the skills he had been taught, engaged them in hand-to-hand combat.

"Excellent!" the Boundarian squeaked, "a glorious battle fought against a dishonorable foe, with right making might and a noble hero overcoming . . ."

". . . hand-to-hand combat," Gold continued, ignoring the Boundarian, "which was a mistake. Though Abe had youth and strength on his side, the others had actually been in a fight or two, which Abe, outside of training, had not. Oh, he held his own for a while, but eventually his foes got the upper hand, and he was beaten, first badly, then unconscious, then finally to death. It was only then that his luck began to change."

"He died?" the Telspong said, shocked. "And *then* his luck changed?"

"He returned as a spirit," the Olexan guessed, "and proceeded after those who had wronged him?"

"He failed?" the Boundarian said. "Not a very inspiring story."

"Your point is?" Al asked.

"My point is coming," Gold replied to Al, "whether the story is inspiring I will leave to you to decide when it's finished, and yes, his luck changed after he died. Moments after he breathed what would have been his last, the automatic shore-leave recall activated and Abe was beamed back to the *Gettysburg*. When the transporter chief saw the condition he was in, he beamed him straight to sickbay and the doctor there was able to revive him."

"Ah," the Telspong said. "Did he report any life-after-death experiences?"

"Brilliant plan!" the Olexan said. "Coming back to life would catch his enemies entirely unaware."

"Worse, much worse, than a simple failure," the Boundarian said, "compounding a dishonorable death by returning to life is . . . obscene."

"Why bother to revive him?" Al asked. "He could just have been reconstituted from his transporter pattern and . . ." Gold shot him a look and Al stopped. "I guess you haven't figured that out yet. Sorry. Forget I said anything."

"No life-after-death experiences that I know about," Gold said, picking up his story, "other than that his life did continue after his resuscitation, albeit requiring a six-month course of rehabilitation before he could resume his Starfleet duties. The whole time he was recovering, he had the images of the Gallamite, the Mausetite, and the Katcherian locked firmly into his mind, and he kept three of the black chips that had beamed up with him clenched in his fist to dull the pain of recovery and keep those three burned into his memory. They had killed him, and he wanted revenge, no matter how long and hard the road to finding it would be."

"I see," the Boundarian squeaked, "he would recover his honor after his death. Interesting."

"The practical advantages . . ." the Olexan began.

"The philosophical implications are . . ." the Telspong began, but Gold cut him off.

"When Abe was finally well enough to return to Starfleet, he was reassigned to the *Tian An Men*, which was on patrol in a sector not anywhere near Carthius IX. . . ."

By the time he was able to return to the planet, three years later, the Gallamite, the Mausetite, and the Katcherian had all moved offworld, in entirely different directions. The young woman who had entertained him that night was still around, and it was a matter of only a little effort to track her down. Abe didn't know what angered him more—what she had done to him, that she had done it so many times to others that she didn't remember him in particular, or that she offered to deliver on the promised culmination of the evening if he didn't hurt her.

But while he was angry at her, she had merely taken advantage of a naïve young officer; by the time he was beaten to death, she was long gone. Maybe she deserved some sort of payback, maybe not. All Abe knew for sure was, the brunette was the type who knew all the scuttlebutt. If anyone could tell him where the three murderers were now, it was her. She had no information on the Gallamite or the Mausetite, but the Katcherian, she knew exactly where he was: Argelius. Presumably continuing his gambling operations on that world. Fine. Argelius was on the *Tian An Men*'s regular route. Getting a short leave there—all he'd need is a few hours, Abe told himself—should be no problem at all.

A month later, Abe found himself standing outside a small stone house in a heavily forested area of Argelius. He had been surprised to find out that gambling and all other such entertainments had been banned from the planet sometime during his rehabilitation.

The Argelians were pacifists by culture and nature and had come to the conclusion that gambling clubs and such were, in the end, simply too likely to cause violent conflict to be allowed. The clubs that had once lined its long streets had moved en masse to a planet called Risa, but, Abe had learned, the Katcherian had not gone with them, but had instead moved to where Abe now found himself: a friendly-looking house in the woods surrounded by multicolored trees, lulled by the harmonic vibrations of the *glanthor* in their burrows under the ground, and cooled by gentle breezes that washed down the nearby mountain.

Hard as it was to maintain an angry demeanor in this genteel setting, Abe's fury at his own murder was strong enough to overcome it. Still, he felt a bit foolish as he pulled on the rope that rang a square metal bell hanging on a post near the front of the house.

The woman who came to answer the bell was cheerful and outgoing, and of a friendly demeanor that would have disarmed Abe had he not already steeled himself against the bucolic environment. There was a bit of gray in her red hair, and two young children, a boy and a girl, were peering from around her skirts.

When the woman saw Abe, her face fell. "You must be here for my husband. Is there anything I can say that would convince you to walk away?"

Abe shook his head and stepped past her into the house.

Resigned, she led him to the back door, and then out behind the house where there, indeed, was the Katcherian that Abe had been pursuing. He was wearing a black robe with silver trimming, standard Argelian clothing, and lying facedown near a stream that ran through the backyard, his right hand trailing in the water.

"We have company," Abe heard his wife say from behind him. The Katcherian turned and saw Abe. He smiled a wan smile and pulled himself up to his feet.

"You are . . ." the man paused, but before Abe could answer, the Katcherian continued. "You are Abraham Silver, once an ensign in Starfleet, now, I see, a lieutenant. Congratulations. Ah, I see you are surprised I remember you, that I know your name. Let me be honest. I know it only because I have forced myself to remember all those whom I have wronged, and what I did to each."

Abe stared at the person who had been a specter in his mind for years. His face was older than the image that Abe had carried with him. The blank cruelty Abe had seen in the man's eyes so long ago had disappeared, and was replaced now by sadness and resignation.

"My life," the Katcherian said, "is by right yours to take. I have learned that no matter how hard I try to make amends, there are some things that cannot be mended."

Abe felt his phaser burning against his hip. He had imagined the Katcherian's death at his hands many times, but looking the real man in the eye and taking his life, while his victim made no move to dissuade him, that was a different matter entirely.

From behind him Abe suddenly heard the rustle of Argelian silks. The Katcherian's wife had come up from behind Abe almost without him noticing, and Abe reflexively stepped back and reached for his phaser.

"There is no need for a weapon," the Argelian woman said. "I have no plans to attack you. This is Argelius. Here violence is unthinkable."

Abe was certainly thinking about violence, but he chose not to express that.

"What I do intend to do," she continued, "is tell you about my husband. True, he fled Cathius IX in fear of the repercussions from the murder of a Starfleet officer, one Abraham Silver. He came to Argelius to work in one of the now-banned houses of chance. That was the only life he knew—at the time.

"But the path of one's life can change. The life of the people of Argelius, one of peace and respect, has a strong effect on everyone, and on my husband stronger than most. He studied our ancient writings, attended our consensus gatherings, and after a while, began to speak out at them. Soon he was recognized as what we call a *parnon*, one whose understanding of the ways of peace and cooperation not only goes beyond that of others, but spreads to others as well.

"It was his words that led us to expel games of chance from our planet. It is his words that have begun to bind our planet together in a web of peace and prosperity that exceeds any we have known before. We have no central ruler, because that always leads to conflict. But if any were known as the first among equals, it would be him.

"You can take his life, if you choose," she continued, "and neither he nor I will move to stop you. The old laws punishing murder have been repealed as being, in themselves, violent. If you kill him, no one on this planet will hinder you afterward, or prevent your leaving to return to your life among the stars. I will certainly be the poorer for his loss, and I will mourn, as will our children. Our planet will mourn as well. What impact his death will have on you is something perhaps even you yourself do not know, but whatever it is, it will be yours to bear."

Gold stopped his story and looked at his four companions at the Captain's Table. Al, the Starfleet officer from the future, had gotten lost in the story and was taking a moment to come out of it. The Telspong was furiously searching through the data on his padd and, reading upside down, Gold could see that the philosopher was scanning over data on Argelius and its philosophies.

At that point the Boundarian spoke up. "I assume that Abraham Silver's honor and duty propelled him to take the Katcherian's life, no matter what the cost?"

"Perhaps, perhaps not," the Telspong said. "After all, the subject of his wrath had changed. Is the person you are tomorrow the same person you are today?"

"Of course," the Boundarian said. "To think otherwise would negate all concepts of responsibility for one's actions."

The Olexan put in, "The rule is that an honorable man will not hear anything said against his honor-quest."

"But is one forever bound by a bad deed done?" the Telspong asked. "Can amends not be made? Can, in your terms, the honor of another be restored by the actions of the one who offended it, rather than by the actions of the offended?"

"No," the Olexan replied, "there are no 'amends' as you call them, only a failure of will on the part of the offended party."

The Boundarian replied, "That depends on the deed. Some deeds hang on one forever, some do not. For example . . ."

"An excellent start," Gold said, addressing his table companions in a tone much like, he realized, that his rabbi wife took when addressing a congregation. "Discussion of such issues has been carried on among my people for thousands of years."

"And what conclusions have you reached?" the Telspong asked eagerly.

"Wait," Al said, his technologically generated uniform shimmering as he spoke, "first I'd like to know what Silver decided to do."

"Well," Gold began. . . .

Abe Silver looked at the Katcherian, then looked at the man's wife, then stepped over to the rushing stream and stared down at his own face as reflected in water dyed red with minerals from the Argelian mountains. He took out one of the three black chips that he had kept with him for years and tossed it into the reddish stream, where it quickly floated downriver and out of sight.

Then he stood up, turned his back on the Katcherian and his wife, and walked back through the house and out onto the path he had taken to reach the small stone cottage. He felt more angry than he had even during his long months of painful recovery. His vengeance had been taken from him in a way that seemed almost cosmically unfair. In a sense, the man who had killed him so violently and painfully no longer existed. He had been replaced by a noted leader and scholar as cleanly as if he had switched with a double from an alternate universe. Silver weighed his needs and his anger against what the Katcherian had accomplished, and let his anger go.

But there were two more men on his list, and he was damned if he was going to be denied his vengeance again.

"So this is the tale of a coward," the Olexan said.

"On the contrary," the Boundarian stated, "it is a tale of a man in whom honor is balanced against other concerns."

"Or possibly," the Telspong said, "it is the tale of an unselfish man, who puts the needs of others over his own need for vengeance."

"Or perhaps," Al from the future said, "it's a tale that isn't finished yet, and that I would like to hear more of." He turned to Gold. "Please go on."

Time passed, and it was six years before Silver tracked down his next quarry, in this case the Gallamite. In that time, Silver's career had prospered and he had risen to the rank of lieutenant commander and was serving on the *Venezia*. The Gallamite had moved to an unallied planet named Carnegie by its earliest colonists, whose intent had been to take the planet's abundant resources and turn it into a worldwide factory. By a hundred years before Silver's time, the planet had become a global industrial park, and for most of those hundred years its specialization had paid off. The planet grew wealthy.

By the time Silver arrived on the planet, however, the need for its manufactured items in the galaxy had been almost entirely eliminated by the development of large-scale industrial replicators. Why order something shipped from Carnegie when you could zap it into existence nearby for a tenth the price? Having taken shore leave while his captain tried to talk the planet into aligning with the Federation after all, Silver walked the dusty, gray, silent streets of the nearly deserted city, wondering why anyone who had the chance to leave here could possibly stay.

The Gallamite's office was in one of the few remaining factories that still had life to it. There was a sign on the side that Silver couldn't immediately understand, but that his tricorder said read "Creative Development" in Gallamite. Silver walked through the front door of the bright red building—the only colorful building he'd yet seen on Carnegie—and asked for directions to the Gallamite's office. The cheerful, brightly dressed young human behind the desk explained that the head of the company typically didn't see anyone without an appointment, but since he was a Starfleet officer and all, and they were working on a Federation grant, he'd be happy to give his name to the CEO's office and see if they'd accept him.

Silver looked around the entryway as he waited. It was brightly painted and decorated with extremely imaginative high-quality art. Silver was particularly intrigued by a holographic display that showed a close-up of the surface of Carnegie as it was transformed from forested to industrialized, and then ran the time frame backward as slowly the artificial constructs were dismantled and taken away, restoring the planet to a pristine condition. Silver had the time to see the entire presentation three or four times before there was a hand on his shoulder.

Silver turned around to see himself facing four Creative Development security guards in uniforms of interlocking pastels, none of whom had facial expressions as cheerful as their outfits.

"Listen, friend," the largest of them said to Silver, "the CEO sends his regrets, but he knows why you're here and he has no desire to see you. We're here," he indicated himself and his three large companions, "to make certain you leave peacefully."

"But," the friendly desk clerk started to object, "we operate on a—"

"CEO's orders," the lead guard said without taking his eyes off Silver.

Silver was tempted to allow the guards to escort him out of the factory and to confront the Gallamite after working hours, and had the situation not been quite so similar to the original scene that had led to his death, he might well have. At first he nodded in agreement and headed for the door, listening for the footsteps of the lead guard right behind him. When his ears told him that he and his target were in the right positions, Silver spun and dropped the guard with a quick chop to the side of the neck. While the other three guards were still reaching for their weapons Silver had pulled his phaser and stunned them into unconsciousness.

Silver walked back over to the desk clerk, who was pale as a ghost and frozen in place. Silver reached past him, looked down at his signaling board, and flipped the "all clear" button, informing the security office, inaccurately of course, that the problem he represented had been dealt with.

"CEO's office?" he asked the desk clerk, who was barely able to stammer out an answer. "Thanks. Take the rest of the day off. You don't look well."

The Gallamite's office was right off what clearly had once been an assembly-line floor, but was now more like an artist's studio, with holoequipment and replicators and even good old-fashioned marble, paint, and canvas, as well as several dozen artists hard at work. Silver barely took in the surroundings as he headed straight for the Gallamite's office and kicked open the door.

There he was, the gamemaster, the man who had conned him and set him up to die. He'd put on about a hundred pounds since then, but somehow looked younger than his years. The Gallamite shrugged as Silver walked in, not at all thrown by the abrupt opening of his door.

"You're here to kill me," he said softly to Silver. "So go ahead."

"But you'll have to get through us first," came a voice from behind Silver, and as he turned, the artists from the factory floor stepped into the room around him and closed ranks in front of the Gallamite.

"Wasn't for him," one of them said, "we'd have starved."

"Everyone else left," someone else said, "and took their money off-planet with them. They left us with nothing, and no way out."

"He's the one who came up with this," another said, waving at the factory floor that was now an art studio.

Silver took a long hard look at the factory floor. So that was what was going on here, he realized. What's the one thing a replicator or a holodeck can't give you? Something you haven't thought of yet. What was the one thing it cost almost nothing to make and nothing to export? Art. Designs. Replicator patterns for useful and decorative items that no one had thought of yet. Holographic dramas that could be generated entirely on one or two small machines and then sent out to the rest of the galaxy for next to nothing, but at a high profit. If the Gallamite had really come up with the concept, no wonder these people thought so highly of him.

Of course, going through them to get to the Gallamite wasn't much of a problem. Silver had a phaser, not a shotgun, and a quick blast or two on light stun would clear the path to the Gallamite and leave nothing on Silver's conscience. Still, he hesitated to draw his weapon on innocents, and while he did, the Gallamite's soft voice came out from behind the crowd that had gathered.

"Thank you all," he said, in the very same soothing voice that had kept Silver putting more chips down on the table all those years ago, "but if you'd just step outside now, I'm sure that this nice officer and I can resolve our problems amicably."

The crowd seemed uncertain, but the Gallamite's words sank in and one by one they left, glaring at Silver on their way out.

"So," the Gallamite said, "either shoot me or take a seat."

Silver sat.

"First of all," he said, "I'm sorry. Things shouldn't have gone as far as they did, and we never should have killed you. I'm glad the condition wasn't permanent."

Silver found the apology oddly comforting, even though the smoothness of the Gallamite's voice left him questioning its sincerity. He felt some of his anger slip away and was annoyed to feel it go.

"However," the Gallamite said, "I hope you know there were consequences for me. I had killed a Starfleet officer, and suddenly I was out of a job and, for that matter, out of a planet. I couldn't settle anywhere without my Starfleet warrant popping up, whether in a month, a year, or two years, and bang, once again my life was gone." The Gallamite held up his hands, cutting off the remark Silver was going to make. "Not in the way that yours was, but in a way. Finally it occurred to me that the one place no one would look for me was somewhere that people were deserting in droves. By all accounts, Carnegie would be almost empty soon after I got here—and that suited me fine."

"So what happened?" Silver asked. He had to steel himself to remember that this man made his living conning people, and that his words should not be trusted. Still, he was curious.

"So I got here, felt safe for the first time since I helped kill you, and I got bored," he said. "And I never could resist a gamble. So I bought out this factory for back taxes, applied under the corporate name for a Federation grant under the Assistance to Unaligned Planets program, and started turning this place around, employing the same engineers and designers and artists who created our physical products in the past to make virtual ones that can be produced by our customers on-site."

"Good idea," Silver said.

"Thanks," he said. "But I have an even better one. How about you don't shoot me, and I'll cut you in for, say, five percent of the profits? After all, if I'm dead, I can't make a dime off this place."

Silver was taken aback. He hadn't expected to be offered a pay-off, and it was clear that the Gallamite, in his own selfish, self-centered way, was doing a world of good—literally—for these people and this place.

Gold paused in his story. His throat was dry, and if it weren't Yom Kippur, he would have asked for a drink of water before continuing.

"Pausing to heighten suspense," the Olexan said, thinking Gold had stopped his tale for that reason, "is dishonorable." His hand began to move toward the weapon at his side, but stopped at a stern glance from Cap, who was, as usual, aware of everything that was going on in the Captain's Table.

"Hardly," the Boundarian put in. "Risking, as the storyteller is, the wrath of his audience, pausing is an act of bravery, greatly to be admired."

"No, it is merely annoying," Al put in.

"Gentlemen," the Telspong said softly, "in music, the spaces between the notes are often as important to the enjoyment of the piece as the notes themselves—sometimes more. I see this as a period of contemplation that enhances the overall effect of the story. For a moment, we remain curious what the star of the story did, and that curiosity, in and of itself, improves the story."

"The only honorable thing would be to accept the offer," the Olexan said. "Blood money is a standard contract, although typically the victim does not rise from the dead to demand it himself."

"I would have refused the offer," the Boundarian said. "Accepting money to abandon a blood debt is dishonorable."

It was unclear to Gold, as he waited for his throat to recover, whether the Olexan and the Boundarian intentionally took opposite sides on every issue of honor simply for the pleasure of annoying each other, or if these differences were the root cause of the conflict between their peoples.

The table's consensus was that it was the Telspong's turn to comment, but he declined. "I prefer," he said, "to wait and see how a story plays out without attempting to get ahead of it. I find that if I guess successfully, the impact is weakened for me, and if I guess unsuccessfully, I am annoyed at my failure to make an accurate prediction and again the impact is weakened."

"I," Al said somewhat fiercely, "am beginning to see how this story relates to my current situation, and would like to hear how this section of it turns out." He glared the others into silence, then turned expectantly to Gold.

Well, Silver found this situation to be far different from the one he had faced with the Katcherian years ago. The Gallamite was unchanged, simply forced by circumstances into behaving as a benefactor, by accident, almost. Now that he had introduced the idea of selling creativity rather than large blocks of metal, it would spread throughout the planet with or without him. There was a sense in which he was no longer necessary. And for that matter, there were, as the Gallamite had pointed out, active Starfleet warrants out for his arrest. Gold could simply stun him, ask for a beam-up to the ship, and execute the warrant once on board. True, it might upset his captain's current negotiations, but those negotiations were pro forma anyway and not expected to succeed.

"That five percent," Silver said at last. "Let me ask you a question—what percentage of the profits do your designers receive?"

The Gallamite's face showed his surprise at the question, and perhaps a bit of suspicion and defensiveness. "They are amply compensated," he said warily, "but you have to understand, the major investment is mine, the equipment is mine, I make the decisions as to which product lines we are going to pursue, and so on. Their contribution, while vital, is only a small part of . . ." The Gallamite trailed off as Silver's hand started moving involuntarily toward his phaser.

"Here's what I suggest," Silver said. "You give your designers the extra five percent you were going to give me, and I'll forget I found you here."

The Gallamite smiled widely. "Certainly! Absolutely! Consider it done!" He tapped some keys on the computer in front of him. "There! The designer compensation fund has already been increased by five percent of the after-tax profits from last year, and will be for this year."

"That's nice," Silver said, "but not what I meant. What I mean is that each designer will receive five percent of the profits from their particular creative endeavor."

The Gallamite's face fell. "Pay them directly? That will cost me . . ."

"A lot less than your life, or a life sentence for killing a Starfleet officer," Silver said.

"But my competitors . . . they aren't online yet, but they will be shortly, and . . ."

"Oh," Silver said, "I'm quite sure your competitors are in start-up mode right now. Once you announce your new percentage plan, not only will you retain your best designers, you'll set the participation standard for your entire industry, and perhaps the entire planet. It's likely I'm only asking you to accelerate a payment structure you would have been forced into anyway."

The Gallamite considered his options for a moment, then agreed. Silver, remembering the guards he had stunned down below and that they were quite possibly awake and angry by this time, called to his ship for beam-up.

"I'll be stopping by from time to time," Silver said, "to make certain that you're following your end of our deal. I'll leave you this to remember me by." He took out one of his two remaining black chips and flipped it across the desk to the Gallamite, who, old gamemaster that he was, caught it deftly. His expression was no more cheerful when he saw it than it had been when Silver had tried to tip him with it, all those years ago. *Good,* Silver thought. *Let the coin remind him of the consequences of his actions, as it has reminded me all these years.* As Silver felt the transporter beam dissolve him, he felt his hatred and anger toward the Gallamite dissolving as well.

•   •   •

"Fair enough," the Olexan said, "a blood price is a blood price, and if the offended decides to spread the wealth, that's up to him."

"Nonsense," the Boundarian said, "a payoff is a payoff, no matter how the money is spent."

The Telspong tapped on his padd and pulled up the current status of the planet Carnegie. "Carnegie," he read aloud, "is a center for art and design known throughout the galaxy. The basic design for the fighter craft used by the Federation against the Dominion came from there, as did the winners of the last four Virtual awards for Best Holographic Scenario. The economy of the planet is stable and the distribution of wealth is among the most equitable in the Federation, of which it is now a member. Is it still known in your time?" the Telspong said to the man from the future.

Al waved the question away. "I'm not supposed to say. And I'm more interested in getting to the rest of the story as quickly as possible. My quarry," he said, although with less vigor than he had before, "moves quickly, and while this story is instructive, I do need to get back to the hunt." He turned to Gold. "So what of the last target of Silver's revenge, and the last black chip he carried?"

It was a few years later, just after Silver had been promoted to captain but before the ship he was to command had returned from its latest mission. Word of the Mausetite reached Silver through—let's say a contact in Starfleet Intelligence who was aware of his situation but should most likely not have offered him the information. Nonetheless the information that reached Silver seemed to have divine energy behind it. The Mausetite was already scheduled for execution on yet another unaligned planet. That part was straightforward.

The penal system on the planet, however, had an odd twist to it that played right into Silver's hands. The right to execute a prisoner was auctioned off by the government. The highest bidder was awarded the privilege of choosing the time and method of the prisoner's death. The latest bid on the Mausetite was actually quite low, and it was simple for Silver to outbid the only other interested party. Soon he literally had the Mausetite's life in his hands. All he had to do was comm back the go-ahead, and the Mausetite's life would end in whatever manner Silver chose.

But the black chip Silver carried still weighed on him, as did the memories of his encounters with his two previous intended targets. A Starfleet captain, even one whose ship was still months out of drydock, had privileges, and passage to the frontier world where the Mausetite was imprisoned was fairly simple to arrange.

Silver found that the prison where the Mausetite was held was a sewer, literally. It doubled as the waste-processing plant for the local city, and the prisoners were forced to wade naked through the waste to retrieve anything the guards thought might be of value—which was then turned over to the guards to sell. After stepping out of the constant stream of waste, the prisoners were hit with high-pressure streams of hot water to clean the waste from them and thrown, still naked, into cells with cold stone floors and nothing else.

It was enough to make Silver begin to pity the man, but the list of his crimes had been sent along with the paperwork surrounding the execution, and the unspeakable things the Mausetite had done since Silver had last encountered him called out for a high level of punishment. While the Federation did not punish even its worst offenders in a way as harsh as this, the Prime Directive certainly gave unaligned planets the right to do so.

Getting an audience with the Mausetite was only a matter of a small payment to the guard captain, who wondered why anyone would want to speak with any of his charges. To Silver's surprise, the Mausetite remembered him the moment he walked up to the old-fashioned metal bars that made up the front of his cell. He not only knew Silver's name, he knew the number of credits Silver owed him and demanded them the moment he saw him.

As the Mausetite yelled at him for his money, Silver read in more detail the list of horrendous crimes the Mausetite had committed, and this list was only what he had done since he got to this particular planet. The number of lives he had damaged or destroyed was impressive, in a horrible way. Silver's other two assailants had in some way redeemed themselves; either they had changed themselves or they had been changed by circumstances. If the Mausetite had changed at all, he had only gotten worse. On top of which, having him killed or killing him himself was totally legal under the laws of this planet. Silver took out his last black chip and stared at it.

Gold paused, again unintentionally, and the discussion began again. This time the Telspong spoke first: "Kill him." The others looked at him in surprise. He remained firm. "Kill him, yes, kill him. Not only is it the only way to be certain that others will be safe from him in the future, but he has shown no growth, no repentance. He has not earned forgiveness, so should not be granted it."

"I thought you preferred not to guess at the endings of stories?" Al said to him.

"That is correct," the Telspong said, "but then I, too, am imperfect and inconsistent. What a boring place the galaxy would be without imperfection and inconsistency!"

Gold smiled at that.

"I agree with the Telspong here," the Olexan said. "Kill him. Kill the Mausetite. He has earned his death."

"Well," the Boundarian said, clearly hating the prospect of agreeing with the Olexan, "yes, kill him. He is dishonorable and dangerous. There is no other choice."

"And yet," Gold said, "Silver found one."

Silver stared at the Mausetite, who ranted on about Silver's unpaid debt. Then Silver came to a decision, and felt a weight he had been carrying for years lift from his shoulders. He interrupted the Mausetite's ranting and said, "I'm here to settle up."

Fear shrouded the Mausetite's face.

"No, not for killing me. The debt I owe you, the debt you've been ranting about. Here you go." And Silver tossed the Mause-tite's death papers through the cell's bars. The papers had cost him just about as much as the amount of his original debt, the one he had been killed for.

"Now," Silver said, "the burden of your life is on you, where it should always have been, and no longer on me. They will never let you out of here, you know that. But now you have a decision to make. With those papers, you can live here as long as you want, or die any way and any time you want. Your life is about your choices, not mine. I'm tired of you, and tired of thinking about you."

Silver turned, ignoring the Mausetite's screams, and walked out of the prison, feeling lighter than he had in years. On the way out he tossed his last black chip into the waste stream in which the second shift of prisoners was standing chest-deep.

"Pointless!" the Olexan shouted. "You have wasted our time with a story of a man who travels great distances to confront his ene-mies, and does nothing when he encounters them!"

"I am not so sure," the Boundarian said. "It seems there is a point to it, but it escapes me. Perhaps it is—" Gold felt his struggle to get the condescension out of his voice. "—a *human* thing."

The Telspong sighed. "It so often falls to me to provide the moral to a story. That's a danger of my profession as a philoso-pher. What the parable our friend the captain has been telling us has a deep meaning, one that—"

"Wait!" the Olexan shouted. "Are you saying that the story we just listened to, on top of being pointless, might never have hap-pened? Might be only a fictional tale?"

"Well, it might or might not be true," the Telspong answered, "in a factual sense. But its level of factual accuracy is hardly an impor-tant matter. There is great truth to be found in nonfactual stories."

"There certainly is," the Boundarian agreed.

"Bah!" The Olexan stood up and stomped off toward a table in the back of the room. "My short leave time, spent listening to pointless events that never even happened. . . ."

It was hard to figure out if a Boundarian was smiling, Gold knew, but he would bet his rank this one was.

"Quiet," Al from the future said. "Quiet, please. After all, this story was meant for me, not for you. And I think I take its meaning. I will reconsider my pursuit of my namesake, and perhaps seek other paths. I thank you for your instruction."

"No problem," Gold said, his voice a little hoarse from telling the tale and still taking no water. He checked his chronometer. "Wait another three minutes, and I'll buy you a drink to go with it."

"I cannot," Al said. "I have family/crew whom I have neglected for my pursuit long enough. You have given me a gift, though, and I wish to give you one in return—but without breaking Starfleet temporal regulations that may be difficult."

Al paused to consider, then smiled and stood up. "I leave you with this. I come from around two hundred years in your future, give or take a few decades. And yet, while I was too intent on my quest to mention it on my arrival, when I saw you sitting here I knew at once that you were Captain David Gold of the *U.S.S. da Vinci*. Two hundred years, give or take, and I knew you *on sight*. You have given me something to think about. Now you think about that."

His piece apparently said, Al nodded to Gold, to the Telspong, to the Boundarian, and attempted to wave good-bye to the Olexan. And then he took his leave.

When Gold turned back from watching him go, Cap was placing a tall glass of water and a large bowl of matzoh ball soup in front of him. To the side of the soup Cap had already set an overstuffed pastrami sandwich dripping with mustard. Gold took a long drink of the water, a spoonful of the soup, and a large bite out of the sandwich, then ordered the drinks he had promised the Telspong and the Boundarian and even had a drink sent to the Olexan's table at the far side of the bar.

The sun had gone down in the Bronx, and Yom Kippur was over for another year.

Tending Bar . . .

Shortly after Gold told his midrash, Chakotay, Shran, Archer, and Porthos all left the bar. After downing his sandwich, soup, and water—and the Telspong and Boundarian had finished their drinks—Gold too left, his ritual complete.

The Ferengi who had been so interested in Archer's canine fable started telling his own tale, a boast involving great profit for him and great destitution for his enemies. Across the bar, the Telspong and the Triexian started comparing and contrasting Gold's and Klag's stories. And at the bar itself, Prrgghh started telling a story of her own, but only Cap and Lizzy were paying attention. Prrgghh didn't seem to notice; if she had, Cap suspected that Lizzy wouldn't be long for the universe.

Soon Demora Sulu came in. She was older than she had been when she entered earlier that day, and older than she had been at the time when she first met Chakotay. Her face betrayed disappointment, as if she was hoping to catch her erstwhile protégé. Cap knew, however, that if they were meant to encounter each other, they would have. Instead, he simply poured her another glass from the same bottle of red wine she'd drunk from earlier that day many years ago.

All in all, Cap decided, it had been a good day. He gave Sulu her drink, and then sat back and waited for the next story. . . .

About the Authors

Peter David is a prolific author whose career, and continued popularity, spans nearly two decades. He has worked in television, film, books (fiction, nonfiction, and audio), short stories, and comic books, and acquired followings in all of them. Peter has had over fifty novels published, including numerous appearances on the *New York Times* best-seller list. His novels include *Sir Apropos of Nothing* (and its two sequels), *Knight Life* (and its two sequels), *Howling Mad,* and the *Psi-Man* adventure series. He is the co-developer and author of the best-selling *Star Trek: New Frontier* series for Pocket Books, and has written over a dozen other *Trek* novels. He produced the *Babylon 5: Centauri Prime* trilogy of novels, and has also had his short fiction published in such anthologies as *Shock Rock, Shock Rock II, Other-Were,* and *Tales of the Dominion War,* as well as *Asimov's Science Fiction* and *The Magazine of Fantasy & Science Fiction.* Peter has an extensive, and award-winning, comic book résumé, and he has co-edited two short-story anthologies, *The Ultimate Hulk* and *New Frontier: No Limits.* Furthermore, his opinion column "But I Digress . . ." has been running in the industry trade newspaper *Comic Buyer's Guide* for over a decade, and in that time has been the paper's consistently most popular feature and was also collected into a trade paperback edition. Peter is the co-creator, with actor Bill Mumy, of the Cable Ace Award–nominated science-fiction series *Space Cases,* which ran for two seasons on Nickelodeon. He has written several TV scripts for *Babylon 5* and its sequel series *Crusade* and has written several films for Full Moon Entertainment and co-produced two of them. He lives in New York with his wife, Kathleen, and his four children, Shana, Gwen, Ariel, and Caroline.

This is the third *Star Trek* anthology that **Keith R.A. DeCandido** has edited, following 2004's *Tales of the Dominion War* and 2003's *No Limits* (in collaboration with Peter David), and he has edited or co-edited more than a dozen other anthologies in the last decade, including the Nebula Award–nominated *Imaginings.* As a writer, his first *Trek* novel, *Diplomatic Implausibility,* was also where he introduced the *I.K.S. Gorkon* and established Klag as its captain. This was later followed by the *I.K.S. Gorkon* series, which consists of three books so far: *A Good Day to Die, Honor Bound,* and *Enemy Territory.* His other *Trek*s include five other novels, two novellas, four short stories, nine eBooks, and a comic-book miniseries, many of which have appeared on various best-seller lists. Keith's first original novel, *Dragon Precinct,* was published in 2004, and his most recent *Star Trek* novel is a look at the world of *Trek* politics, *Articles of the Federation.* He has also written novels, novelizations, short stories, and nonfiction books in the milieus of *Buffy the Vampire Slayer, Farscape, Gene Roddenberry's Andromeda, Resident Evil,* Marvel Comics, *Xena, Magic: The Gathering, Serenity,* and more. Find out too much about Keith at his official Web site at DeCandido.net. Oh, and his story title translates into English as "Brothers and Fathers."

Michael Jan Friedman has written nearly forty *Star Trek* books, scripted more than a hundred *Star Trek* comics, and collaborated on what he insists on believing is one of the better episodes of *Star Trek: Voyager.* In the process, he has stung, annoyed, bruised, embarrassed, punctured, censured, seared, vilified, tortured, maimed,

and outright killed more sentient beings than any civilized individual would ever want to contemplate. But what really horrifies him is all the bridge consoles he's destroyed. Let's face it, there are a lot of interstellar ships in Mike's books, and they've all got bridge consoles. Sometimes a whole bunch of them. It's just too easy to blow one up in the face of some walk-on character, sending him cannonballing across the deck in a shower of sparks and black smoke, and writing *finis* to his noble existence (not to mention his hopes of getting a *Star Trek* show of his own). Certainly, it's a lot less work than character development. But bridge consoles perform an entire array of valuable functions. We can't just go around beating them up. We have to exercise restraint. It is in this spirit that we are proud to make the following announcement about "Darkness," the first account of Jean-Luc Picard's adventures in the seven-year period between his captaincy of the *Stargazer* and his captaincy of the *Enterprise*-D: No bridge consoles were destroyed in the making of this story.

"Iron and Sacrifice" marks **David R. George III**'s first return to the character of Demora Sulu since her prominent role in the *New York Times* best-selling *Lost Era* novel *Serpents Among the Ruins*. David's other contributions to the *Star Trek* universe include the *Deep Space Nine* novels *The 34th Rule*, set during the series, and *Twilight* and *The Dominion: Olympus Descending*, set afterward. He also co-wrote the story for the first-season *Voyager* episode "Prime Factors," and he will be penning an Original Series trilogy to help celebrate the fortieth anniversary of the show. David firmly believes in Robert Heinlein's dictum that "Specialization is for insects." David's passions (after his wonderful, beautiful wife, Karen) include art, dance, film, theater, travel, reading, baseball, racquetball, mathematics, the English language, cosmology, quantum physics, and, unaccountably, the New York Mets. He loves talking about writing, and chatting with readers and fans, both at conventions and online. He appreciates Keith R.A. DeCandido's invitation to contribute to this anthology, and

hopes one day in his writing to revisit Demora Sulu, as well as John Harriman and the rest of the *Enterprise*-B crew. David is not a doctor, nor does he play one on television.

Award-winning author **Christie Golden** has written twenty-six novels and seventeen short stories in the fields of science fiction, fantasy, and horror. She is best known for her tie-in work, although she has written several original novels. Among her credits are the first book in the *Ravenloft* line, *Vampire of the Mists*, a *Star Trek* Original Series hardcover *The Last Roundup*, several *Voyager* novels including the recent best-selling relaunch of the series, *Homecoming* and *The Farther Shore*, and short stories for *Buffy the Vampire Slayer* and *Angel* anthologies. Two more books in the *Voyager* relaunch, *Spirit Walk* Book 1: *Old Wounds* and Book 2: *Enemy of My Enemy*, were released in November and December of 2004. In 1999, Golden's novel *A.D. 999*, written under the pen name of Jadrien Bell, won the Colorado Author's League Top Hand Award for Best Genre Novel. Christie launched a brand-new fantasy series entitled *The Final Dance* through Luna Books, a major new fantasy imprint. The first book in the series is entitled *On Fire's Wings* and was published in trade paperback in July of 2004. Look for the second in the series, *In Stone's Clasp*, in September 2005. She invites readers to visit her Web site at www.christiegolden.com.

Heather Jarman lives a Peter Parker–like suburban existence; few of her fellow soccer moms could fathom that the mild-mannered woman behind the wheel of the minivan might be a writer of *Star Trek* fiction and harbor a deep, abiding love for hobbits, the Hubble Telescope, and blue-skinned Andorians. Heather's recent contributions to the world of *Star Trek* fiction include *Worlds of Star Trek: Deep Space Nine* Book 1: *Andor: Paradigm* and a short story (co-authored with Jeffrey Lang) in the critically acclaimed anthology *Tales of the Dominion War*. In 2005, her creative efforts will be part of Pocket Books' celebration of *Voyager*'s tenth anniversary. She lives in Portland, Oregon, with her husband and four daughters.

Andy Mangels is the co-author of several *Star Trek* novels, eBooks, short stories, and comic books, as well as a trio of *Roswell* novels, all co-written with Michael A. Martin. Flying solo, he is the best-selling author of many entertainment books, including *Animation on DVD: The Ultimate Guide* and *Star Wars: The Essential Guide to Characters*, as well as a significant number of entries in *The Super-hero Book*. He has written hundreds of articles for entertainment and lifestyle magazines and newspapers in the United States, England, and Italy. He has also written licensed material based on properties from many film studios and Microsoft, and his comic-book work has been published by DC Comics, Marvel Comics, and many others. He was the editor of the award-winning *Gay Comics* anthology for eight years. Andy is a national award-winning activist in the Gay community, and has raised thousands of dollars for charities over the years. He lives in Portland, Oregon, with his long-term partner, Don Hood, their dog, Bela, and their chosen son, Paul Smalley. Visit his Web site at www.andymangels.com.

Michael A. Martin's solo short fiction has appeared in *The Magazine of Fantasy & Science Fiction*. He has also co-authored (with Andy Mangels) several *Star Trek* novels (including *Worlds of Star Trek: Deep Space Nine* Book 2: *Trill: Unjoined*; *Titan* Books 1–2; *Star Trek The Lost Era: The Sundered*; *Star Trek: Deep Space Nine: Mission: Gamma* Book 3: *Cathedral*; *Star Trek: The Next Generation: Section 31: Rogue*); two *Star Trek: S.C.E.* eBooks (*Ishtar Rising* Books 1–2); stories in the *Prophecy and Change* and *Tales of the Dominion War* anthologies; and three novels based on the *Roswell* television series. Back in the twentieth century, Martin was the regular co-writer (also with Andy) of Marvel's *Star Trek: Deep Space Nine* monthly comic-book series, and has written for Atlas Editions' *Star Trek Universe* subscription card series, *Star Trek Monthly*, *Dreamwatch*, Grolier Books, Wildstorm, Visible Ink Press, and Gareth Stevens, Inc., for whom he has penned several *World Almanac Library of the States* nonfiction books for young readers. He lives with his wife, Jenny, and their two sons in Portland, Oregon.

John J. Ordover, former executive editor of the *Star Trek* fiction line for Pocket Books and co-developer of the Captain's Table concept (with Dean Wesley Smith), the *Star Trek: New Frontier* series (with Peter David), and the *Star Trek: S.C.E.* series (with Keith R.A. DeCandido), is the happy husband of Carol Greenburg and the proud father of Arren Isaac Ordover. Ordover is currently the editor-in-chief of Phobos Science Fiction and Fantasy.

Dean Wesley Smith, the co-developer of the Captain's Table concept, has published over seventy novels and a hundred short stories under varied names. He has written novels in every *Star Trek* series, including the first original *Voyager* novel, the first original *Enterprise* novel, and the first *S.C.E.* eBook. He currently edits *Star Trek: Strange New Worlds*, now in its eighth year.

Louisa M. Swann is currently on leave of absence from an alternate dimension. Born on an Indian reservation in northern California almost forty-nine years ago, Louisa spent her first six months of life bundled up and carried around in a papoose basket. She spent the remainder of her growing years at Lake Tahoe, California. At one time or another she participated in, made a living as, or halfheartedly attempted the following: student, maid, waitress, receptionist, flight attendant, secretary, teacher's aid (unofficial), ski instructor, ski patrol (volunteer), and engineering assistant. Louisa now lives on eighty acres in northern California with her husband (Jim), twenty-something son (Brandon), two horses, dog, cat, a varying population of rabbits, deer, coyotes, bobcats, cougars, snakes, frogs, birds, bugs, and no electricity. She insists on calling herself a writer, a dementia that is consistently fed by her burgeoning *Star Trek* publications in *Strange New Worlds V, VI*, and *VII*, as well as other science-fiction venues. The human members of the family manage to put up with her eccentricities with only a few minor squabbles. On the other hand, the horses, dog, cat, and miscellaneous wildlife understand her perfectly. She often goes to them for grooming when the rest of this dimension becomes a bit too difficult to handle. While on trips to other dimensions, Louisa enjoys skiing, sailing, hiking, and swimming; however, most of her spare time is currently spent laying bricks, a therapy recommended by her dimensional psychologist.